# Jai

# Jai

S. A. Stitz

Archway Publishing books may be ordered through booksellers or by contacting:

Archway Publishing
1663 Liberty Drive
Bloomington, IN 47403
www.archwaypublishing.com
1 (888) 242-5904



ISBN: 978-1-4808-3258-9 (sc)
ISBN: 978-1-4808-3259-6 (hc)
ISBN: 978-1-4808-3260-2 (e)

Library of Congress Control Number: 2016910370

Print information available on the last page.

Archway Publishing rev. date: 7/26/2016

Dedicated to the few that exist beyond our awareness.
Please remain patient.

# CHAPTER 1

Standing naked in the snow and ice-covered mountains of the Tibetan Himalayas, Jai is in a state of shock. Her face was covered with ice-crystal teardrops as she overlooked the charred bodies of those she had come to love and respect during her training these past two and a half years. But it was the man who'd brought her to this place she most feared lay among the dead.

Now, just three days after having her clothes taken away in order to enter the temple's meditation sweat lodge, Jai calls upon the discipline hammered into her during her training in order to focus her mind on her present situation. Marshalling all the mental energy she could raise, she dispersed it across the temple grounds, but she could sense only a wisp of her teacher's precious energy among those who lay before her. Though she realized that a person's energy source could linger after death, she held but a modicum of hope that she could find him alive.

Finally denying all probability, Jai collapsed to the ground and found herself plummeting from a state of high spiritual exaltation to a feeling of having her heart ripped from her body, leaving her in total desolation and anguish. Her only thought was the promise he'd made to her on her fourteenth birthday to never abandon her or betray her love for him. That gift, his first and only promise to her, now seemed to be fading into oblivion.

Forcing herself to move, she managed to walk toward the still-smoldering temple. As she passed among the many tortured body parts, she searched for the chain he'd worn around his waist, for proof of his demise, but she saw no sign of it or of his distinctive sandals that had sharp fighting blades in the soles. Reaching what was once the altar area of the fighting ring, she saw six mutilated bodies surrounding what was once the holy, vibrant body of Choden, the temple's abbot. Since he was not a warrior, his body had not been desecrated.

Walking around the exterior boundaries of the temple grounds, Jai could find no physical sign of the man she so reverently called Teacher. Yet she could sense his energy somewhere close by, and it felt like it was in a fading state of fury. Knowing that it took a long time for all the energy to leave a dying or dead body, Jai dared to hope she would find Jinhai alive.

Though she had been taught by the monks that hope was a foolish dream of the human mind, dare she hope that her teacher, Jinhai, whom she believed was her sole purpose for living, didn't leave her stranded in a world without awareness or true compassion. She involuntarily began to ask herself, *to whom can I turn to for guidance? Should I look to one of man's hypocritical religions or their Gods? No, I can't! They were some of the many coping mechanisms I had abandoned in the back alleys of Macao.*

For thousands of years, this temple had been a closely guarded secret. Those exceptional men and women who came to study and train rode in and out across the backs of yaks, their hands tied behind them, with cloth sacks covering their heads. They, above all, knew the consequences of revealing its location or even its existence. Even modern technology and satellites couldn't penetrate the force field that kept prying eyes blinded to its whereabouts. In spite of the imminent threat of death disclosure would bring, there was only one conclusion she could manage to come to: they had been betrayed by one of their own.

As darkness fell, the burning embers accorded the dead a fitting farewell. After examining the bodies she could see, Jai decided to give up looking for him until morning. She searched the burned-out hut that she and Jinhai had shared, hunting for clothes and shoes, but the wardrobe chest as well as any other items she could use were in ashes or broken beyond repair. Continuing to search huts belonging to others, she found nothing but ruin and smoldering flesh.

Finally entering the hut that belonged to a friend of Jinhai's, she found a monk's winter robe, an unlit torch, and some pieces of extra cloth that she wrapped around her body before donning the robe. The monastery's robes were made up of a mixture of plant fiber and hemp, and each had a long tail hood and heavy waist cord. As she tied the waistband, she felt a warmth spread through her body and wondered if now she would ever attain the perfection between mind and body necessary to live a life of high spiritual ideals as a devotee of a larger universal presence.

Jai lit the torch in the burning embers, using it to light her way as she walked barefoot on a path through the woods in search of a hollowed-out tree trunk or some other form of safe shelter. Stumbling across a promising home for the night, and not taking any chances, she attempted to smoke out any creatures that might share this fine, old dead tree trunk, assuring them that they would have it back in due time. Settling in, she built a fire alongside the tree trunk for warmth and began to evaluate her circumstances objectively; she found them dire. She believed that everyone she knew was gone, which left her with no one to tell her exactly where she was or which direction it was to a safe haven.

All the temple's stored food and weapons, along with historical documents, tangkas, statues, and scriptures, had been either destroyed or hauled away. She believed that she was in Chinese-controlled Tibet, but where exactly, she had no idea. She hadn't seen an outsider since she and her mentor departed Nepal. As she neared sleep, she still had no idea what she could do to find her way out of these immeasurable mountains but vowed to return to the temple and find more items she might need for survival.

After a short, difficult night's sleep, Jai felt a new sense of determination. After all, she reasoned, she did know what could be eaten in the woods, even if it meant dining on underground creatures in order to survive, and she was more than capable of fending for herself. Crawling out from the hollow, Jai followed her regular morning routine. After taking care of personal business, she began her ritual of stretching exercises, which progressed into a strenuous series of martial arts movements. That finished, she started her yoga practice and ended with forty minutes of silent meditation. By picturing her teacher at her side, she was motivated to work particularly hard at the forms he had designed especially for her. It was her way of giving respect to all he had been to her.

Ready to move on, she searched her immediate surroundings for food. Locating a variety of berries and plants that would give her nourishment and some that could be used to treat illness and wounds, she started back to the temple grounds. Jai ate as she continued to gather as much as she could carry.

She wondered if her teacher may have escaped into the mountains and might be on his way to the area of her retreat. Jai would go back there. Picking through the charred remains, Jai searched for anything that might help her survive.

Finding more cloth pieces, she constructed a backpack and packed it with the food she gathered and some other bits and pieces she uncovered. The items she was most excited about were a flint and striker, a pair of sandals, and an animal-skin water vessel. She was also able to hang two small cooking pots on the outside of her pack. After paying her respects to her friends and training partners alike, she headed out.

The wind picked up as the hours passed, but Jai paid it little heed. Her mind wandered back to her years of training, and to the warm embraces she'd reveled in when making love with Teacher. She knew she'd been seen as a phenomenon from the first day of her training.

Much to the amazement of teachers and students alike, she progressed far faster than any they had seen before. Her lack of size and strength were overcome by her speed, agility, and grasp of all that she learned from her teacher. She was the only one who had a personal guru, and he was far superior to the others. The fact that they were lovers who shared a bed and used all their time either making love or training was recognized as playing a large part in her quick success.

One of Jai's great accomplishments was her extraordinary enthusiasm for the practice of *lung-gom.* She became a lama in the form, which not only developed uncommon nimbleness and the ability to walk or run at an amazing pace but also allowed for extreme endurance. After one year, she could outdistance, at a faster pace, the few other students who attempted the art.

She had become something very rare: a true adept at the practice of that highly difficult discipline.

Ready to travel, Jai chose a point far out in the distance and entered into deep concentration, which put her in a trancelike state. Her eyes were as wide open as possible, and her face was perfectly calm. She lifted herself off the ground with an effortless leap that propelled her in the direction she wished to go. Her first leap landed her about fifty feet away. With each leap, she rebounded higher and landed at a greater distance, finally reaching a stride of close to one hundred yards. When she alit, it was as if her legs were made of tightly coiled springs. Her left arm clutched her robe, and her right moved up and down with each leap, as if she were pushing off the ground with a pogo stick.

Jai's skills allowed her to reach the area of her retreat in less than two hours. She calmed her breathing and refocused her mind, extending her vibrations to search in every direction for an energy aura pulsating from her teacher. It was a short time before she became depressed, realizing that it was a fruitless gesture. Once again she was overtaken by grief, and the thought of allowing herself to die rather than be without her lover crept back into her mind. She picked up her pack and headed into the cave where she had previously spent three days in meditative introspection.

For forty-eight hours, Jai sat in meditative composure, breaking every six hours for water and nourishment, but her expectation of intuitive answers to her predicament was not forthcoming.

"I have to sleep," Jai said out loud, and so for the first time in two days she completely closed her eyes and drifted off. Her dreams took her back to the sounds and smells of her family home in Macao.

**She heard her stepfather's voice instructing her stepbrother to get her into her street clothes and out of the house before her mother returned from the market. To her horror, Jai heard her brother enter the room, and tears rose from within her very soul. Her brother slapped her when she began sobbing. He threw her on the bed. In terror, she tried to get away, but he was too strong. He straddled her and slapped her again. Grabbing her sleeping gown from the hem, he pulled it over her head and threw it across the room, leaving her naked except for her panties. Looking over the seven-year-old girl's shaking body, he said, "These ugly things will not do either." He reached down and pulled her panties down, and as he did Jai started to cry uncontrollably. Peng slapped her across the face and threw her on the bed. As she tried to scramble away, he sat across her stomach and slapped her again. She fought with all her strength, but he was**

much heavier and stronger. Peng laughed at her, calling her a whore, and slut, and the more she fought, the rougher he got. She screamed even louder, which brought her stepfather running into the room.

With one look, he laughed and said, "Do what you have to do to get her ready, but do it quickly, and get her out of here and down to the buyers before her mother returns, and don't mark her up."

For the next few minutes Peng tried like hell to get her dressed, but she fought hard. She managed to grab his hair and pull his head back, and with her other hand she went for his eyes and poked a finger into one, causing him great pain. He jumped off the bed, swearing to kill her. He might have tried, but his father ran in and slapped him hard. Turning his attention to Jai, he told her to get dressed in her best outfit and wait for her brother in the outer room.

Trembling but thankfully alone in her room, Jai got dressed as she'd been told. She chose her best dress. When she emerged from her room, her stepfather smiled and said she looked pretty. She did not feel pretty. Then Peng grabbed her and dragged her through the streets to the market. They reached a warehouse down by the docks, where Peng knocked on the door. Jai saw a small window-like thing open in the door, and she saw a man's face peering out.

"What do you want?" he asked.

"She is for sale," her brother answered.

"Step her back and let me see her."

A few seconds later Jai heard a heavy bolt slide open, and the door opened. "Bring her in," the big, burly man bellowed.

"How old are you, little one?"

Jai was so scared she couldn't speak. Her brother said, "She is seven, nearing eight."

"Where did you find her?"

"She is my stepmother's daughter."

"Do you have permission to sell her?

"Yes, from my father."

"Follow me, and bring her with you."

Jai dug her heels into the ground, but to no avail. Peng drug her across the room into another room, where she saw a steel cage holding four girls. Peng was instructed to put her inside. It took both of them to peel her off the bars and into the cage. Jai heard the man tell Peng that the auction would be held at two in the afternoon the following day, and Peng would receive 35 percent of whatever she brought, but not to expect much.

In a cold sweat, Jai jolted awake, remembering, almost tasting the smell of fear from all those young girls and boys who had occupied the cell before her. That smell, which permeated the Macao warehouse, would never be forgotten. In order to shake her mind loose from the memory, she began her morning practice.

It had been three days since she last practiced, and the motionless meditation had caused her muscles to become extremely tight and sore. Together they forced her to work harder. Each time she reached a point of searing pain, she called out her teacher's name, telling him she would find him. At the end of her martial arts, she chided herself as her teacher would have done for not being perfect, and then she forced herself to do one hundred push-ups in a handstand position, placing her knuckles on the floor instead of her palms.

Finishing the session with meditation, Jai was rejuvenated. She was alive with the chi that flowed strongly through her body as it always did after a strong workout. Her mind was clear, and it struck her that if she could make it out of the mountains into Nepal she would find her way to Hong Kong and Jinhai's junk in the bay. She believed that if he were alive, he would go there to recuperate. This belief also fueled an angry desire to seek revenge against those who had murdered her friends and colleagues. Jai once again found her purpose to live.

Dressed and packed, Jai walked out of the cave to find the sun rising. A moment's thought and she remembered that the mountains ran east and west between Tibet and Nepal. To face south, she turned to her right and chose a spot in the distant sky. Using her *lung-gom* technique, she put her mind in a trancelike state and leapt into the air, bringing her one step closer to what she hoped would an everlasting reunion with her teacher.

# CHAPTER 2

After two and a half days of *lung-gom* without much thought of food or sleep, Jai was exhausted. Her body depleted of most of its fluid and nourishment, she stopped to eat and sleep. Finally out of the trance, Jai sat on a log, took off her backpack, and closed her eyes for the first time since she had started on her present journey.

A few minutes passed before she felt a strange sensation; opening her eyes, she realized that she was floating six or seven feet above the ground. A moment's clarity brought a smile of understanding that by just eating a handful of berries she had increased her ability to make her body lighter with each inhaled breath. She exhaled, pushing all the air out of her lungs, and glided to the ground. Walking from tree to tree while holding onto the hanging limbs, she gathered enough rocks to hold her down. After removing the food, she carefully put the rocks in her pack and placed it on her shoulders.

When she departed the valley where the temple had been located, the almost obscure trail she followed angled sharply downward, ending in a gorge that ran between twenty and twenty-five thousand feet below the peaks of two mountains. At the bottom the ground stayed fairly level, and she bounded along easily. At times the gorge widened to four miles, allowing for small patches of grassland and several stands of trees. Cold, clear water streamlets ran every direction from the thaw high above. Jai sat on a stump thirty feet inside the tree line, filling her body with berries, leafy grasses, and water. She didn't quite feel safe enough to sit outside in the sun, although she would have preferred that.

As the light faded, Jai searched then found a large clump of bushes thick with limbs and needles. She carefully pulled aside the branches, creating enough of a small hole for her to crawl though. Once in the middle she gathered dead leaves and humus for the bed where she would sleep. Looking around, she closed off any holes that might allow someone to see in. Satisfied, she unpacked the extra cloth and made a pillow. Quite comfortable and snug, she dozed off.

Sleep came to Jai, and it was welcome, but she knew the nightmare would come too. Exhausted, she allowed herself to drift off to the inevitable."

After the guard left, Jai sat down and began to cry. The girls comforted her. She looked up.

"We are all going to be sold like dogs," she said.

A girl, who said she was the eldest, reached out and pushed a strand of Jai's dark hair away from her eyes.

"We have to find a way out of this cell," Jai mumbled. "What if I could squeeze through the cells bars before the guard returned with his trained killer dog? Then I could get the key from the peg across the room and open the door, but I don't know what happens after that."

"First things first," said the oldest girl.

Halfway through the bars, Jai squealed, "The door is opening. I see a stream of light creeping closer."

The door opened fully, allowing a stream of light to flood in and highlight the cage and Jai's frightened face.

"Push harder," Jai said in desperation.

With one last gasp they tried pushing her out so she could make a run for the key, but the guard released the dog, and he ran straight at Jai. Seeing this, the oldest girl reached outside the cage in an effort to pull Jai back in before the growling dog could reach her, but to no avail. The dog grabbed then bit down on the limb that was closest to him; it was the elder girl's wrist and not Jai's leg. The dog's powerful jaws clamped down. His teeth broke her bones, and blood spurted out like a gusher. The smell of blood made the dog furious, and he started to shake his head from side to side, tearing her hand completely off. All the girls were screaming, and Jai was able to force herself back into the cage. The guard called off the dog and settled him, but he wouldn't release the bloody hand.

Jai watched as the guard, in spite of all the screaming, took down the key and warned the girls to leave the wounded girl where she lay and go to the back bars. At the back of the cage, Jai and the frightened girls huddled close together and trembled as the guard opened the cage and pulled the hysterical girl out. Placing her in the center of the room, he bashed the girl across her skull with a bully club, which killed her instantly. Blood poured out, and the smell enraged the dog. He ran over and started ripping her apart, exactly as the guard had planned. Banging on the cage bars, he screamed at the girls never to speak about this or he would do the same to them. Then he tore off the dead girl's clothes, threw them in the cage, and demanded that they clean up the blood and throw the clothes back out.

Loud sounds of motorized vehicles entering the grassy plain caused Jai's eyes to instinctively open, ending her nightmare. With all the headlights bathing the open area, Jai was able to look out through the web of branches to see the trucks and small tanks forming a circle. She counted fourteen vehicles before she heard a command, and soldiers began jumping from the back of the trucks. The commander set up a perimeter, and the rest began setting up camp.

Jai believed she was camouflaged enough not to be seen, but she couldn't be sure that they wouldn't do a deep search in the surrounding woods. To ensure that her breathing wouldn't be detected, she began a slow, quiet breathing exercise, which would bring her heart rate down to the point approximating death, while she pressed her body as flat as possible onto the ground until she could figure out what to do.

After warming fires were started, a meal of cold rations were doled out to the soldiers, and they settled down. Jai went over her options; using strict conservation, she figured she had enough food and water to last for about two days. She reasoned that they were just passing through, because as far as she knew there was nothing around for them to defend or attack, so they were probably on patrol.

All at once the peace was shattered by screams. Jai, moving carefully, peeked out and saw a girl being dragged out of the back of a truck. Her head was bagged, and when Jai saw what she was wearing, she gagged. Tears rolled down her cheeks as she watched the men tear away the girl's robe;

it was the same as she was wearing. This very distinct robe marked the order of monks and trainees at the temple where she trained, but who was she?

Thinking back, Jai remembered a new female trainee being unloaded from the back of a yak as she was leaving for her retreat. Until then she was the only female in camp, so she knew this had to be that girl. Jai bit her lip to keep from screaming out as she watched the soldiers one by one raping the girl, turning her from her back to her knees. Knowing this would also be her fate if she was caught, she put herself in a meditative state and blocked out all the sounds but kept her awareness high enough just in case a patrol entered the woods. There was nothing she could do.

Thankfully she heard the commander yell, "Cease your nonsense! The girl is unconscious. You can revive her in the morning, and then the rest may take their turn."

A couple of men dragged the girl to a truck, tied her to the back axle, and with disdain threw her tattered robe over her body. At around two in the morning, all the soldiers and most of the guards had fallen asleep. Peeking out, Jai saw one of the guards slip over to the still unconscious girl, throw off her tattered robe, drop his pants, and mount her.

Jai believed that these had to be these same soldiers who had killed the people she had come to love, but her pent-up anger culminated when she saw this pig spit in the girl's face and kick her after he pleasured himself. That was the last straw.

In a frenzied state, she tried to crawl out of the thicket, but the thick needles held her back long enough for her to regain her composure. Jai knew she would have to try and do something. She wouldn't be able to live with herself if she didn't.

With two and a half years of fourteen or more hours of training seven days a week, her perfected skills had to count for something. She had mastered many forms of ninja, all types of weaponry, including small arms, but her real fighting skill was in garroting, knives, and throwing stars. She also attained a black belt in karate, judo, and three other martial arts. In other words, she was a deadly force in hand-to-hand combat.

*All well and good*, she thought, *but I have no weapons other than my hands and legs, so I guess those will have to do. Unless I wait until most were asleep, do some reconnaissance, and relieve a soldier or two of their arms.*

Jai waited until she sensed most were asleep. Sending out her aura, she felt nothing but calm, so she started working her way out of the thicket.

Now composed, she was able to quietly get through the heavy needles, dragging her now rock-less pack behind her to the edge of the woods. With her eyes well-adjusted to the dim lights, she picked a truck. Then calling on her *lung-gom* practice, she concentrated on its cloth top and leapt in the air, covering the twenty-five feet with no trouble and landing softly. Lying on the top of the truck, she bent over and peeked in, but only sleeping soldiers were inside. She tried two other trucks, each time landing successfully, but finding much the same.

Next was the truck the girl was tied to. She leapt over two others, and this time she landed on the ground next to the sleeping pig of a man. Seeing his bayonet in its scabbard, she reached down and eased it out. There was no question in her mind what she would do next; placing her hand tightly over his mouth, she slit his throat. His eyes opened just long enough to see Jai spit on his face.

All remained quiet. Taking a quick look into the truck, she found the cache of weapons they stole from the monastery. Jai jumped in and was able to fill her pack with all the weapons that would fit, but the biggest treasure was the kegs of gunpowder, also from the temple's store. This changed everything, and she was able to come up with a plan that she hoped would possibly kill most of the soldiers in one blow.

Upon searching his pockets, she found some matches and then cut the dead man's uniform into strips. Two at a time Jai rolled the small kegs of powder to the center of the circle of vehicles. Cutting out the corks, she ran a line of powder to each vehicle's gas cap. Opening the caps, she soaked the strips of cloth by dipping them into the tank and let them hang to the ground, barely touching the gunpowder. Then she ran one final line from the half-full kegs to the edge of the woods opposite from where she had hidden earlier in the evening.

In less than an hour, she was ready to get the girl. Cutting her loose, Jai used her knowledge of fulcrum points and balance to toss the naked girl on to her shoulders like a big pillow and ran to the woods, passing the commander peacefully sleeping by the last small tank. Leaving the girl just inside the tree line, Jai, thinking about the defiled and desecrated bodies, couldn't resist going back even though it meant possibly screwing up her whole plan.

Coming up behind the commander, she used her

knowledge of pressure points and cut off the flow of blood to his brain. When she applied the right amount of pressure, he passed out, but he was still alive. She stripped off all his clothes, hoping to later fashion some kind of outfit for the girl. Jai looked around and found some heavy rope and a board. She spread the commander's legs and placed the board between his calves and secured it. Then she knotted the board in the middle and threw the end over a strong branch and with all her strength pulled him up so that he hung upside down. She put a rock inside his mouth and tied a strip of cloth around his head so he could not scream, then splashed water on his face, and he came around. Then she cut slits in both his wrists so he would slowly bleed out as he watched the show that was about to take place.

All remained quiet, though she knew she was flirting with disaster by hanging around so long. At the edge of the tree line, she lit a gas-soaked rag with a match found in the commander's pocket, and lit the powder. She watched the burning line hit the center kegs and then spread out in fourteen different directions. The first explosion rocked the camp and awakened everyone. By the time they realized what was happening, the next four or five kegs blew, and then they all went up. The sky lit up, and Jai saw the burning bodies, and a smile crossed her lips. She relished the screams and felt that at least some justice had been done.

It was over in a few minutes. In that time Jai didn't move, though she was lit up like a Christmas tree in red, orange, yellow, and black glowing light. She saw only three soldiers run into the woods across the fields, and two of them were on fire. Two more ran toward her. She quickly killed them with her throwing stars.

With the noise of the first explosion, Jai screamed at the top of her lungs, "I hope you all burn in hell."

Jai waited there until all was quiet to see if there were any survivors. She saw no movement, but she heard a few desperate moans. Debating, she decided to show mercy and walked back into camp and killed all those who had survived the explosions but were in terrible pain.

Back at the tree line she said out loud, "Thank you, Teacher, for the courage, the knowledge, and the will to avenge all those who suffered at the hands of these Communist bastards."

Jai put the woman across her shoulders and once again headed south through the trees, hoping to find a village or encampment and have the girl looked after. Moving at a much slower pace than before due to the dead weight, Jai found herself tiring quickly, forcing her to rest often. Thinking that at this speed it would take her forever to reach Nepal, she dallied with the idea of leaving the girl and searching for signs of friendly faces, but she dropped the idea, imagining what would happen if the girl woke up alone in the woods.

For two days and nights Jai carried the still-unconscious girl, stopping often for nourishment, but mostly for rest because her nights were spent in hot sweats dreaming about Macao. The first two nights she dreamt again about the dog attack and the viciousness of the guard, but it was the third night that brought back the auction block.

**At eleven that same morning, one hour before the start of the sale, two new girls were brought into the cage to be auctioned.**

The other five were older than Jai. One was at least eighteen or nineteen, but it was fifteen-year-old, Liling, who was the prettiest, and they would save her for last. All the girls were made to stand on the side of the platform facing out so the bidders could see what was coming. With only one bidder the first girl brought a meager sum, but the next three amounts increased as the girls' bodies were more developed.

Jai was next, and they dragged her to the front. She was the only one they had to tie to a pole to keep her still. Laughter roared throughout the yard as this skinny young girl fought like a wildcat before they were able to subdue her.

The boss opened the bidding, but nobody said a word. He cajoled and tried to persuade the normally easy crowd of her virtues, but to no avail. He ripped open her dress, hoping to excite the crowd, or at least the pimps, but still no one bid. Giving up, he asked the one pimp who normally bought a lot of girls what was wrong.

The man said, "It would take a lot of money to fatten her up, house and dress her. Then, if she's a virgin, I could get something back, she's just not worth the expense. Plus she's crazy."

"Cut her down, and get rid of her. Over there, that's her brother; give her back to him," the boss bellowed.

Afraid to go home without any money, Jai's brother dragged her around the streets, trying to sell her or even pimp her out, but there were no takers. They slept in alleyways at night, usually under a piece of cardboard or in boxes. Finally, after one whole week, he decided to just abandon her, thinking he'd tell his father the true story and add that she ran away while he was negotiating with a pimp. That night, after settling down in an alley and when Jai was asleep, Peng snuck away—out of his sister's life.

It was nearing dawn when Jai awoke, and as usual she checked to see if the girl was still breathing. After her normal exercise routines and eating, Jai once again lifted the girl on to her shoulders and headed out. The unsettling dreams and the trek through the woods went on for another day. On the fourth day, Jai awoke with a fever and chills and was very weak. Her robe was soaked with sweat, and she could barely stand. She drifted in and out of that state for days, once or twice managing to chew and swallow some of the medicinal herbs, but they didn't seem to do any good. She knew they should have been brewed into a tea, but she was too weak to gather wood and try.

On the fifth day, in an apparent state of delirium, Jai was barely able to get her eyes to open when she saw a pair of glowing red eyes staring into hers.

# CHAPTER 3

Frightened because she was so weak and not able to defend herself, she forced her eyes open enough to see what appeared to be an old woman wearing a hooded robe much different than the one she wore.

The woman asked, "Do you know where you are?"

Jai, having a difficult time even understanding the question, said nothing. The woman then asked her name, but still Jai did not answer. Jai was totally convinced that she was an illusion, because every time she spoke, her eyes sparkled and darkened to a deeper red. Jai just closed her eyes in hopes of putting this woman/monster out of her head. But as she did, the old crone reached over and touched Jai's face, and she began to feel a warming sensation starting where the woman's hand lay and slowly flowing down to her toes.

"What is your name, girl?"

"Jai," she managed to mumble.

"Do you know where you are?"

Jai glanced around but could find nothing familiar. "No."

"Well I must tell that you are very sick with a rare bacterial infection that few survive."

"The girl ...?"

"She is at a point just before death."

"She mustn't die, I ..."

"We will do what we can. First I will use my skills to strengthen both of you long enough for you to take her to the master healer. How are you feeling now?"

"Much better. Who is this person you speak of?"

"You will learn all there is to learn if you make it there."

"Make it where? Where am I?"

"You are in the same woods where you contracted the illness. And if either of you are to survive, you must first make it to the land of my people."

"Are you speaking of the place where the ancient gods go to return to their homelands?"

Laughing, the old lady said, "It may be as you say."

"But that place is just from old wives' tales told to children to keep them from wandering off and taken to a mysterious, dark place where all the hideous creatures live."

"Is it?" asked the old woman, chuckling.

"Yes, I heard many tales at the temple where I trained."

"What more did you hear?"

"The monks who believe and teach mystic Lamaism told of gods or dakini that teach secret doctrines of science, mathematics, physics, and astronomy. They often appear as old women with red eyes." Jai stopped short when she realized what she was saying and looking at.

"So they taught you that the dakini or gods, as you people say, weren't just made up stories?"

"No, but when questioned, they all admitted that

neither they nor anyone else they know had ever seen one. But because the stories continued to be told throughout the ages, they believed in their existence."

"Have you ever seen the Buddha?"

"No."

"But you still believe in his existence?"

"Yes, and I understand what you are saying."

"Let me show you a way to believe beyond just acceptance of words."

Jai witnessed the old crone morph into a beautiful young woman, and if that wasn't enough, she once again morphed into a beautiful black wolf with green eyes, and a long gray tail.

"Can you believe now?"

"Yes, as much as I can." Jai, becoming stronger with every passing moment, asked, "Why did you say if I make it to your land? Will I not be strong enough?"

"I only have the power to give both of you enough strength to reach our land. The rest is up to the two of you, but understand you must arrive together, alive."

"But why together? She has not been conscious since I took her from the camp."

"Yes, we know all about the camp, the rape, the killings, and we were also there at the temple when the invaders struck."

"If you are capable of much magic, why didn't you stop it?"

"It was not written."

"By whom?"

"It was not written."

"Why were you at the temple?"

"What took place was written."

"Why do we have to arrive together?"

"When you killed all those soldiers to save the girl's life, your destinies became one."

"What would prevent us from reaching your land?"

"Many things. You will face your fears, your prejudices, your human desires. If you do not overcome these things, you can never reach the entrance bridge."

"Why do I have to go there? I want to leave this land and find my way back to my teacher."

Mentioning her teacher caused chills to run up and down Jai's spine. She looked around but didn't see any breeze blowing the leaves on the trees. She shivered, not knowing the cause.

The old woman continued. "Simple, if you do not make it, you and the girl will die from the diseases you both carry. See the girl, she is much stronger, and soon she will gain consciousness. When she does, I will have gone. It is up to you to make her believe all that you've heard. Now listen carefully. Before I leave you, I will whisper the words that will protect you along the path. There are many dangers you will face, put there to prevent the unwanted from succeeding along the way."

"Do you mean other than our own demons that we must face and defeat?"

"Yes, many."

"Can you tell me what they may be?"

"A few, but only a few. There will be mirages, scary apparitions, and demons of different persuasions, ferocious animals, and fair-haired, beautiful boys. Also you must not eat from the trees or drink from the crystal-clear streams.

You must not be distracted; keeping focus is your salvation. If you lose your way, even once, you will never find it again."

As the old woman talked, Jai pictured Teacher because he always gave her instructions with a warning. She could picture his deep, penetrating eyes, his knowing, warm smile, and she felt a profound sadness. She had to force herself back to focus on what the old woman was saying.

"How will we nourish ourselves if we cannot leave the trail?"

"You will gather all the food and water you will need before you step on the path."

"And how much will we need?"

"How long will you take to get to the end?"

"I have no idea."

"Neither do I, so I suggest you conserve both your food and energy, but do not dilly-dally. The girl is coming around. I must leave now. Come, give me your ear, and I will say the words that you must repeat with every step you take, every step."

After Jai received the formula in the form of a mantra, the mystical person walked off. It wasn't until she saw the wolf change back into an old woman and disappear into the woods that she remembered that she had been speaking to a wolf all this time. She yelled, "Wait, wait, you didn't say where the path began."

A voice from deep in the forest called back, "When you are ready, it will appear."

The girl's eyes sprung open, and she looked around in bewilderment. She spotted Jai, and not recognizing her, she asked, "Who are you, and where am I?"

"First, tell me, what is your name?"

The girl thought for a moment, trying hard to remember, and said, "I don't know, but you must know."

"Sorry, but I don't. You have been unconscious since I first found you. What do you remember?"

Again the girl thought for a few minutes and then said, "I can't remember anything. Where are we?"

Jai now understood that the girl, at least for the time being, knew nothing about her horrendous experiences and decided not to say anything at all. "We are about four days south of where I found you in the woods."

"These are not my clothes, are they?"

"No, your clothes were torn to pieces, probably from the thickets you passed through running in the woods, so when I found a Chinese soldier's uniform, I put you in it."

The girl tried to sit up, but she was very weak and lay back down.

"Do you not know anything about me, why was I running in the woods?"

"Not a thing, and I have no idea why you were in the woods, but I do know that we have both contracted a disease that will kill us if we don't get the proper help."

"Is that why I can't remember anything?"

"That would be my guess."

"What is your name?"

"I am called Jai, a name given to me by my abbot. I will call you Song, which means pine tree in Chinese, because I found you passed out against one."

"So we are Chinese?"

"No, I'm part Chinese and part Japanese, and I'm guessing by your features that you are Chinese."

"I feel very weak, and my body aches so badly."

As they talked Jai was gathering some wood to start a fire to warm them both. She handed the water skin and some berries to Song.

"You have been very restless while you were unconscious, like you were fighting demons. That probably accounts for it. We do not have time to waste. We must reach the people who can cure us before we die."

"How much farther are they?"

"I don't know, but what I do know is that we are about to experience some very strange things in the forest we must pass through. This forest is ruled over by mystical demons that we must avoid at all costs."

"You are kidding, right?"

"Not one word, and there is more. First I must know that you'll trust everything I tell you to do, or not to do. Is that understood?"

"Why should I trust you?"

"I carried you for eight days to get you to this point, and that alone should be enough."

"What else awaits us in this mystical forest of yours?"

"I don't really know, except we've been warned. We cannot eat from the trees or drink the water from the streams. That's all I know, except that if we lose our way by straying off the path, we will never find it again and we will die. Is that clear enough?"

"I guess."

"Let's get started. We have to find enough food for the journey and pack it with us. Why don't you stand up and walk around to see how you are feeling? I'll show you what to pick and what not to."

Song, trying to stand, felt very dizzy and fell two or three times before she was able to walk. Jai, seeing that Song was too weak to stand on her own, helped her get to her feet. When Jai felt that Song was strong enough, they began to look around for berries and fruits to sustain them. Together they gathered much more than they hoped they would need. Jai cut off the legs of the girl's pants and stuffed them with food and then knotted the ends. What was left went into her pack. From her robe's hem she cut a thin strip and tied the two legs together and hung them over her shoulders, knowing that the girl was too weak to carry anything but herself.

"Which way do we go?" asked Song.

"I don't know. I was told that when we were ready the path would show itself. We must not be ready."

Jai, thinking about what might be missing, guessed it could only be one thing. She told the girl to stand up and get ready to move out. Then Jai spoke the mantra, but nothing happened. She tried again using more oomph, and when she finished, they saw a thread like golden light laid out leading into the woods. They headed that way, but as they entered the path, the light started to fade, and fear overtook Jai until she remembered the mantra. As she chanted it loud and clear, the light brightened, and Jai learned her lesson.

Jai led the way, telling Song that she must stay no more than two paces behind, her fearing she might stray off the path. As they walked further along the way, everything alongside the path seemed to fall into deep shadow even though they could clearly see the bright sun overhead. Jai, repeating the mantra with each step, lost track of Song's footsteps until she heard a bloodcurdling scream from somewhere to her right. Looking over she saw Song struggling with a hideous-looking creature, trying to prevent herself from being pulled into a muddy pond.

He looked like a child with purplish-red glowing skin, webbed fingers, and toes that held Song tightly. His head resembled a capuchin monkey, with white hair all around, and his mouth housed long, sharp, tearing teeth. He was naked, and he smelled like rotting fish. Jai's initial instinct was to run to her rescue, but as she took one step off the path, she thankfully remembered the warning not to leave the path or be lost forever.

She made a quick decision and reached into her pack, took out a throwing knife, filled it with instructional energy, and hoped she was still adept at using it. She took aim and threw it. As soon as it left her hand, she willed it to follow the instructions she gave it and cut away the monster's hand to free Song. Jai's physic training worked; it did what it was willed to do and cleanly severed the demon's hand from his arm. There was no blood. Song, still screaming, picked up the hand and ran back to Jai. They sat down so Song could get a hold of her emotions and watched a crying, defeated creature walk into the pond.

"Why are you holding on to the hand?"

"So he cannot repair the damage."

"What did you think you were doing leaving the path?" Jai asked.

"I had to relieve myself, so I thought it best to do it in the pond."

"But I told you not to leave the path under any circumstances."

"I'm so sorry."

Just as they started to rise, Jai saw the creature walking toward them, saying, “Please give me back my hand.”

But the two girls, more frightened than ever, ran away, with Jai repeating the mantra faster and faster. They ran along the lit path for another hour or so until it was time to rest. They sat down finally able to enjoy some fruit when the monkey-boy appeared at the edge of the trees and once again asked for his hand. This time he looked very weak so they didn’t run.

Jai asked, “If it is so important to have your hand back, why did you risk losing it by attacking my friend?”

“It is my nature to eat people. I did nothing wrong.”

“Well it is my nature to save my friend from harm, so I too did nothing wrong. We are at a standoff.”

“You have done what it is right for you to do, and so have I, so why won’t you give me back my hand?”

“I see that you are much weaker without it, and if I give it back you may attack us.”

“I promise I won’t, and if you do, I’ll give you something in return.”

“What can you give us?”

“I’ll give you the secret of the Tengu, which you will meet on your journey.”

“Anything else.”

“Yes, I will surely die if I do not attach my hand back on my arm.”

Jai reached in her pack, took out the withering hand, and threw to him. “Now tell us the secret you promised.”

“Wait, I’ll attach my hand and then I’ll tell.” Then he ran off in the direction he came from.

The girls waited fifteen minutes before Jai said, “We’ve

been fools, and we need to get out of here before he comes back." But before they left, the kappa reappeared and asked Jai to follow him into the woods, where he would whisper the secret.

"I can't do that. I mustn't leave the path. You can tell me here."

"I cannot enter the path; it is forbidden. You must come to me."

Song said, "Jai you go, and I'll stay on the path so we won't lose it."

"Yes," said the kappa. "That will do."

Jai, suspicious of this whole exchange, said, "No, I will not. Once again we are at a standoff."

"Then we will go our separate ways, nothing gained and nothing lost."

"That is not true," said Jai. "You have gained your hand, and I have gained nothing in return. And now that you are whole again, how do I know you won't try and eat us as your nature dictates?"

After a moment's thought the kappa said, "You are right. I can sense what you would taste like, and it is starting to drive me to hunger, so I will complete the deal and then you must leave quickly. Listen carefully: the Tengu lives exactly where you think he does." With that the kappa disappeared into the woods.

Jai called after him, "What do you mean? I don't know where he lives." But there was no reply.

Continuing on their way, the path narrowed to a point where the girls had to walk sideways in order to pass through the thick branches that seemed to want to prevent their progress. Night fell, and the moon cast eerie shadows across the path and the girls. All around they heard sounds of creatures dying, and the trees moaned and creaked. Song, holding onto Jai's waist cord, said, "Can we stop for the night? I am really scared."

Jai, unwilling to admit that she was also, said, "If you are too frightened, then I will stop. Sit down where you stand. We cannot go off the path. We will eat a little and try to sleep."

Jai waited until she was sure Song was asleep and allowed herself to do the same. Though exhausted, she became restless when her dreams of the Macao streets crept in.

# CHAPTER 4

She saw herself at the age of ten, a tough, battle-worn street urchin who neither asked for nor gave quarter when it came to the things she needed for survival. Always the maniac fighter, she lost few battles, which were almost always with older boys. After all, girls were seldom a part of the street scene, and if they were, they didn't last long.

One hot, lazy summer morning she was looking for a mark and thought she found one in the woman going in and out a high-class boutique. She was a well-dressed older woman who came out of the alley and went into the store. Figuring that she could grab her purse when she came back into the alley where no one could see, her choice was made. Things went exactly as planned; she ran up behind the woman and snatched her purse and continued to run past her.

It was a clean snatch, so as she went she was feeling good and counting the money in her head. Then out of nowhere she slammed into a big hulk of a man. She heard the woman behind her yell, "Hold her, she has my purse."

Jai tried to get around the mountain, but to no avail. He had her by the neck and arm. She kicked and fought like a wild animal, but he just laughed.

When the woman caught up the man said, "Should I break her neck?"

"No, look at her fight; she's a hellcat that needs to be tamed and learn some manners. Throw her in the trunk, and we'll take her with us."

Jai continued to fight, biting and scratching her captor as the lady opened the trunk and he tossed her inside, slamming the lid and plunging her into darkness.

Jai lay in the trunk of the moving car, kicking and screaming for them to let her out. Finally realizing that this was useless, she calmed down and tried to formulate a plan. Recognizing that they would have to stop sometime and open the trunk, she reckoned that was her best chance to get away.

They traveled a long way. The last few miles were over bumpy gravel roads, and she was thrown around. When they came to a stop, she heard the woman talking to her through the closed lid.

"Will you come out peacefully? There is no place for you to run."

Jai did not reply. All sorts of crazy ideas were running through her head, but the one that scared her the most was her loss of freedom. Freedom was the only thing that made her life worthwhile. The woman asked again, but still Jai wouldn't answer. Then she heard the woman say something to someone, and there was silence.

A few minutes later she heard a rustling and a voice barking orders. She placed herself in a position to leap out of the car as soon as the lid opened, hoping to catch them off guard. When the trunk opened, Jai sprung forward with all her strength, then let out a scream of surprise as she realized she had been trapped in a heavy cargo net placed over the opening. Two pair of hands quickly wrapped her up and lifted out a very frightened girl, whose reaction resembled any wild animal caught in a trap.

"Take her to the ship and lock her up until we are three miles out to sea."

With those words Jai fought the net, but it had been tied closed and was being carried by two large men holding a pole that ran through it. Once on board she was carried down to the room the captain used as a brig and thrown inside. Alone and frightened, Jai sat on the bed and wept. It had been a long time since she cried, but the feeling of hopelessness overtook her and she lost any semblance of control.

# CHAPTER 5

Jai awoke and found that she was in actuality sobbing heavily. The dawn was just breaking. She looked around for Song, but she was not to be found. She called out again and again, but there was no response. *What will I do? We have to arrive at the bridge together.* Deciding to wait and see if she would show up, Jai started her morning exercises. The longer and harder she worked, the more afraid she became. *Where could she have gone, and why would she leave me?*

Out of frustration she screamed, "Song, where are you?"

Hours passed, and Jai knew she had to come to a decision. Only two things could have happened: either she had been taken or she wandered off by herself. *She heard me say the mantra hundreds of times. Maybe she used it?* Deciding to wait awhile longer, Jai continued to perform her martial arts forms over and over.

Time passed quickly, until she heard a strange noise coming from behind. She took a defensive stance, ready for anything that might happen, and looked behind her. She saw a very strange and hideous sight. The creature was in human form but had wings and very long and sharp nails on its feet and hands, and it carried a good-sized bamboo fan.

Jai yelled, "Who are you, and what do you want?"

"I am your worst fear. I am one that you cannot defeat with your silly antics of flying feet and hands."

"We will see," Jai yelled and charged, but the creature just laughed and stepped aside, whacking Jai across the butt as she ran by.

Time and again Jai attacked, but each time she was laughed at and struck by the fan. Finally she pretended exhaustion and fell to her knees over the top of her pack. Reaching inside she grabbed four throwing stars and a long, sharp knife.

Jumping to her feet, she yelled, "Now you will feel my steels."

But she couldn't find the creature, not until she heard its laughter from above. Looking up she saw him sitting on a branch in the tree, and he had grown to twice the size. Jai, concentrating on the beast's forehead, leapt in the air, intending to attack with her knife, but the creature reacted just as fast and jumped down, landing on Jai's shoulders, where he made himself comfortable and rode her to the ground.

"What have you done to Song?"

"Who?"

"The girl I am traveling with."

"Why do you think it is I who have done something to her?"

"Who else?"

"These woods are full of creatures that are out to do you harm."

"Why? I have done neither you nor them any harm."

"What do you see when you look behind?"

"Whatever is there?"

"Wrong! What do you see when you look inside of you?"

Jai, surmising that "whatever is there" would be wrong, thought for a few minutes and said, "*What I am.*"

"And what are you?"

"Unlike you, I am human."

Hearing that the creature puffed himself up and roared like a banshee. Jai, really frightened now, grabbed her pack and started to run, quickly remembering the mantra she chanted, and the path lit up. The creature, flying above the treetops and screeching, chased her. She ran until she didn't see or hear him any longer and then stopped running. Now she found herself in a quandary. *Should I go back and try to find Song, or continue on?*

Sitting down to rest and collect her thoughts, she heard from above, "What do you see when you look inside yourself?"

Jai looked up, and there he was sitting on a treetop, but now he was twice as big as before and oozing slim. Even more frightened than ever, she screamed, "Go away. I know what you are."

"What am I?"

"You are what the Buddhists call the devil, and you eat people's brains."

The creature roared once again, then flew down and landed behind Jai, but she didn't see or hear him until he said, "What do you see when you look behind you?"

Jai, in a panic, turned and looked but could only see his ankles. Looking up, his head now reached the treetops, and she believed her fate was sealed. She answered, "I see you."

"Now turn around and tell me what you see."

Jai turned once again and said, "I see you, but now you are bigger and uglier."

The creature said, "Now look inside yourself, and what do you see?"

"I don't know," Jai cried out.

"You have until the moon rises to figure out my koans. If you do not, I will surely eat your brains." With that the creature disappeared.

Jai racked her brain, trying to logically figure out the Buddhist-like riddles, but everything she came up with was too easy. *What do I see when I look behind me? Whatever is there. What else could it be?* She could tell that the sun was setting and the moon would rise soon. She told herself that there was no use. So she closed her eyes and thought of her teacher. *At least I'll die thinking pleasant thoughts.* But all she could see was the monster, and every way she turned he was still there.

"That's it," she screamed. "Behind me is my past, and no matter which way I turn, it will still be with me. It dictates what I've become and what I will see in the future. Yes, that's it!"

*Now about the other one. Let's see, what do I see when I look inside of me?* But once again she couldn't figure it out. She knew that the answers she reasoned would be the same. So she closed her eyes and waited for her inevitable death. Her teacher popped into her head, and as he always did, he quietly said to her, "*Act without fear or emotion.*"

Just as she thought that, the monster appeared once

again and said, "Well, my little friend, do you have my answers?"

"Yes, I do," Jai said and stood up. "When I look behind me, I see all that awaits me as I go forward."

"Excellent, but that was the easy one. What did you see when you looked inside yourself?"

"Before I answer, tell me what happened to Song."

The monster laughed and said, "If you get this right, she will be dropped at the foot of the bridge, where you will be reunited."

Jai smiled and in a defiant tone said, "When I looked inside me, I saw my fear of you, and I realized that you only exist because of that fear. You are the embodiment of my fears, therefore not real, and cannot hurt me. Fear is what eats our brains."

As she was speaking, the monster shrunk down until he no longer existed, but before he was totally gone, she heard him say, "Act without fear or emotion."

Hearing that brought a smile to Jai's face, and she asked aloud, "Are you my teacher?" But there was only silence.

# CHAPTER 6

Without the burden of Song to carry, Jai decided to chance running on the path at night. It was unsettling thinking that she might arrive at her destination without Song, but there was nothing she could do but carry on. After resting and eating a small amount of berries and fruit, she headed out. Because the path was so narrow, overrun with trees and bushes, she decided not to use her bounding abilities, and so she ran while chanting the magical mantra with each step forward.

Not allowing herself to be infested by fear, she ran past ferocious animals and ghostly apparitions. She struggled through roaring rivers, across steep rocks that were sharp as a razor, and trees with branches that seemed to want to grab her, but she never parted from the trail. It was almost daylight when she stopped to have a drink of water and some berries. Seated up against a tree, she thought she heard someone whistling a tune. When she looked up, she saw the handsomest young man she had ever seen. Beguiled by his looks, she didn't move as he approached her.

He spoke first. “Hello, let me say up front I have never seen one as pretty as you. What is your name?”

“Jai, and yours?”

“I am Ka Khi. What are you doing here?”

“I am going to the mystery land.”

“But you are on the wrong path.”

“I can’t be. This is the way I was told.”

“You must listen to me. I have always lived on the island with my aunt the healer, so obviously I must know the way. You are on the path to the land of demons.”

“But that’s not possible.”

“Trust me, I know the way.”

“Why should I trust you? I don’t know you.”

“Look to your heart. You will see that you can.”

“You are a beautiful boy, and my heart races when I look at you.”

“Then you will come with me?”

But Jai hesitated and then said, “I just don’t know.”

The boy pulled off his shirt, exposing a beautifully muscular body, and said, “Come, let’s go for a swim. The water is warm, and we can get to know each other better.”

Jai’s body reacted like it hadn’t since she was in bed with her teacher. The old stirrings that she thought she would never feel except with him brought her body back to life. Now confused, she again hesitated. Jai watched as the boy dropped his pants. Seeing that his legs were beautifully shaped and he was well endowed and growing, she felt an even greater urge, and Jai had always loved that feeling of slowly building passion.

Blushing and yet excited, she gave in and said, “Okay, I guess I will follow my heart.”

"Before I can take you, you must kiss me."

"Why?"

"To show that you trust me."

Jai stepped closer, then suddenly stopped, and said, "A kiss proves nothing."

"Please do not argue. We must get going. Now kiss me, and then we can leave."

"Tell me, Ka Khi, if I offered you a choice between my kiss and the beautiful young rabbit that hides in my pack, which would you choose."

"I don't have time for games."

"Answer me, which would you choose?"

Jai watched as the boy struggled with the answer. "Answer me," Jai yelled.

The boy got all ruffled and turned red and blurted out, "The rabbit."

"You are not a boy. What are you?"

The boy said, "I am an anthropomorphized coyote with human characteristics."

"What do you want with me?"

"To seduce and mate with you. Then our children can walk the earth as you do. How did you know?"

"You asked me to trust your words and kiss. I trust in experiences, not words or kisses, plus humans don't look like you and definitely don't smell like you. Be off with you, Ka Khi the coyote."

And so he turned toward the woods and walked away on all fours. Shaking his head, he turned around and said, "Go, the bridge is just around the bend."

Now excited, Jai picked up her pack and ran around the bend, and as he said there was a golden bridge. As Jai left the woods, vicious-looking creatures of all sizes and shapes threatened her. The blades of grass were tipped with poison, but she just kept repeating the mantra that kept her safe.

Arriving at the bridge's edge, she looked around for Song, but she was not there. She sat down and waited, believing that they had to cross the bridge together. Time slowly passed with no sign of Song or anyone else. *How long do I wait? Where is that monster that promised to bring her to me?* she asked herself. Hearing a screech from above, Jai saw a creature she had not seen before flying toward her carrying Song. He swept down and without a single word dropped the girl at her feet and flew off.

Song did not move, and when Jai tried shaking her awake, nothing happened. She put her ear to the girl's heart, but there was no sound. Jai tried everything she could, but the girl wouldn't respond. Giving up, she broke down and sobbed. *Now will I also die? All this way for nothing!*

Jai came to some quick decisions; she picked up Song and carried her back to the edge of the woods, where she built a pyre and placed the girl on top, and with her flint she lit it afire. She thought to herself, *Unlike me, at least you will be purified.*

When she walked back to the bridge, she realized that this time she hadn't said the mantra to and from the woods. Still crying, she walked across the bridge, and when she looked up, she saw what looked like a golden orb glimmering in the sun. Walking toward her was the old woman that she met on the trail, this time in the form of the young beautiful girl.

"Hello, Jai," she said.

"Song is dead." Was all she could manage to say?

"I know. Let us sit down and I'll explain."

"But you said our lives were entangled as one."

"Yes, that is true. When I first appeared to you in the woods Song was barely alive, and I could feel the need in you to keep her alive. After all you had been through at the temple seeing the people you had come to love all dead, followed by the traumatic experience of helplessly having to stand by while she was repeatedly raped, I felt that if she were to die then you would give up your desire to live. I gave her enough of my energy to keep her alive, but in reality it wasn't enough, so I had the winged creature take her dead body away."

"So the creature is one of you?"

"Oh heavens no. I made a deal with him."

"What deal?"

"That he could keep her tortured soul, and she would become one of them. Her soul for yours."

"Why?"

"Many reasons. For one, your training at the temple proved that you have very rare abilities for a human. Then there was your desire to save Song, and A Ma is particularly interested in meeting one such as you. Now we must go. She awaits."

Walking across the golden bridge, Jai asked, "I have seen you as an old woman, a wolf, and a young girl. Which are you really?"

Just as she finished, the girl morphed into a cobra coiled in a strike position, and she hissed. Jai jumped back then she heard the snake laugh, and she immediately turned back into a young girl.

"What else would you like me to be?" the girl asked.

"I'd like to see you as you really are."

"But I am all those things."

"How is that possible? Wait, I know, you are putting it in my head, and I see you as you want me to."

"That would be true if I were a human adept in such a practice, but I am not human. In your words I am a being with powers beyond earthly humans."

"And A Ma?"

"She is the leader."

"So this A Ma can be all those things that you showed me?"

"More, so very much more."

As they walked further in Jai could feel a surge of good energy, and when she turned toward the girl, the girl smiled. Strangely shaped buildings and vehicles began to appear. In the center an orb took shape, and Jai said, "Wow, the orb looks like it's made out of beautiful layers of spun cloth."

"Very observant. It is made out of silk spun into overlapping layers of lace."

"It seems so delicate and fragile."

"There are only a few things that can cause its destruction; hate, prejudice, lies, and a war between good and evil if it is proven to exist. And there's the death of the A Ma, which causes her home to immediately incinerate. Another will be built for the new leader.

"The grounds are amazingly covered by wildflowers of all colors, and a few I've never seen. And look at those beautiful trees laden with fruit and beehives. I think Song would have loved this place. I am truly sorry that I could not save her. Wait, look over there. Do you see what I see?"

"What do you see?"

"It's a big Siberian tiger walking with two small deer, and they are headed this way."

"They're just coming over to say hello."

"Oh gosh, this is a fairyland."

The mystical woman burst out laughing and said, "Welcome to the Island of the Gods. There will be time for you to explore all that lives here, but for now we must enter the A Ma's estate."

Walking through a maze of hanging doors held up by tightly woven, thick bars of silk, Jai and her escort entered the orb. Much to her amazement, there were fairylike creatures standing all around. Every possible size and shape occupied the room. They all seemed to be in deep conversation, not having noticed her entrance at all. There was no furniture, but there was a three-step riser at the end of the room.

Someone struck a gong, and every creature stopped talking and faced the riser. They watched as a beautiful multicolored flower bud slowly descended by a gossamer string. As it neared the floor of the riser, its petals opened to reveal the most beautiful human-looking woman known only to those who inhabit this island. Completely naked, her skin was shimmering and reflected a multitude of ever-changing colors. Stepping out of the flower, she walked to the front of the riser, and with each movement the colors, which were almost scale like in appearance, changed hues, spanning the whole range of their value. It was like watching a living kaleidoscope. The A Ma raised her hand, and everyone sat down on the floor. Jai couldn't believe the spectacle before her and involuntarily gasped.

Then the A Ma spoke. "Bring the girl forward."

As Jai approached the A Ma's aura grew and seemed to rise and lower with each step that Jai took. Now seeing her up close, she recognized that the A Ma was asexual, having no male or female organs. "Come, child, and stand before me. I want to have a good look at you."

Stepping onto the platform, the A Ma's aura darkened, and she said, "Jai, I believe that is your name, your body is still crawling with a disease, one that is slowly killing you, so before I can know you, you must be cured." She looked at a small elflike creature, and he walked over. A Ma whispered something, and he left the room.

"Come with me, my child," said the A Ma. She turned and led Jai out of the room and down a long maze of hallways to a small room containing a bed, a small table, and one chair. "It is in this room that you will be cured of your disease. You will be under a drug-induced sleep so the energy I pour into you can fight the bacteria and germs that have invaded your mind and body. It will not be pleasant, but if your will is strong, we shall win the battle."

"What do I call you?"

"A Ma. It is my title."

"Do you have a name?"

"All of us have names, but they are never spoken aloud, and we should never be seen by mortal humans."

"Are your people born as you are now?"

"Yes, but they are special reincarnates, but enough for now. The herbs have been gathered and must now be seen to while they are still potent. I will return as soon as the potion is finished. In the meantime you need to undress and lay on your stomach on the bed while my assistant locates and traces all the correct areas that we need to treat for your healing. Then I suggest you rest."

Jai watched the A Ma leave the room, and Jai felt that she was alone so she disrobed and lay down on the bed. It was only a minute or two before the elflike creature returned and started to run his hands over her body. She found herself a little embarrassed, but his touch was so caring and warm so she gave into it almost immediately. Then, without a word he left.

Jai dozed off, but it wasn't long before A Ma and the elf returned. The elf was carrying a board of thick needles laid out in a strange pattern. The A Ma spoke.

"Now listen, Jai, what we are going to do is put the brewed remedy on these needles, which are positioned to be inserted into points on your body with the aim of restoring your body to its natural functioning state. These points run along fourteen channels, but we are also going to hit some extra points plus the points where stagnation has taken place. By doing this the potion will spread fast, killing the disease. After that is done, you and I will spend time purifying your energy."

"How long will this take?"

"No one knows, but you will be in a state of delirium the whole while. If your will is not strong enough or your body is too far gone, you will die, but if we don't administer this potion you will die anyway. Relax your body, and we will begin."

# CHAPTER 7

Having taken the potion, Jai was barely conscious and battling for her life. Most of the time she was hallucinating, picturing her younger years.

She saw herself once again at ten years old, locked up, not knowing what her fate would be. In a near state of panic, sealed in a room for three days aboard a rolling ship, she constantly pleaded to be let out. Finally the door opened, and there stood the two men, who carried her on board in a net.

One of the men said, "We are far out at sea, and you have no place to run except into the bellies of sharks, so if you try to escape we will certainly allow that. Know also if you give us any trouble, we will throw you overboard to those same hungry sharks that follow the ship's garbage. Do you understand?"

"Yes. What is to become of me?"

"That's for the captain and the ship's owner to decide. Now come along and keep still."

Entering the captain's quarters, Jai was surprised to see a cabin lavish in furnishings and décor. She was facing the woman who put her in this predicament. The woman said, "Well young lady, I would imagine you are pretty worried. I know I would be."

"Yes, ma'am."

"When you so blatantly stole my purse, I could see that you were a street waif with probably no home. Where are your parents?"

"In a small village. My father sent me to the auction block when I was seven."

"Did you run away from the block?"

"No, nobody would buy me, so my brother left me in a cardboard box in an alley and went home."

"Now that's a sad tale. I can take pity on one such as you. I will put you in the galley; you can start by cleaning the floors and washing pots and pans. If you are obedient the cooks will teach you to cook and you'll have a trade that can carry you the rest of your life. What do you think?"

"What choice do I have?"

"None, and make sure you come to terms with that. Captain, call for the cook, and I will give him my orders."

The woman and the captain ignored her as she waited for the cook, and when he showed up, the woman said, "This is your new galley worker. Make sure you hear me clearly: if you or any of your men lay a hand on the girl, I will hang the offender and you. Understood?"

"What about the rest of the crew?"

"The captain will see to them. Now away with both of you, and be sure she is given the proper clothes."

Jai spent over three years in the galley. She blossomed into a beautiful girl with very long black hair and a body defined by muscles. She managed to keep it all under wraps with baggy clothes and a large scarf for her head. Bunking with the rest of the crew, she made sure that she was never seen without a full set of clothes on her body. There was only one incident, and that occurred when a new officer signed on board. He got drunk one night and crawled into the bed with her. While trying to rip off her clothes, she managed a scream that woke all those in the crew's quarters. They grabbed him and took him to the captain. He had the man tied to the mast and whipped for all to see and then threw him off the ship at the next port.

Six months later while in port, she was called to the captain's quarters, where the owner was waiting for her. Alone together, the owner asked her how old she was.

Jai answered, "Almost fourteen."

"Take off your scarf and clothes. I want to see what you look like."

"But ..."

"No buts, and do not disobey me. Now do what I ask."

Jai, who was very shy, did what she was told. She was now completely naked, and the woman said, "My you are a beautiful girl, tall and shapely. Okay, get dressed. My mind is made up. You have become a good cook with many culinary skills, but I cannot keep you on my ship any longer. It won't take long before the crew throws caution to the wind and goes after you. Understand I wouldn't blame them, but I won't have that on my ship. Make yourself ready to leave the ship forever. I have a friend that runs a respectable house in Macao. You can cook there, and she will probably teach you other skills that could benefit the both of you. Of course I will ask a tidy sum for someone as beautiful as you. Now go and pack whatever things you have."

Jai, going in and out of a hallucinatory state, kept babbling about the angel that saved her from the streets of Macao and then deposited her with another angel. Eleven days went by. Then early one morning the battle was won and Jai's clear eyes opened. The first thing she saw was a smiling A Ma sitting on the edge of her bed.

"You are a very strong young woman, Jai; not many have beaten the combination of viral microorganisms you had. Now you must rest and regain all the physical strength you have lost. How are you feeling?"

"I don't know. I'm just weak, and I do not remember very much."

"Do you remember the temple where you trained?"

"Trained in what?"

"The mystical and martial arts."

"Sorry, I don't remember at all."

"Well, we shall see what you do remember after you return to normal, though I know that you are not."

"Not what?"

"Normal."

Days turned into weeks and weeks into months as Jai regained her strength, but there was no change in her ability to consciously remember her past. Her dreams stopped coming, and her nights were spent peacefully in a deep sleep.

Every day just before dinner Jai joined in with all the residents of the island who were gathered in the forests for talks given by the A Ma. She spoke about the reasons why they, after all the hundreds of thousands of years on this planet, were forced to live separately from humans.

Jai listened in amazement as the A Ma told how they used to live all over the world in consort with the humans, and it all changed when humans came to worship a single deity who it was said gave the humans dominion over the earth and its creatures. So it came to pass that alien beings—they once called gods—were seen as a threat.

Each afternoon after the talk the A Ma held Jai back

from the group as they went to gather fruits, seeds, and grasses to eat. Slowly after a long period of time, she revealed to Jai that Jai was in fact only half an earthly human. Her real mother was one of their kind sent to mate with an earthling in order to bear a child who was partially a humanoid alien and could openly live among them.

"We had hoped you would be capable of performing the same mystical feats as we can and add to it the skills as practiced by the highly skilled lamas of the holy lands but also to be able to transcend beyond her human prejudice and fight for the rights, liberties, and freedom for our people to walk once again among them, openly.

"I did not learn any magical tricks from the temple."

"Yes, my dear, you did. You are the reason we were at the temple. We came to watch you perfect the magic of the lamas. We had to be sure that you were the one, and I know you are."

"But I do not have any of these alien mystical skills that you speak of."

"Again, yes you do, but you do not know how to use them. They lie dormant, and that is part of my job, to awaken the knowledge that allows you to do things beyond normal humans—things that have not been seen or heard since the early stages of humankind on this planet. On top of that, through spiritual growth you will transcend, and with the honing of each set of powers the two species' individual assets will combine and you will be something never before seen on any inhabited planet in any universe."

Upon hearing these words Jai became very anxious. *What will I transcend to? I don't understand any of this.*

"Now, my dear, I am forced to tell you that the human

race as you know it was conceived by the mating of inferior animals of our planet and your apelike creatures. It was a tragic accident on our part. These beasts that we brought on our journey as we were seeking habitation on new planets were to be used as beasts of burden as they were on our home planet. They were successfully transported to other planets over many thousands of years, planets throughout the universes where our people now live in peace. One day, through our negligence, they broke free and scattered throughout the land. When the land masses broke apart, they found different apelike creatures to mate with, and that's why there are so many different races on Earth."

"So if I'm to understand you correctly, we humans are actually made up of two inferior beings, each half a mutation, as is the whole. Am I right?"

"Yes, a bit simplistic, but nevertheless correct."

"I would love to know more about your planet, races, actually the whole universe, but I am curious to know what I will do with all those incredible alien and human powers that you say I will have at my disposal."

"Your primary purpose will be to combat the humans who seek us out with the desire to extract all our knowledge through torture and threats before they destroy us out of fear and reprisal."

"Is it possible to win such battles?"

"Not by yourself. There are a few that have been identified that will help you. Whether you will win or not, I do not know, but we will try."

"You said you knew for many years that this person could be created through the means you described. How could you be so sure?"

"It is written so."

"Where is it written?"

"In the wind. We will start tomorrow."

The rest of that day and night Jai spent trying to make sense of all that she was being told. *Who was I before I lost her memory to the illness? What are these powers I possess, and what new powers will I learn? Exactly which battles will I be asked to fight, and how can I possibly win a war that's been raging for hundreds of years?*

The next morning Jai met the A Ma in the garden. "Today we will begin by attempting to regenerate your abilities gained from the practice of *lung-gom.* It should go quickly because your body will remember even if your mind doesn't."

The A Ma told Jai what she needed to do to regain her powers of *lung-gom.* It was all part of her retraining, and Jai felt suddenly hopeful. Tendrils of past training linked to her time at the temple started to emerge as the A Ma spoke.

"Over time all you have learned will return to you as your body and mind recognize what it is you are attempting."

When the A Ma finished, Jai walked over to an open space amid beautiful wildflowers and sat down. Jai felt the A Ma will her to rise an additional three feet off the ground. Then she removed her hand, and Jai just floated across the lawn as she had previously learned to do using the *lung-gom* discipline.

When the A Ma was satisfied that Jai's mind and body were again accustomed to flight, she brought Jai out of her trance and said, "Do that again, but this time try and reach your trance state a lot quicker."

Jai, trying not to be enraptured by the aroma emanating

from the flowers, reached a trance state in half the time and levitated off the ground by herself. She then followed her previous route over and around the forest ceiling.

Satisfied, the A Ma sent a message for Jai's weapons to be brought to where they were. While they waited Jai said, "I don't see how my skill with ancient weapons can be used to fight modern artillery."

"You must master all your previous skills before this month is out. Then we will teach and train you to master as many of our abilities that a superhuman such as yourself is capable of, things that your world call paranormal, and it will take as long as it does. There is a definite urgency to get you in prime condition in order to mold and lead the operation, and of course to get it underway.

"But I do not have the knowledge necessary."

"I will place all you need to know in your subconscious, and when the time comes that it's necessary for you to use it, it will automatically enter your conscious mind. As for all else that needs to be known, the people who are the leading experts in their fields will be working for and with you."

"If they are the experts, why would they follow me?"

"Because you will have the strength and paranormal abilities to gain their respect and hold them all together as a highly proficient group.

# CHAPTER 8

When the month was over, Jai had mastered not only her weapons but also the four martial art disciplines she had mastered in her previous training.

In the early morning as Jai was exercising, she listened carefully as the A Ma began to explain what her missions would be once she was finished training.

"You must see your mandates as one and the same. After all, without a clean, purified planet our people would eventually die off anyway. So your task is to destroy what and who is destroying the planet and the peace between our peoples. This living planet is fighting a losing battle against man's greed and technology. Man follows no rules in attempting to fulfill his greed for power, supremacy, and wealth. You will lead the crusade against our enemies and the planets."

Jai continued her push-ups. The physical activity felt good and made her feel stronger than she ever had before. She knew her strength was vital to winning the war that would come against the enemies of the aliens and the planet itself. The pollution of the air, water, and land that humankind had let happen now threatened her people with extinction. Such an event seemed unthinkable to Jai. She exercised with renewed vigor, the sweat pouring off of her. She tasted salt, and it tasted good. It tasted like her very essence, her very soul.

"We taught the earthlings much of what they know today, in science, math, astronomy, even music. But due to the abundance of tainted food, water, and air, our bodies are slowly losing their ability to reproduce, and like many of the Earth's creatures, we will become extinct.

"The battle for the Earth to survive is almost lost, but for one fact, and that is there are a few such as you that can help bring the Earth a long way back to nature's original design. Until you, no one else had the necessary abilities to lead them.

"When you are ready, all the paranormal skills that you acquired will be stored in an energy form within you. There will be one exceptional man who will take you through transcendence of your human boundaries achieved by powerful energies that the two of you will create using human sexual methods. For this to be accomplished, you must give yourself to him totally, and without reservation. He will more than satisfy your human sexual needs, but you will not carry the burden of what humans call love toward him, because what they call love is selfish and has nothing to do with true love. Having transcended, the desire to be with others in a sexual way will be heightened. This man is also a warrior, but he will not be one of your best. His further purpose is to continue to create purified energies within you, allowing you to maintain the highest level of transcendence. You might say he recharges your batteries.

"The people who were identified as the best choices for your teams are waiting for you. As the director, you will command and direct training, technical support, information gathering, supply accumulation and dispersion, and mission profiles, all under your guidance. You report to no one and answer only to yourself and the A Ma or her representatives. The task is daunting and the responsibilities even greater, but hopefully in your training you will be made ready to undertake what lies ahead. Now let us eat and rest, for starting tomorrow you move into realms that you have never seen or even heard of."

Jai, trying to absorb all that she was being told, asked, "These others, where were they trained? Here I assume?"

"Oh no, you are the only one that has ever been inside this land of ours. The others are masters of the highest rank in their respective disciplines but still not worthy of entering this land. There is also one other element, a very powerful secret international group of people that you will be allied with if you prove to be successful in your missions."

"Are they environmentalists?"

"Some are, but for the most part, no. Known as the Company, they have been in existence since the end of the Franco Prussian war in 1871. Then as now, they are the best to be found in humanitarian and environmental causes. They control governments, dictators, spy agencies, military leaders, and religious leaders and always have. Their cause is to rid this world of any and all that threaten its peace or environment."

"If they are as you say, why have they failed so miserably?"

"Simply put, since the 1920s they have made horrendous mistakes, most of them political and economic. Their motivations are true and just, but their common sense and intuition are lacking to say the least."

"Why should we do their bidding?"

"You won't! You'll be strictly autonomous, picking and choosing your own missions and priorities."

Jai, feeling a little confused, asked, "How come, with all your capabilities, you haven't been able to stop the ongoing destruction of the planet?"

"Because we waited far too long, and now we cannot go outside the ever-decreasing area we are able to survive in."

The next day Jai was awakened at five in the morning and told to return to the gardens, where the A Ma would be waiting. Casually walking to where she believed she was expected, Jai sensed a strange energy coming from the thick bushes on her right. It took her back to the path and the negative energy she felt before being confronted by potentially dangerous creatures. Anxiety crept in. *I must get a hold of my anxiety and allow my training to take over.* She instinctively put her mind in a trance state. Then with a single leap, she rose high enough above the thicket and in a flash she was above the creature that crouched in hiding, prepared to throw the spear it was holding. Jai floated above and behind it, waiting to see if there was another reason this creature was waiting in ambush. After a minute or so she was satisfied that she was the one. Suddenly she felt she was back at war with the Chinese contingent, and her survivor instincts kicked in.

She quickly and quietly landed, and with a single movement of her arm, she unarmed the creature, and with her other hand she grabbed its neck in such a way to render it unconscious.

Instantly the A Ma appeared and said, "I see that all your instincts are returning, including ones that we have not practiced." Then she touched the unconscious creature's head with her palm, and he recovered in an instant. "Any after effects?" she asked the creature.

"No, none. I do not feel any different."

"Thank you for your help."

"I wouldn't want to face her in real battle," he said and walked away.

"Before we get started, I want to examine your brain and physical structure. Please sit on that stump and I'll begin."

Jai did what she was told, and the A Ma placed her hand on Jai's head. Jai saw the A Ma's aura change to a brilliant white sparkling light while she was pouring her energy into Jai. The A Ma smiled.

She said, "As I thought, you are different, your brain and physical internal structure are not as the others. You do in fact have the natural capability of performing the same feats as we can. As I told you, you are a mutant, part human and part us. Now it is time to awaken the alien in you. You are what you are, and you are predestined to do what you are training to do.

"The skills you master from me are necessary just to be able to control the people under your command. Remember, humans with genius IQs or those perfecting great physical prowess have a great inclination to rule. Unfortunately their egos grow in direct proportion to the size of their muscles or IQ number."

A Ma continued. "An example might be your ability to do astral travel and to enter the person's mind you are out to destroy. It will give you the information necessary to set up the mission. Actually my sense is that profiling may be one of your weakest assets, so it might be necessary for you to find one who is better."

Jai interrupted. "So profiling, or understanding normal people might be a downfall. What then is my best asset?"

"Your greatest asset will be your instinct to think beyond any human or machine man has built. You will also be able to process information at a speed greater than their best computer. Then as time goes by and humans create even greater artificial intelligence computers, you will be able to outthink them."

"So I'm some kind of freak."

The A Ma, chuckling, said, "Aren't we all? But let's not think about that. It is time for breakfast, then on with your lessons. Where are you going?"

"To breakfast."

"Not today. Today we will eat from the earth, while we expand on your previous knowledge of medicinal herbs and berries, without going into them at this time. There are five methods of medical procedures that you will be able to provide or perform."

"Unbelievable!"

"As part of your training I will take you on a meditative retrospective tour of the changes on this planet since the mid-eighteen hundreds. It will be like watching a super-fast movie of the hundreds of thousands of creatures that have been killed off, the lush forests that no longer exist, the pure, clear oceans, lakes, and streams that are now so polluted that nothing can live in them, and the wonderful grasslands that are now contaminated with chemicals and its soil barren. These pictures I promise you will sicken you to the point that will make you aware and angry enough to do the job that needs to be done."

"A Ma, some times when I am strolling on the grounds, I hear strange noises I have never heard before. Will you tell me what they are?"

The A Ma laughed and said, "The high-pitched notes are coming from the lake that surrounds our land. It is the merpeople, or mermaids as your people call them. They were also known as sirens in ancient times. What is left of them reside here because they can no longer live in the oceans or seas. The fluttering sounds are the pixie fairies. They are mischievous by nature. They are also the only fairies that can still live in the outside world. Their breathing and swallowing apparatuses have a multitude of filters that can eliminate impurities from the air, food, and water. But most choose to live with the rest of us. They do not have the ability for imagination or creativity; if they did, they could help you. They are barely two inches in length and have wings that make that noise you hear."

"Are there any others out there?"

"Yes there is the Sidhees that live in subterranean dwellings, never to come above ground. They are in the deep, untouched jungles or beneath mountains. Any other questions before we begin your first lesson?"

"No, not now. I am anxious to start. Oh wait, how long will all this take?"

"Let's see, you are approaching seventeen human years. I hope that we can be finished by the time two more of your years are done. Is that all?"

"Yes."

"Then let us continue. Since some form of energy is a major part of everything that exists, your ability to control all its forms is your primary purpose.

"It seems to me that no one human can master all this in two years, no less," Jai pondered out loud.

"Remember that you are only part human so your brain is different, and second most of this information will be stored in your subconscious and will automatically be brought forward into your conscious mind the exact moment it is needed. The time differential will be minuscule.

"Always remember the utilization or introduction of the forces of energy unknown to humans in any way is forbidden. The consequences are dire to you and our mission. Understand?"

"I understand the words, but the difference between known and unknown energies I do not."

"Trust me, when the time comes for you to, you will. Let us start with a good example of different ways to utilize energy and yet achieve the same result. Let's look at the ability to make yourself invisible to those around you. First we have the slowing of the flow of energy and your heart rate to the point approximating death. Being perfectly still and taking very shallow breaths while in a meditative state does this. Second, by creating an energy shield around you that cannot be penetrated by light, the human eye cannot see beyond it. Third, directly removing your image from the observer's mind, and fourth, the very old shaman's way of shape changing, which uses a great deal more energy than the others.

"Now I'll demonstrate; can you see me?"

"No, you have totally disappeared."

"What method do you think I used?"

"Either you created an energy field, or you wiped your image from my mind."

"That is correct. I stand right in front of you, but your eyes cannot see beyond the shield. For the next few weeks you will learn how to do all these things and put them into practice. We will begin with your energy. Are you ready, Jai?"

"Yes, A Ma, I am."

# CHAPTER 9

Two weeks later Jai was sitting in the midst of a magical place, surrounded by magnificent flowers whose colors were so brilliant they would almost blind her, and the odors they emitted made her feel a little dizzy. The richness of the soil was obvious, as it appeared to be black and crawling with worms, known to the aliens as nature's farmers.

She began her meditation, hoping that this time she would be able to lower her energy level to a point where the multitude of creatures that lived in this part of the land would not be able to detect her presence. It had been two weeks since she began this practice, but she was never able to accomplish a perfect result.

Within a few minutes she reached the level where her energy began to lower. She became aware of the blood flowing through her veins and arteries as it begin to slow, and her breathing was very shallow. She felt like she was in a movie that was being shown in super slow motion. Her senses became super sharp, and she could hear the busy bees and butterflies moving all around where she sat. Her eyes were open but unfocused, so she was able to see images of animals grazing all around her. They had scattered as she first approached, and now thinking her gone, they returned. They moved closer, some even came within one or two feet, and she realized they still didn't know she was there. Excited because of the success, she finally achieved forced her energy to increase dramatically, and a wall of energy flew outward, spooking all the animals around her, and they bolted. Jai just sat there and laughed out loud. It was the first time in a very long time that she had.

Suddenly Jai felt a strange sensation overpowering her. It was like all she was doing what she had done before. *Is all this a replay of my forgotten past?* No answer was forthcoming.

Another week of practice and Jai had mastered the technique and was able to achieve a state of extremely low energy output in an instant. Then she and the A Ma began the next phase, which was the complete opposite: the building up of her energy and then the utilization of it.

All the while the A Ma was pouring information into Jai's subconscious. Sometimes there was a communion between the two, but most of the time Jai found that she just knew things. She sensed that her body was a computer and her mind the software. Her subconscious felt it housed stored files that were to be used by her mind only when it became necessary.

A Ma trained her in illusion in order to create scenarios in the enemy's mind so they may give away important information. Jai learned to separate her conscious mind from her subconscious. Thereby she was able to switch the two, allowing her to keep her focus away from what was happening around her or to her.

One year after Jai began her new practice, the A Ma came into her cave and looked carefully at her. Then she reached inside her and found that she was completely rid of all disease. A Ma saw that Jai was turning into a beautiful woman. In the outside world a female's looks were quite an advantage—superficial yes, but true nevertheless.

Time flew by as Jai lived only to train, learn, and gather as much information from the A Ma as she possibly could. The animals became her playmates, and as her skills were honed, she was able to outpace them in the game of tag she made up. She honed her abilities to appear and disappear, leap and float, throw her energy with pinpoint accuracy, heal wounds, sense the smallest energy within a quarter of a mile, instantly put up her shield when attacked, and enter and exit other people's bodies or minds without being detected. When she was able to interpret the thoughts and moods of those she entered, the A Ma knew that with a little further instruction Jai would be ready. She was one of them.

It had been two and a half years since she entered this land, and Jai was now approaching her nineteenth year when the A Ma said, "Well, my daughter, we are reaching the point where you must leave us and enter the outside world.

"People and machines await your arrival so that it can all begin. As much as we all regret you having to leave your new family, we all recognize that you are the only one who can lead those that await you. You must go and do what you are meant to do; after all, you have become all that you are meant to be. Before you go, we must discuss what awaits you. First of all, know that the people have been setting up the physical operation so it can start when you arrive. A billion or so has been siphoned out of accounts of eco-terrorists, and countries that fund them, but most of that has already been spent.

"We have a highly secret satellite waiting in orbit. Its country of origin has tried everything to reboot the onboard computers, along with its designer deliberately having admitted to possible mistakes and mishaps have written it off as unsalvageable. It was built with a new material that made the satellite invisible to the eye or electronic devices. This material was designed by the man who, for the time being, is overseeing the operation. His name is Denton. He is also the man who designed and created the satellite's communications computers and all the satellite's functioning software. He is waiting to reprogram its onboard computers to do our bidding. Right now he is designing what it will do in the future. You will study those functions with him, adding the things he can't possibly think of. Then you yourself will put in a failsafe system to prevent him or anyone from changing its functions.

"Denton is the person you will want heading up the tech department. His genius cannot be measured. He is an expert in many fields, but even better, his learning curve is off the charts. He has never answered to anyone, and that will be your most difficult task. You have the ability to outthink him and express it before he does. You must prove to him that your mind's capabilities are beyond his, something he has never faced before, but he may never fully know of your abilities. Because Denton is a huge key to the success of your operation, he must be immediately dealt with.

"We have hologram capability that will allow communications to oversee the whole mission as it is taking place. We have highly developed heat-sensing and x-ray equipment to help locate hostiles and electric sources, plus other spy equipment that Denton is developing now.

"Any nonterrorist hostile personnel that is brought to headquarters must be drugged and therefore unable to see or figure out where they are so that they may be released when you are finished with them.

"Another important thing you must remember: you are part human and part alien, and therefore you have two competing natures. So besides your alien intellect you also have the lower animal nature of the earthly human. Therefore there are times when you will act out as they would in disparity to your higher self. Recognize this when it happens and learn from it.

"And now it's time to tell you that there is an organization out there that is dedicated to destroying us. This group is governed by capitalists and governments whose interests and welfare depend on keeping the oil and coal industries in production. They have put together a small army of highly trained mercenaries, and their leader actually comes from the same temple that you were training at. He is as proficient as you in all the martial arts taught there."

Jai asked, "Do they know where this land is or where my headquarters are? Do they know about me?"

A Ma, looking rather dejected, answered, "I'm afraid we do not know the answers to your questions. I have to surmise that if they don't, they are actively searching. We do know from an inside government source that they exist, have a big budget, and will stop at nothing to complete their stated mission of destroying anyone trying to disrupt their big profits. I am hoping you are unknown to them.

"Now I believe you will want to spend the next day or two saying good-bye to all your friends and those who have helped you along the way. I will visit you tomorrow night just before you go to bed."

"Then what will happen?"

"You'll see. In the meantime, enjoy your remaining time here."

As Jai began to protest, she realized that the A Ma was no longer there. The rest of the night and following day she sat or played with the animals she had gotten to know so well, and made it a point to sit with each and every creature she had come to love in her time in the magical land of fairy like aliens. She became very emotional throughout this saying good-bye process and cried most of the time.

The following evening while she was preparing for bed, the A Ma appeared before her. "Well, Jai, there is so much I would like to say to you, but there are no words for my feelings. I see you as the daughter I never had or will have, and I am truly thrilled by what you have grown to be. I believe I now know that I would have been a good mother to my children had I had any."

"But A Ma, is it not possible for me to remain here? Can't there be another to do what I am trained to do? I love you so much, and somehow I feel deep down inside that you are not the first love I have lost. I don't know if I can be who you say I am without you guiding me."

"But my dear child, I will always be with you. I am in your head and heart for always. Never forget that. Now drink this tea I brought to help you sleep because I know you will be restless tonight and you have a long trip ahead beginning very early in the morning."

Jai drank the tea while the A Ma watched over her. Jai heard the fluttering sound that always made her smile, and the last thing she said before falling asleep was, "I love you, Mother."

"I love you too, my child."

# BOOK II

# CHAPTER 10

Jai's eyes sprang open, sensing something unfamiliar. Immediately awake, she looked around the dark room and recognized that she was not in the cave where she spent the last two and a half years. She tried to get up and out of bed, but she was hooked up to a heart monitor and had various other tubes attached to her body. Looking around she saw what looked like a stark hospital room. Her bed was alongside a large window, and she managed to see outside. There was a courtyard with a large fountain and what appeared to be Buddhist nuns moving around.

As one happened to approach the window, Jai called out, "What is this place? Can I see the A Ma?"

The nun, hearing a strange noise, moved closer to the window and peered in. Surprised to see the girl's eyes open, she responded, "Wait, my child, I will get the doctor and someone to speak to you in Mandarin. That seems to be your language."

"Yes, thank you."

She understood immediately that she was speaking in a

strange language. The door to the room opened, and a nun walked in. "Good morning. My name is Lavyana, I am the abbess of this convent and also your doctor. I am sorry but my Chinese is not very good. What is your name?"

"Jai. Where am I? You look Indian." When she said that, they both realized that Jai was now speaking Hindi.

"Yes, that is correct. You are in India, in the city of Dharamsala. Where did you learn to speak Hindi?"

Jai had no answer but continued to speak in Hindi. "But I don't understand—how did I get here?"

"You were brought to us almost three years ago by a young man who said he carried you a long way."

"What! That's not possible. Can I see the A Ma?"

"Sorry, I do not know of whom you speak. We have no one here by that name."

"You said I have been here for almost three years?"

"Yes, that is correct."

"What year is it?"

"Two thousand eleven."

"But that means I am still nineteen. I don't believe you."

Lavyana said, "You were brought here in a delirious state, having been found in the mountains by a young man.

"I have sent for him, the one who brought you here. Actually he's quite a young man now. Maybe he can explain better. You should know that you have been very ill since your arrival. At the beginning you were delirious, and then you went into a coma. You hadn't opened your eyes once until today. It was lucky that he brought you here. We are a training facility for female doctors and nurses."

"This is not possible, just yesterday I was …? I don't know where I was, but it was not here."

"It must all have been a dream. You have been here for almost three years."

"That just can't be."

"You are switching languages every sentence or so. I think I recognize English, French, Mandarin, and Spanish. Where did you learn all those languages?"

"I don't know. I just remember the A Ma."

Seeing that Jai was fully conscious, Lavyana unhooked the monitor and disconnected the feeding and elimination tubes. "I have to leave you for now. I will return with the young man, whose name is Makeen. In the meantime I think it best if you do not try to leave this room. You are very weak, and your body's muscles must have atrophied by now. We should be back here within the hour."

"Thank you. I won't go out."

Jai, in a state of total confusion, was able to get off the bed and sit on the floor without knowing why. She placed herself in her meditation pose, and shortly thereafter she was in a meditative state. Sitting in silence, her breathing very deep, she reached a state of calm and was able to free her mind of all she had heard. Time passed, and she became aware of people entering her space. She heard a scream. She looked around for the source but didn't see anyone.

Then she heard a woman say, "Dear Buddha, what is happening?"

Jai realized that the voice was below her and looked down to see the abbot and a man staring up in amazement. She naturally released her breath and floated down to the floor.

"What was that? Where did you learn to do that?" asked the nun.

"I don't know. I was sitting on the floor, and the next thing I knew I heard your scream and I looked down and then floated to the floor."

"Where had you been before you became ill with delirium?"

"I don't know."

"Please do not do that again, especially in front of the others. Here let me introduce you to Makeen, the person who brought you here."

"Hello, Makeen, my name is Jai."

"Glad to finally make your acquaintance," Makeen said.

The abbess said, "I must attend to some business. Jai, I am so amazed. You, for some unexplainable reason, seem to be fully recovered. Jai, if you feel strong enough, I'll take the two of you outside the property so that you may talk together. Men are not allowed here and especially in a woman's quarters. But before we go, I must say that you two are the most handsome people I have ever seen."

Lavyana, shaking her in disbelief, continued, "I think we might be looking at some kind of miracle."

Jai was feeling frightened, having no memory or understanding of what was going on in her life, and being asked to leave the grounds with a strange man was at the least unsettling. *What do I do? Will I be safe? I guess I will have to find out. They say he did bring me a long distance to the convent, so his interest in me must be good.*

Jai turned to Makeen and said, "Shall we go?"

As they walked through the courtyard, all the nuns stared and some even gasped. The abbess left them at the entrance gate and said, "Jai, please return no later than dusk or I cannot allow you back in till morning."

"Yes, I will. Thank you."

There was a beautiful park with a small lake and koi surrounding the convent, and they decided to explore it as they talked.

"So, Makeen, they tell me that you brought me to the convent three years ago. Is that correct?"

"Actually it's more like two and a half."

"I guess I owe you my gratitude."

"Maybe, but I think anyone would have done the same."

"Where was I when you found me?"

"On the southern slopes of the Himalayas. Actually you were in a wooded area lying up against a tree. You were pretty ill, and I couldn't make any sense of what you were babbling."

"So you just carried me here?"

"Actually, I carried you to a village about sixteen kilometers from where we started. It is the place my aunt and her family live. The local doctor said he could do nothing and suggested I bring you to the Buddhist convent. I believe it was because of the robe that you are wearing. It comes from a temple long ago destroyed by the Chinese in Tibet. Do you remember ever being there?"

"No, I do not remember anything at all except my name."

"Would you like some tea or maybe a coffee?"

"Yes, that would be great, but I have no money."

Laughing, Makeen said, "I do. There's a place across the street. Let's go there."

As they approached the café, Jai saw her reflection in the mirror and gasped. "My God, is that me? I had no idea I looked like that."

"When I first saw you, you were shorter and a lot thinner. You have grown into a magnificent woman."

Jai, looking at herself in the window, couldn't help but study the image standing with her. He was a gorgeous hunk of a man. He was taller than her by about three inches, with broad shoulders and chest and thin hips. He was very muscular, yet he seemed to move like a cat. She turned and looked at his face. He had blond, almost white hair and wore dark reflective glasses. The features of his face that she could see were angular, and he had a deep cleft in his chin. His skin was very pale, yet he looked oriental.

"Can you take off your glasses? I would like to see your eyes."

"When we are inside, I will."

Entering the café, Jai had this feeling of being displaced. Everything was new, and she had no memory of ever being in a place such as the café or even a big city. Yet with that she had a feeling of being where she should be. Having no memory of her life, she was both apprehensive and comforted at the same time.

Once seated and having ordered iced Indian tea, Makeen took off his glasses. Seeing the surprise on Jai's face, he said, "I am an albino. My skin can't tolerate very much sunlight, and neither can my eyes."

She saw that his eyes were two different colors, one almost pure yellow and the other hazel. Then he put his glasses on and said, "I hope my eyes don't upset you. If they do, I think you will get used to them. I have."

"No, it was just the initial shock. But seeing your eyes, I had this distinct feeling that I have seen them before."

"Well you have. As I said, it was years ago."

"Will you please help me remember? I have no recollection of how I got here, where I was, or even who I am. You said you found me on a mountain Do you know how I got there or who I am?"

"No, I do not," replied Makeen.

"Well then what took place after you found me?"

"As I said, I eventually brought you to the convent and handed you over to the sisters. They took you in, and that's all I know. I inquired as to your well-being on occasion, and until today I was told that you were in a coma and nothing had changed."

"How much longer will I be able to stay in the convent?"

"I doubt that they will allow you to stay. They will probably ask you to find a place and work so you can leave."

"But I don't know what I can do. What do you do?"

"Presently I'm a karate teacher at a dojo nearby. I also teach three other disciplines. Have you taken any martial arts classes?"

"I don't know."

"Would you like to come to my studio and watch for a bit?"

"Yes, that would be good. Is it far?"

"No, it is just two blocks from here. There are classes going on now so you will be able to see different levels of karate."

They finished their tea and walked over to the dojo. When they entered, Makeen bowed to the room, and Jai followed his lead. Everyone in the place stopped what they were doing and bowed to their head teacher. He announced that they would put on a demonstration for his guest starting with the two best wearing the white belts and proceeding to the black.

"As a final demonstration, I will spar with whichever of you feels he or she can give me the best match. Now let us begin."

The matches went on for an hour before they reached the black belt level. Jai was impressed with what she saw but was confused. She somehow knew that she had witnessed inferior fighters. *Maybe when Makeen fights I will see something better.* Makeen stood, and the silence was deafening. Finally Makeen called to the floor his best student-teacher and explained that he would do nothing to cause him to lose face.

After a minute or two, Jai recognized that Makeen was being soft and allowing blows that would never have struck before. He called an end to the sparring and thanked the class for the wonderful exhibition. *Why does all this feel so familiar? It's as if I have been a part of this type of thing before. Why can't I remember?*

Her thoughts ended when Makeen asked Jai what she thought, and she said, "I would like to try."

"Okay, pick a white belt and she will demonstrate some moves with you."

Jai bowed to the class and addressed them. "Who here would like to spar with me? Please stand." The whole class stood except for Makeen. Jai laughed, turned to him, and said, "I see you alone would like to spar with me."

"I do not think that is a good idea," he said.

Jai walked over to him and whispered, "Then take me to another room and we will spar."

"But this is foolish."

Jai said, "I have this gnawing feeling in my head and body that I am good at this. Please let me demonstrate either here or alone."

"Okay, we will do it here."

They walked to the center of the room and bowed to each other. Makeen immediately tried to sweep Jai off her feet, but she reacted instantly and stepped out of the way and kicked him in the side as he flew by. He gave her a questioning look, and she just shrugged her shoulders. He tried again and again, using different skills. She avoided him every time, but she didn't take any offensive action. There was a trickling of applause each time Makeen failed. If it had been two different fighters the class would have gone wild at the mastery of her moves. Suddenly Makeen called a halt to the action, and they bowed to each other. Then he stepped back and applauded her, and the class joined in.

Walking back to the convent, Jai said, "When we were sparring, I felt this incredible energy coming from you. What was that?"

"My chi. It builds, and I must be careful not to overdo it. By the way, I felt it in you also. Are you telling me that you never had lessons in either the martial or tantric arts?"

"Not that I can remember, but obviously there is a lot I don't remember and it scares me."

"I can't imagine that a girl who looks like you hasn't been reported missing somewhere."

"Maybe I have been, but right now it doesn't matter because I can't remember anything anyway."

"Here we are at the convent gate. With five minutes to spare, we better ring the bell."

"Yes, I had a great time today."

"Me too. Can I see you tomorrow?"

"Yes. I do not know what the abbess will expect of me,

but I'm sure I can get away. If you come by around ten, I'll know more."

"Good, I'll do that."

The gate opened, and the abbess said, "You just made it, my dear. Now hurry along. I must lead the services."

Walking to the stupa, Jai asked, "How long may I stay here?"

"You have been here much too long, I expect you to leave as soon as you find a place to stay outside these walls. I'm sorry, but those are the rules. There is a lot I do not understand about you and your condition. How can you possibly be so healthy? You should be headed for at least a year of physical therapy. You really are quite amazing."

"Believe me, there is much more that I am amazed at than that. I am so confused. Who am I, and where did I come from? How did I rise to the ceiling, and where did I learn martial arts? But I understand your predicament, so I'll begin looking first thing in the morning."

"Fine. Dinner will be in the dining area at six forty-five. Then we will clean, and after that everyone returns to their rooms for contemplation. There is no electricity. We get up at four thirty for prayers, and breakfast is at seven. You should join the kitchen staff at five thirty to help prepare the morning meal."

"May I leave the grounds at ten to search for a place to stay?"

"Yes, of course. I'll see you at dinner."

After dinner and clean up, Jai went to her room. She was having a hard time trying to concentrate on anything but Makeen. She could still feel his energy and smell the scent that came from his sweat as they sparred. She would describe it as musky sweet, and she pictured him naked, circling her in an attack position. Picturing this, Jai's energy began to rise. The feelings were beginning to overwhelm her, so much so that she needed a release. She felt this small explosion inside her, and her energy flew from her body, striking the small dresser up against the wall, and it splattered into a million pieces. That plus a loud knock on her door brought Jai out of her state.

"What happened in here?" asked a frightened nun, opening the door.

"I don't know," answered a still-shaken Jai.

"What did you do to the dresser?"

"As I said, I don't know."

Just then the abbess walked in and asked everyone to leave except Jai.

"Listen carefully, young lady. I don't know who or what you are, but I do know that you must leave this place no later than the day after tomorrow."

"But ..."

"No buts. My word is final." With that the abbess left.

Jai, in a near state of panic, couldn't figure what she was going to do. Everything was strange to her, the people, city, customs, and complicating matters, she couldn't remember a thing. She sat on her bed shaking and sobbing out loud. Then she heard this strange fluttering sound, and as she listened she began to calm down. It was like an old friend was telling her that everything would be all right. Jai sat in a meditation position, and in a moment or two, beautiful visions of flowers and grassy hills flooded her mind, and she became completely calm. One hour later she lay down in her bed and slept like a baby.

# CHAPTER 11

At four thirty she was awakened by a tentative knock on her door. She put on her robe and looked around for anything else that might be hers, but there was nothing. She helped prepare the morning meal, ate in silence with the others, helped clean, and then went to the front gate and sat down to wait for Makeen.

He arrived ten minutes early, and they left together. "Why do you look so sad?"

"The abbess threw me out and said I couldn't return."

"What happened to cause her to say that?"

"I don't know. I was in my room thinking about stuff and trying to figure out how I became comatose when all of a sudden the dresser exploded into a thousand tiny pieces."

"Really?"

"Yes, that's all."

"Did you cause that?"

"I don't think so, but I honestly do not know."

"Okay, I brought last night's ads. Let's see if we can find you a job and a place to live before the day is out."

Jai interviewed at five different places, making up a background. She nevertheless came up empty. After she left her last interview as a receptionist at a law firm, Makeen asked, "How did it go?"

"Just like my first interview, I could have the job but there were strings, and they made no bones about what they wanted."

"What?"

"Me."

"We have to hurry so you can get into the convent for your last night."

"I would rather not. Can I stay with you and never go back?"

"But they took good care of you."

"So everyone tells me, but it didn't take them long to think I was some kind of devil and throw me out."

"I have some money saved. Maybe you would rather stay in a hotel until we can get this thing sorted out."

"Why don't you want me to stay with you? Are you married or have a girlfriend?"

"No, I was just thinking that that's what you might like."

"No, I would rather have some company in a place and time where I am a perfect stranger."

"Okay, let's do it then. But first I'm teaching a class in a half hour. Do you want to watch?"

"Can I join in?" Jai asked with a teasing smile.

"Okay, but if you join in the sparring, you really might get hurt. Last time everyone, including me, just pampered you."

"I'll remember that."

Jai decided not to participate. Instead she just enjoyed the activity. They spent the next three days looking for a job for Jai, and she was becoming extremely irritated, desperate, and depressed. At night they would go to the dojo, where she joined the white belt class, learning to kick a large, heavy bag that hung from the ceiling, but her mind was not there. She wore an oversized gi, and nobody at the school paid any attention to her while they were training. Her black hair was braided and fell to her waist, which reminded everyone of the beautiful woman who was among them.

After classes on the fourth night, a guest who was also a Tibetan master of the highest rank honored them with a demonstration. Jai was really not interested, so she sat by herself in the boxing and kicking room and fell into a deep meditative state. Hearing the explosive grunts coming from the master, she saw herself in a temple courtyard with about thirty others all wearing the same robe and practicing karate or some form of it, a form far different than she had witnessed since coming to Makeen's dojo. This was a far advanced deadly art. One who mastered this form could kill another with a powerful energy, propelling one or two fingers that would deeply pierce any bone, including the very dense skull. The noise coming from the breaking of a two-inch plank brought Jai out of her trance, and she entered the other room as the class was bowing to the master in appreciation of his art.

Jai walked to the center of the circle that surrounded the master and bowed but not deeply as would have been expected. She said, "That, master, was very impressive."

"But how do you know? You weren't in the room."

"I know." Then she said, "With your permission, I humbly ask to try your form."

"It is dangerous because you may break that beautiful hand and fingers, deforming them for life. I ask that you do not."

"There is much about me that is deformed, so please do not bother yourself with such details. May I?"

The master turned to Makeen, who just spread his hands in defeat. And so the master chose a board from among the many that lay around and handed it to her and said, "Is this satisfactory?"

Jai looked at the board and realized that it was a very thin piece that the beginners used. She said, "I am sure that this board is a worthy choice, but with your permission I would like to choose another."

There was a huff of air let out by those in the class, all realizing that what Jai just did was an insult. "As you wish, my dear. What belt do you wear?"

"None."

Then the master turned to Makeen and said, "She is an impertinent girl who needs a lesson, so I will allow it."

Jai bowed and walked over to the pile and chose a board equal to the one that the master had splintered. But instead of placing it across the bricks as the master had done, she handed it to Makeen to hold. Everyone knew that this was a more difficult test because the give of the holder's arms would not allow for as much resistance.

Makeen whispered to her, "Are you sure you want to do this?"

Jai looked at him in a questioning way and said, "What do you mean? I just feel that I can."

Jai bowed to the visiting master, then the class, and last to Makeen. "Please hold the board as far away from your body as you can and take a powerful resistance stance."

Everyone in the dojo held their breath in complete silence while Jai gathered her chi; it took her less time than it took the master. She stood facing the board. Then, much to the amazement of everyone there, Jai, without the normal release of sound, punched a hole in the board with one finger on her right hand and immediately punched another with two fingers on her left. There was complete silence; no one moved. It was almost like they were afraid to breathe.

After a minute the visiting master walked over to her and bowed deeply. Jai returned the bow, and then everyone followed.

"Young lady, may I talk to you in private?"

"If you mean with Makeen present then yes."

Makeen stepped in and said, "I will dismiss the class. There is no more to show them tonight."

When they left, Makeen asked, "Shall we go to the tea shop around the corner? They have private areas, and we can talk freely."

They chatted about nothing on the way over, but once seated, the master introduced himself to Jai. "My name is Master Tsewang. Does that sound familiar to you?"

"No, why should it?"

"I'm not sure, but let us find out. The discipline and form that you showed tonight you could have only learned in one of two places, both temples. I was a teacher in one that ceased to exist about three years ago, destroyed by the Chinese government. I left the temple shortly before that happened to start another, because our practice was becoming obsolete. Not many were brave enough to defy the Communist regime and join us. There was a young girl among the students who was brought there by her teacher, and she was his only student. Does any of this ring a bell?"

"No, but before I attempted to pierce the boards, I had a vision of a temple in the snow-covered mountains."

"Do you remember more?"

"No."

"You do not look so much like the girl that I remember, but she was younger, shorter, and not so pretty. I just cannot imagine any one female being able to do what it took me forty years to accomplish. Let me ask you, do you know *lung gom*?"

"No, why do you ask?"

"The girl that I speak of was a master of its powers and became so far sooner than anyone at the temple before her."

"What exactly does the practice accomplish?"

"An adept can leap into the air and propel himself for twenty feet or more, allowing him to cross great distances very fast. But this girl could also levitate to the treetops and balance herself on a leaf with one toe, or just float around."

Jai turned white, and Makeen smiled. "Why do you look like that?" Master Tsewang asked.

Jai said nothing, but Makeen said, "A few days ago I walked into a room and found her floating at the ceiling."

"Why is it that she seems not to remember anything?"

"She has just recovered from a long illness and came out of a coma with no memory."

"So she is from here?"

"No, I found her in the Himalayan foothills. She was

almost unconscious and babbling. I brought her to the monastery, where the nuns took care of her."

"What was she wearing?"

"A robe."

"Can I see it?"

Jai answered, "Yes it is here in my bag."

Jai took it out, and now it was the master's turn to turn white. "It is the robe of the temple that was destroyed. Unless you stole or found it somewhere, you must be that girl."

Parting company with the promise of getting together once again soon, Jai asked Makeen, "Back in the dojo, what did you mean, 'am I ready'?"

"Be patient, Jai. I believe that you are something other than you appear to be, and I also believe that it will all come back to you shortly."

# CHAPTER 12

Back in Makeen's apartment, he put on some slow music and asked Jai if she knew how to dance.

"I honestly don't know."

"Let's try."

Makeen took Jai in his arms and immediately took charge of her movements. Pressed to his body, Jai felt some amazing energies starting to fill her body, and it responded.

When the song ended, Makeen looked into Jai's downcast eyes, and said, "You move so beautifully. I would like to ask you if you have ever made love before, but I know that you wouldn't remember."

Jai found it harder to lift her head and look into his eyes than anything she tried in the dojo. She easily recalled all the moments when he was not with her that she thought of him only, his body, and his movements, and it always excited her to the point of almost losing control. She had wondered what it would be like to have this beautiful man make love to her but didn't dare show this desire. With no memory, she really didn't know anything about her past.

Had she made love before? Was she married? So many unanswered questions, and that proved to be scary. Gathering enough courage, Jai lifted her head and looked into his eyes and shrieked.

"What's the matter? Am I that ugly?" asked Makeen.

"No, it's your eyes."

"What about them?"

"They are dark brown, and very intense."

"Do they bother you? Would you prefer them the way they were, mismatched?"

"No."

"Then look into my eyes and don't be afraid."

"But I am afraid."

"Of what?"

"You told me that you believed that I was something other than I appear, and I believe the same holds true for you."

Makeen thought for a moment and said, "Maybe you are right, but I can promise that who I truly am will bring you no harm."

"Then tell me who you are and what you want from me."

"That's not possible. I must show you, but not until you are ready."

"I don't know if I can trust you. It is really hard to trust when you have no memory."

"I am your friend, believe me. Let's just dance and forget all else."

Jai relaxed back into his arms, and once again she felt his energy surge through her, but this time she didn't back away. She could sense that Makeen felt her resistance lessening as he started to press her deeper into him. He was growing hard against her thigh as he spun her around the floor. When they came to a stop, he looked into her eyes, and she felt that her doubt was gone. Gently he kissed and licked her lips as he bent her backward while guiding her to the floor.

"You do know that you are the most beautiful woman I have ever been with or seen?"

"Since I have no way of knowing how many women we are talking about, I don't know if that's much of a compliment."

"Trust me, it is."

"Well I may be beautiful as you say, but I have no idea what I'm doing."

"Trust your instincts. If you have made love before I'm sure your body will let you know."

"What if I'm a nun sworn to chastity?"

"Then we'll go to hell together. You are worth any price I must pay."

"My body and mind are screaming for you to take me."

"I will, but first I must learn every inch of you, and I am a very slow learner."

While kissing Jai's lips, Makeen carefully opened the jacket part of her gi, exposing one breast. He slowly kissed and licked her face and ears, then continued down her long neck, never touching her with his hands, only his lips and tongue. He heard Jai sigh, so he began circling her breast with his fingers. Her nipples reacted immediately, hardening even further and deepening in color. Gently caressing her breast with his whole hand, he squeezed it just enough to force her nipple upward, painfully pleading to be in his mouth.

Instead Makeen took Jai's hand and had her cup her own breast before he said, "Offer it to me."

Those simple words and his eyes intently staring into hers brought Jai to a climax, and when she did he accepted her offering, biting down gently, which deepened Jai's climax even further.

Jai could feel the animal coming out in her, which seemed to cause a similar reaction in him. He tore at her top, exposing her to her waist, but Jai felt he stopped guessing that he wanted this to last as long as possible. Kneeling across her thighs, he held her arms above her head, and he looked at her. She sensed that he enjoyed seeing her perfect breasts and nipples and that her whole body was covered with beauty marks testifying to that fact.

As he looked at her in the way a dominant male cat might, she felt her body squirming, asking him to enter her. As she arched her back and moved her hips in a circular motion, he grew harder against her pubic bone. Makeen bent over and licked her between her breasts and then licked his way down to her belly button. Jai was building once again. She wanted him inside of her, but she was enjoying these new sensations she was feeling. *Let him take it slow,* she thought, but when he started to pull her pants down as he glided his tongue down to where her pants used to be, she climaxed again. Keeping her thighs locked together with his knees, Makeen teased her lips with his tongue, knowing that she wanted it inside her. Oh, it was easy to tell because she was trying hard to spread her legs, but he kept them closed until he tasted her sweet nectar. As he did he released her legs and pressed his tongue inside her as far as he could. Then with a slow upward stroke, he found her clitoris and continued to lick it, never allowing it to slip away. The intensity was causing Jai's energy to build to a point where she had no control over her body. In a single motion she arched her back up as high as she could and wrapped her legs around his back and then exploded with a gut-wrenching scream and climax.

Makeen wanting badly to continue was stopped by Jai.

"But this is only the beginning," he said.

"Maybe so, but something is happening to me. I can feel a change coming over me, and it frightens me."

"Maybe it's your memory coming back into focus."

"Maybe, but for now I need to stop."

He mildly protested but knew that it would be no use. She was a very strong-minded girl, so he let it go.

That night Jai dreamt of flowers that gave off sweet, overpowering odors that she could almost taste. She saw herself naked straddled across a deer's back as he galloped across a luscious green meadow. Her hair was flying behind, and she was laughing. It was a feeling of freedom like no other.

The next morning Makeen woke Jai with kisses. Though she would allow that and his simply playing with her nipples, she wouldn't allow him or her to go any further. "Now it is your turn to be patient, my friend," she said in a serious tone.

Jai spent the day job hunting, but to no avail. At three in the afternoon she headed to the dojo, figuring to kill some time while she waited for Makeen to take her to dinner as planned. She was wearing a Western-style dress, which was rather form fitting, that Makeen had bought for her to interview in. Walking through the alley alongside the dojo,

Jai was lost in thought, thinking about the night of love that they shared, so she didn't see or sense the man that had been following her for a while. He came up behind her and grabbed her around the waist with his left arm and held a knife to her throat with his right.

He whispered, "Don't scream or move unless I tell you."

Jai was shocked. Caught by surprise, Jai felt a rage building inside her. A van pulled up alongside the entrance to the alley, and the driver jumped out and opened the sliding door.

The guy holding Jai said, "Now walk to the van, and get in. If you cause me any trouble, I'll slit your throat and be done with you."

Jai, who was stunned by what was happening, didn't gain her composure until she realized that they planned on abducting her, for what purpose she could only guess. Acting on instinct alone, she reached up and grabbed the wrist of the arm with the knife and spun out of the guy's grasp, breaking his wrist and pulling his arm out of its socket. As she spun she karate kicked him square in the groin, and he went down like a sack of shit, crying about the pain.

As soon as the guy from the van saw Jai fighting, he ran as fast as he could to help subdue her. With one man disabled and Jai's senses at full alert, she knew the second assailant was coming for her. She spun and waited in her power stance. Jai waited until the right moment, and when he came within striking distance, she, with tremendous force, punched him in his chest plate, completely shattering it; some of the large fragments pierced his heart, and he died instantly.

Jai took one look at the guys lying on the ground, and she knew they wouldn't be going anywhere soon. She calmly entered the dojo, and seeing Makeen standing to the side watching a class, she walked over and whispered to him that he needed to come outside with her. On the way she explained what happened, and when he saw the scene, he realized that this was no laughing matter. He couldn't afford to have her be known. He told her that she was to go back to his place and stay there. She was never here.

After she left, he called the police, and when they came he said that it was he they attacked despite the guy on the ground mumbling something about a girl.

"Yes, but I'm sorry that that man died. When I spun around, he was already on top of me, with his knife ready to strike, and I punched him with all I had."

"Never knew a breast bone to be shattered by a punch before," said the cop.

"Neither had I. It just happened so fast. Can I go back inside to my classes now?"

"Yes, go ahead, but we may want to ask you some more questions later."

"No problem."

After the police left, Makeen left the dojo, picked up some food for supper, and headed home.

# CHAPTER 13

Jai sat quietly in Makeen's apartment. She replayed the incident, and for some odd reason, she wasn't bothered much. She wondered why. *Who am I?* she thought. She heard keys in the lock, and Makeen walked in. They embraced.

As they headed to the kitchen, Jai asked, "What happened after I left?"

"I told them that it was me they were after, leaving you out of it altogether."

"Why?"

"Because you have no papers."

"I would like some tea with dinner. Would you like some? What papers are you talking about?"

"Well simply put, you have no residence, no family, no memory, and no passport. Who knows what they would have charged you with? Anyway, I'm not exactly through with you yet. We have unfinished business. And yes, I would like some tea."

"Yeah, I guess your version of what happened is better. It's more believable that a man could do what was done."

"True, I wouldn't have believed it either unless I had seen you in action. I brought dinner. I think it best we aren't seen together for a few days."

"Does that mean you plan to feed me and then once again seduce me with your wily charms?"

"Yes, but of course I plan to exact a price for defending you so gallantly in the alley."

"Oh, you do, do you? So now I may have to defend myself?"

"I'm not planning on you doing so."

"Then you better convince me somehow why it is that I should yield to your obviously lecherous advances."

"Believe me, I plan to win you over without a fight."

"Are you expecting to hear a meow or a growl as a response?"

"A meow. Your growl might prove beyond my ability to master."

They spent part of the afternoon theorizing about what those guys might have wanted with Jai. Then it was Jai's turn to put on the music, and she turned to Makeen and asked, "Would my hero like to dance?"

"Why of course."

Together once again in an embrace, Jai began to sense his energy quickly rising. She looked into his eyes, but instead of seeing the desire for her she expected, she saw something completely different; she saw her face reflected directly back at her, and she jumped back.

"What's wrong?"

"I saw my eyes in your eyes, and they were blazing

yellow. There was no iris, just slits of blazing yellow, and I was startled. Did you see my eyes like that?"

"No I just saw your beautiful purplish black eyes."

"But I would swear that I ..."

"It was probably the overhead light reflecting off my eyes."

"Yes, you are probably right. But you should know that I am so worried about these things I am capable of. Maybe I can learn more about the temple training Master Tsewang said I was at when next we see him."

Makeen said, "Can we go back to what we were doing, please?"

Jai walked back into his arms, and they once again began to move to the rhythm. Makeen asked, "Jai, do you trust me?"

"Yes, I believe so."

"Then let me make love to you. I know that's not a very romantic way of approaching this, but believe me, you will forget that you weren't romanced when we are through. I promise you will be happy with the result."

Jai, not knowing what he was really talking about, said, "Have you treated all your women like this?"

"Never before, and there will be no others after you. You'll see."

"Well since I'm to be your last than I'll sacrifice being pampered. Anyway I want this as much as you do, maybe more."

Makeen had been preparing for this moment since his training in the tantric arts. He became skilled in the art of unblocking passageways in the body and brain, allowing energy movement and purification. He was trained by two women at a secret location in a forest located in the Himalayan foothills. He was brought there by his karate teacher, who claimed Makeen's ability to raise his chi and control was unprecedented. The women lived on a small farm, and they had just one other male student in all their years as masters. After they tested his abilities, they accepted him.

He loved the energy work, which was inevitably accompanied by sex. After a year or so he had reached the proficiency point where they were satisfied. Another woman appeared and took part in his final test. She, in fact, was the person in charge of his training and the person who recommended him to be brought here. After Makeen raised her energy to a place approximating transcendence, she was pleased that he had achieved the high results.

The next morning the four sat together having breakfast while discussing the direction his life was about to take. They talked very little about the goals they were trying to achieve, instead concentrating on his relationship with Jai. The new woman explained that Jai was the very special person who was to be made ready to take charge of an important organization. The final step was the unlocking of all she was programmed to be. That called for an energy key that would unlock her energy flow passages and subconscious. He was that key. The scenario of their meetings before and after her training was gone over carefully, and if he were successful, and there was no reason he shouldn't be, he would be at her side until the goals were met. Compensation would be generous, before, during, and after it was over.

As Jai took off her outer garments, Makeen flashed back to that day when he first saw her in the woods and how surprised he was at her young age, but when he saw her two and a half years later in the convent, he was thrilled at how beautiful she was. Jai lay down in the bed in just her undergarments while Makeen undressed himself.

Lying beside her, he whispered, "Just surrender yourself to me, and buckle up for a cosmic ride that will take us both to a place neither one of us have been before."

"How could you know that?"

"I know. Just wait, and I promise you will know too."

As he was trained to do, Makeen imagined Jai as a living goddess, one who had been asleep for a long time. His wonderful task was to slowly bring her back to life. He had to massage and tease every cell in her body to the point where they were pulsating with anticipation and hunger. He knew that sexual hunger in humans was mostly mental, but with the right techniques, the physical desire could be made to be just as commanding. Energy, if brought to such a state, seeks more energy, and he was about to build her energy to such a point that it would suck the energy out of his body. The method would cause a fusion and create an explosion from a single purified energy that would open all her passageways, including the ones to her subconscious and also her power of intuition. That done, her circuit would be complete and she would have access to all the knowledge that had been programmed into her conscious and subconscious mind. Of course, that would leave him completely drained and vulnerable, but that didn't matter to him. He trusted her.

Makeen, keeping his energy at a low level, massaged Jai's complete body, starting with her back and then turning her over. He was sure not to miss a single inch.

Makeen felt Jai sense what he was doing, and began to feel her body responding to every nuance of his movements. Now laying on her back with Makeen straddling her thighs, her body naturally sought more. She began a slow grinding movement, trying to excite him to a point where he wanted to be inside her. Makeen, feeling her desire building, slowed his movements and energy flow. He had no idea how long this would take, but he wanted it to last forever.

*What kind of man I must be to be able to hold such a magnificent creature in my power? We may make love many times more, but after this I will be under her power, and the ending will probably never be the same. I will savor every moment, every single quiver I cause in her body. When I come, I will explode with utter passion and fierceness.*

With that thought he began using the techniques he was trained in. Using his hands, tongue, lips, and thighs, he forced her energy higher and higher. Interchangeably she cried for more, yet begged for release. Her climaxes were coming faster and faster, but she was not ready. At one point it became so intense she let out a scream that sounded like nothing he had ever heard before, but still she was not ready. Makeen flipped Jai over and spanked her butt hard, causing a conflict of pain and pleasure; she fought like a crazed animal, yet moaned with pleasure. He flipped her on her back once again and started kissing her face and neck conflicting her.

Because she believed she couldn't go any further, she cried, "No more I can't."

"I promise you are capable of so much more. You will be surprised how much higher you can go. Just relax, surrender to my will, and just feel. Trust me, it will be worth it."

Over two hours had passed since they began, and Makeen could feel that the time was getting close. Using even further advanced techniques that created an even greater movement of energy throughout his and Jai's bodies, he began to pour his energy into her until her body took over and drew out most of what his body had to offer. Her yin energy being dominant over his yang encapsulated his. The high thermal heat and speed of movement created an internal explosion, causing their energies to fuse into one. Because of its great power, the energy raced through her body and brain, opening all the passageways and released all her stored energy. This internal explosion of energy was so powerful it threw Makeen up against the furthest wall and knocked him out cold.

Jai was stunned, her body was tingling, and what felt like blood rapidly pulsating through her veins caused her to feel a power in her body and mind that she could never had imagined. Her senses were a hundred times more acute, and her mind was processing all the information it was being fed at what seemed like ten times the speed of light. Her eyes still shut, she saw brilliant flashes of lights in colors not visible to the human eye. They surrounded her and then embraced her like a blanket, and it comforted her as if it was an old friend. She opened her eyes to find her vision extremely acute. Looking out the window, she could see with intense clarity even at great distances. Then she noticed a body lying on the floor. It took her a millisecond to realize who it was and what he was doing there. Without thought she placed her hand lightly on his head, and he immediately came out of it.

"Wow!" he said.

"Yes, wow, but that doesn't cover the experience or the result. How do you feel?" Jai asked.

"I feel like I have had all my energy drained out me. I'm not even sure I can move. But god, what an experience."

Jai was looking carefully at Makeen's face, and then she smiled and said, "I am sure now that I have seen you before."

"Yes you have. When I first saw you, you were carrying another girl, and you both looked very ill. I tried to get you to follow me so that you could get help, but you were suspicious and wouldn't go. Then you collapsed in delirium, so I was forced to carry you out of the forest."

"What about the other girl?"

"She had already died. After I took you to my aunt's farm, I went back and buried her, but I believe you were not aware of any of that."

"Her name was Song."

"Who?"

"The girl you buried. Maybe it was a good thing that she died. So you are telling me that I actually spent the past almost three years in a convent."

"As far as I know, yes."

"Then explain what I've become and all the things I seem to know."

"I can't."

"Are you supposed to contact someone as soon as I awakened to this state?"

"Yes."

"Then do it, so we can get started on all we are supposed to do."

"Before I do, tell me do you remember your past life?"

"No, so far I can't remember anything except Song's face and yours. All I know is what and who I am now, and what I'm supposed to do; I can't even remember if this was who I was before you found me, and if not then how did I get this way? Maybe I'll find out after I start my new life."

# CHAPTER 14

The necessary people were contacted, and Makeen was instructed to immediately take Jai to a private flight center where a plane would be waiting. When they arrived to their destination by Town Car, Jai asked, "Is that our blue plane on the tarmac?"

Walking to the plane, Makeen answered, "Yes it is, but it will be a different color when we land. The skin is made up of millions of multicolor dots that can be changed to almost any color or combination."

"The tail numbers and registration?"

"Those also."

"And the pilots, I'm assuming that they are the best?"

"The very best to fly that Gulfstream 550. They are also trained in air force tactics and maneuvers. This plane is equipped with long-range capability at a very fast speed. It houses all our latest satellite and communications equipment and is updated whenever it is warranted."

"What, if anything, do any of the others know about me?"

"Absolutely nothing. There is a lot of talk about when the director will officially take his post, also scuttlebutt as to whom it will be. Most of the money is on Denton, but some of the others are picking a certain military person who seems to fit the bill. Only two or three think it will be someone they haven't met."

"You said 'he.' Is no one betting on a woman?"

"Are you kidding? I can't wait to see their faces."

"Whom do the pilots think they are picking up?"

"They have no clue. After I made the call, they were sent a series of numbers, which told them where to fly to and how many to pick up. It is up to you to tell me where you want to go and I'll tell them. I took the liberty of bringing a hooded cape that reaches the floor in case you didn't want them to see that you are a female."

"That won't be necessary. They will see me as I choose them to see me."

"Really? How will you do that, Jai?"

*Simple*, thought Jai. *I will appear as a man to everyone on the plane, but I will not tell you how. I can shape-shift or I can put the image that I want them to see in their minds.*

"Never ask questions or question what I say. You will learn soon enough, as they all will, that I am capable of things that humans can never even imagine. Also I prefer that you call me Director from here on, as will the others. It is important that they connect me directly with my position and therefore my power to rule. Until I say so, do not introduce me to anyone. How many crew, and how is the plane laid out?"

"There are two pilots, one American, one Israeli. There is a flight engineer who sits in the extended cockpit, a highly trained and capable tech and communications person and his assistant, and an attendant. The layout is simple. It is designed as your backup control post. Besides all the technical equipment, the main cabin has four club seats, a desk and chair with com and computers, a bathroom, and a small kitchen. The rear of the plane is a closed-off bedroom, with a sitting area and bath. The cargo bay can hold enough food, clothing, and spare parts to last at least a year and is accessible through the main cabin bathroom."

"Why is the plane's door not open?"

"When I call with a code it will, and we will be in the air right afterward. Where do you want to go first? I must put that code in also."

"There is a main headquarters and three substations. Where is my headquarters located?"

"Headquarters is located directly under a heavily fortified and guarded military base in Eastern Germany. Occupied then rebuilt after the Second World War, it was a troop training center and important monitoring post during the Cold War, and continues to be one.

"Why was this place chosen?"

"Many reasons. First is the amount of communication traffic in and out that will disguise ours. Second, the fort itself is heavily populated most times of the year and we wouldn't be noticed, and since it is a training facility, the noise from the tanks and artillery will cover us twenty-four hours a day. But the most important reason is its proximity to the terrorist-leaning countries that train and finance terrorism and supply weapons."

"So we enter from outside the fort?"

"Yes, but there is also an entrance on the fort itself. If

need be we can enter the fort as military or civilian workers, but that is just a precaution."

"That's where we will go first, but I don't want anyone to know we are coming. Please have them drop the door, so we may be on our way."

The door opened, and the two entered the cabin. A Japanese girl greeted them, but they ignored her. Jai stood by the cockpit door and asked, "How long before we lift off?"

"Sir, as soon as everyone is seated, we will roll to the strip. We will be first in line, sir."

"Thank you, and please leave your com sets open so that I may hear all the traffic during the entire flight."

"Yes sir!" said the copilot.

Jai turned to leave and said to the girl, "Come with me to the rear of the plane."

"Yes sir," she replied.

Jai led a startled Makeen and the girl through the cabin, stopping only to glance at the equipment on board, and when they reached the bedroom door she asked Makeen to wait in the main cabin. When he left Jai asked the girl her name. "Lei," she replied in Japanese.

Jai switched over to Japanese. "A beautiful name, it means graceful, right?"

The girl blushed and said, "Yes."

Jai asked, "What exactly are your duties? Are you just the plane's stewardess?"

"Oh no, it is my duty to take care of all your personal things and residences. All the things that you will have no time to bother yourself about."

When Jai saw the girl blush once again she asked, "Why do you get so embarrassed?"

"Excuse me, but I was trained to take care of a woman. I really know nothing of men's things."

"Then you will be uncomfortable taking care of me?"

"It will be an honor for me to learn, but I'm afraid many mistakes might be made before I am competent."

"Will you also never raise your eyes off the ground when you talk to me?"

Saying that she was so sorry, she lifted her head and saw the beautiful Jai standing in front of her. Lei's knees buckled, and she slid to the ground. Jai smiled, and said, "I will get you a glass of water." When she returned from the bathroom, the girl was sitting on the edge of the bed staring at her.

"But I saw you as a man."

"Yes, you did. It was my choice."

"So you are a woman?"

"Yes, as you will clearly see when you draw my bath."

"But how ...?"

"Listen to me very carefully, Lei. You will see and hear many so-called strange things when you are around me. It must be your sworn duty never to speak of them or question me about what you see. Do you understand?"

"Yes, I most humbly do."

"You understand that if you do not follow my guidelines, you will be dealt with in the harshest of ways?"

"Yes, it was drummed into my head throughout my training. I will never speak of you or anything you do or say as long as I live. That is my solemn oath."

"Good, then let me ask you, have you been to my quarters at headquarters?"

"No. Excuse me, but what do I call you?"

"My name is Jai, but I'm to be known as Director to all in the company, except you. You may call me *obasan.* That's ma'am or lady in English. Please be seated. We are taking off, and as soon as it is safe please ask Makeen to come back here. Yes, he is the tall, strange white-haired one."

"How did you know what I was thinking? Oh, never mind, please forgive me, but I think it will take some time. Best I just never speak again."

Makeen, walking into the room, said, "Except for Denton, who is at his home outside the compound, everyone else will be at the headquarters when we arrive. You will create quite a buzz when you enter."

"We will go to Denton's house first, and when we get inside the compound, the people will only see you enter." Jai responded. "I assume you have been there?"

"Yes, just before you awoke from your coma."

"Is it fully operational?"

"Yes, except for your quarters everything is finished. They are running tests until the Director is chosen."

"What about you? What is your job?"

"Whatever you make it."

"I think I know, but for now let's leave it open. I see we are about to land. Is there one of our cars meeting us?" asked Jai.

"Yes."

"If you will go to the main cabin, I want to rejuvenate my energy through meditation. Today is an extremely important day, as I must immediately win everyone's respect and obedience."

# CHAPTER 15

As their plane was making its approach, Jai was thinking, *I wonder how many different lives I have led in my short life. And now I will start a new one. Who am I really? Will I ever truly know?*

On the ground their silver and black plane rolled to a stop inside a private hangar. Makeen knocked on her door and said, "Customs and immigration will be on board in a few minutes. I have the papers for you and Lei, and the captain has the rest. They know this plane very well, and we will not have a problem."

"Okay, let me know when it's done. By the way, am I a man or woman?" Jai asked.

"I have both."

"Use the man, but let me see the picture so I may appear that way to them." When alone with Lei, Jai said, "Since I have not had a wardrobe designed as yet, tell me which outfit will most allow me to look like a warrior."

"Okay, but we have nothing on board."

"It's not necessary. I will use my powers as I did when

I came on board to force people at the compound to see me as I wish. The problem is it takes a great deal of energy to do so, and that's not a way I necessarily want to use it. Just watch, and when I'm through tell me which outfit fits the profile."

When Jai was finished, Lei chose, and Jai told her, "You have good taste. It is the one I would have chosen."

A half hour after customs was finished, Makeen and Senor Juan Mendoza, Jai's male identity, climbed down the stairs and into the waiting car. Makeen told the driver to take them to Denton's home, which was a farmhouse that was located in the opposite direction from the town to the compound. After trying his home, they found him in the barn, which he had converted into his laboratory. Being deep in thought, he didn't hear them enter and was startled when Makeen tapped him on the shoulder.

Makeen said, "You do recognize me, don't you? We met at the compound a short while ago."

"Yes, excuse me. You see, I am working on my favorite project, one that I have been at since my freshman year in college. And who is this studious-looking young lady with you?"

Makeen, momentarily taken back by the words *young lady*, hesitated, so Jai jumped in and said, "My name is Jai. Do you mind if I look at your work?"

"Look all you wish. I doubt that you will even begin to understand what it means."

Jai looked carefully at the three huge blackboards. Two of them had mathematical formulas and the third physics diagrams and formulas. After nodding her head a few times, she said, "I see you are trying to either prove or dispel the idea of antigravity. Thousands of great minds have tried before, and since no one has proved that it can exist, it is generally accepted that it doesn't. So I will conclude that you are trying to discover a formula to prove its existence."

"Very good, young lady. You are either a mathematics or physics student, am I right?"

"Neither, but let me ask you, of all the unsolved mysteries in and out of this world, why did you choose this one?" Jai asked as she stepped closer to the blackboard for a better look.

"I have many interests in my fields of study, but let's just say this is my hobby and passion. It started when I was five years old with my fascination of the pyramids in Egypt. I was told that scientists contend that it took around five thousand men twenty years to build the great pyramid. It baffled me, and so I researched the topic finding nothing that I thought plausible, until I read theories of them using sonic or magnetic levitation.

"I came to believe that an antigravity, which frees an object from the force of gravity, is a greater possibility though more obtuse."

"Excuse me," Jai interrupted. "Are you trying to prove that antigravity exists or could be manufactured, so that you might justify the massive amount of effort and time you are expending, or are you simply trying to discover its existence through formulas or elimination?"

"Either way. I believe the ancients possessed the methodology to induce antigravity, even as late as the early religions in Tibet," stated Denton.

Jai, again looking at the formulas on the board, said, "I'm sure you know there have been many machines that claimed antigravity properties since the 1920s, but none ever proved the designer or engineer's claims to be true or justified. It's been a monetary folly of huge proportions."

"Yes, but all it costs me is chalk and time."

"I beg your pardon, but you are costing the people you work for a lot of money and time spent away from what you were hired to do."

"How dare you, you impertinent twerp. Remove yourselves from my property."

Jai responded, "First of all, it is the company's property, not yours, and second of all, if I choose I'll have you removed before the day is out and of course everything in here would remain because all the equipment that you have spent a fortune of the company's money on trying to prove that antigravity is possible belongs to us. We have allowed you to do this to keep your genius mind occupied until we were ready to begin operations. Now is that time."

"Who are you to tell me these things and order me around? I am the person in charge of the whole operation awaiting orders to begin."

"From whom?"

"Nobody knows. Every single order given comes through our specially built communication computers by fuzzy images that looked like a group of three, but their voices are clear."

"Did you try and back track the signal?"

"Yes we did, but it led us nowhere. We kept losing it somewhere on the Tibetan, Indian, and Pakistan boarders."

"Do you have one of those com-computers here?"

"Yes, right over there by the desk."

"Good. Let me do something to put your mind at rest,

because from here on out your mind belongs to me. I'm sure you have a company scanner among your things, so please get it."

Denton appeared to Jai to be intimidated, having never been talked to like this in his entire life, and made a show of looking for it while he tried to figure out what was going on. Not being able to do so he, said, "Ah yes, here it is."

*What an interesting juxtaposition. Here I am one who should be bowing to this man's intellect and accomplishments, but I am in fact taking control of the situation and his mental state.*

Jai said, "First of all, I want you shut down the main breaker switch, shutting off all power to this room. Then scan the room for any power sources I may have planted."

That done to Denton's satisfaction, Jai said, "Now I will remove my outer clothing, and you will scan me for any objects that I may have on or in me. When you are satisfied that I have none, please take this flashlight and be seated with Makeen at least six feet from me."

That done Jai said, "Good, now shine the light on me."

Denton turned the laser light on Jai. She was sitting on the floor in the middle of the room still in her bra and panties. Jai rose to the ceiling and floated around the room. Tapping into Denton's thoughts using her ESP capability, she knew that Denton still doubted that what he was witnessing was due to her being free of gravity, thinking instead she was countering gravitational force by an opposing force of a different nature like energy. Jai, transmitting directly to both Denton and Makeen's minds, told them to follow her outside. Once outside Jai led them to a large boulder, and she floated down and sat on it. "How much does this boulder weigh?" she asked Denton.

Denton, in an obvious state of shock, replied, "Half of a ton, maybe even a ton," he replied.

"Closer to a ton, I'd say," she retorted. "Step back, both of you."

As she and the boulder rose into the air, Jai said, "As you know, gravity is not a force in the traditional sense of the word but a result of the geometry of space itself, which by its very nature causes attracting forces. Am I correct?"

"Yes, that is the theory that replaced Newton's law."

"So, my dear Denton, if a being such as I changed the geometric space where I was, shouldn't it be possible to free myself and everything in it of the effects of gravity?"

"That's what I am attempting to prove. How did you manage to do that?" stated Denton

"My dear man, you are looking at the proof. What else is there to prove? What you should now be looking for, if you choose to continue during your spare time, is the mathematical formula or physics model of how to change geometric space. Careful below, we are coming down."

When she landed, Denton saw that Jai was dressed. He asked, "I didn't see you take your clothes with you, did you?"

"You may say that. Now let's quit wasting time. I am the new director. I am sorry that it comes as a surprise to you, but in fact it is true."

"I still have my doubts, and until told that by the people who hired me I will remain unconvinced."

"Let's go inside and turn on your com-computer."

After about two minutes the com-computer came to

life with a fuzzy picture of three beings. The three of them couldn't recognize the faces on the screen. Then the one in the middle spoke, "Denton, this is Command. Do you recognize my voice?"

"Yes."

"Now you have met Jai, the director of the entire organization. She is the top in the chain of command, and no one, including you, will contradict her orders. Her power of thought is greater than yours, and her abilities are far greater than any being you will ever come in contact with. Do you understand?"

"Yes, both have been shown to me. She has proven her worth."

"Good, then this will be the last time you hear from us. Now both you and Makeen please go outside to the car and wait for the director."

After they left, the A Ma spoke. "Jai, it seems that you have won your first battle. The next should have the same outcome. How are you feeling?"

"I am fine, but I am very confused about what happened to me in India with Makeen. What did he do to me?"

"He just forced a transcendence of you by energy, and that act transformed you into the being you were trained and made prepared to be."

"But I have this feeling of loneliness and uncertainty that I can't shake, because I have no memory of my past before a certain point."

"It will come back to you sometime in the future, but in the meantime you have an extremely important job to do and do successfully. Now unfocus your eyes and look at me. What do you see?"

“I see the three of you have morphed into one, and that figure is sparkling with different colors.”

“Look closer.”

“You are familiar, but I don’t know you.”

“You will remember me soon, my child. Your memory is playing tricks on you. In the meantime look and listen to the fluttering for comfort and direction in your time of need.”

“What does that mean?”

“When the time is right, you will understand. Now go and take charge of your clandestine agency and fight the battles that must be won.”

# CHAPTER 16

The three having reached the entrance to headquarters, Jai was questioning Denton's acceptance of her as the director regardless of him saying so. Her thoughts were interrupted by Makeen asking her, "How are you going to handle meeting the people who are waiting for our arrival?"

Instead of answering directly, Jai turned to Denton and said, "Please walk me through what will happen as we enter."

"The entrance is unique. Its opening is fully camouflaged at the base of the mountain. The door is opened by a laser signal emanating from buttons hidden in three different boulders, each approximately two hundred feet from the entrance. Each one is strategically placed along the hard-to-spot paths. Once someone enters, the door closes behind them, and a preliminary scan takes place; if they do not have the correct chip implanted in them, they are gassed with a combination of a psychotropic agent and a nerve agent that will render them unconscious. They will be kept in a side cell off the entranceway until the psychotropic agent does its work. Are you familiar with its effects?"

"Unfortunately yes," Jai stated

Makeen spoke up. "I suppose it is better than death, and its effects will dissipate in three years or so depending on the state of mental health they were in before the gassing; they will remember nothing of the experience and go on with their lives."

Denton continued his description. "Passing the scan opens a very thick, vault like door into the cylinder, and yet another scanning room, and this time it's a full scan of DNA, eye structure, voiceprint, and x-rays that will show any foreign objects not cleared. That scan also tells the computers which levels the person may travel to. That done, you enter a pod that can hold up to four people. You press the level that you wish to go to, but only the buttons of the levels you are cleared to enter will operate. If you press an unauthorized button more than once, the pod will lock and can only be opened by security forces. Both go across the diameter of the available space and rise to eight feet."

"How high are the ceilings?"

"The entrance is about twenty feet, and the pod room exactly ten feet."

"Denton, the scan when we first enter and the final one at the pod, what is its diameter and height?"

"Then it will be a simple matter. I'll just flatten myself against the ceiling, and the scanners will not know I'm there, and that, my dear Denton, will be your first assignment—to reconfigure both scanners to cover the entire entranceway and pod room. Make the call and tell them that you are on your way. Tell them you want everyone, no exceptions, to go the training level, and have inventory bring the list of equipment I'm handing you now. When the pod opens, no one will be able to see me. Denton, you will ask them all to be seated in a circle, leaving a six-foot circumference in the center. I'll do the rest."

"I can't wait to see this," Denton said.

Everything worked just as Jai planned. Before they entered the large training room, people were milling around, and the buzz was that they were finally going to be able to settle their bets. Everything came to a standstill as the pod door opened. Denton and Makeen walked into the room. Denton took charge as he had done since the project began, and following Jai's instructions, he asked everyone to sit. The buzz ended when the lights began to dim. Jai stood in the center of the circle that was surrounded by her energy shield, which made her invisible to the naked eye. She looked at everyone's faces to detect their level of anxiety, especially the military ops people. Then Jai made her decision on how to proceed.

When the room was totally dark, Jai slowly changed her aura, starting at her feet, from black to a bright white. She slowly raised it up, lighting the entire circle, revealing herself as a beautiful woman wearing a light gray business suit. Her long black hair was loose and down, and she wore no makeup or jewelry. The crowd was stunned, and the silence was deafening. Then as Jai expected, the buzz started: Was this a trick or a hologram? Who was this person, and why the show?

Satisfied with the results, Jai said, "This is no trick nor is it a hologram. I stand before you as real as you yourselves are. It is my aura that lights up the space. I am the

Director—the person solely in charge of all that will take place here."

When she finished speaking, most people looked to Denton, and he, after getting a nod from Jai, said, "She is indeed in charge, and as you are just beginning to find out, she is a remarkable person in many respects, one of which we are witnessing, and I'm sure there's more to come."

Jai spoke again. "First of all, I want the present heads of strategy, tech, military ops, and finance to approach me. I will open a pathway that you may walk through one at a time so that you can reach out and touch my body."

The four stood up and walked forward, where they found a space in the light, and they entered the circle and hesitantly reached out and touched Jai's skin. Satisfied, they returned to their places outside the circle. Then Jai said, "Now those who hope to be military ops go to the rear and pick up the loaded weapons from the head of inventory. Everyone else hug an outer wall."

While that was taking place, Jai changed the energy circle from her aura to an energy shield that was thick and impenetrable. When everyone was safely in place, she called for the military people to step forward to a distance of twelve feet from the light and surround her on all sides.

Then Jai said, "You people are holding an array of powerful weapons. You will look at the ammunition in your pieces to see that it is the most penetrating that we possess and probably that exist today. When you are finished, lock and load your weapons and wait for my command. When given, you are all to fire a full clip at me."

Jai looked around to be sure everyone understood what was about to happen, and then she instantaneously changed her appearance. Jai suddenly appeared to them in a skimpy outfit made of a thin black metallic material, and there could be heard a loud breath of air that escaped from everyone. Her breasts were covered in a halter with straps that crossed her body and attached to a skirt that reached midthigh. Her stiletto boots ran up to the top of her calf, and her hair was now braided and reached her waist. She seemed to be at least seven feet tall or more.

Again satisfied at the reaction, she said, "Now without hesitation, all of you open fire."

Every person carrying a weapon emptied their clips into the energy field, which stopped the projectiles' progress by either embedding them or they bounced off and fell harmlessly to the ground. There was a gasp from the crowd, and one girl fainted. Jai made a mental note of those who cowered to use later in her evaluations.

When the ear-shattering noise ceased, Jai saw that everyone, including Makeen and Denton, stood in awe. She said, "What you have seen today is just a small sample of what I am capable of, and the reason I am the director of this organization. I know that everyone here today is qualified and passionate about the work we are about to undertake. In order for us to succeed, I will need your full cooperation, and instant compliance from those who will be retained by me. I will be meeting with all of you in the next few days, and when that is concluded, I will attempt to appoint everyone to his or her post. As you will learn, my decisions are final. Be prepared to state your case of qualifications for the position you seek. There is nothing else for the moment, so go back to what you were doing before I arrived."

The overhead lights flickered on as Jai's energy shield dissipated, dropping all the spent ammunition, making a loud crashing sound. Jai disappeared altogether from view. Everyone left except Denton and Makeen.

Jai reappeared and said, "That went well. I don't think I left any doubt as to who was in charge. Now let us tour the place, and then I'll begin my interviews. Makeen, you will coordinate telling each person when to come to my office after I decide."

Denton, interrupting, said, "Madam Director, is there any more to your paranormal abilities than your mind-blowing antigravity ability? I mean obviously you can perform these things using yourself as the object, but I really wonder if that's as far as it goes."

*Well, my friend, I guess it's time to prove you wrong again. I hope you are not afraid of flying.*

Jai then spent a moment building her energy and aimed it at Denton. In a flash Denton was headed to the ceiling, and when his head hit he cried out, "Bring me down, please set me down."

Jai and Makeen were laughing and Jai retorted, "Not until you enjoy the full ride." With that Denton flipped upside down and started to rotate, first one way and then the other. Summersaults followed, and Denton screamed even louder.

"Okay, I'm convinced. I will never question you again. Now please put me down."

Jai sent him down so that he softly landed on his feet, saying, "Now I want you to know that every minute of your time I am demanding that your energies to be spent on moving the technology of this organization forward. If you don't follow my lead and instructions, the next demonstration will be a lot more powerful and possibly harmful. Do you understand me?"

"Yes."

"Okay, now let's begin the tour of the facility."

"Yes, of course."

"How many levels are there, and what is on each?"

"The scanning rooms, as you saw, were on level one. The second level houses all the training rooms, the hospital, and the offices. There is a fully equipped gym, plus two martial arts practice areas. It also has every person's private changing and sleeping quarters for those on standby, and a food court.

"Third level is the briefing and debriefing rooms for incoming ops and hostiles; it also has the holding cells for hostiles brought in for questioning, and houses the inventory and maintenance chief, his assistants, all weaponry, and the parts department.

"Fourth level is the think tank where the missions are prioritized, researched, and profiled. Operations team leaders all have offices on that level as well as the head of finance and procurement.

"The fifth level is operations; that is where all the present and ongoing maneuvers are controlled. It contains the complete working banks of computers having our latest AI capability, analyzing and updating the operations on a momentary basis.

"The sixth level houses the heart and brain of the whole system. Starting with the fusion energy plant designed by me, which supplies the power to everything, including the huge rebreather oxygen tanks, artificial sunlight, water purifier tanks, all electrical equipment, and backup generators, which store enough energy to run the whole operation for three months. The seventh level houses only your personal quarters, except for Lei, who should have a small apartment alongside yours. This level is unfinished, waiting for you to design.

"One other very important feature is your private place of operation. It is a tubelike structure that runs in a complete circle all around the interior wall. The whole piece moves up and down, from operations on the sixth level to the training on the second level. It rides on compressed air, so it is completely silent. It is fully equipped and tied into every piece of computer and com equipment in the place. That about sums it up, madam."

"And don't call me madam."

On the second level Jai stopped to watch training for a moment, and she asked Makeen, who was also watching, "What do you think of the martial arts training facilities?"

"The facilities are fine, but that trainer is anything but a master. At least not in karate, which he is demonstrating at the moment."

"Denton, is he the one that's up for head trainer?"

"Yes, and he's the best we have."

"We can't send our ops into the field this far under trained. Let's do the interview right here and now. Makeen, clear everyone but the trainer out of the ring."

The ring cleared except for the two combatants. Jai said, "Makeen, you'll spar with him and tell me what you think."

Makeen and Jai entered the ring, and Jai said, "What is your name?"

"Huan."

"I'll hold your interview for the position you covet right here. This is Makeen. He will spar with you, and for the moment please, use only Karate techniques."

Jai, hearing every word of his thoughts, and knowing that those in training were all watching and listening, said, "Okay, Huan you may have your wish. Since Makeen is a true master, and I not even a top-level novice, I will give you the opportunity to make me beg and spread my legs as you wished for."

"But I ..."

"Don't but me or lie to me. Were you not thinking those very thoughts?"

"Okay, yes, but who would blame me?"

Jai turned and said, "Someone get me a marking pen." After receiving the felt pen, she said to Huan, "Remove your gi."

He did what he was told, and standing there in his Jockey shorts, Jai walked up to him and marked an X on his rib section, then one on the femur of his opposite leg, and finally his jaw. Then she stood back and said, "Prepare yourself well, Huan. I am going to break every bone I marked, and you will never touch me, and if I don't I will certainly lay down for you so you may ravage me as you wish."

There was the expected buzz from the crowd, and Jai turned to Makeen and said, "You may take on all the others that think they can be my head trainer, but for now, Huan, let us begin.

They bowed to one another, and Huan circled Jai, but she just stood there. When he was behind her, he knew he had the advantage and tried to sweep her off her feet, but Jai, sensing his intention, waited, and when he made his move, she leapt in the air and spun hitting, him in his side exactly where she had placed the X, breaking two of his ribs.

She bowed and said, "Oh, excuse me, I only marked the one."

Huan mumbled, "You bitch, I'll ..."

But before he could finish his sentence, Jai jammed her palm into his jaw and broke it in two places. She said, "You were about to say?" But he wouldn't speak. He was down on his knees, and she stood over him, legs apart and her fists on her hips. "Are you going to continue this charade?" she asked.

Huan shook his head no. Jai said, "I want you to replace that mark I placed on your thigh with a tattoo of an x, so that you will always remember if you or your thinking gets out of line again, not only will I break that bone, but also both your knees. Understood?"

"Yes."

"Yes, what?"

"Yes, Director."

"Good, now you two over there hidden behind the others, take this man to the hospital on the next level, and come back down. The rest of you gather around. This, for those who do not know, is Makeen, and for the time being at least he will take on the duties of head trainer. Believe me, when he is through you will know what it is to be a martial arts black belt of high degree, and you will be prepared to face our enemies out there in hand-to-hand combat."

Makeen, realizing that Jai was finished speaking, bowed to her, and the rest followed suit.

"Everyone not in martial arts training, go back to your stations," Jai said.

# CHAPTER 17

When they reached the three people, Jai, walking quickly past them, said, "The head of finance, come with me. The others, wait until I ask for you."

Once seated Jai asked, "What is your name?"

"Abdul-Haady. I am Lebanese."

"Tell me, what is the status of our finances?"

"We have a steady flow of income being siphoned out of shadow accounts of terrorist organizations around the world. Our brilliant tech department has found a small loophole and window of opportunity to change the amounts deposited to read as less the actual amount. Then our computers post the lesser amount, and we send the difference to our accounts. We don't take much from each account, just enough so that nothing is detected, but due to the fact that terrorist activities are on the rise throughout the world, I expect the amounts we receive will be growing."

"How much are we getting now?"

"Around one hundred fifty million a year."

"Is that our only source of funds?"

"At the present time, it is the only one we are using."

"How much did it cost to put this whole operation together?" Asked Jai.

"Almost a billion dollars."

"What are our expenses running per year now?"

"Right now around one hundred million. Our payroll is in the millions, and the rest is operating expense. But, and that's a big but, operating expense will probably double or even triple once you start missions."

"How much of a reserve do we have?"

"Around sixty million."

"Of course. What about actual cash?"

"Almost none."

"Thank you, now bring in the others. Oh, and I'm now officially appointing you the job of head of finance."

The temporary head of strategy and mission research and Denton, the overall head of tech and R&D, sat around the table. "As you all know by now I am the director of this organization, and Director is what I will be called. Now the present head of mission strategy, your name and background?"

A short, powerfully built man stood and introduced himself. "I am Gavriel Gavish or Gabriel Kristal in English. I am Israeli born and bred. I served in Mossad as a strategist then worked in the oversight branch of military intelligence before I received command of that unit."

"Why is it that I do not see an acting military commander present?"

Denton spoke up, saying, "As I said I assumed that I will be that person as director."

"And you are capable of leading troops into battle? What are your qualifications for doing so?'

"I have no experience, but I thought I could do that from headquarters."

Jai said, "My dear man, not only is that impossible having never led men into battle, but quite honestly it shows a total lack of common sense, and I promise you the men you send will not have any confidence in your ability to get the job done, and more importantly get them out safely."

Denton said, "I guess there are things I must learn rather than thinking I know it all."

"True," Jai said. "Now does anyone here know of such a person who is a victorious leader in many battles and would be in harmony with our causes?"

Denton said, "There are whispers of an individual who supposedly fights against the oppressors in mainland China and throughout communist Asia. He is like a ninja that leads a small army of men and women. They move in and destroy as much as possible and then disappear into the night. They say he has never lost a man and is respected by all the poor and oppressed people throughout Asia. We have heard he has no political aspirations or motives; justice is his motivator. But he is also known as one who metes out punishment without thought to a trial or tribunal verdict. They say he has struck in different countries at the same time, so it is all hard to believe."

Jai was seemingly interested asked his name. Denton spoke up. "He has no name. They say he only fights in the name of Choden, meaning one who is devout."

Hearing that name, Jai turned ash white and became a little dizzy, though she didn't know why. When she gained her composure, she asked, "Is there any possible way we can reach out to this man?"

"Many have tried, including some of the most powerful countries in the world, but nobody has succeeded that we know of," said Denton.

"Never mind. I think I may know someone who can help. Let's move on for the time being," said Jai.

Denton stood up, but Jai interceded, "That won't be necessary. I know all I need to know about you.

"Kristal, you will remain head of military strategy and will report directly to me. Denton, you will head up the R&D department, and you will report directly to me. Any questions? No? Good.

"Starting now I want all training time and effort to double for any and all assets. I also want everyone in a key role to be training another to replace them if something should happen to them. Either promote or hire the best you can.

"One top priority is to find a very healthy pile of illegal cash money that we can confiscate, because we will need it in the field. Once found, the whole organization will take part in achieving a successful withdrawal of their funds. That is all for now. Let's get to work. Our overall mission in life starts right now."

# CHAPTER 18

Deep in the Appalachian Mountains of Georgia, Atticus Boone, a diagnosed megalomaniac, who was the founder and leader of a secret mercenary group specializing in murder and mayhem for hire, had just hung up a burner phone. Seated around an old hand-carved table in a large log cabin sat members of the Inferno, recently labeled by the FBI and Homeland Security as the scum of the earth having no thought of country, mercy, or allegiances.

Addressing these leaders of his military cells Atticus began by saying, "As you all will remember, we have sworn that no outside people would ever be allowed to pull our strings. Money and power would dictate our choices and as a further reward the thrill of the hunt and kill. Now a new opportunity has presented itself. One that could change our lives forever.

"We have been asked to become the military arm of a very important cabal whose members are counted as some of the wealthiest in the world. These faceless people are the true leaders of the governments and corporations. Always behind the scenes, they are the king makers who control their human puppets without interference."

There was a lot rustling and murmuring around the table before the question was asked: "What exactly are we being asked to do?"

Atticus replied, "I do not have the particulars yet. What I do know is that we will be up against a formidable force. We are not only to eliminate a newly formed militia but also the people they work for. Also it is rumored that the military is run by a person with highly unusual powers and skills. I was told that no one in our group can defeat him and to that end we are to work with and support an individual who has those same abilities."

"What will be the compensation for these missions?" someone asked.

"Each mission will have its own price. Bottom price is five million, and it goes up depending on the difficulty and danger."

"Do we have a price for the missions they are talking about?"

"Not yet, because I haven't accepted their proposal. We need to vote, and if yea then we will know."

Atticus called the vote. In the end, after much discussion it was a unanimous yes.

After agreeing to accept the offer, the Inferno leader addressed his men. "Gentlemen, and I use that word sparingly, after we complete these assignments and expenses have been paid, we will all be multimillionaires, but I'm thinking that will not stand in the way of reaching our goal of world domination. The success of these missions will attract a great many more like-thinking men and women, making us even stronger than we are now."

On a junk in Hong Kong harbor off Sheung Wan lived a man of unusual beliefs and skills. Trained by the best in Tibet, Germany, America, and Japan, he was an artist when it came to stealth warfare and the use of highly technical weapons and electronics. Although he felt all the disciplines added to his skill, it was his tantric training by a secret religious order of monks in Tibet that he depended on in the most difficult situations. Spending six years under rigorous scrutiny, he earned his ring in the shape of twin cobras, which was the order's highest honor. Combat was not the only discipline he trained for; the art of sexual domination of both men and women was the other skill he acquired.

He was known throughout the shadow world as Jun Shan, master assassin, but in the halls of the world's governmental agencies that dealt with such things, he was just the Whisperer. It was rumored that before he killed his victims, he was so close, he could whisper in their ears. However, how they would know such a thing was a mystery since no one ever survived to tell the tale. Neither employer nor pursuer had ever seen him, nor did they know where he lived or how to contact him. It was a mystery how when a person or nation wanted to use his services, he would contact them in a timely manner.

After finishing his short talk with his American contact, he threw the burner phone overboard into the bay.

*This is an unusual assignment,* he thought, *a true*

*departure from the usual political adversary, dictator, mob boss, rich businessperson, or authoritarian of one kind or another.*

*Over the years, I successfully terminated about fifty targets, ridding the world of bits of evil. However, this one is different. There was no reason given and no background dossier enclosed with half payment of $5,000,000. Upon completion, I will receive the rest. Of course, no task has ever proved simple, and the prep work sometimes takes me months, but still, $10,000,000? I am fairly well off, but my work's expenses for preparation and travel are heavy, and yes, I do lead a lavish lifestyle.*

At the appointed time, he chose a new cell phone, this one with a Spanish country code, and he called the number he had been given for this date.

"It is getting close. Are you ready?" asked the disguised voice.

"Almost. I will be going to Germany soon, where I will continue preparation and await your go-ahead. Ciao!"

Knowing that this call could not be traced, he still dumped it another part of the bay. Never more than one call per phone, one victim per client within any five-year period, and never the same suppliers for equipment. Most of his weapons he designed and built himself.

# CHAPTER 19

Three intense, heavily volatile months passed, but not without fallout. Due to the intensity of the training and the pressure Jai put on all the leaders, the organization lost many people, including some that were targeted for leadership. A few were drugged and sent away and others demoted to lesser positions.

She was standing behind Hiroshi and Hoshi, identical Japanese twins whom Jai had hired and assigned as equal heads of tech operations. Together they could outperform any single person by three.

She spoke to Denton and Kristal. "We need to replace the people we have lost with a tougher, more disciplined type of individual. Those who remain must be able to handle two, maybe three missions at a time, and that is not nearly enough."

Gabriel Kristal said, "You are right, but the personnel we have remaining are well prepared and disciplined. Let's remember, Denton acting as director hired everyone without any knowledge of what it takes to be a military operative."

"Yes, I know that. I'm not looking for excuses. What I want to know is where the new people we need are. What are we doing to find these people?"

When no one answered, Jai said, "Hoshi, who is better suited to research the military world from personnel files, you or your brother?"

"Though I am a female, either one can do the job equally."

"Okay, Hiroshi, you stay with the training missions, and Hoshi, you work with Kristal putting together a resume of the perfect soldier for our purposes, and then find them, quickly. From what I'm seeing, our people are close to being able to successfully carry out a mission. Where are we in identifying the target we need?"

Kristal said, "We have the target well researched, but as you suggested, we need site recon before we can profile successfully."

"Do we have the people necessary for this?"

Kristal answered, "No. We have people that we can use in the Arab areas, and a couple in the Orient, but this mission must take place in three places: the United States, Russia, or on the Atlantic Ocean. When I get all the information from research and tech, I will put together a mission profile."

"Damn it. We have to operate much faster and with greater efficiency. I need minds that can keep up with the computers. Denton, listen carefully—I want you to research the scientific community and find me the most capable cognitive scientist who fits the profile I sent you a week ago.

Drop whatever you are doing, and get this done immediately. Immediately—do you understand?"

"Yes, I'm on it now."

"Kristal, get me what you have on the first mission. Yes, Denton, what is it?"

"I found your person, no question."

"How did you do it so fast?"

"I have been working on it. Actually I identified the person two days ago but couldn't track her. She is a twenty-two-year-old genius in her fields of study, which are the sciences of neural decision and cognition, especially in the development of concepts in individuals and groups. She is the whole package. The one problem is she has applied to work for Greenpeace. She apparently loves what they do."

"Denton, do you think we can persuade her otherwise?"

"I honestly don't know."

"That's why we need her on board. She would know."

"Hoshi, have Makeen get ready to travel with Denton and me for a few days. Denton, have the plane ready to leave for Paris at six a.m. You, Makeen, and I will be leaving immediately. Be sure to bring all the information on the girl.

"Kristal?"

"Yes, Director."

"I'm leaving for a day, maybe two with Denton and Makeen. You'll have control while I'm gone. I expect to see a list to complete our asset roster when I return."

"Yes, it will be done."

The next morning in a field approximately ten kilometers from headquarters Jai saw the helicopter waiting to take them to the airport in Frankfort.

"Denton, have we set in motion my plan for the girl?"

"Yes, by the time we get there, it will be done and we can act."

"Has the girl been notified as yet?" Jai asked

"No, they are waiting for the go ahead from us."

"And the Greenpeace voice print?"

"It is perfect," replied Denton.

Jai said, "Okay, that's good enough. I'll can bet she'll be on the plane when we return to Germany. A call to her setting things in motion should be made now. We'll show up at her place right after we land."

Two hours later Jai stood outside Amira Moreau's apartment door. She could hear sobbing within and knew that the call had the effect intended. She rang the bell, and a teary-eyed girl opened the door. The women stared at each other for a moment or two, both stunned by the incredible looks each other possessed.

Amira spoke first. "I'm sorry, but what is it you want?"

"My name is Jai, and I am the director of a newly formed international defense force. May I come in? I would like to speak with you.

Once inside and seated, Jai said, "We specialize in defending the Earth against environmental rapists as well as governments and businesses that enslave people. It's an organization that, if my information is correct, you may be very much interested in becoming a part of."

"How do you know that, or of me?"

"Your reputation in your fields of study plus your recent attempt to join Greenpeace made us aware of your skills. May I come in?"

Jai saw her hesitate and placed a thought in the girl's

head of Jai being someone who was honest yet very serious. The girl relaxed and said, "Of course, please do."

"You seem to have been crying. Is everything okay?"

"I just received word from Greenpeace that they were not interested in hiring me."

"Well, we, on the other hand, need a person of your skills, to make our organization even more potent than it will be."

"I don't know why they didn't hire me. Why didn't they hire me?"

"I don't know the answer to that question, but I do know that you will be happiest working with us."

"Tell me about your organization."

"Our people and equipment are all cutting edge. We have an R&D department that surpasses any in the world. It is headed by a man named Denton."

"Abraham Denton?"

"Yes, why? Have you heard of him?"

"Yes, everyone worth their salt doing any scientific research knows of him. The man is a genius."

"That's what he called you. He is the one that has recommended you for the newly created position of cognition and neural sciences."

"Will I work for him?"

"No, you will work directly for me and alongside him. So, what do you say? Will you join us?"

"Can I speak to Denton before I give you an answer?"

"One moment. Denton, would you come upstairs? There's a young woman that would like to speak to you."

"He's here?"

"On his way up."

"Oh shit, I don't know what to say to him. I was just trying to see if what you said about him working for you was true."

"Are you going to join us and do work that will satisfy your creativity and desire to save the planet?"

"Yes, without question. When do I start?"

"Pack your things, only the essentials, and we will be on our way."

"To where?"

"You'll see—you'll see."

# CHAPTER 20

Once on the plane, Jai immediately walked to the rear and turned on the com device. She found a message to contact her superiors. It sounded serious, so she felt a little apprehensive while tuning into the correct frequency. The woman she had spoken to at Denton's place appeared.

The woman began speaking. "Listen carefully, Jai. I know you don't remember all that I told you before you lost your memory. So I will repeat it. I told you that there will be a very dangerous group that is out to destroy not only you and your company but also me and my people. We believe that they are getting very close to discovering who you are and where you are located, and quite possibly where we are located."

Jai, feeling very uncomfortable with this seemingly new information, asked, "How do they know about me?"

"I'm sorry we don't know. It might be possible that there is a spy in your organization. Unless you can think of another way?"

Jai responded, "Not at the moment. Do you know where they are located and who is in charge?"

"I'm sorry but no. We are working on it but are at a big disadvantage not being able to leave the land where we live. It's up to you. You better have people watching your back and stay alert twenty-four/seven. Also, whatever safeguards you have in place around the headquarters, you might think about strengthening them. I strongly suggest that you address this problem directly."

Their plane touched down in Germany at nine thirty, and they boarded the chopper, all to Amira's amazement. When she said so, Denton responded, "Wait till you see where you work and live."

When they arrived inside the cave entrance, they went up to operations. In the conference area on the hoop sat Kristal, Hoshi, and Hiroshi, the communication twins.

"Where are we in recon recruiting?" asked Jai.

Kristal answered, "We don't seem to be able to make it happen without money or revealing who we are."

Jai asked, "Okay, then if necessary I'll do the recon. What about the first mission? What have you got for me?"

Kristal answered, "The best is a shipment of Russian mafia money being shipped by freighter from the United States to their bosses in Russia. This is money from their illegal operations, largely the illegal drug trade. It is rumored that the number is in the neighborhood of three-quarters of a billion dollars US, but honestly that has never been substantiated."

"Okay, bring me a mission profile for the job. I want modes of transport, beginning and ending points and everything in between, timing, number for guards along the way. I'm also assuming our forgers can handle whatever papers we need. I want it on my desk in two days. Put everyone on it twenty-four hours a day if necessary. We are jacking up the proficiency of this organization, and people better start understanding that we are fighting a war that will be shortly lost if we and only we don't get our shit together. Playtime is over; now get to work. Amira, you stay with me.

"Amira, we have a few minutes. Do you have any questions?"

"Jai, I don't exactly know what my job is."

"First, call me Director anytime we are in a public area or if there are people around; in private you may call me Jai. To begin with, we will use your two areas of expertise. Using your knowledge of cognitive science, I want you to help Denton and his people in predetermining what possible moves and conclusions artificial intelligence computers will come to when we better design the software.

"Second, you will use your neural expertise determining the ability of our people when it comes to their decision making and functioning in all situations. Third, you will evaluate all potential military and tech ops for their ability and willingness to do this job then hire or dismiss them."

"When do I start?"

"You are working now. Just let me give you a list of people with their responsibilities, and you observe them under all conditions. Start a computer file on everyone, and use a system of passwords that cannot be broken. Ask Denton to help you. You will be in all my meetings with military and tech, and you will learn a lot about each of them then.

"Hiroshi? Come up here, I want you to take Amira,

my new assistant, around and show her everything. She is cleared for all floors, so take her top to bottom."

At the end of the tour Hiroshi left Amira off on the fifth floor with Denton and returned to his desk alongside his twin sister. "Isn't Amira just stunning? She is as beautiful as the director, but so much softer."

Hoshi said, "I can't believe her dark chocolate mud pie eyes, perfect mocha skin, and straight black hair. You are right. She seems to be much softer, but equal in every way. My dreams will be full from here on out."

Hiroshi responded, "Maybe we can make your dreams come true. But remember, I will not be left out."

"Don't worry, my brother. You know I always take good care of you."

"And I you, sister."

# CHAPTER 21

The following day Jai was talking to Hoshi. "Did the Russian mafia heads agree to buy the coke supply from Columbia?"

"Yes, the brothers did and everything is in place. They called Columbia to check to be sure that our people were legit, and we intercepted the transmission. We told them that the two, Delores and her husband, Alvaro Ramirez represent the drug cartel and the Lunas personally, and they are empowered to negotiate a final deal. We faxed them a photo of the two. The meeting is tonight."

"Hiroshi? Has the number-one team and equipment arrived in Bremerhaven?"

"Yes, on schedule."

"Good, is the freighter on schedule?"

"Yes, everything is a go," Hiroshi answered.

Four hours later, Jai said, "We are entering the brothers' compound."

"Park your car in front of the house, and go in," one of the guards at the entrance said.

Hoshi said to the field ops, "Okay, we have great sound and video."

Jai rang the bell, and the door was opened by another guard. "Please remove your coats, and step over to the guy with the hand scanner."

When the guard reached out to direct Jai where to stand, she jumped, "Hey, you can scan me all you want, but keep your hands off of me. Where do you want me to stand?"

"Okay, don't be so touchy. Stand over here."

Watching the whole thing on a monitor, one brother said, "That girl has a lot of spunk."

"Keep your hands off, Michael, at least until this first deal is done. There is a lot of money at stake here."

"I know, don't think I'm stupid, but I promise you her husband better be careful. She's my type of woman."

The two ops walked into the room with a guard, who was immediately dismissed.

"Hello, my name is Luigi, and this is my brother, Michael. Can I offer you a drink?"

Jai answered, "Not until we conclude our business, thank you."

"As you might guess we checked the two of you out with Carlos in Columbia, and he speaks highly of you," Michael said.

Jai said, "Carlos? I assume you meant Fausto Luna?"

Luigi jumped in, "Yes, yes of course. I apologize for my brother. Sometimes his memory fails him. I've told him many times to lay off the booze."

"How long will you be staying with us?" asked Luigi.

"The moment we reach a deal, we are gone. There are others that await our services," said Jai

"So what is it you are proposing?" asked Luigi.

"We will deliver the amount of uncut coke to your ship five miles off the coast of Aruba twenty-four hours after the funds reach our bank. Can you get a ship there that fast?"

"Yes, of course. Did you bring a sample of the product?"

"Yes. I'm sure that you know we deal all over the globe and have never had a problem with product or delivery."

"Yes, that has also been confirmed. Let me see what you brought. Are you sure you don't want something to eat or drink while my brother tests it?"

Over com Jai heard Hoshi. "Slow it down. There's a problem outside."

"Well okay, I think I'll have a rum and coke if that's available."

Hoshi said, "Back-up team, there are two hostiles headed to the south wall for a smoke. Take them out, now.

"Did you hear me, team two?"

"Yes, we'll take care of it."

When he handed her the drink, Luigi said, "I have to ask, you are seemingly Spanish. How is it you have beautiful blond hair and white skin?"

"I am of German descent. My family escaped to Columbia after WWII."

"So like my family, yours was on the losing side of the war?"

Jai ignored the remark and instead said, "This is fine rum. If I'd known that Americans had such good taste, I would have had it straight."

"My brother buys only the best. Remind me of the price once again."

"Fifteen million, which, when cut properly, will bring fifty times that on the streets of America."

"But the price quoted was twelve million."

"True, but our commission was not figured in. That was always to be left to us to negotiate."

"Three million is quite high."

"We are worth it. Without us you cannot make a deal. The Lunas will only deal with us."

"If I call, will they say the same?"

"Try, and you will see that the number you call no longer exists."

"Alvaro, what is taking so long? I'm ready to go," asked Jai.

"Okay, I hear you. What is the problem, Luigi?"

"This product doesn't seem right. It's appears to be nothing but ..."

Everyone at operations watched, as Luigi never got to finish his sentence. Jai pulled out her stun gun, and Luigi dropped like a log.

"What the hell!" Michael said as he turned toward Jai, drawing his gun and firing.

But he soon realized he was shooting at an empty space. Looking around for Jai, he saw nothing. Then she whistled, and he looked up and saw Jai hanging in space above his head. He raised his gun to fire, but he was too late as he hit the floor, stunned by Jai's weapon.

The Jai and her partner put thin wire harnesses around each of the men, attached them to a drop mechanism, and lowered them out the window to the waiting arms of the backup team.

"We'll wait for 2$^{nd}$ teams signal before lowering

ourselves out the window. I need to be sure the grounds are clear. I'm downloading their computer files to Hoshi now."

"We've got all we need," Hoshi said. "Okay, get out of there."

After stunning the gate guards, the teams made it to their plane, and once everyone was on the transport plane, the pilot said, "We have clearance for liftoff, and we follow the original plan, Greenland then Bremerhaven?"

At the compound Hiroshi switched the main monitors over to the Bremerhaven team, and Kristal, standing behind him, said, "Team leader, the plane is on its way, and your freighter is about to dock. It will take the ship about four hours to clear immigration and customs. Is your team and equipment in place?"

"Yes, two of the backup team are signed on as replacement sailors, and the containers have been cleared for loading."

"Director?"

"Yes, Hiroshi."

"The five containers are loaded in the domestic hold, which is alongside the international hold, and are scheduled to be the first to be unloaded in Cuxhaven. They are untying and lifting anchor now. The trucks are headed to the rendezvous. So now it's a matter of timing."

"How long before they begin?"

"The second mate does his rounds one hour after they leave port, so right after that."

"Did they place the cameras in the hallway outside the holds?"

"Yes, we can see the whole stretch."

"Kristal, we are landing, and I will be at the dock shortly. I will take over the op," said Jai

Fifty minutes later, Jai was on board. "This is Jai. We are finished converting the domestic containers to international. Is the hallway clear?"

"Yes."

"Three and four, start switching the containers around. Two stay on guard, but move to the stairwell."

Two hours later the empty containers were stowed in the international hold, and nobody would be able to tell they weren't the originals. In the domestic hold, the money containers had been changed in appearance and appeared to be domestic containers. All the papers had been switched, and thereby they would bypass customs. The assets hid themselves among the working crew, who were readying the ship for docking. Jai was last to leave, making sure that everything appeared normal.

When safely in port they all left the ship and disappeared. Local stevedores would unload the containers with the money onto waiting military transports operated by Jai's team. They delivered the cargo to headquarters with no complications.

Once money was safely put away and counted, Jai asked, "What was the count?"

"Four hundred seventy-five million," Makeen replied.

Amira asked, "What happened to the brothers?"

Jai answered, "The KBG has been notified of the containers, and they will meet the ship in St. Petersburg, to confiscate the supposed contraband. To their great surprise they'll find five empty containers, plus the two drugged brothers. They have been wanted in Russia for many years, accused of killing at least eight government officials, two policemen, plus a number of others. They were in their twenties when they escaped to South America, then five years later moved to the United States and eventually took control of the Russian mafia in the States. Even though not part of our overall mission, we can take solace in the fact that the world will be rid of them.

"Makeen, meet me in my apartment in thirty minutes."

"So Amira, how did you find the mission and its aftermath?"

Amira answered, "The missions went well. I just can't believe that you can handle these stressful times with such coolness. How do you do it?"

"Simple—I make myself think of the cost to the planet if we fail. There are a lot of creatures that are depending on us to succeed; to that end I must remain serious and very dedicated."

"What made you believe in protecting the environment and act the way you do?"

"I do not know. My memory is a blank up until recently, but I do know that what we are doing is beyond reproach."

"I couldn't agree more."

"By the way what do you think of the Japanese twins, Hoshi and Hiroshi?"

"They are unbelievable. They're like one person split in two. Their reactions both mental and physical are identical."

"And emotional also," Jai said.

"Maybe. I haven't seen that as yet, but there have been no identical circumstances for me to judge."

Jai said, "Anybody looking at them would not think they were computer geniuses, would they?"

Jai said, "Theirs is an amazing story. Born in shame to a very young mother, they were separated at birth. Throughout their childhood they both had an imaginary sibling that they talked and played with. By the age of ten they still held onto these imaginary people, and no matter how much their mothers threatened, the twins swore that they existed.

"Then one day each of them, in an attempt to prove that they were not lying, asked their stepmothers to take them to park in the center of Kyoto where they both lived on opposite ends of the city. They were old by their children that they would never speak of them again if their 'imaginary friends' weren't at the park. The parents, in desperation, finally gave in, hoping their kids would give up for once and all this nonsense.

"Hoshi told her mother that she would meet her friend in a tunnel in the center of the park. Hiroshi did the same. The pair approached the tunnel from different sides and asked their mothers to wait at the entrances. Reluctantly they agreed. The two children walked to the center of the tunnel. Later they claimed that they were talking to each other all the while, and who could argue? When they physically met for the first time, there was a moment of silence as they looked at each other and saw a reflection of themselves. Then Hiroshi grabbed his sister, and they both cried. The mothers, hearing the sobbing and unable to see what was going on, ran in, and as they approached, they saw their children holding each other in frenzied relief. It took a moment or two, but the mothers finally realized that aside from being different sexes they were looking at identical twins, and they were flabbergasted. After a moment

Hoshi's mother grabbed the other woman, and they too started to bawl. Hiroshi's mother said, 'How could we have known?'

"The four spent the rest of the day in the park. As it turned out, both women were divorced, and Hoshi and her mother moved in with her bother. They haven't been apart since. The pair are a phenomenon in computer journals, and they were protégés of Denton's from the age of twelve."

"Wow, that's quite a story."

"Yes it is, and believe me it goes further, but that's for another time. I've got a bit to do before things heat up again. You should probably add to your files. I'll call when it's time to return to operations."

"Hoshi? I'll be out of communication for two hours."

Jai whet up to her apartment and found Makeen waiting for her. "You know, Makeen, the last day or two my energy level seems to have dropped, and I'm not sure that I have performed at my best."

"I don't think anyone other than yourself would notice. The mission went well, and all was accomplished."

"You know, Jai, it's been a long time since we've been together sexually. I think it's time, and necessary."

"You make it sound like I am a machine, not a human being with emotions."

"In some ways you are expected to be like a machine, and machines need top-grade fuel to operate efficiently. Your fuel is energy, and dare I say sexual energy seems to work best for you."

"Are you my only gas pump?"

Makeen responded, laughing, "I would like to think so, but I'm sure that's not the case. But hey, you can always count on me to do my job. What man wouldn't want to be in my position? The pay is good, the work is meaningful, and most of all the benefits are fabulous."

"Then why are you standing around wasting company time Come here and do your job."

Jai watched as Makeen walked over in that stalking cat way he had and picked her up and threw her on the bed. Slowly, so very slowly, he caressed and massaged every part of her body, building her energy, but not allowing her to climax too soon. Falling back on his training, he allowed her body small releases, but each time she did, he softened the pressure so that her body and mind were begging for that one explosive climax that they craved so badly. Jai felt that she would have to have multiple and powerful climaxes before achieving the goal. He hadn't yet removed her clothing; it was one thing he always took his time with. It seemed to her that unveiling her perfect body gave him such pleasure. That, and the powers she knew she possessed were prizes to be won over, but she knew he would never be able to conquer her, and that too brought his sexual desires to a peak.

Almost every night since they had been together sexually she wondered what it would be like if he could bring her to a climax that would break any control she had over her own powers. *I'd probably kill us both.* Now naked except for her panties, she could sense that she was lost in his power over her body.

He whispered in her ear. "Not yet, young lady. I'm not finished with you."

Then with his teeth he started to pull her panties off, and Jai's body arched anticipating his tongue. Ever so slowly he probed her lips, barely licking her clitoris, and she began to moan in a way that told him she loved what he was doing, and she was no longer in control of herself. Sensing the perfect moment, he whacked her butt cheek hard, and she lost the last remaining bit of control she had and let out a scream as she experienced a huge climax.

Makeen increased the pressure, which brought her quickly past the point she was before, and just as she was about to come again, he mounted her and rammed her as deep as he could. Again she screamed, and this time she started to shake, causing every inch of her insides to spasm, magnifying every movement of his pulsating, hard cock. She started climaxing one after another, each one more intense than the last. She threw her legs around his broad back, crossing her ankles, and held on for dear life. When Makeen exploded, she joined him, and together they screamed with an animalistic roar. They collapsed into each other.

After a while Jai said, "I feel like a wet rag. How can sex, which causes me to use so much energy, actually create more in me?"

"I don't know, but what I do know is I'm certainly not going to analyze the process. As long as it works that's my only concern or should I say hope."

"I guess we'll just have to wait and see. As of right now I don't have any energy."

Makeen said, "Maybe we need to do it again."

"Yes, and maybe you'd like to bury me."

"No, I want you around forever."

"For just you?"

"I would like to think so, but I already know that's not going to happen."

"How do you know that?"

"Let's just say, if I were you, I would go with what is quite obvious, at least to me."

"And that is?"

"I'd rather not say."

"Is this a game?"

"No, but if it was I would love to play. Keep that in mind."

"Shit, what time is it?"

"Four thirty."

"I have to get back in communication with operations, and also read the debriefings. It's been great, I just hope I can walk."

Makeen, laughing, said, "Well if you can't, you can float."

"Cute!"

# CHAPTER 22

"Hoshi, I'm back on com. I'll be in my office on the hoop. Send up the female who was on the last mission, and Amira."

With a little time to spare, Jai went over in her mind the words of the women on the com, wondering how big a threat they faced and knowing that if she was being warned that it must be imminent. *I just can't imagine how someone found out about me and my paranormal abilities. On the other hand, I must figure it out.*

"Excuse me," Jai heard the female she requested to join her say.

"Yes, come in. Sorry, I do not know your name."

"Zelda, Zelda Pederson."

"Zelda, I have some very important questions to ask you. Normally I wouldn't ask ops if they would do the things necessary for success in our missions, but since there are times when it can become very personal, I prefer to know up front what your thinking would be."

"I can't begin to imagine what that would be," Zelda said.

Jai continued, "Zelda, there may come a time, and I imagine that it may happen, often when we are going to need a female to get very close to either a target, or a go-between person to help us gather information or complete an important mission."

"By very close I'm assuming you mean have sexual relations with?"

"Yes, that's exactly what I mean. We will try to learn all about his or her appetites, whether deviant or normal, before you are asked to do this. Are you comfortable with that?"

"I am comfortable with any sexual behavior, especially my own. I have experienced about all there is to experience. In my home country sex is not as taboo as in other countries. My family promoted my experimentation at all ages, believing it natural to do so. I believe that answers your question, Director."

"Yes it does, and thank you for being so upfront."

"And you, Director."

"You may leave, Zelda."

A knock on the door and Kristal entered. "Where are we in missions?" Jai asked.

"We have two small ones in progress, nothing much, just research," answered Kristal.

Jai said, "I have received some potentially valuable information of the kind we have been looking for from outside sources, but it's based mostly on speculation. What we have has been sent to your computer in the file M-I. Please look it over, research it, and then put together a potential strategy that will bring it to a successful conclusion. We will, of course, need recon to gather as much vital information as possible before the profile can be finalized, and since we don't have our recon sources in place, I will pick a team from within to do the job. Any questions?"

"Not until we see the file," Kristal replied.

"Good then let's meet again at eight a.m. That is all."

# CHAPTER 23

I *can't believe it has been four months since I've taken over this operation. I feel as though we've accomplished a lot, but I am beginning to wonder if I have what it takes to do this monumental job. No memory, not knowing who exactly I am working for, or who I can trust given the latest information.*

With these thoughts on her mind, Jai began to fall asleep, and for the first time in a long time, she spent a very restless night filled with disturbing dreams of things she couldn't understand.

Jai saw herself being dragged from a ship by a woman through the streets of Macao and deposited in a large old house in a rundown neighborhood. Running through the hallways. She saw all shapes and colors of young and old women scantily clad standing outside their bedrooms and laughing at her. They were vicious, telling her that they were she, and then began ripping at her clothes. She ran, but the hallways never ended, and men began to appear, laughing at

**her as she tried to hide her naked body. They grabbed her and threw her to the floor, laughing all the while holding her down they were putting their hands all over her body and face. One young boy who looked familiar, but she couldn't remember from where. He was sitting across her chest.**

She screamed in her dream and bolted awake, sweating profusely as she tried to catch her breath. The speaker over her bed blared out, "Director, are you okay?"

Jai suddenly realized that she must have screamed out loud and answered, "Yes, I'm fine, just a bad dream."

Jai couldn't go back to sleep. The dream remained vivid in her mind, especially the boy. *I know that boy,* she kept thinking, but from where she couldn't begin to fathom. *Was this a clue to my past?* That question kept running around in her head.

She got dressed, and taking the kitchen shoot to the entrance, she left the compound. Luckily it was around three in the morning, and the German training guns were silent. Wandering around the dense forest, she came across a small meadow, where she startled a sleeping deer and her fawn. Jai attempted to send out good vibrations, but the two ran. After a few yards, the mother stopped and turned to look at Jai. She cautiously walked back to Jai, with her fawn following. Jai slowly reached out her hand and touched the mother's shoulder, all the time whispering words of comfort and allowing her to feel Jai's peaceful energy. The fawn, feeling her mother relax, came out from behind her, and Jai nuzzled her head with her own. After a while they sauntered away and lay back down in the tall grass to finish their sleep. Jai smiled, reminding herself that harmony and coexistence among all creatures was what her life's task was all about. Walking back to the forest edge, she sat down up against a tall tree trunk and fell asleep to the hum of what sounded like the fluttering wings of hummingbirds surrounding her.

At sunrise Jai awoke, still wearing a smile, and made her way back to the compound. She found herself thinking, *How auspicious that that experience came at a time when I needed a reminder of the powers necessary to complete my undertaking*

Back in the compound she took the pod up to the hoop and surprised the techs because no one had seen her leave. Looking a little disheveled, she nevertheless smiled and then asked if there was anything unusual that occurred during the night. Receiving negative responses, she went into her apartment to get ready for the day.

"Director?"

"Yes, Hiroshi."

"Kristal is headed up with the report you asked for."

After reading their report, Jai said, "I agree with the summary you wrote. It is useless to try and outline a mission without the proper intelligence. We are a long way from ready. Do we have anyone in the area?"

"No, I'm sorry, but we do not."

"This is our biggest problem right now. We need operatives in all the hot spots of the world. How many have you got in the field recruiting?"

"Three total, and they have been unsuccessful so far."

"We sound like a two-bit insurance company trying to recruit sales agents. We are faced with fighting a war in the blind, and that has got to change.

"I want two men who will fit into the area, with the

correct physical and religious backgrounds. I will lead the recon team in myself."

"But Director, the locals will not accept a woman as trustworthy or important enough to help out."

"Turn your backs to me and then turn back again."

Kristal did as he was told, taking his eyes off of Jai for barely a second, and when he was facing her again, she asked, "Well, do you see a woman?"

Kristal, with a look of shock on his face, admitted that he did not. Before him stood a typical Arabian-looking male with a tooth missing in the front of his mouth. "Holy crap how the hell do you do that?"

"Do what?" asked Jai in Arabic, and with a male sing-song voice.

"Never mind. Can I ask a question?"

"Yes."

"Do you have a penis too?"

Jai stood up and asked, "Would you like to see?"

"No thanks, I meant it as a joke."

"Did you now?" Jai asked, though it was obviously a rhetorical question.

Six hours later Jai stood behind the briefing and hologram table and addressed Hiroshi, Kristal, and Denton. "I will be leading a recon mission into Azerbaijan. What is important to us is that during the Iraqi and Iranian war, Iraq used chemical weapons against Iranian forces and Kurdish separatists using a mixture of poison gas and nerve agents, killing around five thousand people, mostly women and children.

"To make a long story short, we all know that the Iraqi government agreed to disarm itself from all nuclear and chemical weapons, but because of a slew of misinformation and conjecture, the American president chose to invade the country in search of those weapons and found nothing. In the process he destroyed the infrastructure and stability of Iraq, and unleased a civil war that had been held in check for many years by Saddam Hussein.

"We have good intel that at least a third of those so-called nonexistent chemical weapons containing nerve agents and poison gas are now being held in the region of the Talysh Mountains of Azerbaijan by a rather large group of terrorists, the Golden Warriors of Allah. The use of those weapons would have a devastating result on the environment and innocent people and creatures. It will be recon's job to find out exactly where they are hidden and the various ways we can get to them and destroy or confiscate them. We leave at five thirty sharp. That's it for now."

"Denton, stay behind a minute. I'm leaving you in charge while I am gone.

"Okay, Director, and good luck on finding the weapons."

At noon the next day, three male foreign geologists disembarked in Baku, the capital of the Republic of Azerbaijan from an Armenian flight, where they were met by Jai's initial contact.

"I thought I was meeting a woman?" he said.

Jai introduced herself as Jose Valdez from Chile and said, "Your name please?"

"Hadi."

"The woman you were supposed to meet couldn't come. She was stricken by some sort of bug at the last minute, but believe me, we are more than capable."

"Okay, let's get a move on it. The faster we get into the mountains, the better I'll feel," Hadi said.

# CHAPTER 24

They got into a small, old car that appeared held together by thin strands of wire. They drove through the city and the suburbs and then headed southwest through the cities of Puta then Karadagin. They turned south, going deeper into the Talysh Mountains, which border Iran. For roughly two hours they rode on bumpy, rocky mountain roads, until they came to a halt on what was obviously a junction of old mining roads merging from all directions.

When they stopped Jai said, "Is this as far as we can go by car?"

"Yes, as far as we dare. The mountains echo even the smallest of sounds, as me and my partners came to learn."

Jai said, "Okay, let's hide the car off the road over there and begin our climb."

Being duly cautious, it took them close to an hour to reach the site of the encampment. They could hear the people long before they reached a point where they could look down from behind a bunch of rocks. When Jai was satisfied that they were well hidden, she turned on her camera and sound equipment.

"Hiroshi? Can you see and hear me well?"

"Yes, perfectly. We see the people below, and we have the coordinates. The satellite is picking up the images clearly so we can monitor the whole area around you. So far I see no hostiles except in the camp below."

"Can you see us?"

"Yes, the four of you are hidden behind a bunch of rocks, and the local guy is picking his nose."

"What else do you see?"

"There is a large cave opening on your far right with guards all around, and four more inside."

"As soon as I decide how we are going to get a look inside, I'll let you know," Jai said.

Formulating a plan, Jai said to the three men, "Hadi, leave now and go back about one hundred meters, and wait. You two spread out and cover me from two directions. Keep alert. You will not be able to see me at times, got it?"

"Yes."

"Now go pick two good sights. Remember, those stun guns have a range far less than our normal guns, so move in a lot closer. I'll wait until you are set.

"Hiroshi, did you get all that?"

"Yes."

"Let me know when they are positioned correctly and then I'll leave."

When they were ready, Jai, summoning her *lung gum* practice, leapt into the air and bounded her way toward one side of the mountain valley. Arriving safely, she leapt and then floated to the overhang above the cave entrance and waited to be sure no one had seen her. Hearing no disturbance and making sure no one was facing the cave, Jai floated to the ground. Putting up her shield of invisibility, she walked into the cave and past the interior guards.

"Hiroshi, are there any more hostiles ahead?"

"Not that we can pick up."

Jai said, "It appears like there are many tunnels coming off this main one. I'm going to search them all. Are you picking up my video signal?"

"Yes, everything is working."

"Good, here I go."

Once again using *lung gum,* Jai moved in and out of the tunnels with amazing speed. She had seen caches of rifles, grenades, missile launchers and missiles, and various other assorted conventional weapons, but no chemical weapons.

"Hiroshi, intensify the infrared to see if we can pick up liquid or gases."

"Yes, you were right. We see something. Go back to the main tunnel and then go right 150 feet and look above you. There is a shelf that goes back a long way. We are picking up something from within; we are just not sure what."

Jai floated up to the shelf, and using her highly tuned senses, she began to crawl through the four-foot-high tunnel. She sensed an electrical system in front of her long before her flashlight beam fell on the alarm system.

"Hiroshi, get me through this alarm."

"It's a rather old and crude system hooked to a battery, with one exception, if you unhook the cables, you will trigger another alarm situated in a hole four feet left from where you are. That one needs to be disarmed first. The wires are buried below pressure mines, so you have to get around them first. Disarming the secondary alarms will also disable the mines."

"Okay, got it."

Jai flattened herself to the roof of the tunnel so as not to disturb the mines and moved toward the hole. Once there she undid the cables and headed back to the main alarm leading to whatever they were guarding.

"Director? There are two guards coming toward you from the entrance. They must be doing rounds. Are you going to take them out?"

"No, I can't do that. If these people know someone has been here they would move everything to a different location long before we could act. If I have no choice then we will have to destroy everything now, and that will put us in real danger. Do not contact me again until I contact you. I want no sound at all. Tell the ops outside to do nothing at all no matter what happens in here."

Jai turned off her light and put on her night vision glasses. She heard the unsuspecting men long before she saw them. Deciding that she would have to see what they were going to do, she waited. The men came into view and were heading toward whatever cache was hidden. One of the men stopped, and reached above his head to touch the wall, and a metal door swung open. Jai immediately saw that there was a panel of lights, of which three were green, but the four others were red and blinking. Instinct told her that they were attached to the second alarm and the mines. She sent a visual image into the mind of the man who was standing back and looking up at the panel.

He said, "They are all green. Shut the door, and let's go to dinner."

After they were out of earshot, Jai said, "Hiroshi, are they still in the cave?"

"Yes, but they are being replaced by two others."

"Okay, let me know if they too are going to do rounds."

"It doesn't appear so; they must be satisfied with the report they received from the others."

"Okay, here I go." Jai unhooked the cables from the main alarm system and moved toward the crates that lay back another hundred feet or so.

After a short pause, Jai said, "I have found the chemical and biological weapons, but they do not say what types they are. I'll count the crates and backtrack my movements, rearming all the alarms again."

With everything back in working order, Jai was once again invisible to the interior guards. She walked out of the cave and floated to the ledge above, then made her way back to the rocks. "Okay, team, move back to our first position. I'll back you up."

They picked up Hadi on the way back to the car, and he asked, "So did you find what you were looking for?"

"Yes, and more so. I would strongly suggest that you do not come back into these mountains for a long time."

Jai sensed that there was something amiss and asked Hadi if he had stayed where she told him to all the time they were gone. He turned uncomfortable, and Jai realized that he had gone back to the car to most likely go through their luggage.

"Did you find what you were looking for in our bags?"

"What do you mean?"

"You know what I'm talking about, but I'm guessing that you were smart enough not to try and cut or pry them open, because there is no way you could open those locks. It is foolish to lie to me, and if we are going to have a future relationship, you must trust that lying would be useless."

"You are right, I did as you said, but couldn't open the locks as you also said."

"In spite of your misstep I will pay you four and a half million New Manats, or fifty thousand US dollars when we reach an airport hotel for the job you have done for us. Does that suit you?"

"It is more than I expected, but I will not quibble," he said with a broad grin.

"Listen, Hadi, if you want you can work for us, we can be very generous."

"What is it you want me to do?"

"I want you to recruit others who can move in and out of Iran, Syria, Iraq, Saudi Arabia, etc. Also many who live in those countries. You will be the go-between, so that all information they gather about things I will tell you about, you will pass it on through highly sophisticated equipment we will supply. Does this interest you?"

"Very much. Yes, very much so."

They reached the car and headed to the city. Even though it was pitch black outside, the driver was speeding at an uncomfortable rate. The car was bumping along, and the air was hot and dry.

Jai continued, "Okay all arrangements will be made. When my team comes back, you will lead them back to the encampment."

"Very good, very good indeed."

"Use only people that you can trust. Numbers do not matter, only the quality and dedication of the people."

On the way back Hiroshi informed Jai that there was a flight back to Armenia in four hours, and the three were booked on it. They went to a hotel near the airport, and Jai entered the lobby bathroom and changed clothes. She put the money for Hadi in a travel bag and ditched the clothes she had been wearing. Walking to the table in the restaurant where the others waited, Jai approached, and Hadi's jaw dropped as she sat down.

"So now you know that the woman you had been expecting was with you all along."

"You are not serious?"

"Oh yes she is," one of the team said.

"How is this possible?"

"How and why are not questions we are paying you to ask, understood?"

"Oh, yes, but really ... okay, I'll stop.

They all ate a full meal, said their good-byes, and watched as Hadi gleefully strode out of the hotel. "We've accomplished more than we came for," Jai commented.

"Can he be trusted?"

"Believe me he can, as long as we pay more than our enemies."

# CHAPTER 25

When Jai arrived at operations, she was greeted by Denton and Amira, "It appeared to go well," said Denton.

"Yes, much better than even I expected. We picked up what could be a good person to head up a field recon team in that area. Amira, join Kristal and me for debriefing in one hour. For now I'm going to clean up."

"Can I speak with you before the debriefing?" asked Amira.

"Yes, come with me to the apartment. Lei is out."

Entering her suite, Jai said, "Sit here in the living room while I shower, I'll leave the door open so we can talk. Is there a problem?"

"Potentially, if something isn't done to dispel it."

"What is it?"

"I believe that someone, and I'm not sure who yet, is trying to undermine your authority."

"What makes you say that?"

"Of course it's just a hunch, but I have noticed people

leaving their posts and heading to rendezvous in dark corners. It has given me an odd feeling."

Jai caught a glimpse of Amira looking at her naked body slipping into the shower and felt her blood rush to her head, making her a little woozy. *What is happening to me?* she thought to herself.

"Go on, Amira. Are there any other incidents I should know about?"

Amira, caught in her own thoughts, didn't hear Jai's question. "Amira, are you all right?"

Amira, focusing her mind, said, "Yes, I'm fine. Just thinking, and no, no other incidents that I can think of."

Jai, finished with her shower, reached for a towel, slipped it around her, and stepped out of the stall. The towel just barely covered her body from the top of her breasts to her upper thighs. Amira quickly looked away. Her heart was racing.

Jai caught every word Amira was thinking, and so she walked out of the bathroom in a way that accentuated her femininity; and like a cat she walked over to where Amira was sitting, fully realizing that she was making it very difficult on her, but that was exactly what she had in mind. Jai thought, *I too have no idea what is going on here, but she is such a splendid-looking woman with a mind and body to match, and I'm finding the combination irresistible.*

She could see that Amira couldn't take her eyes off of her as she moved and decided to allow her to look all she wanted. Not saying a word, she found excuses to move around the room. Amira stood up, and excusing herself, she wobbled into the bathroom and immediately threw cold water on her face. Jai pretended not to notice any of this.

When Amira came back out, she found that Jai had gone into her bedroom, and closed the door.

Jai decided that Amira and she could be lovers sometime in the future, but now was not the right time. *I'll let both our desires build, and I'll entice her enough that she makes the first move.*

The debriefing was simple, and then Jai added, "First, we need to destroy the caches of weapons held in those caves without allowing any chemicals to escape; second, we must capture a couple of the leaders and see if they know where the rest of the chemical weapons are hidden; and finally we need to do this without loss of life on either side. A successful mission would mean a lot in recruiting undercover agents and field recon ops for future missions. Bring me two, possibly three mission profiles. You have all the intel you need. That's it."

Alone, Jai called Makeen on her com. "Makeen, are you in the compound? Good, meet me in my place as soon as the lessons are over." Walking to her suite, Jai wondered if Amira was too much of a distraction. *Will I lose sight of all I need to accomplish?*

Makeen entered Jai's apartment. "Have you seen or heard anything that could possibly be trouble while I was gone?" asked Jai.

"You know nobody will say or do anything around me, but I did happen to walk in to a strange scene at a restaurant in town. It was probably nothing, but I thought it odd at the time."

"What exactly did you see?"

"Sitting at a table were, Kristal, two weapons guys that work for Denton, two operatives, and a level-five team leader."

"Why is that strange?"

"Two reasons. One, nobody is supposed to be seen outside the compound with other people from here, and two, they acted really weird when I came in. Three of them got up and left immediately with food still on their plates."

"They left together?"

"Yes."

"Who stayed behind?"

"Kristal and the team leader. I picked up my to-go order and left."

"Why the hell would they bring suspicion on themselves like that? Stupid! Too stupid to be in the positions they hold. I wonder what they are up to. Who is monitoring operations right now?

"Hiroshi."

"Hiroshi, come up to my apartment, now."

"What are you going to do?" asked Makeen.

"Find out what is going on and put a stop to it."

Hiroshi knocked on the door. Jai asked him to enter and said, "Hiroshi, here is a list of names. I want them monitored twenty-four/seven by you or your sister only. You are to notify me when any two or more are together."

"Got it."

"You don't seem to be surprised."

"I'm not. I saw Kristal talking to each one on the list when you were gone. Plus, a tech has been searching the files and I believe trying to back door his way in to levels he's not cleared for."

"Why haven't you told me this?"

"I've been waiting to tell you, but you have been tied up since you returned. Here is the chip I had prepared to give you with all the information, including the files he was trying to access."

"Good, now leave us and talk to your sister. She knows, right?"

Hiroshi hesitated and then said, "Yes." Then he left.

"Makeen, who do you think I can totally trust?"

"Of course, there's me, Amira, Denton, Lei, the twins, probably Abdul Haady, the financial guy, Zelda, and most of the foot soldiers."

Jai, pacing around the apartment, said to Makeen, who was sitting on the couch, "That leaves just the five at the restaurant?"

"More or less."

"What about the team leaders?"

"I would make sure before you deploy them on sensitive missions."

"Unbelievable. Amira, please come to the apartment."

Amira knocked on the door and without waiting entered. Jai explained to her what she learned and asked her if she had seen or suspected anything beyond what she already told her.

"No, I was busy monitoring everybody during your recon mission, then entering my observations into my computer files."

"Do you really think there could possibly be something devious going on? Any signs at all?"

"No, but if you are thinking about Kristal being involved, I wouldn't doubt it."

"Okay, what we need to do is find out if we are right, what they are up to, and if there are others involved, inside or out, before we move on them."

That night Jai had another dream.

Jai was in the middle of an army of soldiers fighting for her life, and Kristal was their leader. There were bombs blowing up all around her, but she couldn't escape because she was chained by her ankle to a truck. A guy wearing a strange robe leapt into the battle and managed to unchain her before he died. The next thing she was running through the forest carrying a barely clad Amira over her shoulder. She came upon a grass meadow, and exhausted, she laid the girl down in a bed of colorful wildflowers. Different types of creatures approached from all around and surrounded them. Jai found herself staring hungrily at the beauty that lay before her and reached for the one button remaining on the girl's dress, but she was startled awake by the sound of her alarm.

She lay in bed, her sheet wet from perspiration, trying to remember the details of the dream, seeking some insight into her past life, but there was nothing that brought back conscious memories.

Jai worked closely with Kristal and Zelda over the next two days, formulating a mission plan to destroy the weapons in Azerbaijan. Nothing unusual happened with the group of five. When all was set, Jai approved the profile and called a briefing with Hoshi, Kristal, and the team leader he chose, Denton, Makeen, and Amira, but Hoshi called Jai and asked to meet with her before the briefing, saying that it was extremely important. When they met, Hoshi passed on the information she and her brother had gathered, including a strange transmission they intercepted on a channel no longer in use.

"Who received the call?"

"Kristal."

At the briefing Jai said, "We are ready to take out of play the chemical weapons we found. Hadi, our man in the field, is waiting for the team. Your profiles are on the chips in front of you. I can't tell you how important this first mission's success is, but I can say that I want it done and done right. You leave in two hours. Kristal, you have oversight. Follow your profiles and all will go well."

After they broke to get ready, Jai spoke into her com. "Zelda, are your teams ready? Good, Hoshi are you tracking Kristal?"

"He's headed to the infirmary. Should I have Makeen go with him?"

"Yes, but he should not be seen. Let's wait and see what he has planned. Zelda, you and your men take off; I'll handle Kristal and his men. Follow the profile to the letter. Having been where you are going, I'll be on oversight.

"Denton, have the four agents I asked for meet me in weapons."

Jai found the two weapons conspirators huddled together in supply. They didn't see or hear her come in. "You boys seem very busy. What is that you are writing down?"

When they didn't answer, she said, "Hand it over."

They hesitated, and one of the men reached for his sidearm, a weapon that he shouldn't have been wearing. Jai leapt into the air spinning, and with one of her legs she kicked the arm of the hand reaching for his gun and broke it in half. The other guy just froze as the four agents Denton sent came up from behind and grabbed him.

"Two of you put them in separate interrogation rooms and strap them in. Then call infirmary, and get a doctor for his arm. The other two wait here for the cancelled team to show up for their weapons and supplies and take them to interrogation also. Everybody wait there until you hear from me."

"Makeen, what is Kristal doing?"

"He's about to give himself an injection, but I can't tell what it is. Do you want me to stop him?"

"No, he is going to make himself ill, so he has an excuse to be away from operations, and then he'll try to leave the compound. You stay with him in case I'm wrong, but remember, he belongs to me. After he shows signs of a sickness, put him in a holding cell and make sure you have guards you can trust outside. I'll deal with him after the mission. Hiroshi? I want a deep background check on Kristal. Penetrate the surface layers. I want to know everything. Have we tracked the person or place of the call he received? Virginia in the United States—do we know from whom or what agency? Okay, stay with both. Hoshi will handle the mission with me."

# CHAPTER 26

At the compound the next morning things were jumping with the rumors of the arrest of Kristal and some of the others and the first real mission getting underway. Everyone was in a controlled panic.

Jai and her team were close to an intersection of many roads leading into the mountains. Jai, leading the mission, asked control, "Any unexpected happenings?"

"None, except that Hadi showed up with his two-year-old, spacious Range Rover. There was plenty of room for the eight of them plus their gear. Interesting what a little money will buy."

"Good, I hope he and his friends get hooked on a new lifestyle that will keep them with us."

Jai spoke again. "I am turning on the cameras and will not move closer until Hoshi sweeps the area. Hadi and his mate are ready to infiltrate the militia. We need them to tag or at least identify the three leaders."

Hoshi said, "The perimeter is a clear move to your first position."

Jai reported, "We are in position."

"Hadi is down in the encampment."

Fifteen minutes later, Jai said, "Hadi has identified the two leaders. We'll tag them."

Com responded, "Yes go ahead. You and the other agent go on down also. The perimeter is still clear."

Jai reported, "We can see two men getting ready to take over guard duty inside the cave."

Com reported back, "Position the four of you just inside the mouth. Infrared shows the inside guards are doing rounds. When the new ones enter, take them out and hide the bodies, then greet the others and allow them to leave. Any sign of suspicion on their part and take them out of play also. When you are ready, Jai, you and your partner head for the rear. I'll have you on infrared and guide you through all the tunnels."

"Two new guards are down. We'll wait for the others."

Silence, then Jai spoke. "Okay, they are out of the cave."

"Go straight ahead. Agents three and four, keep a close eye on the comings and goings outside the cave. Okay, Director, take a right at the next cross roads, then about fifty feet ahead make a sharp left. Straight ahead about twenty feet on your left side there is a panel about six or seven feet above the floor. See it?"

"Not yet. Okay, yes, I got it."

"Open the door and look inside and see if there is a main breaker switch."

Silence, then, "I see seven flashing lights but no breaker switch."

"Look all around the box."

"I need to rise to see above. Hold on. Yes, you are right—it's here."

"Raise up high enough for your camera to see it. Okay, good. It's the main breaker. Throw the switch, but be ready for anything to happen."

That done Jai said, "The lights in the panel went out, but that's all."

"Great, now we don't have to disconnect the mines or batteries. Go straight back and you'll see the crates with the chemical weapons."

"Okay, we got them," Jai reported

"Open the crates and take out the containers that house the chemicals and nerve gas. Once that is done, open the lead boxes you brought in, then put on your bio-suits and check each other to be sure everything is covered."

There was ten minutes of silence, and then before they got the okay to proceed Jai said, "I'm ready to open the missiles."

"Okay, when that's done, pour the contents into the lead boxes, which contain an agent that will greatly reduce the effectiveness of the chemicals. It should take an hour or so to empty them all, and when you are done solder the lead boxes shut. Keep your cameras on so we can monitor your work."

Approximately eighty minutes later, Jai said, "Okay we are ready for the next step."

"Remove your bio-suits and place three charges in that tunnel. When that's done, I'll take you to the tunnels that house the conventional weapons, and then you'll place two charges in each. That being done, head to the cave entrance and wait for further instructions."

A little while later Jai said, "We are at the entrance."

"Okay, take the two unconscious guards out and into the woods, then go to that large tent on the north side. Right now the two tagged leaders are in there eating lunch by themselves. There are no guards around them. Go in from behind and stun them and carry them to position one where the other four are waiting."

Everything went without a hitch, and when they were all together, Jai said, "We are ready."

"Good. As soon as you blow those charges and they go running to the explosions, head on out of there. When you're near the car, we'll blow the tunnel charges from here."

As soon as they were safely at the car, Jai said, "Okay, Hoshi, blow the tunnels."

They watched as orange and red flames came shooting out of the tunnel's entrance, and they could see the rubble falling and sealing the entrance. There was a cheer in operations as well as in the car.

High above the cave entrance a pair of strong binoculars were trained on the proceedings, watching carefully every move being made. At the same time an infra-red eye kept track of the bodies inside the cave. Having received an insider tip describing the operation that was about to take place, and with the possibility it might be led by the person he was contracted to kill, Jun Shan watched intently. The one thing that caught his attention was the levitation move inside the cave. He studied carefully the people who exited the cave, making a mental note of their faces and body language. There seemed to be one man who stood apart from the others, and he could tell that he was their leader. He put into play his camera with its telephoto lens and began shooting, concentrating on the leader.

Always working alone had its disadvantages. He knew that by the time he packed up all his expensive gear and made it down to his rented vehicle, they would be too far ahead for him to catch up. *I'll just have to wait until I get another chance given that I am getting information from an unknown source through my American contact. Hopefully that will continue.*

# CHAPTER 27

Jai, her team, and their prisoners made it back to headquarters in good time. Stepping out of the entrance, they were greeted by Hoshi and Amira. Jai's thoughts went immediately to the two beautiful women standing before her. *I couldn't have chosen a better welcome back home.*

Amira said, "Congratulations on a successful op."

Hoshi asked, "What about Kristal? What will you do with him and the rest of them?"

"Nothing until Hiroshi penetrates deep into his Mossad files and we figure out why he has turned. Then I'll figure out what to do with him and the others," Jai responded.

Two days later, Hiroshi, sitting in Jai's office, said, "I was able to penetrate Kristal's Mossad file. The reason we didn't see it before is that it had been deleted, but I dug out a discarded backup drive. Here it is. It's not pretty."

"Thank you, Hiroshi. That will be all."

"Amira, my office." Five minutes later, Amira arrived. She dropped everything when she heard the tone in Jai's voice. "Look at this. It speaks for itself. Hiroshi, is there any mention of what happened to the girl—or if there are any others? Okay, do another search and see what you can find. Put everyone on it. I want to know ASAP.

"Makeen, my office, please. Well, Amira, what is your assessment?"

"He is obviously a sadist, one with particular needs. My guess is that being in here is crimping his style, and the desire to fulfill his perverse sexuality forced him to find a way out, but also he must have been planning on something to earn money on the outside. My guess would be it has to do with the sale of our weapons and technology. He certainly must have connections into the terrorist world considering his background."

"Director? I found the girl. She is living not too far from here in Nuremberg."

"Hiroshi, what do we know about her?

"She was found by a landlord who had complaints of strange noises coming from the small warehouse he had rented out. He must have interrupted what Kristal was doing. He called the police and an ambulance. The doctors in the ER gave her zero chance of survival, but she made it. The hospital records show she was operated on seven times and then went through therapy, both physical and mental, before she was released about a year ago. She works at home as a computer geek, fixing whatever she can to earn money. But a search of her computer drives says that she is really an agent for the Palestinians, supplying any information of value she can find on the Jews in Israel and Germany. She has also been searching for Gabriel Kristal."

"Thanks, Hiroshi. Well, obviously Kristal is Jewish and this is the girl's way of getting revenge until she finds him."

Amira said, “I bet that she has been looking for him since she was released from the hospital.”

Makeen walked in.

“Amira, go with Makeen to Nuremberg, and talk to her. See if she won’t come here. Use a promise of possibly knowing where her torturer is located.” If she will, we will send the plane, and she must be blindfolded.”

The following day Jai heard from Amira about the girl, Wanda Ruyter. She saw his picture, and though she hadn’t left her apartment in years, she agreed to come to the compound if they would promise that she would be left alone with Kristal for one hour. Makeen added, “Let me say that he did some really horrible shit to this once-beautiful woman, and she is twenty-six today. What should we do?”

“Bring her along,” Jai said after thinking for a moment.

Four hours later, after doing a number of deceptive maneuvers and keeping the girl blindfolded, they arrived at the compound. Jai met them on the third level in a debriefing room.

After formal introductions, Amira said, “We do not want you to relive your experiences with Kristal if it is too painful. What we want is enough evidence of his behavior to make a decision on how to proceed with his case. Is there anything you can tell us?”

Wanda replied, “I’ll give you all you or anyone else will ever need if you think you can stomach it.”

“We can,” Jai said.

“I was just about to turn nineteen, and I was working as a hostess in a small restaurant where I met this girl and we hit it off. One day she invited me to a party, supposedly with a bunch of people my age. As it turned out, there was to be only three of us at this party held in Kristal's rented warehouse. For a whole week I was repeatedly raped and beaten in every way possible either by one or both at the same time. All the while they were comparing me to the other girls they had done the same things to. I fainted many, many times, but he would revive me and tell me I had to pay for what the Nazis did to his family.

"My gag finally fell out of my mouth, and I screamed like a howler monkey. That's when the landlord heard my screams and called the police. Luckily they were just around the corner. Kristal heard the sirens approach and ran out the back door. They took me to the hospital, where I could hear them saying that I would die within the hour. I guess my desire for revenge kept me fighting, and in the end I won that battle.

"They did a lot of reconstructive surgery, especially on my eyes and mouth, and they were saved, but the rest of me is useless. My breasts had to be removed also because the cutting games of tic-tac-toe he played on them were just too deep and they became infected."

Jai was thinking, *Why didn't I know this about this man? I can sense the evil in people. How did this escape me?*

"My god." Amira gasped. "Are you sure it's the man in the photo? Never mind, stupid question. It's just so hard to believe knowing him."

Jai said, "Okay, you have given us what we need. I'll allow you one hour with him. Makeen, move Kristal to a soundproof room and strap him lying down to a table. Then leave him by himself. Let me know when it's done."

The door to Kristal's room opened, and this figure walked into the room and shut the door. Wanda didn't say a word. To begin with she just ripped open his shirt and then cut away the rest of his clothes. Then she emptied her little satchel and placed everything on his chest. The first words she spoke were "Welcome to my hell."

"No, don't. I have a lot of money that I will give you if you just help me get away."

"There is nothing in this world or beyond that will help you escape what it is I'm going to do, absolutely nothing, but you may beg some more as I did, and that I will enjoy."

Wanda copied everything she could remember that Kristal had done to her. The screams were horrific, but no one could hear. The cameras were recording, but the screens were turned off outside. When she was satisfied she did all she could, she went into the water closet and slowly washed the blood off of her hands and face. Before she came out, she felt Kristal's pulse and found that it was very faint but still there. Satisfied, she walked out of the room and down the hall to where two agents were waiting.

"Director, she's out."

"How is she? Is she all shaken?"

"No, she's as cool as a cucumber."

"Keep her there. Amira and I will be right down."

When they approached Wanda, Jai asked, "Wanda, what will you do now that your revenge is complete?"

"Kill myself. I have nothing else to live for."

"What if I can offer you an alternative?"

"And what could that possibly be?"

"Before I go any further, you must allow Amira here to do a complete psychological workup on you. If you pass, I will tell you what we are about and how you can become a part of it, but if you want you may just kill yourself and be done with it, but that would be a waste of your talents and dedication to a cause."

"You may want to do it quickly, because we have less than four hours before we all die."

"What do you mean?" asked Jai.

She told them all that Kristal told her about the bombs and timeframe.

In the meantime two agents went into the room that held Kristal and came out looking very pale and asking to speak to Jai privately. Then told her what they saw.

Jai said, "Can he be brought out of his coma?"

"Believe me, there is no way," one responded.

"Then put an end to it, and incinerate the body. A fitting end considering what he had planned for us. Denton, come down to level three immediately."

When he arrived, Jai explained the situation and asked what equipment they had that could find those devices. "We have the right equipment, but if the bombs are shielded in the same type of material as our satellite and planes are, they can't be detected."

"Okay, Makeen, get everyone out of the compound now. Denton, you safely shut everything down, and set our destruct timers for four hours. You and the twins will stay with me until the last moment in case we find the bombs and need to quickly abort our destruct sequence. Can you handle that?"

"Not without messing myself, but yes I will," a shaking Denton replied.

"Makeen, you and Amira stay with the girl at Denton's house across town. Be sure and blindfold her. Everyone get out, now."

"Okay, here we go. Hiroshi and Hoshi, go to the main frame on seven and do a sweep of the entire complex. If Kristal didn't use our new skin to cover the bombs, the sweep will uncover all of them. If you have no luck, then Denton, you set the destruct mechanism. Then the three of you join me in operations. Amira? Ask Wanda if he told her how many bombs he placed."

"She says five, but he could've lied."

"Okay, thanks."

The three took the pod up to level seven, and Jai carefully monitored their movements from the hoop. The sweep didn't reveal any anomalies throughout the system, so Denton set their timers for four hours. Jai placed herself in the middle of operations and sat down while she waited for the rest to return. Once they were there, she told them to watch from the hoop, but not to do anything. Jai put herself into a deep meditative state, and building her energy, she sent it out to cover a quarter of the area, but she felt nothing. Withdrawing her energy, she built it up again and sent it out to cover another quarter, but again nothing. On her third try she first sensed the heat from the timer, and then concentrating on that spot she was able to feel the bomb hidden inside a spare electrical fuse box.

She said, "Denton go to maintenance and supply and bring me everything you have to disarm bombs. I want it all here just in case we are up against something you haven't seen before."

Then she rebuilt her energy and searched the rest of operations, but found nothing more. When Denton returned, Jai and Hoshi, using infrared, searched the interior of the box but found no explosives attached to the door. They then searched the area around the box; still nothing. Jai then slowly opened the door, which revealed the bomb covered in Denton's "invisible" skin. It was attached to an individual timer, which read two hours and twenty-three minutes and running.

"This means that all the bombs have their own timing devices, so disabling this one won't stop the others from blowing. The one good thing is that it is a simple connection as long as there are no hidden devices to set it off. Denton, what do you think?"

After looking it over, he replied, "I don't see anything other than what is obvious."

"Okay, all of you get back in the hoop while I try and disable it," Jai said.

The others safely out of the way, Jai took another look just to satisfy herself and then started to reach for the connection wires. The fluttering sound of wings stopped her dead still, and she had a very bad feeling all of a sudden.

"Denton, do you have the mine sweeper with you? Good, bring it to me."

Denton swept the box, and sure enough it found a pressure sensor switch under the bomb with a hidden wire attached. "How are you going to remove that wire?" Denton asked.

"Not necessary. I'll burn it off. That won't change the pressure on the plate."

"But you can't reach it without moving the bomb."

"Just watch."

Jai put herself into a high state of meditation and began her Bardo practice, which creates a tremendous amount of high heat. When she felt the temperature was right, she shot it out, aiming at the pressure switch, and in a second the thin wire melted.

"Wow!" said Denton.

"Okay, go back to the hoop, and I'll do the rest. Hiroshi, you keep track of the time. Starting now we have two hours seven minutes," said Jai.

Jai had no problem disabling the timer, and after another sweep of Operations, they headed to the seventh level. Denton mentioned that Kristal didn't have clearance, but Jai said she would rather be safe. There was nothing on seven, so they headed to the fifth level, where they found two others that were rigged exactly the same way. There was another in inventory and maintenance on the fourth level, and then one more in a briefing room.

"Hiroshi, time?"

"Sixty-four minutes, but that's five. Shall I call everybody back in?" Hiroshi said.

"No, let me try a few other places. I can think of two places I would place them if I was doing this."

"What are they?" Hoshi asked.

"The pod for one and the hoop for another. I going to check them out. Why don't the three of you wait on level two?"

Jai rode down in the pod with them and sure enough found a sixth device attached to the side of the pod. After dismantling that one, she found one on the hoop in the conference area. These last two didn't have pressure switches. *All done and still nineteen minutes left,* Jai thought.

"Thank you, whoever is watching over us," Jai said, looking up to where she normally heard the fluttering wings.

"Hoshi, all is clear. Call everyone back in."

But the fluttering began again, and Jai said, "Hoshi wait. No, stay put until I call again."

*I must have missed something,* Jai thought. *What level haven't I checked out?* She went up to the eighth level, but found nothing, then down to two, and still nothing. *Where else?* She checked her apartment on the hoop, nothing. *What am I missing? That's all there is.* But the fluttering continued, and Jai realized that she had less than twelve minutes to figure it out. She sat down to meditate, but her mind was running wild. *What would I do if I wanted to destroy everything and kill everyone inside? That's it!*

Jai yelled out and started running to the pod. She reached the level and ran to the place most likely to hold the bomb. She hoped beyond hope she was right because there was only time for this one shot. She built her energy as she ran, and when she got there she spread it out and found what she was looking for, the eighth bomb. It too had a pressure plate, but with as much practice as she had had already she was able to disable the whole thing in three minutes. When the timer stopped it showed eighty-seven seconds before it was to blow.

Jai sat down and waited ten minutes to be safe and then called Hoshi to bring them all back in. "I don't know who or what you are, but stay close," she said to the tiny breeze she felt on her face.

When Hoshi came back in, she asked Jai, "How did you figure out where the last bomb was located?"

"It was when I realized that he not only wanted to destroy the complex but kill us all in the process that it came to me that in order to assure that end he would have to blow the entrance so no one could leave, and actually that device was set to go off two minutes before the others."

Hoshi, shaking her head, said, "You are a wonder beyond human."

Jai just smiled.

# CHAPTER 28

Later that evening with things back to normal, Makeen contacted Jai. "Director?"

"Yes, Makeen."

"After we were told to return to the compound, Wanda took flight out of the bathroom window. I assume you want us to bring her back."

"Yes, of course. She now knows what town we are in or near. Any problem finding her?"

"No, I tagged her before we left the compound. Operations can pick her up on their screens."

"Okay, Denton has shut down our destruct mechanism and turned on the mainline computers. The twins will be on line in a moment."

"Hiroshi? Wanda has been tagged. She was at Denton's home five minutes ago. Find her and report to Makeen. Play the tape from the room where Kristal was held for Wanda on my screen in my apartment. I'm headed there now."

As Jai was viewing the recording, she heard, "Director, the team has returned with the girl."

"Makeen, hold her in the clinic. Did she say why she ran?"

"Yes," Amira responded. "She believes that we are an anti-terrorist group out to destroy those that have become her friends."

"Have you told her the truth?"

"Yes, but she didn't believe either of us."

When the tape was done, Jai went down to the clinic and spoke to the girl. "I'm sorry that you believed that we are your enemies, but maybe it is for the best. Makeen, give me a hand."

They strapped the girl down on a table, and Jai said, "Give her a three-day knockout, and then wipe out her memory going back to when she worked at the restaurant. Let her stay in the clinic under the doctor's care for a day to be sure her vitals are fine and then take her back to her apartment, and leave her to awaken."

Amira asked, "Why can't we try and rehabilitate her?"

"Even if it were possible, the time and effort it would take we can't afford. This way she will live some kind of life without the mental scarring. The physical may prove to be too much for her to bear, but that will be her choice."

"What did you see on the tape?" Makeen asked.

"It was gruesome, but in the end Kristal twice told her there were eight bombs. Seeing an opportunity to destroy us and herself, she purposely lied to us. Amira, come with me to the apartment. I want a preliminary debrief on everything you were able to observe during this crisis."

When they reached the apartment, Lei was there waiting. Jai was exhilarated from the explosive situation she had just experienced, and needless to say, watching Amira walk in front of her around the hoop quickened her pulse and breath.

"Lei, please prepare the table for my massage. I am very tense at the moment. You don't mind, do you, Amira?"

"No, not at all. Please do."

After showering Jai laid down on the massage table, and when Lei covered her with a sheet, Jai slipped out of the towel she wore. While Amira talked about the limited time she had to observe during the crisis because she was at Denton's, Jai was able to hear the slight tension in her voice, and as much as she wanted to send out her vibrations to touch her, she felt it might be a mistake with Lei so close.

"Director, excuse me, but you have an incoming communiqué from Hadi in Azerbaijan."

"Patch it through, Hiroshi."

There was a brief pause, and then the com set went active. "Jai? It's Hadi. Are you there?"

Jai said, "I'm here. What is it?"

"We have found a second store of chemical weapons in Iraq. But I'm afraid they won't remain there much longer. They just learned of what happened to the others."

"Is this all the remaining weapons?"

"I do not know."

"Okay, give the details to the next person you speak to. I'll put together a team, and they will meet you in the mountains on the Turkey-Iraq border at dawn tomorrow. We will send you the coordinates. You will be there, right?"

"Yes, of course I will."

"Hiroshi, are you getting the details? Good, come up to my apartment on the hoop when you have it all. Lei, wrap it up. We have to move fast. Amira, I do not want to use the same team. Have you cleared six other people for deployment?"

"Well five anyway, but I can clear one more if necessary."

"Let Hiroshi in. He's approaching the door."

"Let's see what Hadi sent."

After scanning the information, Jai said, "Hiroshi, get a team list from Amira and call a briefing in one hour. I will do the mission outline. Amira, who are you suggesting as backup team leader?"

"Hannah."

"A woman to lead in Muslim territory—are you sure?"

"I gave it a lot of thought, but she is the best, and the best qualified. She also has the respect of all the other agents. So yes, Hannah."

One hour later with everyone seated around the table, Jai walked in and began the briefing. "We have information as to the whereabouts of a second cache of weapons being held on the Iraqi-Turkey border. I will lead the first team. Hannah, you will lead the backup team, and Hiroshi will do oversight from here. After the last op you can be sure they are waiting for us and are trigger-happy. Everything you need is on your chips. Any questions? No, then we leave in one hour."

The transport helicopter had been dispatched, and the two teams left by jet for Turkey an hour later. It wasn't too long before they hooked up in Batman, Turkey, and the teams headed for the rendezvous with Hadi in the mountains. When they arrived, a very despondent Hadi and two of his new recruits greeted them.

"Good to see you again, my friend. Why so sad looking?" asked Jai.

"You have missed the terrorists by an hour or more."

"Which way are they headed?"

"Southwest, in the general direction of Syria."

"How long will it take them to reach the Syrian border?"

"I think a long time, because the roads are very rocky, steep, and curvy. I'm guessing they can't safely move at more than sixteen kilometers an hour in most places."

"What kind of trucks are they in?"

"Old Russian half tons."

"Hiroshi, are you with me? Good. Can you pick up the convoy by satellite? Once you do infrared x-ray tell me in which truck the weapons are."

Having the information, Hiroshi said, "Director, there are four trucks. The lead truck has eight soldiers carrying weapons plus two in the cab, the second is carrying what appears to be women and children and no weapons, the third houses the cache of chemical weapons with the driver, and one other in front, and the fourth has six soldiers, plus boxes of rifles, rocket launchers, and rockets. They are spaced around thirty yards apart."

"Okay, send us a close-up satellite picture of the road they are on and keep sending as they go. Once I have that, I'll figure out what to do. Well, as I suspected would be the case, we are doing it on the fly."

After Jai received the photos, she asked Hiroshi his opinion, and he mentioned a sheep ranch with a large herd very near the road that they could break out and use to block the caravan. Then they could ambush them from the sides if they got there soon enough. Thinking it over, Jai believed that there were too many things that could go wrong, including interference by the civilian family and workers.

So using the same concept, she set up a plan and then briefed both teams and headquarters on what everyone should do.

Both teams plus Hadi and his men climbed aboard the chopper, and Jai gave instructions to the pilot to make a far swing and drop both teams ahead of the convoy and as close to the narrowest point between the two mountains as he safely dared. Then he should fly the chopper to a point where it couldn't be seen nor heard and wait. After landing she checked with Hiroshi and found that they were five miles ahead of the caravan, which gave them only ten minutes to set the ambush.

"Hannah, split your team in two and climb up on both sides of the road just far enough to place your charges so that the pass will be completely blocked. Do not under any circumstances set them off until given the order to do so by me, understand?"

"Yes, Director," Hannah answered. She looked at her team, and they all nodded yes in return.

Jai continued, "After the boulders come down, stay in position to cover first team from above, got it?"

"Understood."

Hannah split her team in two, and they started to climb. Meanwhile, Jai explained the rest of the plan to her team. Everyone had barely taken their positions when they first heard then saw the approaching caravan of trucks. "Backup team, are you ready?"

"Yes, and the charges are all set to blow. Know that because of the mountains formation I believe you are going to get a fairly large landslide of boulders and debris," Hannah cautioned.

Jai said, "Okay, first team, I'm going to leave you now

and try to separate the last two trucks even farther apart from the first two. After the explosions, get to the rear truck and control the situation. I'll take care of the one in front."

Jai, unseen and moving down the road, allowed the first two trucks to pass, then went into a meditative state. She concentrated on a scenario where a small herd of sheep and their tender were making their way across the road, completely blocking it. She sent this out to the cab of the third truck, infecting both men's minds.

The driver suddenly slammed on the brakes, yelling out, "*What the hell! Hey, you Turkish ass fart, get those sheep off the road or I'll blow your brains out.*" The driver's headphones came alive from the trucks in front and back.

"*What the fuck is going on, Farik? Why are you stopping?*"

Jai, satisfied that the trucks in front were far enough away, said, "Hannah, blow the boulders."

Once again positioned high above the fray, Jun Shan peering through his binoculars watched with amazement as the third truck stopped for no apparent reason. Then there was a huge explosion, and a good piece of both mountains came plummeting down, causing all sorts of havoc among the combatants in the trucks. He watched as Jai's team took advantage of the confusion. With his directional microphone he heard a woman's voice say, "Okay, first team, move on the last truck," and at the same time he saw Jai draw her weapons and jump on the hood of the stopped truck. Clearly seen by the two men in the cab, they froze, and in Arabic Jai said, "Do not move no matter what happens and you will live. Otherwise I'll blow you both away."

*And so I believe I am finally able to identify the leader*

*of this ragtag army. It might be easy just to try and take her out during all this commotion, but if I miss I might be seen and I will lose all further advantages. I'll wait and see what transpires.*

There was a problem behind them; the soldiers in the rear truck had been well prepared for any type of action against them. They leapt out of the truck and opened fire on first team as they were moving in. Two men on first team went down in a hail of flying bullets before the rest returned fire. Jai, being stuck with the two men she was guarding, couldn't help, and at the same time she realized that Hannah's team had opened fire, directing it on the men from the front vehicles who were now trying to work their way over the fallen debris to help out. Jai, seeing no other way, shot the two men in the cab with her stun gun and started running to the rear to help out. As she reached the truck's rear, she spotted two men with a rocket launcher getting ready to fire at the chemical weapons truck. She leapt in the air and opened fire on them, instantly killing them both, and then she began firing at the others, who had successfully pinned down the rest of her team. She killed four before she landed, and her team took out the remaining four.

"Hannah, how are you doing?"

"We are fine. They are totally pinned down, and it would take them an hour or so to reach your position after we stopped firing."

"Okay, when you see the chopper approaching from behind my position, you and your team break off contact and get down here as fast as possible."

"Bird one, do you copy? Come get us from the rear.

We do not have time to get rid of the weapons in this place without many more being killed, so you will have to fly them out. I'm thinking that because of their weight the teams will be forced to make our way out until you can unload and return for us. Bring Hadi; we will need him to help us with the locals if necessary."

"Director?"

"Yes, Hiroshi."

"What are you going to do with the two stunned men in the cab of the truck?"

"I believe the one riding shotgun is the leader, so we'll take him with us for questioning and leave the other. Got to go, the chopper is landing. Hannah, how close are you?"

"We are practically on top of you. Look above you."

One half the team loaded the chopper while the other half tried to keep the unexpectedly fast-approaching terrorists pinned down. "Now get our two dead and put them in the chopper also."

The pilot addressed Jai. "The already loaded weight allows us to safely take five of you with us, leaving the rest behind. What do you want to do?"

"Hannah, you pick three to go with you and take the prisoner. Find a good place to safely take the weapons, unload, and then follow the profile and destroy them. Make no mistake that is really bad stuff. We'll move ahead and find a good place to hide until the chopper can safely get back to us. We will head out on a diagonal and get as far away as possible. I will take Hadi and the other team members."

Hannah, with a deep look of concern on her face, said, "It is you that should go with the chopper, and I should stay behind."

Jai retorted, "You are as good as advertised, but I am much more capable of handling any situation that might arise. So pick your men and get on the chopper now. Those soldiers are starting to close in, and we have to move."

The chopper took off safely, and Jai said to Denton, "I'm going to blow the ammo truck then leave." When the charges were set, Jai moved everybody safely away set them off. The explosion disoriented the rest of the terrorists long enough for Jai, Hadi, and the others that stayed behind to head out. "Hadi, I hope you are in good shape. We will be running and climbing for a while."

"I better be, there is an awful lot of your money awaiting my return."

Climbing out of the valley in a northeasterly direction, they stopped at a vantage point on top of a hill and watched as the remaining terrorists went through the debris looking for wounded comrades and any weapons they could salvage. In a holding position, they waited to see if the terrorists were going to come after them, but instead they headed back over the boulders to the remaining trucks and the women and children.

"Hiroshi, does the satellite show any place for us to hide until we are picked up?"

"There's an empty barn about five hundred yards directly north of your position."

"Where is the house?"

"All I see is a bunch of rubble about one hundred feet to its west. I'm guessing that it's been down for a long while. Infrared shows no signs of people or animals in or around the barn. There is also an open field before you reach it, and it looks perfect to land the chopper."

Two hours after settling into the barn, the three heard a faraway explosion, and Jai was told by Hiroshi that it was the demolition of the weapons. "The chopper is about to take off and should arrive there in fifteen minutes or less," Denton reported.

"Director, Hiroshi here. There is a jeep of sorts with five men carrying conventional weapons headed your way."

"Can you tell if they are military, police, or civilians?"

"My best guess is that they are civilians, and they appear to be moving rather fast. Wait, they are being chased by two vehicles also with armed men."

"Do we have a safe way out?"

"If you leave now through the side door and head directly north," Hiroshi said.

"We're headed out. Call off the chopper until we can find another pickup point."

"The two vehicles doing the chasing are Turkish police," Hiroshi said.

Jai told the others to head for the small clump of trees, and she would catch up. With the others safely hidden, Jai leapt to the top of the barn and then made herself invisible in order to try and decipher what was going on. The lead jeep, seeing that the police were catching up, veered off to the east, and the police followed. Jai thought, *It is obvious that they were headed to the barn but couldn't make it in time. So what is so important with the barn?*

"Hiroshi, keep a close eye on things I'm going back into the barn and look around."

"Okay, they are still moving away from your position."

Jai jumped down and entered the building while Jun

Shan, who had followed close behind, watched the whole scenario from a close vantage point. Trying to decide when and where would be the best place to take her out, he decided to wait.

Having spent almost two hours looking, she couldn't imagine what could be in there, unless that's where they were planning on making a stand. Jai built up and then spread her energy, searching for anything out of the ordinary. Feeling nothing, she decided a closer look was needed, but again there was nothing out of the ordinary, so she exited the barn and headed to the stand of trees where the others were waiting. Less than halfway there she tripped over a small pipe coming out of the ground.

"Hiroshi, can infrared tell where this pipe leads?"

"No, from the blank space on my screen I'd have to say that wherever it goes is protected by some sort of energy-repelling screen, but before it disappears it runs back toward the barn."

"I'm going back. Are the police still chasing that jeep?

"Yes, they are still moving farther away from your position."

"Team one, you and Hadi return to the barn, and let's see if we can find out what is going on in here."

"Hiroshi, draw a line between the pipe and the barn, and tell me if it hits the barn."

"Yes, it does."

"Exactly where?"

Digging down at the point Hiroshi told her, Jai found that the barn was in fact sitting on concrete that continued a long way into the ground. The other two showed up, and Jai said, "There is something under this barn, and we have to find out what it is. I'm guessing there's a hidden doorway that leads below, but be very careful if you spot something. The entrance could be booby-trapped."

For twenty minutes the trio searched and found nothing. About ready to quit, Jai said, "We are looking for the unusual. Let's look closely at what would normally be in a barn before we leave. Hiroshi, are we still clear?"

"Yes, they are still moving away from you."

With the change of focus one of the men, hoping to clear away some hay, grabbed a rake that was hanging from the rafters, but it would budge. Calling Jai over, he said, "This rake will not come off the beam."

Jai looked it over and said, "Move back let me try something."

She grabbed the handle and leapt up and when the rake moved up about twenty degrees they all heard a pop. Looking around they saw that some floorboards had risen above the ground.

Jai came down and said, "Don't touch anything until I examine it for mines."

Her energy couldn't find anything of the sort. She reached under and found a handle and moved it to the right, and the floorboards rose up, leading to a stairway, much like the hood of a car would operate. You two stay here and stay in touch with operations. I'm going down."

At the bottom of the stairwell, Jai sensed a small electric vibration and realized it must be a light switch. She flipped it, and the lights lit up a tunnel that led in a southerly direction. Keeping in touch with Hiroshi, she followed the passage until she came upon a large opening that led to a room, but it wasn't until she turned on the additional lights that she was able to see how big the room was and what it contained.

In it she found a manufacturing plant for heroin in all its forms. Stacked up in the corner she found finished product bagged and ready to go. There was also a computer that appeared to have only local access, and a cache of weapons and ammunition of all kinds. Her best guess was they are either selling it to terrorist organizations to help them finance their operations or to anyone for export. *Either way I have to destroy this place.*

"Hiroshi, how far away is the chopper?"

"It's about to land."

"Have them hover to keep them away from any debris. Team two, bring down all the explosives we have."

When they arrived Jai handed over the computer and all the discs and told them to get Hadi and move a long way away from the barn in a northerly direction.

Jai, working carefully with a rag around her nose and mouth, placed the charges in the room and along the roof of the tunnel to be sure it collapsed. She set and coordinated the frequency with a small device that would set off a sequence of explosion caps. Then she planned to join the others about one hundred yards away. Making sure the chopper was far enough away, she hit the button and waited. They could hear a small bang just before a series of muffled explosions rocked the earth they were standing on. The barn collapsed with a groan, and smoke and debris flew everywhere. As soon as it all settled, Jai called for the chopper to land. Then she walked back to the barn and found, to her satisfaction, that everything had collapsed as she planned. *Good job all around,* she thought to herself.

As Jai ducked down to examine an unexploded ordnance, she heard a shell go whizzing past where her head would have been. She immediately dropped down and lay flat and rolled to her right and scooted behind a boulder as two more shots hit the ground, just missing her. Once safely out of sight of the shooter, she made herself invisible and stood up and walked out from behind the rock.

Looking squarely at the tree where the shots had come, from she saw nothing, and there was no movement in a 180-degree arc. To be sure, she pushed her energy out and swept the area but again to no avail. She then searched the area for any signs of the assassin, but there was nothing, not even a shell casing. *Who could this be? One of the drug dealers, someone who followed them from the caravan, or someone with a totally different agenda?* Satisfied they were no longer close, Jai joined her men, and they boarded the chopper.

# CHAPTER 29

With no further distractions, the teams made it back to headquarters in good time. After the debriefing, Jai found herself totally exhausted and went to her apartment and fell into a deep, peaceful sleep. Shortly a persistent sound of fluttering and the feel of a gentle breeze on her face caused her to become restless. She instantaneously went on alert, sensing the unmistakable presence of others in her room. Before she dared move or open her eyes, she sent out her energy to locate the intruders. She felt nothing but then heard her name being called by a familiar voice. She opened her eyes, and to her amazement there stood the woman from the computer. Now able to see her face and shimmering body, strange sensations went through Jai's body and mind.

The woman smiled and asked, "Do you remember me, my child?"

"Yes, you are the face on the screen, but I feel deep down inside that you are more than that to me."

"That I am, but it will take more time before you awaken to the truth."

"The truth of what?"

"Who you are, how you came to be what you are, and who I am."

"Many times I have strange dreams of things I do not understand. Is it because I can't remember those things?" Jai said.

"You have lived through a lot, both bad and good. But what is important is who and what you are now, and what you accomplish with that power."

"Why did you come to me? Is something wrong?"

"No, quite the contrary, you are doing quite well. There is another reason that I came to you. If you will recall, I told you that the most powerful and intelligent collection of people on this Earth will be following your exploits."

"But I thought we were anonymous and autonomous, with our identities and location a secret."

"You are, but there is this one very significant organization consisting of important and wealthy people that have heard of your group's exploits. We have been in contact with them through secretive methods of communication, and I have agreed to take up their cause in addition to ours. In return we will have access to military and intelligence agencies throughout the world. They are willing to give us one team of the most highly trained covert military forces that exist, and they will be placed under your direction.

"Those that want will join you. This will expand your outfit of fighting men and women immediately."

"How do we communicate?"

"On a channel that doesn't exist except through your satellite. They know you as the director."

"When will I be hearing from the team?"

"I thought it would be better if you contacted them; they are awaiting your call. Anything else?"

Jai asked. "We are missing a person to head up the military operations, and also a person to replace Gabriel Kristal, the previous head of military strategy. The person to head the military is most important. I was told there is such a person who nobody seems to know his name or where he is located at any moment in time. They say he fights for Choden, a name that seems to resonate within me. Also most of his battles are fought in communist countries in Asia. How can we find this person?"

The A Ma replied, "We know this person of whom you speak, but I am not so sure he is the right person to join you."

"Why? We need him very badly."

"For reasons that I cannot divulge at this time. But I will talk to our people and see if we can make this happen sooner rather than later. Now child, I must go. Go back to sleep. Things will become clearer in the daylight." With that said, the image just faded away like mist in the hot sun.

# CHAPTER 30

Once again in a deep sleep, Jai saw herself standing over a stove cooking. Hearing her name being called from another room, she left the kitchen to see who it was that was calling her. Entering the living room, she saw the usual sight of barely clad women all being fondled by hideous men, but this time they all seemed drunker than normal. As always, the sight revolted her, so she cast her eyes down as she walked over to the girl who was calling out her name.

"Look at me," the girl bellowed." Jai couldn't bring herself to. "Look at me, bitch," she cried out again.

All the while everyone in the place was laughing. The fat, hairy foreigner whose lap she was sitting on grabbed Jai's waist with both hands and with a quick strong jerk pulled Jai on top of the girl. Jai, caught completely off guard, fell and just lay there. The man grabbed Jai's hair and shoved her face into the girl's large breasts, demanding she suck on a nipple. Jai started to struggle, and everyone started to laugh even louder while chanting for Jai to suck. Jai bit down, and the girl screamed with excruciating pain. This caused a frenzy, and a few of the other girls grabbed Jai and managed to pull her off. The men, in a state of fury, held Jai down and were ripping off her clothes and beating her into submission.

The house's madam and the man she had been entertaining in a bedroom upstairs heard the commotion. Naked, they both ran down and into the living room. The madam ran to the screaming woman while the man rushed to aid of Jai. His body showed deeply scarred signs of many battles. He entered the fray using a multitude of martial arts techniques and fought his way to the naked, semiconscious, and bleeding girl. When it was over seven men lay in pain, some with a variety broken bones, some unconscious, and the fat, hairy man who started the whole affair lay dead.

The madam screamed at her john, "Get the girl out of here before they kill her and possibly you."

Taking his time, he gathered some of the clothes lying around and dressed Jai and himself. Then he lifted her up and threw her over his shoulder and carried her out.

Jai bolted awake, and from somewhere deep inside of her came a scream of recognition. "Teacher, Teacher, is that you?" she cried, and then she collapsed into a fetal position with a flood of uncontrollable tears pouring out of her.

Finally getting herself together, Jai forced herself to relive the dream. She began to understand that this was possibly more than just some dream. She was coming to believe the events might be real, and that her memory was starting to return. But as hard as she tried, she couldn't remember anything further—not even the face of the man she called teacher. Putting it out of her mind, Jai readied herself to face the day's challenges.

Having reached her office, Jai called Denton, "Are you

up? After a short pause he answered, and Jai continued, "I want a mechanical voice to answer any call coming in on a new channel that I will give you."

"What's this all about?"

"I'll explain later, and in front of everyone. What about the computer and discs I found? Was there anything on them?"

"I'm waiting for a report; they have been working on it all night. Each file is coded in a different way, so if we break one it doesn't clear the others. Smart move on their part. I'll upload the two decoded files to you now."

"Will what I read give us any good information?"

"Absolutely!"

"Okay, I'll read them now. Ask everyone to stand by for a possible meeting at eleven this morning. That includes all off-duty personnel."

Jai called Amira on the com. "Hello, Amira. Come up to the office and bring the twins with you."

Hearing Amira's voice had sent a sensation through Jai's body. She had already accepted the fact that if Amira was willing they would become lovers, but she needed to be sure of two things: first that the affair wouldn't interfere with their work, and second that Amira knew it was her decision to make. But there was another factor—Makeen. How would she explain him? Possibly she could keep it secret long enough for Amira to accept her need for his energy. Her thoughts were interrupted by a knock on the door.

"Come in," Jai called.

The three entered, and Amira sat next to Jai and the twins across. Jai could sense the twins looking at Amira then at her with admiration. At that moment she raised her energy just to tease the twins, but what she got in return was an energy filled with a sexual hunger emanating from each of them.

Jai saw them look at each other with an understanding; it wasn't until that moment that she knew brother and sister were lovers. Jai began to think, *That has to be an interesting coupling. It is obvious that they both want us and probably together.* Jai was surprised that the thought of the four of them together in bed or even the three of them didn't set her back at all. But then she thought of the twins with only Amira, and that didn't sit well, even to the point of making her angry. *Wow,* she thought, *I'm jealous of my own sexual fantasy.*

Getting herself together she said, "We have joined with a new arm of already trained assets. We will be getting a lot more equipment and intel."

"These other assets, will we control their movements?" asked Hiroshi.

"Yes, they are now one of us, and in time they will be integrated," answered Jai.

After a short pause Jai said, "Okay, let's get back to work. Amira, you stay with me. We have an important mission that stems from the information gathered at the drug house."

With the twins gone, Jai asked, "Amira, are you aware that the twins are lovers?"

"Yes, for a while now," she answered.

"Did you catch the sexual tension between them as they sat across from us?"

Amira, a little taken aback, paused for a few moments

as if she was deciding how to answer and then said, "Are you referring to the same explosive energy that exists between us?"

Now it was Jai who became slightly uncomfortable. She had no idea that this was going to surface so soon and without her being prepared. "Yes, how long have you known?"

"Two seconds after I met you. I felt that you were the most magnificent creature I'd ever met, and I had an extremely strong desire to know your mind and body. What about you? When did you know?"

"The same. You knocked me over the moment I laid eyes on you. You are an absolutely beautiful woman. I've wanted to possess you since that moment and even dreamt about it at times. But my biggest fear is whether it will affect our work."

Amira, thoughtful as always, said, "I think we can keep our feelings separate. You are the director, and I will always see you that way, at least in the workplace. My respect for you and your unbelievable abilities is without question."

Jai asked, "About the twins, do you think their private life interferes with their work?"

"No, actually I think it enhances it. One is always trying to outdo the other."

Jai, laughing, asked, "Are you aware of their desire for us?"

"Very much so, and I think Hoshi is the dominate one of the two."

Feeling it necessary to change the subject before it got to a point of doing something to seal their understanding, Jai said, "As I see it, you are probably right. Now let us get to work on the mission I spoke about. This one will be unusual, and our thinking must be out of the box, so to speak."

"Yes, I believe you are right. By the way, you are not ever going to allow me on a mission, are you?"

Jai, expecting this question, answered, "Why did you say that?"

"I just feel it in my heart."

Jai, thinking for a way to say what she wanted to say, said, "Probably not now, and maybe never, and that comes from my heart. Now please leave. I have a lot to do, and you are a definite distraction."

Appearing unhappy yet smiling inside, Amira turned and left. Jai called Makeen, "Please come up to my apartment in thirty minutes." Jai, knowing her team's chips were programmed, headed for her apartment to be with Makeen.

"How are you, Makeen?" Jai asked, realizing they hadn't seen each other for a while.

"Physically I'm fine, but mentally I'm getting down. The training is going well, but honestly I'm bored with it."

Jai, wondering if that was all, asked him, "Is there anything else that's bothering you?"

"Yes, now that you've asked. I really want to get onto the missions, or at least take part in some way to begin with."

"Anything else?" Jai asked, knowing full well that their lack of a relationship was causing him tribulations.

She figured it would be better said if it came from him.

Jai could tell that he was thinking about how to say what he wanted to express.

After a minute or two, he said, "I will be truthful. I full

well know the part I'm supposed to play in your personal life, and I was trained well to do it well, but honestly I fell in love with you the moment we met. Now trying to remain objective where you are concerned has become very difficult. Don't get me wrong, I will continue to do my job, because being in bed with you is what I live for, but I'm coming to realize that my love will never be returned. Actually, I don't know if you are even capable of loving someone."

Jai, feeling a little uncomfortable thinking about what he said and knowing how much she felt for Amira, decided it best if it was left unspoken.

"I can imagine how difficult this must be," Jai said, allowing her inflection to be sympathetic. "But you and I both know that we didn't choose this path or each other either. I was created to do what is necessary to save this planet, and you were trained to see that I am at the peak of my energy at all times. I know that after having expressed your feeling that what I am saying must sound very harsh and cold, but those are the facts."

"Is the reason you asked me up here now to energize you?"

"Yes, I must admit it is. I am leaving on an important mission in the next two hours, and it is necessary."

Makeen replied, "Funny thing, but I guess I'm happy that it is me. At least I have you in some way, and who wouldn't want to be me?"

Jai decided to lighten things up and said, "Hey, have you ever left unsatisfied?"

"Absolutely not," he replied. Continuing with the thought, he said, "But it would be nice if you bought me dinner every once in a while, and maybe a kiss good-bye when it's over."

"Take a rain check on the dinner, but I promise you a lot of kisses."

Makeen made love to Jai, but he was rougher in his technique, much more than normal. Still he brought her to the levels necessary to cleanse and rejuvenate her energy. Jai figured that under the circumstances she would forgive him his rough handling. She had returned his efforts in a much softer and loving way and ended it all with deeply felt kisses and caresses.

As he dozed, she found herself thinking about how he would be a good husband and a wonderful lover to some lucky girl out in the world, maybe an Oriental, with creamy skin and warmth far beyond what she herself could give, maybe even younger than her, with an innocent twinkle in her eye, without the years of hardship and pain, great responsibilities, and a cause much greater than human love.

She wondered what she would do if she were a man. There are so many beautiful women out in the world, so available and willing to please. Looking at him, exhausted from their love making, his face strong, especially his chin, she decided that he was the type of man a woman would want. If she were he, she would try to possess them all.

Leaving the bed, she headed to the shower. On the way her mind snapped back to the upcoming mission. She turned on her com and said, "Hiroshi, is everyone ready to leave? Good. Are both the helicopter and plane fueled and ready to depart? Amira, you take communications behind Hiroshi on this one. I have a feeling he will be very nervous with his sister on the mission. Because of the profile and the possible scenario that may take place, we will be using voice communications only. Team two will be our eyes."

When Jai came out of the bathroom, Makeen was gone. She guessed he thought it would make things easier for both of them if they didn't see each other again before she departed. Lei had packed Jai's things as instructed, so she headed down to operations for a last-minute briefing with Hiroshi and Denton.

# CHAPTER 31

At the office Jai picked up the phone and after using the prearranged sentences said, "This is the director. To whom am I speaking?"

"This is the team leader of Alpha squad. I was told to make contact immediately. You should know that we have heard some rumors about your abilities, and my team and I want to know if there is any truth to any of it."

Jai laughed and said, "I guess that depends on what and from whom you heard it, but we'll talk about that later."

When Jai was notified that the Black Ops team was on com, she asked Hoshi if she could track where the call came from.

Jai, hearing Hoshi on her direct com, said, "Tell me how it is in Alaska this time of the year. I could only imagine the difficulty if one needed to do a task outside."

After a stunned silence, Alpha leader said, "We heard you were good and had the latest technology at your disposal, but we believed that it was impossible to trace our position. Did oversight tell you our location?"

Jai responded, "If they had, I wouldn't be talking to you. I wouldn't have anything to do with people who might compromise their soldiers. No, gentlemen, we not only have the latest in com equipment, arms, drones, modified planes, and satellites, but we also have developed equipment far beyond anything ever seen."

"That sounds impressive. It's no wonder you have been successful thus far."

Jai chuckled. "You can bounce your signal all over the world, and from satellite to satellite, but we traced it in less than ten seconds."

"Wow," mumbled Guy, the team leader. "As I mentioned, we had heard rumors about your unworldly abilities. Is any of that true or just fantasy?"

"Tell me what you heard before I answer."

"We heard rumors relating to your ability to change your appearance, to make yourself invisible, and also some crazy things about your fighting skills."

Jai was serious when she said, "Let me just say I have defeated some of the great masters of the individual martial arts. I have also been known to take out potential assassins desirous of doing me bodily harm. As for the rest, let me assure you that if we are in combat together, I will dispel any other rumors you might have heard with fact.

"Now let's get down to the business of our relationship. I have been told that your team will come under my command, and thereby you will be in full use of my people and all our technology. At some point in the near future your team will merge into our organization, and our two oversight committees will work as one. Understood?"

After a moment's pause, Jai asked, "Do I detect a hesitation on your part?"

"No, just thinking," was the reply

Jai continued, "Now if you have a mission ready for us to plan and research, tell my people. Anything else?"

Guy replied, "Not at the moment, but there is one we have been trying for years to plan but have been unsuccessful in doing so due to lack of good intel. It seems that the head of the outfit we are after is very well protected by his country's very powerful government. I'd like to dig up what we have and turn it over to your people and see what they can find."

"Sounds challenging," said Jai, "Put what you have together, and let us look at it. For now I have to sign off because I have a lot to do and I'm sure you all do too. Sayonara."

Jai, on her way back to her private quarters, heard a fluttering of wings close to her ear. She headed to the com center and turned on the monitor that connected her to their oversight. The A Ma immediately appeared and said, "Oversight is very pleased with the way you handled the meeting between yourself and their team."

"I felt it went as well as it could, but I believe it will take a mission or two before their people will be completely satisfied with the new arrangements."

Then she asked, "A Ma, do you know when my memory will return? Sometimes I feel like a tree with no roots, and it is very strange."

"Patience, my child. It will return little by little or something will happen that will jolt it back to you. It's all inside you. It's just a matter of connecting with it."

"On another matter, are you any closer on finding the man we spoke of recently, the great warrior?"

"My child, we know who he is and where he is at any time, but we are still debating whether he is right for you and your group. Then there is the matter of him wanting to move under your direction willingly. I promise a final answer very soon."

Jai said, "We are in desperate need of a military leader, so if the answer is no, we have to move on to someone else."

"I know, my child. Now go on and do what you have planned and know I approve wholeheartedly," the A Ma said with a large grin. Then she faded away.

On com Jai said, "Hiroshi, Amira and I will be in conference for a couple of hours, and I do not want us disturbed for any reason except a dire emergency."

After shutting down Jai's coms, Hiroshi turned to his sister and said, "My money is on something other than a discussion between those two."

Hoshi replied, "Mine too. I wish it was me and the director."

Hiroshi just smiled.

Jai reached her quarters before Amira, *I have some decisions to make,* she was thinking. *How do I want this to go?* She stood in front of her full-length mirror and thought about how she wanted Amira to see her. She tried different looks with her naturally beautiful long black hair but couldn't make up her mind because it had to follow the look that her outfit would portray.

Jai pictured many different scenarios she would enjoy and decided that the one that turned her on the most was the one she would go for.

Amira left her suite and headed to Jai's quarters. She knocked lightly and heard Jai walking to the door. The door swung open, and Amira was stunned. There stood Jai in a beautiful black silk gown with specks of sliver highlighting her breasts and waist, and they also circled the hem. The gown was split on the side from the floor to her upper thigh and from the plunging neckline to her belly button.

Amira became light-headed as she all of a sudden realized that she had no choice to make; it had been made for her. She was lost in Jai's beauty and began to feel that she was not worthy of this magnificent creature. It was strange because all of her life, she was the Jai and everyone bowed to her beauty, but now she knew that she would become just a slave to her own desire and Jai's will. With that thought Amira dropped her eyes and looked at the floor. She couldn't look Jai in the eyes, knowing that she knew what she was thinking.

Jai reached out and cupped Amira's chin, lifted her head, and made her look deep in her eyes. Amira felt like she was floating in a vortex of brilliant colors lit up by the specks of silver, not only on Jai's gown but also on her face and body. She reached out to feel Jai's skin, but Jai wouldn't allow it as she stepped back.

Jai whispered, "Take my braid in your hands, and follow me wherever I go."

Jai turned her back to Amira, and Amira took Jai's long, thick braid in her hands and followed Jai as she started to walk away, knowing that she was yielding her complete mind and body to Jai's will. She realized that not only did she want this, but in order to have what she had been yearning for, she needed to surrender herself completely.

Jai walked Amira into her bedroom and reached up and pulled her braid from Amira's hands. Then she turned around and faced her. "Stand very still," she said.

Jai reached up and pulled the pins from Amira's hair and caressed it as it flowed down to her chest area. She reached across and started to run her fingers around Amira's face. Touching her lightly, Amira started to swoon, and feeling a touch of faint, at the same time she began to feel as if an electric wave was pulsating throughout her body.

Amira reached out to Jai for support, but Jai lightly slapped her hand away and said, "You will not fall. Now stand up straight and close your eyes until I tell you differently.

Amira followed Jai's order, and she began to lose the feeling of faint though she was still very weak in the knees but promised herself she would not faint.

Jai reached out and removed Amira's jacket and let it drop to the floor. Then she slowly opened the buttons of her blouse and pulled it out from her skirt and allowed that too to fall. Undoing the bow string on Amira's skirt, Jai held it closed, and when she was ready, she slowly brought it down around her knees and stood back a little so she could take in Amira's body from head to toe. Jai thought, *This will be a feast that will last for a while.*

In a blink of an eye Jai dropped her skirt, and with a quick snap of her fingers, she opened Amira's bra and slid it off her shoulders.

Amira was feeling helpless, her nipples reaching out to be touched. They ached with longing. Now very wet with excitement, she wished she could return what was happening for Jai. She knew that unless Jai released her from her imposed bondage, she should do nothing.

Jai smiled as she stepped closer to her and with her left hand cupped one breast, holding it high, then caressed it with the other, being careful not to touch her nipple. As Amira's large nipple grew still harder and harder. Jai stepped in closer and placed it between her teeth. She bit down lightly, and circled it with her tongue.

Amira was on the verge of a climax, which Jai could feel, and releasing the nipple, Jai said, "Don't you dare climax until I tell you."

Hearing that, Amira lost complete control and let go with the biggest climax she had ever had. Jai grabbed Amira by the hair, sat down on her bed, and pulled her across her knees face down.

Amira cried out, "No, please don't."

Jai responded, "What did you expect when you disobey my orders? And from now on, you do not speak unless spoken to, and when you do you will address me as mistress. Do you understand?"

"Yes, mistress."

With that Jai lifted her hand and slapped Amira hard on the butt, then again. Amira moaned. As she did, Jai caressed her butt cheeks with a loving touch, then slid Amira's panties down around her knees. She ran her fingers into the crack of her butt, seeking her anus passage, and when she reached it, she started to probe. Amira, never having this done to her before, naturally clenched her butt cheeks together and held them tight. Jai removed her hand and slapped her again, this time harder. Amira cried out, but said nothing.

Jai said, "This body you are carrying around belongs to me, and I will do anything and everything I choose to do with it. Do you not agree?"

"Yes, mistress, I agree."

Jai told Amira to stand up and not to move. Then Jai removed her panties and told her, "Take my braid and come with me."

Jai led her into the bathroom shower and told her to face the wall, leaning with her hands stretched above her head, and close her eyes and stay that way.

Jai stepped out of the shower and removed her gown, revealing bare breasts, a leather thong, and a silk kerchief around her neck. She reached into the shower and turned on the water, adjusting it to a comfortable temperature as it poured down on Amira.

Jai stepped in, and with the silk kerchief she tied Amira's hands together and secured them to the shower head. "Now, my dear, we will see to it that you are scrubbed clean enough to my satisfaction," Jai said with a threatening voice.

Amira quivered with fear, but at the same time she felt herself have a small climax in anticipation of Jai's hands on her body. Jai shampooed her hair with long strokes, making sure that every strand was covered with soap and her scalp was suitably massaged. She soaped Amira's neck and shoulders, massaging everything as she slowly went down her back to her butt. Stepping to the side and with one hand, she parted her butt cheeks, and with the other she slid her hand in, rubbing as she went.

Amira involuntarily clenched her cheeks together again, but before Jai could slap her, she released them. Jai smiled to herself, seeing that she had a good pupil. Using a lot of soap as a lubricant, Jai once again probed Amira's anus and slowly, gently pushed her one finger in. Amira moaned as she accepted Jai's finger, and she involuntarily began to rotate her hips. Feeling this Jai slid her finger out and slid her hand down between Amira's legs and down the lips of her vagina. As Amira's hips swayed, more overtly asking to be entered, Jai squeezed her lips together, and with a side-to-side movement, she massaged Amira's clitoris and Amira exploded with a heavy climax.

Jai stepped out of the shower and got a white facial mask that didn't have eye holes and slipped it over Amira's head. She thought, *I could have made myself invisible, but that would defeat the purpose of her feeling in bondage.* She turned her around and once again looked her over before she began to wash her.

Starting with her face, she worked her way down to her breasts, rubbing them with a lot of suds she tweaked both nipples until they were once again hard as stones and then kissed each before moving down. When she reached a point between Amira's thighs, she found that she was perfectly lubricated and needed nothing more to be comfortably entered.

Jai, using her finger with a circular motion, slowly entered Amira, and when she could go no more, she rubbed and tickled everything she could reach. All the time Amira was climaxing and building to an even greater height. Slowly withdrawing her finger, she reached and played with Amira's clitoris until Amira gave out a scream from intense pleasure. At the same moment Jai rammed two of her fingers into her vagina, bringing Amira to a state of multiple climaxes.

Jai kept it up until she felt Amira's body begin to slacken, and she withdrew her fingers. She untied her hands from the shower head and dried her whole body with a soft towel and then carried her over to the bed. Jai laid her down face up and tied her hands to the bedposts.

Jai slipped down to the foot of the bed and starting with her toes licked and nibbled her way up to her thighs. Using her own legs, she pressed Amira's legs together and started licking her vagina's lips. Then she pressed her tongue into her just deep enough to reach Amira's clitoris and tickled it with her unusually long tongue.

Amira was going crazy as Jai kept the pressure up. She tried hard to separate her legs, but Jai held them together with a vicelike grip. When Jai was ready to enter her, she released her legs, stood up, and retrieved two more silk scarves. She pulled Amira's legs far apart as they would go and tied them to the bedposts at the foot of the bed.

Jai, straddling Amira's thighs, pushed her tongue as deep as she could into Amira's vagina, and using a slow in and out motion, she again brought Amira to a state multiple of climaxes, but this time they were even stronger.

She kept it up while reaching up with her hands and tweaked both Amira's nipples with her fingernails. This went on for quite a while until Jai felt that Amira was about to pass out. She withdrew and looked at her face and saw that she was crying.

She asked, "Why are you crying, my beauty?"

"Because I feel so free," Amira responded.

Jai, feeling that Amira was at the point of falling asleep, told her to go to sleep for a while. She placed her fingers at the point where she would cause her to pass out and applied the right pressure. Amira fell into a deep sleep.

Jai, looking her over, decided she was going to fix a few things. She went and got a pair of scissors and a razor. She then shaped Amira's pubic hair into what she felt was more to her liking. When she was finished she got some indelible pens and drew a very colorful hummingbird high up on the inside of her thigh and signed her name.

She sat down and wrote Amira a note: If you like what I have drawn, we can do it as a permanent reminder. Do not return to work until you are ready to assume your regular persona.

Then she got dressed in one of her usual work outfits and called Hiroshi and told him that she was back on duty, but Amira was taking a little personal time. That done, she contacted Lei to come in and remove Amira's clothes and bring her some new ones from her suite.

# CHAPTER 32

Headed down to com, Jai was thinking, *I wonder where that type of sexual desire and behavior came from. I was such a cold-blooded bitch, and yet I feel a love for her that is quite contrary to my actions. I wonder if I've lost any chance of a loving relationship with her.*

Hiroshi called Jai, "We have received a coded file through our new dummy com center from the Black Ops teams. Shall I decode them, or will you do it?"

"You go ahead, but except for you it's for my eyes only."

"Yes, Director, as you wish."

After a while Jai, having read the decoded message, called Guy, the leader of Alpha team, and recited the password of the day and hour.

After he gave the appropriate response, she said, "I can see why you have been desirous of shutting down this suspected operation. Do you have any idea who is supplying the fissile materials to build the bombs? What are they getting, uranium, plutonium, U-235, or U-238?"

"No we don't, but we figure that it is someone or some

group that has tremendous backing and influence, possibly from the former Soviet Union or one of its states. We have been trying for years to capture someone who has this knowledge, but everyone we do get knows nothing about where it comes from. We did uncover one eight months ago, but he bit into a cyanide capsule before we could question him."

"Okay, I'll put my best people on it and see what we can learn. If you are correct, this is well worth pursuing without prejudice. I'll be in touch as soon as I know. Ciao."

"Hiroshi, get together all my top mission people for a meeting. Call in anyone who might be out on break, and let's all meet in the conference room in one hour.

Jai headed to the conference room. On the way she ran into Amira and was duly surprised to see her so soon. "I'm glad to see you are rested, Amira."

Jai was watching Amira's face and feeling her energy. She was happy to feel and see that Amira was both her normal self and a great deal more humble. She said, "It is all right for you to show me what your feelings are toward me when we are alone, but make sure they do not show when others are present. Understood?"

"Yes, Director. Oh, and please I do want that hummingbird with your name permanently attached. Not as a reminder because I will never forget, but as a symbol of my esteem and love for you."

"As you wish, but never forget unless we are alone, you are just like everyone else around here. Now join us in the conference room for an important meeting."

*That was better than I anticipated from her. Actually I have this feeling of joy and sexual tension. This is good!*

In the conference room Jai explained to the group what she had learned and stressed the importance of successfully researching and then planning and carrying out this mission. "A lot is riding on this—our future with oversight, and our own ability to pull off a seemingly difficult job. Any further questions?"

When nobody said anything, Jai said, "Okay, let's get to work."

With nothing more to do at the moment, Jai went to her suite to shower and renew her energy through meditation. Jai found herself very restless, and her mind was wandering back to the experience with Amira. She laid down on her bed, thinking she better take the edge off so she could concentrate, but instead she fell asleep.

She immediately began to dream, taking her back to the incident at the madam's house.

Totally exhausted and in a partial coma, Jai felt herself being carried away to where, she had no idea. She saw herself being laid down on a bed still in her ripped clothing and sleeping. She could see a man standing over her and feeling her pulse to assure himself that she was still alive. In her dream she opened her eyes, and after focusing them, she saw the man bending over a sink in the bathroom. He was naked, with a muscular swimmer's type body. His thighs and legs were big, well defined, and his butt was tight. After a couple of minutes she fell back into a deep sleep.

In her dream Jai found herself asleep and dreaming. She saw herself healthy and happy. She seemed to be training at a beautiful temple with the same naked man who was now in the bathroom. She was jumping and flying and laughing. Suddenly she was in his arms making love, and Jai was in ecstasy. Without warning she saw herself wandering among a lot of dead bodies in robes the same as she was wearing. She was searching and calling out for her teacher and lover, but no one came. She was running, and flying, lost in a nightmare of desperation.

Then there was a girl in her arms and a monstrous-looking creature trying to rip her away. In her dream's dream she awoke with a start and was looking straight into the eyes of this beautiful creature who had a kind face and smile. This beautiful female took her in her arms, and she felt safe and secure, not worrying about who she was. She was once again training, but this time it was different. She trained with horses with horns, goats, lions, and tigers instead of robed people.

In her dream she awoke because she was being shaken by the naked man. He said, "It's time to get up and move your body and stimulate your mind."

As soon as Jai was able to speak, she asked, "Where am I, and who are you?"

He replied, "We are on my junk in China, and who I am doesn't matter. What matters is that you get better. Then we'll see if I'll tell you who and what I am."

"How long have we been here?"

"Eleven days."

"What's to become of me now?"

"If you are as strong minded as I think you are then I will take you to a place far away into the mountains, and you will learn to be a woman of great value and independence."

Jai saw herself spending the next month eating, drinking strange liquids, and doing all kinds of exercises, including yoga, and when the naked man (he still hadn't told her his name) who was now dressed in a robe felt she was ready said, "My name is Jinhai. I am a fighting monk of a secret order whose mission is fighting those who disturb the peace wherever I can. I think you can become like me if you are willing and dedicated to the fight. What do you say?"

Jai replied, "I will try."

"Not good enough"

Jai said after thinking, "I will give it my whole being, and I will succeed."

"You may now call me teacher. We will leave in the morning."

Jai, still dreaming, then saw a beautiful creature, and the creature said, "I love you, my child."

Jai sprung awake and cried out, "A Ma."

The A Ma appeared immediately, having waited until Jai came awake "Yes, my child?"

Jai asked, "Are my dreams the reality of my past or just dreams?"

"They are real and your true past. From your first dream when you were a child, to the slave trader, to the streets, to the ship, to the house of prostitution, to your monk and your training, and finally to me. Now you know where you came from, who and what you were before, and finally how you came to be with me and what you are now. Considering your age, you have experienced more than most will in two lifetimes."

"I seem to have had a tough life till I met you."

"Yes, I would agree, but it all led to what you are capable of now and the good you are trying to accomplish with the missions you successfully complete."

"Any news about the people I am seeking to fill the two important roles in this organization?"

"You will have your answers as soon as you finish your upcoming mission. It is the most important to date. If you feel it becomes necessary to go on this mission, be sure that you are the leader. Insert the new Black Ops team when you feel they might be necessary."

"I will. Thank you, A Ma, for being here with me when I awoke. You, as usual, made things easier and clearer."

The A Ma smiled and faded away.

# CHAPTER 33

"Director, Hiroshi here. I believe we have a good lead that may help us to track down at least one of the principals in the proposed Black Ops mission."

Jai, upon entering the com center, asked Hiroshi what they had come up with. "Hoshi found a strange article online authored by a former bank teller in Iraq. He now lives in Jordan, where he posted an article claiming that he was unjustly fired from his previous job because he told the truth concerning deposits being made into different accounts, all having sequenced numbers on one hundred US dollar bills. Luckily he escaped with his life by leaving the bank and walking straight to the bus stop without going home to pick up any of his possessions. He thinks the money is counterfeit, but Denton believes it may be the money trail we have been looking for."

"Have any of our people tried to contact him?"

"Not yet. We were waiting for your orders."

"Zelda, get a small team ready to travel to Jordan. Make sure you have an Iraqi or someone who speaks the various dialects. This should be an in-and-out mission with no problems but you never know, so bring at least two other soldiers and a quarter of a million dollars. When you are assembled and armed, I'll meet you at the departure door."

Zelda replied, "We'll be ready in half an hour."

"Denton, how do you assess the situation?"

"I think it is probable that the Iraqi terrorists have also read the article or it was brought to their attention. I believe he is in great danger if not already dead."

Jai said, "You may be right. How old is the article?"

"Three days."

Jai suited up and armed herself before heading down to meet the team. When they saw her, they were surprised, thinking that this would be a simple extraction.

Zelda spoke up. "Are you coming with us, Director?"

"Yes I am, because as Denton rightly pointed out, if the article is real the Iraqis would be after him to shut him up. I thought of one other simple reason. We may be walking into a trap. We'll make contingency plans on the plane. Also, we will take the cargo plane and carry our own vehicles. In the meantime pack your battle gear. It may not be necessary, but just in case I want us to be ready."

On the way over to Jordan, they planned for every possible scenario, hoping they would find him alive. "Hoshi, have you located Mahmad?"

"Yes, Director, unbelievably he's working at a bank, and he is there as we speak. They get off at four, and then he rides his scooter home. It is about two miles to his house. You should be landing just in time to unload your transportation and get to the bank. It's about a twenty-seven-mile drive on a good road."

"Do we know what position he holds at the bank?"

"Yes, he is the new accounts manager."

"Perfect."

"Okay, I will go in as a wealthy man looking for a new bank to open an account. Josh, since you look the part, you'll be my bodyguard, so just carry your 9 mm shoulder piece. Zelda, you and one other should be in the bank watching our backs, and the rest outside. Both groups do a detailed sweep to see if there is anything suspicious looking. As we discussed, we will take the mark with us, hopefully peacefully, if not then by force. This move is to save his life in the foreseeable future. Any questions?"

As prearranged they landed at an air force facility in the capital city of Amman and unloaded their armored cars with all the equipment they might need in the trunks. When all was ready, they headed for the city of Al Salt.

Upon arrival Jai said, "Park a block away, and outside team do a sweep while the inside team enters the bank and does a sweep, pretending to fill out forms. Josh and I will follow after you both are satisfied that we are clear. Zelda, be extremely careful. Remember, a trap is very possible."

"Of course, Director, and as planned, if we see anything out of place, we will try to handle it without a commotion."

"Okay, teams, let's do this and get safely home."

"Team one reporting. We've spotted Mahmad's scooter, and it's being watched by a woman and a man, both dressed as Westerners."

Jai said, "Take them out, but make sure you do it in a way so that they cannot speak into any com systems they may have. Zelda, you heard so I'm guessing they have someone in the bank also. Make sure that the outside team acts first and then quietly walk them out, hopefully without a struggle."

Six minutes later the outside team reported that the bogies were neutralized. They were sleeping peacefully in a large garbage container behind a closed restaurant.

Jai spoke, "Zelda do you see any threats in the bank?"

"Yes, I am standing right next to him, and my partner is behind. Now that the exit is clear, we are about to walk him out.

"Excuse me, sir," Zelda said, addressing the man. "Do you feel that small pressure in your back?"

"What the hell?" he responded.

"That, my friend, is a 9 mm with a hair trigger, and know if you look down at my side, you will see that I'm holding a syringe filled with a deadly poison. If you move or even blink, you are dead. Also you should be aware that your friends outside are no longer there, so expecting any help or calling for any will be meaningless and you will die a nasty death. Understand me?"

"Yes."

"Let's make this simple. Just turn around and walk outside and you'll live to a ripe old age."

The man, with the gun still in his back, walked out the bank door to the waiting second team. He was immediately neutralized and joined his comrades.

"All clear," Zelda said.

Jai entered the bank, looking and dressed like a wealthy middle-aged man. Jai spoke to the bank guard. "Where may I find the new accounts manager? I believe his name is Mahmad."

"He is in his office by the ATM to your right. I see he

is free, so just tell his assistant seated outside his door that you would like to speak to him."

"Thank you," Jai said in Arabic and headed over, with Josh just behind.

Two minutes later Jai was sitting in Mahmad's office, and he said, "So, Mr. Sharif, how may I help you?"

"Let me make this simple for you. It is I who is here to help you get out of a very bad situation."

"What—what do you mean?"

"There were two bogies outside by your scooter and another in the bank. They were here to see that you didn't live to see the sunrise tomorrow. Fortunately we arrived when we did, and for the time being you are safe."

Mahmad looked out the window for his scooter and saw nothing unusual.

"What happened to the men you speak of?"

"They have been neutralized by my team."

"You mean they are dead?"

Jai replied, "No, they are just knocked out, and they will live to come looking for you again. But even if they were dead, there would be many others to replace them."

Mahmad, looking very nervous with drops of perspiration beading his forehead, said, "Who are you, and why should I believe you?"

"Who we are is of no importance to you, and you can see for yourself, if you wish. Just walk out into the alley and look in the big trash can, but make it quick. We have limited time."

"So what do you want from me?"

"As you can guess, your own people want to shut you up. Writing and having your article published has caused them a great deal of concern and money. We, on the other hand, want the opposite. We want you to talk to us. Give us the name or names of the people who were depositing those large sums of US dollars you wrote about."

"If I do I'll be dead in a week."

"You are a dead man walking right now unless you cooperate with us. That is the only chance you have of surviving. Where would you like to live?"

"Either Canada or the United States of America. Is that possible?"

"Yes, anything is possible when you deal with us, but you must act immediately. By that I mean you will walk out of the bank through the rear door and into a waiting vehicle and give us the names then. We will start to head to the airport, and if the names check out, you'll be on your way to your new life right then."

"What about my things in my apartment?"

"They are being gathered as we speak and will be on the plane with us."

"Really?"

"Really!"

"What happens if I choose to take my chances alone?"

"You do not want to even think about that. We will take you out of here and force you to tell us everything, and you will wind up with nothing. The way I see it, you have no choices, or maybe two: a new safe life or a painful death. What do you say?"

"How do we do this?"

"Ask your secretary for the safety deposit box keys, and we'll head to the vault. We'll just walk out the back door and into the car."

"But the alarm will go off."

"Don't worry about that. I will take care of it when we get down there. Anything else? No? Then, let us go. Time is wasting."

Jai, Josh, and Mahmad headed toward the exit, and Jai raised her energy just enough to fry the alarm wiring. They walked out the back door into the waiting vehicle, and a few moments later Zelda and her partner walked out of the bank into the car with the outside agents.

On the way to the airport, Mahmad revealed the names on the accounts and anything else he could think of. Once he opened up, it surprised Jai all he knew about what was going on in Iraq as far as the nature of the relationship between the US representatives and the Yazidi people.

"Hiroshi, did you get all that?"

"Yes, Director, we did, and we are checking the accounts now. We are also looking into some of the other names he gave us. From what we can see so far, the accounts exist, but we will need a little time to look into the actual account transactions."

"Okay, let me know as soon as we can prove at least two accounts. We will be at the airport in twenty minutes. Have them ready for immediate liftoff."

Once up in the air, Hiroshi relayed the info they had gathered. "It seems that most of the accounts have been closed, but we will continue to follow the trail to other banks in and out of the country. The ones that remain verify the info that Mahmad gave us, and most important we were able to find out the real name of the person depositing the money in all those accounts. We are in the process of locating his whereabouts. I think we will have that information soon. We are very close, Director."

"Great, as soon as we return to base have everyone gather for a meeting. Then notify the Black Ops leaders that I will be in touch soon with an update. Give your lowest person the job of finding a place in the US for Mahmad to live and work as an artist. I want him picked up when we land and taken to wherever you find. Have a new passport and life experiences ready to give him. You know what he needs, so let's get this done. He is one of the good guys."

# CHAPTER 34

Once back at headquarters, Jai was talking to the leader of the Black Ops team. "Guy, we have the name and location of the man who handles all the money given to the Yazidi sect by the US government. Capturing him and getting him to tell us who is actually handing him the funds, if there are any other US middlemen, and how they are distributed in Iraq—that is the critical first step to finding out if the United States is funding the purchase of nuclear material and from whom.

"We have a mission plan that we feel is the safest and surest way of succeeding in his capture. As per our understanding with our oversight, your team will accompany us on this mission. We will supply you with the details and the necessary equipment if different or more advanced than your own, and we will monitor the operation from our headquarters. Any questions at this point?"

"How, where, and when do we get the mission plans? Will you be joining us?"

"You will fly your own plane to a rendezvous point,

which we will give you once you are in the air. When you have reached that destination, you will switch planes, and we will fly your team the rest of the way. You will understand why when you see our plane and what it can do. Nothing else like it exists. Any further questions?"

"Not until we see the plans. What if we don't like the plan or feel we have a better one? Can I change them?"

"That is your choice, but remember if you change the plan in any way, we drop out and you will have to explain to oversight why you countermanded their specific orders." Any other comments?"

After she paused for a minute, Jai said, "No? Good, then you should have wheels up in one hour."

Jai, taking a break until the operation was to begin, was taking a bath when she realized something was bothering her. Going over everything that was said and done, she couldn't get it out her mind that the Black Ops team hadn't been able to gather any information on what was going on even though they had supposedly been trying.

She jumped out of the bath and picked up her com. "Hoshi, has the Black Ops team taken off yet?"

"No, Director, they are gathering their equipment and discussing the possible scenarios we have given them."

Jai asked if any of them had been alone for any length of time.

"No, not that we could determine."

"Okay, keep your ears open and let me know if that changes."

"Will do."

Twenty minutes later Hoshi reported that they all stayed together for the whole time.

"Hiroshi, anything unusual happening with our target?"

"No, he's just making a lot of phone calls, which is not unusual in his case. He still is at his home and should be leaving for his office at any time."

"Okay, I'm on my way down. I just need to see Amira for a moment."

Arriving at Amira's suite, Jai knocked and without waiting for a reply, just walked in. She didn't immediately see her, but hearing her crying in the bedroom, Jai went in and saw Amira lying on the bed sobbing.

"What is the problem?" Jai asked.

Amira hid her head in the pillow and said, "Please leave me alone. I'll be all right in a moment."

"Listen, my beauty, I understand you think you are not able to handle the emotions that you are experiencing, but trust me, you will come to a point that you will accept your position with me. Love comes to one in many ways and is also expressed in many ways. I know you feel that you have lost yourself and all you believed in before we got together, but you must accept your love for me and whatever it brings in any form.

"There are many things that you don't know about me, but you will come to learn what they are and who and what I am. Believe me, Amira, in my way I love you too."

Amira, still crying, said, "I feel that I have no control in this relationship. You didn't even let me touch you. Am I your slave? Am I just an object of your sexual desires? If so I don't think I could live with that."

"Listen carefully, Amira: you will come to fulfill all your desires toward me, but only when you know what I am and why I am so different. Only then will you be able to touch me in ways that will bring me to heights I may be capable of."

"Why can't you just tell me now?"

"Because you are not ready, and words will not be adequate to explain. You will have to experience, and then you will come to understand. I promise. Now I must go to ops. We are starting a mission, and I would like you to be there with me."

"I'll be down in a couple of minutes, and thank you for understanding me," Amira said.

"Oh, but I do understand you. Make it one minute."

Jai left, wondering what Amira would think of her sexual relationship with Makeen.

At ops Hiroshi said to Jai, "Something stinks. I don't like what I am seeing."

"Tell me what you see or feel."

"I started to see large withdrawals from the accounts we've been tracking. Also nobody has left the target's house yet, and that is against his usual pattern."

"Do we have anyway of seeing inside his house?"

"No, we only have listening devices planted, and they are at a distance."

"Start tracking the money that is disappearing. Get the pilot of our ops plane, and tell him to stall as long as possible, even if he has to divert because of some weather or ground control equipment problem. Get two of our fastest planes ready now!"

"Where are they going?"

"To Alaska. I want their compound searched thoroughly for any clues that may prove that someone in their group tipped off the target. Send Denton and Zelda.

"I'll be flying to the rendezvous point in the other plane with a battle-ready team, including Makeen. I'm going to get ready. Also I want to speak to the head of their oversight committee. On second thought, cancel that call."

Back in her apartment Jai called upon the A Ma on the scrambler. When the A Ma appeared, Jai asked, "A Ma, how deeply have the oversight committee's people been vetted?"

The A Ma answered, "Very deeply. To the best of our knowledge, they are all clean. Why do you ask?"

"Something is amiss. I believe the reason no one could get anything on the people running a dual operation is because someone is tipping them and their operatives off. By the time we are ready to proceed, hopefully I'll have some clue as to whom that is so I can stop what I believe is a doomed mission and a possible trap that is being set."

"I hope you get this cleared up; it's an important mission for oversight and our first with them. If you are wrong, what then?"

"I'll just let the mission proceed, and they'll never know what I suspected."

"I have some news for you which can wait until this is resolved." Before Jai could ask, the A Ma faded.

By flying over the ice cap, Denton and Zelda reached the Black Ops' secret headquarters quickly. They did a thorough search and found nothing out of place. Walking back to the plane, Zelda turned around and saw something she thought unusual. One of the air ducts was faced upward, facing the sky. She asked Denton if there was any reason that it should be that way. Denton, after thinking about it and then checking online about the air flows in that region, found nothing that made sense.

"I'm going to check to see if it is just loose and has possibly turned in the Artic winds."

After a comprehensive search, she found what they were looking for.

Zelda said to Hiroshi, "Tell Jai we found our leak. I know she's offline except to you, so tell her I must speak to her immediately."

Jai switched on her main com, and Zelda told her what she knew. Leaving nothing to chance, Jai made ready another team and told Hiroshi to do everything possible to track their target and formulate a plan to pick him up wherever he was running to.

Jai's plane passed the other one, and when she was fifteen minutes ahead, she told Hoshi to tell the mission pilots to land, pull into the hangar, and not to open the weapons hold until she gave the order.

When Jai and her team landed, they parked on the tarmac, changed the look of the plane to make it seem like a regular corporate jet, and then deployed her team inside the hangar and waited.

When Black Ops left their plane, they had no weapons, so they moved away to wait for the unloading of their vehicles, weapons, and explosives.

In the flash of a second, they found themselves surrounded by heavily armed troops, and realizing they were defenseless, they immediately raised their arms to a position of surrender.

In the center of all the troops there came a small whirlpool of energy and what looked like shimmering squares of colored glass lights making the tickling sound of a perfectly tuned set of chimes. It grew upward and spread out like a tornado until it reached the ceiling, and when it started to dissipate, Jai was seen standing in the middle with her fists on her hips. She was in her black battle gear, and even in their bad situation the Black Ops team looked at her in amazement. She was stunning.

"What is the meaning of this?" Guy asked.

Jai stepped closer and began to speak. "First of all, you may put down your hands, but be aware that my men have orders to shoot anyone who makes a sudden move toward me or them.

"The meaning of this is quite simple. Haven't any of you reasoned that since you have chased down some good leads in the past you have never been successful in catching your target?"

Guy spoke, "Yes, of course we did, and we checked and rechecked any possible sources of a possible leak. Much to no avail, I might add."

"What about your own team members? Did you have any suspicions about any of them?"

"Yes one, and he has since moved on, so to speak."

"Have you had any misses since, in any of your missions?"

"Yes, but the only real failures have been with the nuclear problem."

"Well I'm here to tell you that you got the wrong man before. The man who has been selling you out stands among you as a brother at this moment."

The team started to get restless and were looking at each with questioning eyes.

Guy said, "Do you know who this is and do you have real proof, and if so how did you get it?"

"Easy we were keeping an eye on the bank accounts of the mark, and after I spoke to you, they all started to empty. It wasn't too hard to figure out that the leak was coming from inside your group or that one of you was in fact the American contact. Cross checking we learned that when money was being handed over, most of the time you guys were predisposed with a mission. So there had to be a mole in your team.

"After you flew out today, I sent my people to your headquarters to see what they could learn."

Guy commented, "But nobody can break into our headquarters or barracks, or at least that's what we believed."

"We are not nobody or even anybody. It was a snap. It took three minutes to disarm the alarms and open the place. In a period of fifteen minutes we had your computer files open, both military and personal.

"But luckily it took one of my operatives to spot an anomaly as they were leaving to head back."

"What was it?" someone asked.

"One of the air ducts was turned to the sky, a different configuration than the others. So they went back into the building and climbed onto the roof to see what they could see. There it was inside the skyward vent—there were two laser lights, one green and one red, but there were no wires attached.

"So then we knew that there was a mole, but figuring out who it was turned out to be an easy answer for our in-house genius, Abraham Denton. He simply used a volt and amp meter, and by switching on the various lights in the bedrooms of each individual, he was able to determine which one drew the most energy."

Everybody stood still and very quiet while Jai spoke, anticipating the name of the person, but she didn't have to say another word. Guy's second in command put his hands on his head and dropped to his knees. Everyone gasped.

Guy said, "What? Are you kidding me? He's like my brother. He saved my life more than once. This can't be true."

Jai said, "It is. Meet Falah Nazari, your mark Hanif Nazari's real brother. They have squirreled away a fortune in US dollars over the past four years."

Alpha team's leader said, "What are we to do now? This is a mess. Does my oversight know all of this?"

"Yes," answered Jai. "And as you can imagine, they are very unhappy."

Jai continued, "I'm leaving the questioning of this traitor to you. When my team is able to track his brother, my team and I will formulate a new plan, which we can carry out. Same as before."

Alpha team's leader said, "I just have to ask what kind of trick or equipment you used to make such a wild entrance."

Jai just smiled. Then with an unspoken command her team lowered their weapons and headed out the hangar door. Jai said, "Get me the information we need from this traitor, and then deal with him as you wish. I'll be in touch as soon as we have the mission outlined."

With that Jai began to radiate white light, and as it got hotter to the point that the teams could feel the heat, Jai vanished.

"What the hell was that? Is she real or a hologram?" the team leader asked to anyone who would listen.

From a distance they heard Jai's voice, "As real as any of you, but different, oh so different."

# CHAPTER 35

Back at headquarters Jai relaxed in her suite, swirling the contents of her drink around and around as she stared into the glass, as if it were a portal to the elusive presence she often felt from a distant place in her heart. Was it the island of the home of the A Ma she missed? Exactly what was that anyway? A place she made up in her troubled mind? Or was the island and the A Ma truly an element of reality, her reality? The lights were dim and the hour was late, but she was still wired from the previous mission.

She had called Makeen up to her apartment, and he sat on the couch beside her. "I think I need some of your energy. Do you need some of mine?" Jai asked.

Jai, having spent a few rejuvenating hours with Makeen, saw her com light up. "Yes, Hoshi," Jai responded.

"Director, we have the location and accounts located for Hanif Nazari."

"Where is he?"

"He is in New York City. Apparently he owns an apartment in Trump Towers under a dummy US corporation. We believe he plans to stay awhile because he showed up with a lot of suitcases and one trunk."

"Where are the bank accounts?"

"All over the globe."

"Okay, do not touch them. We do not want him getting suspicious. Hiroshi, call together my top people and I'll meet them in the conference room in fifteen minutes.

"Makeen, you were wonderful as always, but we have to go and take care of the impending business."

"I know, but it is so hard for me to give you up for any reason."

Jai looked deep into Makeen's eyes and said, "You know that your role is not to be my love interest. Your role and what you have been trained for is to help charge my energy to the point where I'm at peak efficiency."

"Yes, Director, I know, but that doesn't change what I feel toward you, nor does it stop me from wanting to consume you."

"Believe me, Makeen, I know what you feel and how hard it is not to express it to its possible conclusion. I too sometimes have those feelings, but we must remember who we are and what we are here for."

In the conference Jai said, "A snatch and grab in New York City should be rather easy, with one major exception. I'm told that Mr. Nazari doesn't leave his apartment for any reason. He has bodyguards inside and out, and the place is fully staffed with a maid, cook, and whatever else he may need.

"So we need a major distraction, or a way to flush him out. Any ideas?"

Denton said, "Jai, you can do all sorts of things like

make yourself invisible to the naked eye and enter whenever the door is opened. Or possibly you can enter through the air vents?"

Jai said, "I am planning on using Guy and his team to do the mission. I want to see how they operate."

Jai had a temporary plan in mind but was hoping her team would come up with it or even something better. After all, that was what they were hired for.

Then Hiroshi said, "What if we give him a really good reason to leave the apartment?"

"Like what?" Denton asked.

"What if the US government froze his accounts in the states?"

"For what reason?" asked Denton.

"Suspicion of laundering money for terrorist activity. After all, he deposited relatively large sums in a rather quick fashion."

Denton said again, "But if the government is part of the doubling-dealing scheme they probably won't do anything. Anyway the money is back in the US, where they can get their hands on it at any time."

"Yes, but if he were made to believe that this was real, and here's the key—we open an extension office of the NSA where he must go in person with the proper documentation to prove the money was indeed legally his. Then we would have him in a trap."

Jai said, "The place has to look real. There must be security when they enter and that would remove any weapons his guards would be carrying. Then only Mr. Nazari would be allowed to enter the office, and his guards would have to remain outside."

"This could work." Amira said.

Abdul said, "This is a very good plan if we were going to set it up, but how do we know the Black Ops team can pull this off?"

Jai said, "We don't, but we will have a backup plan for us to get it done if they fail. This man is too important to let slip away again. Okay, team let's get the details down, and I'll contact Guy."

Hiroshi contacted the Alpha team and switched the com to Jai. "Team Leader Guy, we are ready with your planned mission. It will take a little time for you to set it up, but it's well worth the expense and time. One other thing, when you set up a temporary headquarters, we suggest that you go north from the city so if something goes wrong you will have clear access out of Manhattan.

"This time the plans will be sent to your headquarters beforehand so you have time to set it up. I suggest that you send a small contingent to New York immediately because there is a lot of prep work to do. Contact me if you have any questions."

"Okay, Director, will do. Alpha out."

Hanif Nazari felt safe in the United States. After all, it was for them he had been working all these years. He had also figured out how it was possible for him and his brother to keep receiving all that money. He believed that no one, even if they had the right contacts, could follow the money trail back to the top people running the operation, and that was his ace in the hole. He believed that the people who were the brains behind the whole scheme had to be high up in the US government—someone or ones who made a lot more money than he did.

He wondered what they would do with his brother if or when he was caught. He believed his brother wouldn't give up his name but he couldn't chance it, and that's why he ran.

Luckily he had secretly bought this beautiful apartment years before. With twenty-four-hour protection he has enough money for more than one lifetime, and there was no reason to leave the building he was also reasonably comfortable in his belief that he would never be found.

He wondered if his connection in the Taliban, and the people who received the greatest cut of the funds, had been compromised also.

Anyway, he was sure the game was over and the American mucky mucks would see to it that everything was shut down and well hidden. He had enough money to last at a very high level of comfort. He smiled and called for his dinner to be served.

As he did every morning, Hanif checked on his accounts, and when he opened up his US accounts he found they had been locked out by the US Treasury's New York Office. There was also a letter on the account stating that he could download an explanation of the government's move and that he should call and make an appointment to get his actions explained.

He immediately called the bank to see if this was true and found that in speaking to the branch manager it was indeed true. Of course, his call had been intercepted and rerouted to headquarters, where an electronic voice had been initiated to sound exactly like the manager. Hiroshi was actually talking to Hanif and confirmed the hold.

Hanif immediately placed a call to the number supplied on the downloaded form and after waiting on hold for a minute was put through to the local treasury director, also an electric voice. Hiroshi told him the treasury's concerns and that he needed an appointment to show proof of his legal transactions. He said that this could be put to rest instantly if the proper proof was shown and checked out.

Hanif inquired if this could be done by e-mail, fax, or wire. He was told no, that he must appear in person and he could bring his lawyer or accountant, but not both. It was explained that electronic documents could easily be tampered with. An appointment was made for the next day at ten in the morning.

Hanif knew that this might be a trap, so he set about planning an escape just in case. The next morning at nine thirty in the morning a group of five could be seen walking out of the towers in a protective formation. They entered a limo and were driven to the address given to him.

When they arrived, they cautiously entered the building, where they were met by a security detail and a screening machine. After clearing security and having the two guards give up their guns, they walked with the man they were guarding in the direction of the manager's office. The other two were asked to leave the building and wait outside.

The three men entered the office and looked around. There was one receptionist plus three secretaries in front of three interior offices. They were pointed the way to Mr. Golden's secretary, and when they reached her desk, Hanif bent over in apparent terrible pain. His guards put his arms around their shoulders and carried him to the door.

Before going out Hanif called back, "I'll make another appointment when I'm able."

In the meantime Jai and her crew were watching very closely, and at the same time they were doing a face recognition scan on the party of five. They found that the man who was supposed to be Hanif was an impostor.

Hoshi said, "Shouldn't we tell Guy?"

Jai responded after a little thought, "No, let's see how it plays out."

Guy was nervous and said to Jai on com, "I think we should stop him now. On the other hand we could wait and see what's up Hanif's sleeve. I'm taking my team and following him."

Jai looked around and at her team and said, "Guy, the Alpha leader, is only partially right.

"Hoshi, scan the office building. Does anyone see anything out of place?"

Since there was no reply, Jai continued. "Watch carefully what happens when the Black Ops team leaves the building. I have a feeling we will see our mark appear."

As soon as the Black Ops team and the phony secretaries walked out of the lobby, a man in a maintenance uniform carrying a mop and bucket appeared from the far hallway and had a slight smile as he lifted his middle finger and said, "Screw you, you bastards.

On her outside com Jai said, "Okay, Makeen, pick up Hanif. He's headed right for your position, and bring him here. How long before you arrive on site?"

"The traffic is heavy and we have to get to LaGuardia

Airport. We will use a scheduled commercial airliner's call numbers and be gone before they know it. Because we are in one of our transport planes, I'd say we'll be there in seven to eight hours."

"Okay, we will be ready to interrogate him."

"Hiroshi, get me oversight, and have Amira join us for the questioning of Hanif when they arrive. When Black Ops calls to report in, stall them until I'm finished with oversight."

Ten minutes went by before Jai heard that oversight was on her com. "This is the director. I assume I'm speaking to the entire committee?"

"Yes you are. How did it go?"

"Simply put, not well, in a manner of speaking." Jai went on to explain what happened and that Guy made some wrong decisions in the field.

Oversight asked, "Why? It seems to us that they are doing everything right. They have him in sight, and if he tries to run they will get him, right?"

"Not exactly. The man they are following is a decoy set up by Hanif to see if it was a scheme to trap him."

"Shit, that means he's on to us and is getting away," replied oversight.

"Not really. We got him. He's on his way here now.

"But why didn't you plan for this contingency from the beginning?"

"Oh, but we did. We just needed to see how your team would react to a sudden snafu if it took place. They did at least two things wrong. The first was not having a team remain behind to search the rooms he was staying in and to see if there was also another team guarding their back. Second, they should have anticipated the possible ploy."

"As you did?"

"Yes, exactly, as we did."

"So where are you in terms of with working with us?

"One thing jumps out: not all your men are well trained in operations of this sort. They are tough fighters and capable in that area, but as for sophisticated operations they will not do."

"What do you suggest?"

"As soon as this op is done, we'll train all the people who want stay with us. The rest will have to be let go."

"We'll have to discuss this. In the meantime let us know what you find out from Hanif."

"Will do. Director out."

# CHAPTER 36

"Inferno leader, I'm afraid that you have missed your primary target. It appears that Hanif has been picked up by either one of two groups in New York. We believe that he is being held by that mysterious new group who we are calling White Dragon. So if you can find out where they are holding him, you'll have your two targets in one sweep."

"Any clues as to where that may be?" the Inferno leader asked.

"None, but we are working on it. Nobody seems to know who they are or who is controlling them, if anybody."

"This is very strange. Are you sure it is not Black Ops?"

"We are not sure, but we don't think so. We have been watching them closely. Recently there has been a lot of their activity in Manhattan, but we couldn't pinpoint exactly what they were working on. They picked up and were tailing a man who we could not identify, and the rest of the teams seemed to go off in a different direction. Then by chance a man they later found out was Hanif was spotted coming out of the same building, being led away by unknown forces. That is why we believe it's White Dragon. We don't know if the first Black Ops team was a decoy or not, but either way somebody has Hanif and unless we can get to them before he talks, we are screwed. If that happens before you get to him, a lot of top people may go down, and your contract will be nullified, and that will be the end of our relationship."

"Understood. I'll get on it right away. If they are going to leave the city, it makes sense they will be going by plane. I'm sure they want to interrogate him ASAP. Did your people follow them?"

"Unfortunately no, they chose to follow Black Ops because that was their assignment, and Hanif wasn't positively identified until we ran a facial recognition."

"Okay, I have people at all the major airports and I'll alert them to look for any unusual events. In the meantime I'll get my air wing in the air headed for New York. Let's hope we can catch them and knock them out of the sky." Inferno leader signed off.

---

With nothing else pressing, Jai, feeling a bit tired, went to her suite to lay down. Not realizing how tired she really was, she dozed off.

---

**Jai found herself back in the mountains of Tibet, where she was standing looking at the devastation created by the communists of China. She once again saw all the mutilated and dead bodies, and she was calling out the name of her teacher, but to no avail.**

**She saw herself searching among the bodies, and they seemed to**

**stretch from one end of the Earth to the other. Then the scene started to morph into the ocean, and again she saw nothing but dead bodies and she heard herself calling out the name: Makeen, Makeen.**

Jai bolted upward out of the dream and felt she had this premonition of what was about to happen. In a panic she called Denton and asked, "How fast can you get the satellite armed and ready to fire over the Atlantic?"

Denton answered immediately, "Arming it will only take a minute or two, but placing it in position to fire will depend on where and when."

"Where is best in the western part?"

"Best would be around mid–South America, but it can reach as far north as northern Columbia. If we have enough time then we can go as far north as the Bahamas."

"Hoshi, what is the status of our plane leaving New York?"

"It's about forty minutes out, heading directly to the British coast."

"Get in touch with the pilots and tell them to change course and head directly south over the Atlantic, and be prepared to take evasive action. But they are to try and avoid any confrontation.

"Okay, Denton, get ready to fire the lasers as soon as we have confirmation that our plane is being targeted. And keep trying to position it so that it's as far north as possible."

"Inferno leader, we got them. They left New York's LaGuardia about one hour ago, they are headed dead south over the Atlantic. They are one hundred miles east of the South Carolina coat."

"How fast are they going?"

"One moment. Around four hundred to four and a quarter miles per hour because there is a strong southerly wind."

"Got it. We'll pick them up by satellite radar. Do you know the kind of transport or call numbers?"

"It's a converted Lockheed L-10, and its last transmission was FX C 943."

"Okay, we are on it."

*My god not again. I don't know that I can handle another great loss in my life. First my teacher, Jinhai, and now Makeen. I need to stop this, now!*

"Hiroshi, have we spotted anything that seems like they are being tracked?"

"Not yet. Wait, wait a second. There are two unidentified fighter planes taking off from a private airstrip in the jungles of Columbia."

"What is their heading?"

"Directly east. Our computers show they will intersect us in forty minutes, but if they are carrying the latest missiles, they will be in firing range in fifteen minutes."

"Does nobody know who the hell those people are?" Jai blurted out.

Denton answered that they had no clue.

"Hiroshi, tell our pilots to correct their heading to one hundred thirty-five degrees southeast, and to open up the throttle. That should give us a little more time."

Hiroshi called out, "We have five minutes before they lock on."

“How are we doing with the satellite, Denton?”

“We need about seven minutes more.”

“We don’t have seven minutes. Hoshi, does anyone have a drone in the area?”

After a quick scan Hoshi responded, “Yes the United States has a spy drone over French Guiana.”

“Denton, is our satellite in range to blow it up?”

“Yes, but why?”

“It will give off a large heat signature, and hopefully the bogies will lock on and turn south. Then they will bring themselves in range of our lasers, and before they figure out it’s not us we will use our weapons,” replied Jai.

Denton said, “Not sure that will work. It depends on how sophisticated their equipment is.”

“Does anyone have a better idea? No? Then let’s do it. We’ll worry about the consequences later.”

“Okay, here goes. Too bad our first real test for the laser is this one.”

The satellite fired a salvo of laser beams at the drone and blew it to pieces. They watched from the control room as the bogies altered their courses to due south, putting them in range of the satellite, and as soon as they were Jai calmly said, “Take them out, now!”

With a flash of light both fighter jets were blown to smithereens, and there could be heard a very loud cheer in the control room. Jai calmly turned away and headed for her suite so nobody could see the smile on her face.

She turned back around and said, “We were lucky. Now we have another priority: who the hell is after us and how do we stop them?” And with that she walked out.

# CHAPTER 37

"Good evening, Hanif. My name is Amira. Can you hear my voice?"

"Yes. Where am I, and what the hell have you strapped me into?"

"One thing at a time, Hanif. First of all you are with the people that saved your life, actually more than once. Second, you are being held in a secret facility where there can be no escape, and finally we made you comfortable because you are about to watch a lot of news footage taken by your sworn enemies. We hope that what you are about to see will help loosen your tongue and give us the information we seek from you. Otherwise we have much stronger methods to extract that information.

"I am the first of many you will speak to. You should know that I am not a combatant, and therefore I have been given the chance to persuade you to talk without the pain and degrading events you will face. If you test our resolve I promise even I would not like to watch in spite of how I feel about you and your kind of degenerate."

"You are making a very big mistake. When the people I work for find out that I'm missing, they will hunt you all down. I am too valuable to them."

"My dear man, you are living an illusion. It is those very people you speak of that have tried to have you killed so that you could not reveal their names and contacts. We believe that you have already been replaced, and they will be back in business within a week or two."

"I don't believe a word you say," Hanif responded.

"Okay, then I am to assume will not talk to me about your line of contacts and the people who are heading up the organization."

"That is correct."

"Before we begin, there are two things that must take place. First we will put your head in a vice so that you cannot turn away from the screen overhead, and second, if you dare close your eyes, we will have to slice off your eyelids making it impossible to do so."

After the chair was laid flat down and his head held in place so that he was looking at the ceiling, Amira turned on the video.

Hanif watched as his people were being slaughtered and tortured by the Taliban. Then the rapes of the innocent children and women as their husbands and fathers were made to watch, followed by the disembowelment of the men and their sons before they were killed.

Amira, seeing tears in the eyes of Hanif, turned off the video and asked, "Are you ready to tell us what we want to know?"

Containing his emotions, Hanif replied, "Never. We know what they do. My people have given their lives for Allah and will be rewarded for doing so."

Amira turned the video back on, and Hanif watched as his wife, two sons, and three daughters were brought into focus. Amira said, "Hanif, I really don't think you want to watch what is about to happen. This is coming to you live, and we are filming it. Now you should know that we have snipers surrounding the camp, and they will kill your family's captives if you agree to our demands. Only you can stop it, and if you don't your mind will be tortured forever and Allah will never forgive you."

Hanif just shook his head no after giving out a scream. He watched as his wife was stripped of all her clothes pushed to her knees. They brought over the eldest son and daughter and stripped him of his pants and underpants, and then they ripped off the girl's clothes. Hanif saw the leader grab Hanif's wife by the hair and say, "Get your son hard and put him in your mouth, and show the girl what she needs to do to get him off. Do what I say or I will have your youngest daughter raped in front of you."

As his wife did what she was ordered to do, Hanif shut his eyes tight and gave out a maddening scream. Two guards grabbed his head as a woman dressed as a nurse walked over with a scalpel.

Amira said, "I warned you what would happen if you closed your eyes."

"Don't do it. I'll watch, I'll watch."

The nurse heard Amira say to back away and see what he did. Hanif continued to watch as his twenty-year-old daughter brought her twin brother to a climax, and when he came all over her face, the guards pulled him away and cut off his genitals. As a reward for the eldest daughter's cooperation, she was allowed to die with a bullet to the brain. Then they brought the next two children into the camera's view.

Hanif gave a blood-curling scream and said, "Okay, stop them; I'll tell you everything I know." Amira shut off the video but left the audio on so Hanif could hear the shots being fired and the cries of the dying soldiers.

"Are you aware that the money you are helping to hand over is going to the very people you hate, and are you aware that it's being used to buy nuclear materials to build bombs?"

"Impossible! It is going to my people."

"You are so wrong, Hanif. Are you there when it's all given out?"

"No, because the Americans finish up the last of it."

"Do you know who those Americans are?"

"No, we are not allowed to see them. We are taken off the base and driven away."

The overhead bright lights went on, and Denton walked into the room. They immediately started questioning Hanif.

Amira heard Jai say, "Good job, Amira. Your timing was perfect the moment you turned off the video as I instructed you to do."

"Yes, but I think it might have helped us even more to get the information if he saw his family's captives suffer."

Jai responded, "Yes that may be true. If only it actually took place."

"What? What do you mean if only?"

"I mean what really happened even he shouldn't be subject to. We were never there. The video, as you know, was taken by one of their captives and shown on their local television stations. It all took place when he left Iraq weeks ago, but he never knew. We added the gunshots and phony sounds of men dying.

"Why are you crying, Amira?"

"It was so cruel. Sometimes I can't believe what men can do to each other."

"Let's not forget the animals and the environment. We know what they do to women and children. Keep these things in mind, and you'll never forget why you are here."

"I know, but I'm still not sure I can live with what I see and hear."

"We have time while they debrief Hanif. Why don't you come up to my suite and we can talk further?"

"I'll be right there."

"Hoshi, Amira and I will be off the com for a while. I'll call you when we are ready to return."

"Yes Director," Hoshi replied. She turned to her brother and said, "I think Jai is going to help Amira take the negative edge off."

Hiroshi grinned and said, "Maybe someday we'll get to take both their edges off. Anytime Jai is close the sexual energy in the whole room skyrockets, and Amira is a close second."

"What about me, bro? Are you losing interest?"

"On the contrary, my interest in you gets heightened as they are an aphrodisiac. Haven't I proven that to you?"

"Well, yes, I was just teasing you, though I understand what you are saying. I too get crazy when they are near."

On her way to her suite Jai thought to herself, *I think it's time to show her a great deal of love and tenderness. She doesn't really have the life experiences for this kind of work, nor does she have the relationship experiences to be with someone like me. I believe if I'm to keep her with me she will have to see another side of me. Question is do I tell who and what I really am? I guess I'll let events dictate the answer.*

# CHAPTER 38

"Inferno leader, this is control. What the hell happened? There were three explosions in the area of our mark then nothing."

"Leader here, something took out a drone, which we believe was a US spy drone, and our planes locked onto the heat signature and turned to pursue. A minute later they disappeared in a cloud of debris."

"So we lost our mark and have no clue who has him, nor do we know our enemies?"

"That seems to be the case."

Control said after a minute, "You are on your own. We will no longer fund you or help you with diagnostic information."

"You are making a grave mistake. We have protected you for years, and with this one slip you are leaving yourselves open to attack. I don't believe you people."

Control said, "There are many such as you out in the world, all looking for backing to do their dirty deeds. You have an agenda that we have been keeping an eye on for over a year, and we don't like where you and it is headed. If it wasn't for this so-called slip we would have found another reason to part company.

"Good luck to you, and don't do anything stupid. If we feel that your organization will seek retribution, we will have you all cancelled. We know everything about all of you, and you know nothing about us. So be very, very careful and smart."

The Inferno leader was boiling mad, and his first reaction was one of revenge by any means necessary, but he quickly got control of himself and said, "I understand. I don't like it, but know that we will never lift a finger against you. There are plenty of jobs out there for people like us, and we will continue to pursue our aims under a different banner."

"Good! I wish you luck with your pursuits as long as they don't clash with ours. Good-bye."

Jai dressed in a soft pastel summer frock and greeted Amira at her door. "Come in, Amira. Would you like a stiff drink? I'm going to have one."

"Thank you. Today for the first time in my life I will have one, because I need it," she replied.

Jai asked her to sit on the couch and proceeded to pour each of them a double rye blend. She handed it to Amira and sat down very close beside her. Jai lifted her glass and said, "Here's to successful things that must be done."

Amira lifted her glass and took a big drink and then started to cry.

Jai put down her glass and placed her arms around

Amira and held her tightly. Amira felt Jai's loving touch and her sexual energy all at the same time. She started to relax, and at the same time she couldn't help but feel her own sexuality begin to stir. Jai, feeling Amira begin to lose herself in Jai's touch and energy, said, "Sometimes, my love, we must do what is necessary so that others do not face the same pain."

With tears running down her face, Amira said, "I know, but most times I feel that I am not the person to see and do the things that are necessary."

"Most aren't, Amira, but even so some have a driving force deep within them to do what is right. Whatever it takes to motivate one to do things they wouldn't normally do in the name of what is just is right and pure."

"I am so glad you are in my life," Amira said. "You are my driving force. I feel a deep love for you that I never thought possible with any person, but I don't know where it comes from. I don't know who you are or why I feel this way. Sometimes I feel so confused, but sometimes I feel so wanting you to love me and take me to places I have never been. It scares me like it did the day we made love, if that is what you can call what we did."

"Honestly it was a release of emotions and desires that you brought out in me," Jai said. "Things I didn't know were there, and I love you for it. Who I am is everything you have seen in me, and as we stay together, you will see so much more. What I am is difficult to explain and dangerous to know. When the time is right I will explain, but now is not the time. You'll just have to trust me."

As Jai was saying this, she was removing the barrette from Amira's hair, and she let it fall. She leaned in and softly kissed her lips, and when Amira responded, Jai reached down and undid the buttons on her blouse and slid it off her shoulders. Jai leaned Amira back slightly to take in Amira's reaction and also to see her breasts. As Jai ran her fingers through Amira's long hair, she let it fall over her bra and thought, *What a beautiful creature she is. I want to make love to her like Makeen does to me.*

Thinking about how Makeen would handle her, Jai began to stroke Amira's face in a loving manner. She leaned in and flicked her lips with her tongue and then pressed her tongue between her lips but withdrew it quickly, teasing Amira's tongue. As soon as she could feel the tension building in her, Jai licked her face, lips, and neck. Slowly she licked her way down to the cleavage between Amira's breasts and pressed her breasts together so that Amira could feel her tongue on both breasts while she licked the very sensitive spot that resides there.

Amira was starting to feel lost in passion as she felt herself slowly starting to melt. Having slid Amira's bra up to her neck, Jai placed one of Amira's nipples between her teeth and licked it, and it became so very hard that Amira felt a combination of pleasure and pain caused by her straining nipple. She moaned as her hips started to slowly gyrate, beginning the dance of invitation wanting to be entered.

Jai tried hard to stay objective, but she too was quickly building her sexual desire for release. She began to slide down Amira's body, using her tongue to continue to tease and arouse Amira even more. She kept her eyes open so she could see as well as feel Amira's beautiful, youthful skin. She noticed for the first time that she had beauty marks all over her body and smiled.

Having reached the top of Amira's bikini panties, Jai slipped down to her knees and gently pushed Amira down so she lay flat on the couch. She lifted both Amira's feet to her mouth and licked her toes. Not expecting this, because nobody had ever done this to her before, Amira moaned aloud as she climaxed with each toe Jai put in her mouth.

Jai stood up and removed Amira's slacks, blouse, and bra, and then she undressed herself, leaving nothing to the imagination. Amira, sensing what Jai was doing, looked over and saw Jai's exquisite body and her thick raven black hair, which she had unpinned and allowed it to fall freely down to her thighs.

Tears came to Amira's eyes, and she softly said, "I love you so much."

Jai looked deeply into Amira's eyes and said, "I love you too, my beautiful angel." This made Amira lose control, and she began to cry uncontrollably.

Jai took her in her arms while whispering, "Hush, my baby. Let me do as you asked. I'll take you to places you have never been before."

With those words Amira let go of Jai and lay back and said, "I am yours forever. Take me as you wish."

Jai slid back down, once again using her tongue to heighten Amira's senses. When she reached her panty line, she teased her by licking her way across. Amira reached down in an attempt to remove her panties, but Jai stopped her and placed Amira's hand between her thighs. Cupping her hand, she began to have Amira rub herself between her own legs. Amira opened her eyes and saw Jai watching her, and that excited her even more. With Jai still holding her hand, Amira slid her hand under her panty line and began to masturbate in earnest. She came with a yelp, but Jai wouldn't let her stop, pressing Amira's fingers deeper inside with her own fingers attached. Amira had four fingers deep inside her vagina, which was never done before.

She called out, "Mistress Jai, please, please I can't. My god I'm coming, oh my god stop. Oh shit, what's happening to me? I can't stop coming." Her multiple climaxes, which she had no control over, were becoming more and more intense, and when Jai felt it was time to release her hand, she pulled both her and Amira's hands out.

Jai wanted so badly to mount this beauty and fuck her like a man. She thought about Makeen's movements on top of her while positioning herself as he would to enter her. Once there, Amira was moaning and gyrating her hips, wanting so badly to have Jai inside her. She wanted to be fucked as much as Jai wanted her to be.

Then a strange thing happened. Jai's energy was reaching a peak, and Jai felt herself gathering it between her own legs. In her mind she envisioned her energy becoming a penis growing big and hard. She could feel Amira's labia under her energy rod, and Amira's legs began to part as she felt this thing pressing against her. Then Jai just naturally pushed down, and her energy penis entered Amira just like a man would.

Amira went berserk and screamed out "Oh my god, my god, please fuck me. Don't stop, don't ever stop."

After a while Jai realized that Amira was in a place that most females never reach. She continued to push and withdraw slowly as Makeen would do to her and then push even harder and faster. Amira lost all control over her own body, and she knew she had left the Earth and was flying.

Her climaxes felt like one big sunspot bursting with energy, and it was lifting and pushing her higher and higher, with no limits as to where she go in the universe. Nothing existed except she and Jai entangled in web of energy soaring and then floating in space.

Amira cried out, "Don't let me go. I'm free. I'll never come back. Stay with me please. I'm spinning out of control. Oh god, I'm coming. Oh god, please don't stop.

Amira and Jai both reached a point of overwhelming passion and explosive energy, and at that very moment they both screamed when they hit the apex of their major climaxes, which lasted for what seemed like an eternity. Then they collapsed.

Amira passed out, and Jai allowed herself to slowly return to Earth.

Jai lay alongside Amira, softly caressing her sleeping body when she whispered, "Next time, my sweet, I will let you see what I really am. I hope you'll be able to handle it."

At the very moment Jai was whispering to Amira, the A Ma appeared alongside the couch they were lying on. When Jai felt her presence, she looked up and said, "Look at her, A Ma. Isn't she the most magnificent creature you've ever seen?"

"You cannot ask us to judge the earthly human since we are not attracted to them. You, on the other hand, I find quite appealing. It's probably the alien half of you."

"Why have you come?" asked Jai.

"I have come to tell you a few things. We have agreed that you may seek out the fighter we have discussed and try and recruit him as your military commander. But the latest op must be completed before you start searching for him. Finding the people who are behind that operation is of utmost importance. We will give what information we have on where he is when you are ready, and since that changes day by day, there is no sense of us discussing it now. The next thing is most important.

"My child, you have reached the time when your memory is to be restored."

Jai, unbelieving what she was hearing, said, "You mean you are capable of doing that?"

"Yes, Jai, I am. You see, it was me who blocked your memory when it was time for you to leave us. Everything that took place in our land was of course real, but it all happened on a different plane of consciousness. We knew that it would be very difficult for you to awaken in the convent only to find that you had been there in a coma for the same amount of time you were with us."

"How is that possible?"

"I'm afraid what I'm about to say you will still not be able to grasp, but when you thought you were dreaming, you were actually reliving your life as it happened. The life you had with us was on a dimension where time does not exist."

Jai, pacing the room, occasionally glanced at Amira to be assured she was still asleep. She asked, "So what happens now."

The A Ma answered, "I will put you back to sleep and unblock your memory so that you will be normal in that respect."

"Will I be able to recall it all, even the time I spent with you?"

"Yes. Now lay back down, and let's get started. It will only take a few moments."

Jai awoke and as if nothing had taken place asked, "What else did you want to discuss with me?"

"I have decided to wait and see what you plan on doing with Amira in the future. I heard you say you will show her who you are next time you two are intimately together. That, my dear, may have consequences."

"I understand, but are they negative?"

"It depends on how she views you in the future. That's enough about that."

"Okay. It's really good to see you, A Ma. I miss you and our home so much sometimes it hurts."

"I know, my child, but the work you do here is too important for either of us to allow you to come home presently."

"I know, and the more I see out here, the more I know you and our cause are right."

"I must be going now. Keep up the good work. I will awaken your lover up as I leave. Good-bye for now." With that the A Ma placed her hand on Amira's forehead and then faded away.

Amira's head started to clear, and she said, "Oh my god, what happened to me?"

Jai responded, "Don't you remember anything?"

Amira took a moment, smiled, and said, "Yes, of course I remember every look, every touch, and most of the words, but where did I go? I felt like I left the gravitational pull of Earth and was flying throughout the universe. It was beyond belief, beyond anything I have ever experienced.

What, other than the incredible sex, did you do to me? Did you drug me?"

"Whoa, slow down. First of all I did not drug you or do anything to you outside our sexual love making. Second of all, it was all natural. It's just my enhanced abilities and your willingness to be free that allowed the creation of the sensations you had. That's all."

"Unbelievable!"

"Yes it was, but now we have to get back to work.

"Hiroshi, we are back on. Have we learned anything new from Hanif?"

"No, Director, nothing of any use. It seems like he really doesn't know anything more than what we already know or surmised."

"Okay, ask all the section leaders and squad leaders to meet me in the conference room in half an hour."

# CHAPTER 39

When everyone was seated, Jai walked in and said, "It seems like we have to figure out the solution to this problem by ourselves. Whomever is leading this operation has covered their tracks very well. We have to try and find the weak point in their scheme. So let us start with what we know. Hiroshi, working backward, what facts do we have?"

"Only that the money arrives at the destination as per the shipping form and are met by Hanif and his people. From there the four hundred fifty million is broken down into smaller amounts to be distributed as per the instructions laid out by the CIA."

Jai, after a moment's thought, said, "Is there any way we can find out what was the original amount of money and weapons allocated to Iran for each shipment?"

Hoshi said, "We have done that, and they always match."

Jai said, "If the bill of lading reads four hundred fifty million dollars and the CIA acceptance form is for the same, then how can we know that money is being stolen, or diverted?"

Denton said, "I don't know. That is the information that Black Ops gave us. We just assumed that it was correct."

Jai said, "Okay, let us move on."

Hiroshi said, "Are you going to call control to find out what they did to confirm?"

"No, I am not. Somewhere, somehow there is something fishy going on, and I'm not about to tip our hand."

Jai began again. "So it seems that we have the correct amounts arriving in Iran according to the paperwork issued. So now we must retrace that back as far as we can."

Hoshi said, "We have checked the paperwork at the receiving end at the airport, and it checks out."

"Where do they load the trucks?" Denton asked.

"The money is picked up at a mint, so it is all new bills and the numbers are in order. Armored trucks do the hauling," Hoshi said.

Jai asked, "Are they military or private contractor?"

"Private contractor," Hoshi replied.

"What do we know about them?"

"Interesting situation. They are a subsidiary of the contracting group that manufactures heavy metal. That manufacturer is a subsidiary of a large weapons manufacturer."

Jai jumped in and said, "I suppose they are the ones supplying some of the weapons going to the Iranian forces?"

Jai responded, "Hoshi, Hiroshi, did either of you check out the ownerships or stockholders of all those companies?"

Hoshi responded, "There are two people in today's administration that have past affiliations with one or more of those companies."

"Who are they, what positions did they have, and where are they now?"

Hiroshi answered, "Albert Beasley was with the transport company as president. He is now transport operations chief with the DOJ, CIA branch."

"Really?" Amira mumbled.

Hoshi said, "Yes, really, and Ingmar Williamson was the president and COO of the mother company. Both were big stockholders until they were forced to sell all their holdings before joining the government."

"Is it a publicly traded company?" Amira asked.

"Yes, and the stock was sold on the open market to various brokers and individuals."

Jai said, "Sounds clean, but dig deeper, you two."

After some thought Jai said, "We are missing something, something quite obvious."

Denton said, "If we go back to the very beginning, we know that congress has nothing to do with authorizing the money or arms. It comes under the president's discretionary budget and his right to send money, arms, and troops as he wishes without approval from any government body."

Jai said, "Funny, so you are saying the United States is under a partial dictatorship? Is there a document someplace that records the amounts the president approves to be shipped and to whom?"

Hiroshi replied, "Not that we can find."

Jai continued, "So if there is no paperwork to begin with, who does he tell?'

Denton said, "It seems we need to go backward again. So far we know the CIA handles everything from the pickup point forward, and they are under the DOJ/CIA branch headed by Albert Beasley."

"And whom does he report to?" asked Amira.

"In this case he gets his orders from the undersecretary of the department of defense."

Jai jumped in. "I'll bet that's Ingmar Williamson."

Hoshi, shaking her head, said, "That is correct, and I'll bet that's where the paperwork initiates from."

Jai said, "The answer lies in speaking with the president of the United States. Problem is what if he himself is involved? They'll cover it up, and we will probably never know the truth."

Amira, thinking out loud, said, "What about the people who handle the money? If there is a discrepancy, they might know where it takes place."

Jai said, "Yes, somewhere along the line the paperwork and the money won't match. Amira, you said that everything checks out at the loading dock, but what is the amount that checks out?"

"Four hundred fifty million dollars. It is on pallets and shrink wrapped so no one can actually count it. It would be a big job, and everything would have to be taken apart."

Jai said, "What if the president ordered a larger amount to be shipped? Since nobody actually counts the money, the paperwork really doesn't matter. The question is at what point can the money be stolen?"

Hoshi, sitting there listening, drew a timeline map. She jumped in and said, "The only place that makes any sense to me is either somewhere between the mint and the delivery at the plane, or on the plane itself."

Denton said, "But how would that be possible, especially once it is on the transport truck?"

Jai said, "That's what we need to find out. Hiroshi find out about the company's drivers and guards—who they are and anything at all we can know. Do the same for the plane's crew, and see if they are using the same guards that came with the delivery. In the meantime let's break until we have further information."

Two hours later Hiroshi contacted Jai. "Director, Hoshi and I have found out a lot. We need to meet. I think we have enough to act."

"Good, have everybody meet in the conference room."

In the conference room with everyone seated, Jai said, "Okay, Hiroshi, tell us what you found out."

"We found out that the transport company has no record of the guards they send on the land transport, and they do not go with the air shipment. We cannot find anyone who knows anything about the two guards on any shipment. It seems that with each shipment they send new guards, and most of the other employees believe that is for security reasons. Why, we asked, and they all said they had no clue and they had never met any of them before."

"That is strange or at least it seems unusual," Denton commented.

Jai said, "I think we have enough to go on, but we need better than secondhand information. We are going to have to get inside and see what we can find. Any suggestions?"

Zelda, who had not spoken to this point, said, "It seems to me that the best place to infiltrate and also find out what is going on is the guards. If they are changing them every trip, then they must be getting them from somewhere."

Jai said, "Hoshi, look into it and see what you can find."

It wasn't five minutes before Hoshi had what they needed. Speaking to the group, she said, "Every place I look that transport company is looking for experienced guards, ex-military, mercenary, or police. No family preferred due to extensive travel and possible relocation."

Jai said, "I guess I'm going to be a highly trained guard, and I will need another person possibility from Black Ops. Hoshi, get me Guy."

After a couple of seconds Guy was on the line, and Jai said, "I need you on this mission. You should leave immediately and fly to Washington's Dulles Airport, and we will pick you up there."

"Our plane is ready to go, Director, so I'll leave in fifteen minutes."

Jai turned to Zelda and said, "Pick your best man. You are going with me. Hoshi, did the want ads give any indication of when they want people to start?"

"Yes, immediately."

With the whole team gathered, Jai contacted Hiroshi. "Have we learned anything new?"

"Hell yes. Unfortunately it seems that the shipment is going out tomorrow. That means your idea of getting hired on as guards must be out. What are you going to do?"

Turning to the other team members, Jai said, "Things have changed. They are picking up a new shipment tomorrow morning. Instead of two of us hiring on as guards, we have to take out the new guards and replace them."

# CHAPTER 40

The teams split up at eight in the morning. Jai staked out the nearest coffee shop to the mint, and Guy and his man did the same at the Starbucks a couple of blocks away. Zelda watched the mint employee entrance just in case they were wrong.

At a quarter to nine Jai, having been sent a picture of the guard's uniforms from Hiroshi, spotted two men walking into the coffee shop she was watching.

"Listen up, Guy. I've got them in sight. Come to my position and wait with me. Zelda, go get the van and park it were we agreed upon, and as soon as I tell you they are coming out, start it up, open the sliding door, and be ready to move out. We need to do this quickly because the guards have to be at the mint by nine or before."

When the Guy's team reached Jai's position, they were stopped in their tracks. There stood Jai in a very short black skirt, high heels, and a satin shirt with the buttons open to her belt.

Guy, staring at her, said, "Let me guess, you are the bait, right?"

"Right. I'll stop them in their tracks, and you two walk up behind them put your guns in their backs and follow me to the van. If they resist, shoot one in the kneecap. Believe me, they'll do as they're told. Are you ready?"

"Yes, Director, everybody's here if we need a quick plan depending on what they say."

The two guards walked out of the shop, and when they turned to go to their car, they bumped into Jai. Jai said, "Now, gentlemen, there is no reason for you to give up your lives for the job you are about to do. Is there?"

In tandem they said, "No ma'am."

"Good, just walk into the open door of the van and you'll be home for dinner tonight. Men, relieve them of their weapons."

Once in the van everybody was looking at Jai because she appeared to have changed her clothes and was now wearing a military jumpsuit, which she wore to the coffee shop.

"How the hell do you do that?" asked Guy.

Jai laughed and said, "I didn't do anything. Your minds did it for me."

"Okay, you two guards, tell us exactly what you are to do when you get to the mint, and don't leave out any details."

In less than five minutes, the guards told Jai everything she needed to know.

Jai said, "Okay, you two, strip down to your shorts and then lay on the floor face down with your hands behind your backs. Quickly!"

That done, Jai shot the guards up with a potion that would force them to sleep for ten to twelve hours and remove any memory of the last three days.

Jai said, "Guy and myself will take over for the guards."

Guy interrupted and said, "But you are a woman. I doubt that they hire women."

Zelda laughed and said, "Look again." There stood Jai in the guard's uniform, and she looked just like him. She even had the mustache.

"Fuck, I'll never get over this shit. Are you a magician?"

Jai laughed. "You might say that. Before we head out, check their weapons and action kit. Make sure we have enough ammo, first aid, and gas masks, plus anything else you feel comfortable with. Just make sure that you are carrying only small-barrel combat weapons so we can maneuver in close quarters."

That done, Jai said, "Zelda, you two tail us from a distance. They will be looking out for a possible robbery. Also they themselves may have cars along the route and trailing to the air base, but be ready to close in on a moment's notice. After the drop their security should fall off to practically nothing, so stay really close. Everyone ready?"

They all shook their heads or mumbled yes. Jai said, "Okay, here we go. Are you guys ready back at base?"

Hiroshi answered, "Yes, we are all here. Good hunting, everybody, and stay sharp."

Jai and her partner showed up at the mint and reported in. Their IDs were casually verified, and they were shown to the transport van. They watched as the money was loaded and then they entered the back of the van. They became aware that the door was locked from the outside with no handle in the interior.

As soon as the van began to roll, a false panel began to rise to the ceiling, much like a garage door. Following what they were told by the guards, they unwrapped the top of the pallet and removed ten stacks of money and lined them up against the wall. That done, they banged on the wall and stepped back into the van and sealed the pallet back up, making it look as if nothing had been touched.

Jai whispered, "Jai here. Can everybody hear me?"

"Yes," they all replied.

"It's going just as the guards said it would."

Ninety minutes later they had reached the hangar at the airport. The remaining money was unloaded and placed in the cargo plane. So far nothing else unusual took place. Jai and Guy were in the back of the truck, and it took off.

Jai said, "Zelda, close in tight if you see no tails. Unfortunately this only solves one piece … wait hold on. Partner, do you here a hissing sound?"

"Yes."

Jai, looking around, saw nothing until she looked at the ceiling. There she saw four jets spewing out gas. "Put on your mask. Hurry, hurry. I'm betting this stuff is lethal. Zelda, get an explosive device onto the back door, and after it blows, stop this van."

"Already closing. I'll get alongside and slap it in place."

"Sounds good, but hurry."

Two minutes passed; then inside the van they heard then felt an explosion, and the back door blew apart. The Black Ops leader started to crawl to the empty space, but Jai held him back, saying, "Wait for Zelda to stop the truck, and hold on to the straps on the side walls."

Zelda pulled alongside the transport, hoping to cut it off and force it to the left, where there was no traffic or pedestrians, but the driver swung to the right and smashed into the van. Zelda held her steady. She knew if the cops started a chase, they would be the ones they would go after, seeing a legitimate transport seemingly being hijacked. Since the transport tires and body were bulletproof, she had to come up with something different.

She sped up, and when far enough ahead, she said to her partner, "Did you ever play chicken when you were a kid?"

"No, what's that?" he answered.

She quickly did a U-turn and sat facing the transport. "Hold on tight. This is going to be hairy. Take off your seat belt, and get ready to jump if he doesn't stop."

She floored the van, heading straight for her target. Her partner and everyone at headquarters yelled, "She's crazy! They'll all be killed."

The truck didn't veer, and neither did Zelda. At the last moment she yelled, "Jump for your life."

The truck driver saw what was happening too late to do anything and hit the brakes as is a natural reaction. The van and truck hit straight on, but because the van was so much lower, the truck climbed on top of it, and they both slid forward for at least one thousand feet before coming to a stop. The driver was knocked out cold, and his partner was dazed.

Jai yelled, "Now, get to the front, and let's not let them get away. They are in on this up to their necks, and we may be able to get more information from them. Hiroshi, Zelda, can you hear me?"

"Yes, Director," they replied.

"Zelda, get the hell out of here, and take the two drivers with you. The van is clean, no way for them to trace it to us. Hiroshi, get Black Ops control. Tell them we have a lot of evidence implicating the United States in fraud and possible terroristic activities going high up in the government and our location. Tell them we need the top people from congress at this site immediately before the locals screw it up. Remember, just congress heads, nobody from DOJ or the White House."

"Got it. We are already on com with control. Do you want to speak to them?"

"No, don't have time, you do it. I'm staying as a company guard to be sure we are not compromised. When I'm done, I'll want a meeting with everyone at headquarters."

"Got it."

The local police showed up almost immediately with the press and police and news helicopters. Jai was explaining to the police detective that there was a robbery attempt, but when they blew the door apart, the truck was empty, having already made their delivery. The detective just shook his head and laughed.

He said, "We will need you two guards to come to headquarters so we can get an official statement. Where are the drivers?"

Jai responded, "We don't know. As soon as we cleared the back of the van, they were gone. As soon as our company representatives and our insurance people show up and I tell them the little, I know we'll be free to come to the station."

"Director, Amira here."

"Yes?"

"You have the senate and house majority whips headed your way right now. Along with them a member of the Black Ops control board is on his way. He will be wearing a red boutonniere in his lapel, and you should speak to him ASAP. He is the one that got the whips to come."

Just as Amira finished speaking, three limos pulled up together; two were government and one privately owned. As soon as they identified themselves, they asked that the police step back until they were finished. After the detectives checked with the chief of police, they stepped back to the barricades.

While the government people were talking to the detective, the control guy asked, "Which one of you is the director?"

Jai acknowledged that she was. Of course he saw her as a man, and said that he believed that the director was a woman.

Jai said, "Believe me sir I am all woman, but, proof of that will have to wait until later."

Confused, but wanting to hear what they had to say, he said, "Okay."

Jai asked that he bring over the government officials so they could witness what happened next. When they were standing next to Jai, and the detective was at the barricade, Jai said, "Will you three please step inside the transport? Guy, you go to the cab and find the switch to open the wall."

After they stepped inside, Jai directed them to the false wall just as it began to raise up. The house whip asked,

"What are we looking at?" Just in time for them to see the ten stacks of money.

Jai looked at control, and he nodded his head in the affirmative. Jai proceeded to tell them everything she knew about the operation except who they believed to be the men behind it all. Of course they wanted badly to know, and Jai told them that they would have their answers in forty-eight hours or less. She didn't want to accuse anyone without definitive proof.

"Now gentlemen, if you'll please get me and my partner out of here without further time wasted, we'll get the evidence you need. I think you three should not speak of this to anyone because you really don't want them covering their tracks or skipping town. Agreed?"

They all did, and so with a few words to the police detective in charge and a promise for a later date for his interview, Jai and Guy were on their way to the airport.

# CHAPTER 41

Jai said after everybody was assembled, "Well, we have two parts of the puzzle solved. First we know for sure where and how the money is being pilfered, and second that the guards are all murdered after one delivery. Now the big question remains, who is running this operation, and of course how is the money being distributed once the plane lands?"

Hiroshi said, "Before we get to that there is the paperwork, and I think there are only two possibilities; one is that the president verbally orders a payment of half a billion dollars twice a year to one of the armies and that it's loaded on the transport with the paperwork reading the correct amount and destination, meaning that the paperwork is changed without his knowledge after the pickup at the mint. The second shipment reads the same way but after the pickup not only is the amount changed but the destination is also."

Amira jumped in, "Yes, but that still doesn't tell us if the president is involved."

Hiroshi continued, "As I said, without his knowledge. Now I believe that either way he is not going to have a trail of paperwork leading back to him. So who fills out the original paperwork, and who makes the switch?"

Jai jumped in. "If the president gives the original order to the head of the DOD, then he could easily pass it down to his undersecretary, and that is, as we know, Ingmar Williamson. What if he makes up two sets of orders, one for the mint, and one for loading on to the plane and further unloading in Iraq? What happens after that is simple. He gives the first order to the mint and the second order to Albert Beasley, the operations chief from DOJ and the CIA. He in turn passes it on to his CIA driver and it's done."

Hoshi says, "Sounds right, but how do we tie it all together? We need to find out where the drivers take the stolen money and what they do with the bodies of the guards."

Denton says, "That won't be easy. They have nothing to gain by talking and everything to lose, especially if they get a nice cut of the pie."

Jai said, "We can tell them they have two choices—to be held as terrorists and then executed as traitors or we can wipe their memories back to the point before they were hired on.

"I have a problem with that. That would mean they get clean away with their crimes," Denton said.

Hoshi chimed in, "True, but think of the alternative. The top brass would get away with the money, their crimes, and we would never find out what happened to the bodies of the murdered guards."

Jai after a little thought said, "Okay, you are both right, so it's up to us to find the evidence linking the top men to the crime, and we have forty hours to report our findings. So I guess what I'm saying is, I'll give the tech team thirty hours to do just that, and if they don't we go to the drivers with that deal. We can argue this all night, so I'm making that that plan without further discussion. Any questions? No? Then let's get started."

While everybody was leaving, Jai caught Amira's eye and motioned her to stay.

"Come upstairs. It is time to have an essential enlightening talk. See you in five."

Once they were together in Jai's suite, she said, "Amira, please have a seat."

"Is there something wrong?"

"No, but it is time for you to hear the truth about who and what I am, the question you have been asking me and yourself since we met."

"You are making me very nervous. Even though I really want to know, I'm afraid to find out because it might change everything."

"That's true, but I feel it is only right since we have reached a critical point in our relationship.

"First of all, if we are still together I will tell you where I came from and the devastating childhood I had, but for now you have to know what I am. To start with I am human."

"Whew that takes a load off."

"But only half."

"Seriously? Are you part witch or something like that? That would explain your unbelievably strange powers."

"No, Amira, the other part of my people are a humanoid people from a distant planet outside this solar system."

"You are kidding? Right?" Amira said is a state of shock.

"No, it is the truth. My alien people have inhabited this planet longer than the human species of today."

"Are there more of your type here now?"

"No, not like me, but yes there are aliens that live on Earth, and it has become my mission in life to protect them.

"Against whom?"

"Against all those that are out to destroy them, but they are not our only enemies. Our main enemy is the impurity of the environment, which your humanity is slowly but surely destroying. We cannot live in a polluted atmosphere, and eventually neither will humans be able to."

"Are those the main reasons you put together this team?"

"Actually I didn't. It was put together before I knew who I really was, and it was waiting for me to lead it."

"Why you?"

"Because I have within me the unusual combination of human tantric powers, which I learned as a young girl, and the powers of my alien people. But mainly it's because I can survive anywhere on this planet and they cannot."

"Wow, this is so much to handle all at once. How does this all affect me and our relationship?"

"That's strictly up to you. The alien leader is called the A Ma. After we made love last time she told me that I took you to such a high level that there may be consequences for our actions. I do not know what she is speaking about, but I will soon. I just wanted you to know, because my human self is in love with you. Whatever it is she tells me, I promise we will deal with it together."

# CHAPTER 42

Zelda was feeling sick and tired over all this pussy footing around. *Somebody has to step up and do what's necessary around here. The others are great, but am I the only one with a pair?* Walking into the room where the prisoners were being held, she found no guards, cameras, or com devices. Both men were standing up tied to beams in the ceiling. She walked over and saw they were both conscious and looking at her.

"Gentlemen, I'm going to end this bullshit right now. One of you will tell me all I want to know and live to be free, and the other? Well, let's just say I'm going to enjoy myself, because I'm known as the sadistic one who takes a lot of time enjoying herself. Now because this is going to get messy, I'm going to remove most of my clothing, and the first to get nice and hard will have the pleasure of watching the other suffer."

Zelda stripped slowly down to her bra and panties, keeping an eye on both men. It was the younger guy whose body betrayed him.

"That's great," she said. "I like young bodies. How old are you?"

He didn't say anything, and Zelda smiled. "Not a good start for you."

She took out her hunting knife from its scabbard and began cutting off his clothes. She stepped back when all he had on was his underpants and said, "Let's see, I'd say you are twenty-eight, maybe nine. Am I right?"

The guy looked down but didn't answer her. "Bad boy," she said. She slid the blade up between his thigh and underpants and with one motion cut them so that they hung on the other thigh. "I think I'm right," she said.

Zelda grabbed his cock and stroked it until it was as hard as could be and continued as she spoke then said, "Gentlemen, I only have three questions. One, who are your bosses, and two, where do you take the stolen money, and finally, what did you do with the bodies of all those guards you murdered?

"No answers? Good, and so I shall continue with my little game. Not to worry, mister shotgun, your cock and balls are safe until the end. If neither answers my questions by then I will cut them off and cook them for our friend here to eat. I want you both to understand something. If you don't talk, you two are useless to me, and I will owe you no favors so you both will die a very painful death and then you'll both disappear and nobody will be the wiser.

"I have an idea. Let's play a game of who is the better man." She cut off the driver's boxers and now held both their cocks in her hands.

"Let's see who can hold out the longest."

After a couple of minutes senor shotgun yelled out and

came with a strong stream. Zelda said, "Wow sir, that was really powerful. The women in your life would be proud, except they will never have that again, at least not from you.

"Anybody ready to answer my questions?"

"No? Okay, game time is over. Watch and listen carefully. Mr. Driver, you will be next, and torture will follow."

Just as she was about to start, she heard in her earpiece Hoshi telling Jai that they found out the name of the driver through facial recognition. That he has a beautiful wife age thirty-two named Amy, and a twelve-year-old daughter named Kris, and now they had their address.

Zelda thought, *Now this is information I could use*. She said aloud, "So Mr. Hotshot Driver, I think you are seriously thinking you can watch this kid get tortured and play for time in hopes of getting rescued. Let me simply say that will not happen. Nobody outside this organization knows where this place is. On the other hand, would you be able to play that same game while watching the men here do to your wife, Amy, and daughter, Kris, what I'm doing to the two of you? If you have any doubts know that they were picked up in Alexandria and are on their way here. I hope they are wearing pretty panties."

"You are bluffing."

"And you are willing to chance that? When they get here, I'll have them put in the next room and you can listen while they get raped and tortured. My friend we are very serious people, and all your money and friends will not stop this from happening. Only you can, only you!"

"Will you let them go if I talk?"

"Yes, they will be let go even before they board the plane. While you were drugged we flew you out of the country. Your girls have not seen the men' faces, and the van they are in is clean so we can let them go with no worry. It's up to you. My guess is they have thirty to forty-five minutes before they board, and then it will be too late. We will need that time to check out your story, so you better start talking right now. Tell me from the beginning, and leave nothing out."

It didn't take long before Zelda knew everything and said into the com, "Tell Jai I know everything we need to know to hang those bastards."

When they were all together, she told them that the people they were looking at were the right ones, where the drivers dropped the money, and that the bodies were dropped off late at night at the steel plant and dumped into a hot vat of molten ore.

"Where's the money?" Hoshi asked.

"They bring it to a twenty-four-hour very secure storage facility. When they get to the door of the unit, the outer door automatically opens, and they unload the money in an outer room. Then they leave. They believe that the principals came later and open the inner room, and that's where all the money is."

Hiroshi said, "That's why we haven't been able to find even a trace of it anywhere in the world with anything to do with their names or under any aliases."

Jai said, "Okay, then we have to be there when they open up the vault to be able to prove it's them. I'll bet they are making plans to move it now because their cohorts are missing and they are in danger of losing it all. How did you get all the information, Zelda?"

"I have my womanly wily ways. You'll see they are

unharmed, except that their clothes seemed to have fallen into shreds. In my opinion they should be terminated."

"I agree," both Hoshi and Hiroshi said.

"Okay, let's get together a team. We need everybody for a twenty-four-hour watch. We need a lot of film, and as much sound as possible. We need them going in, loading, and leaving. Remember, people, these are powerful men who will have the best lawyers money can buy. And we need to start immediately."

Zelda asked, "What should we bring for weapons?"

Jai said, "I know this may sound silly, but it is possible that they will bring their own private bodyguards, so prepare for that possibility. If they don't then this will be a walk in the park.

"Okay let's move people. I'll take the first watch with Makeen. Guy and one other of us will be our backup. This team will leave right now, to be replaced in six hours."

Amira jumped in. "Why not have the capital whips standing by so when it's going down the can see it for themselves?"

"Great idea. Call Black Ops control for me and tell them what you said, but under no circumstance are they to know what, who, where, or when until I say so."

Washington, DC

"Albert, have you seen the news?" asked Ingmar Williamson.

"What is going on?"

"Somebody has hijacked the transport after the airport delivery. The police have it, and the money, but the drivers are missing. I think this is not just a simple robbery because they left the cash. I'm afraid somebody is on to the operation, and they will eventually get the drivers to tell about the drop offs."

"I'm going to get one of the company's armored cars then we will meet and get the money out of there. We can hide the armored truck in plain sight in the warehouse with some phony mechanical problems. That will give us a day or two to find a new place to move it."

"Okay, I'll make some excuse and meet you there. I can leave in half an hour."

At eight thirty at night Jai spotted an armored car headed down the street toward the storage and vault compound. She said, "I think this is it Zelda. Get ready; Hoshi, tell Amira to call the whips, and as soon as we confirm what is going on, tell them to get here ASAP. Are all our cameras and sound equipment online?"

Hiroshi responded, "Yes and we have cut into the feed of their cameras also. We have the inside and outside fully covered with no blank spots."

"That's great. Did Amira reach the whips?"

"Yes, they said they have been ready since we called. They still don't know who we are after."

"Okay, an armored car is turning into the vault, and wait a minute, there is a government vehicle close behind. They both have only one driver. Ladies and gentleman, we are about to witness the end of a major series of crimes by people high up in the US government. Hopefully everyone involved will get the maximum possible sentence."

Eleven o'clock that same night—the White House, Oval Office.

In attendance were the house and senate whips, the secretary of defense, the secretary of state, the vice president, and various heads of the FBI, CIA, DOJ, and Homeland Security. The president walked in in his bathrobe and said, "What the hell is going on? There better be a nuclear war about to start."

The senate whip was the one who laid out what had been going on for three and a half years—who was behind it all and how they were able to pull it off. Then he said, "The people that took down the whole operation are now in Iraq dealing with the CIA personnel who are responsible for separating the money used for buying nuclear materials coming out of a few former USSR states. They hope to follow a trail to the stockpile they previously purchased."

The president, in a state of near shock, said, "How come I'm just now hearing about this, and who brought down the operation?"

The house whip said, "Honestly, sir, the senate whip and I were the only ones told about this, and that was only a couple of days ago. The reason is simple: the people who brought it down didn't know how high this went. Even you, if you follow the evidence, could easily have been a suspect. I'm sorry, sir, but it did originate in this office with your discretionary budget and your order on how it was to be used."

"So who put it all together, and are the leaders in this room?"

"No, they are not here, nor are they ever going to be recognized. They are a privately funded organization built around stopping crimes against humanity and the environment. They wish not to be known, believing they can be more effective that way."

"So have they cleared me?"

"Yes, or we wouldn't be here right now."

"Let them know we will give them whatever they require in any amounts to help them recover the nuclear material and further to eliminate whichever group is responsible."

"Yes sir," said the senate whip.

The house whip spoke next. "According to their director, after they locate the material or at least its approximate location they will turn the information over to our DOD and the Israelis."

# CHAPTER 43

The A Ma was deep in thought as she watched Jai sleep. *There are so few of us left on this planet. Once we were so strong, so right for the universal plan. Throughout the Earth's history we have seen its downward progression. The ever-increasing lies, the propaganda, the corruption, and the decay that power manifests. We were forced into hiding and couldn't fight for the greater causes. We will never forget who we are and why we are on Earth. We were the space travelers seeking new Earths and negotiating peace throughout the universes.*

*Our original concept was based on the reality of change. Of life and death, in perpetual motion, not on some fanciful ego illusions. We were the guardians of the new earths, and also the old ones needed us to survive. There are so few of us left, but we are committed to the Earths and our own salvation. We have everything necessary to save the planet except the ability to live in its newly polluted atmosphere. It has been decided we need to evolve so that we might walk easily on this Earth and save it from destruction.*

"Wake up, my child. We have a lot to talk about."

"Hello, A Ma. How long have you been here?"

"I just came in, because, but what we must speak about can't wait. I feel that you have had your energy renewed by Makeen, and that is good."

"Yes, A Ma, it had been a long time and a lot has happened."

"I know. Now there are two very important items that need immediate attention. First let me congratulate you and your team for the op you just finished. I believe your team will locate the missing nuclear material and it will be recovered."

"Yes, A Ma, they are close to the final source."

"Now we should start with a delicate subject; we believe and I agree that you should have a baby to raise."

Jai got out of bed. Shaking her head as if there were cobwebs she needed to shake loose, she said, "What? I'm I hearing you correctly? A baby, me?"

"Yes, to raise not to bear."

"Then who does this child belong to, and why aren't they raising it?"

"Simply because it hasn't been born or conceived yet."

"Pardon? What? I don't understand."

A Ma, laughing, sat down on the bed and said, "You will in a moment. We want this, and we believe this is correct for many reasons, which I will explain later. Until then let me find out how you feel about it."

"I don't really know. I have never given the idea of having children any thought. It has never entered my mind. At least not consciously."

"And now?"

"Whose baby will I be raising?"

"Not I will, but *we* will be raising."

"Who will be the father?"

"You do not know him. He is one of us. A very good specimen of our people. Probably the best we have."

"And the mother?"

"Amira."

"What? You can't be serious. I don't think she will accept that. I know she is in love with me."

"Listen carefully, Jai. When you were with her intimately the last time, you raised her energy extremely high, and in the process you disrupted the makeup of her DNA. You also added to her gene pool, creating a slightly different human.

"We believe that her eggs will contain these different changes and along with the one hundred percent alien sperm we can help humanity evolve, on this planet, pushing them farther away from their animal roots to a more intelligent being, leading to a better end for them and us.

"Also that experience changed you as well. You went from a woman with strong sexual desires and needs to a woman deeply in love."

"I know. Does this mean I can no longer be the head of this agency?"

"Oh no, everything remains the same. You'll have Lei and plenty of others to help along both lines."

"There is still the matter of convincing Amira."

"It may be the time for her to meet me in person. She will then recognize my energy, which she has become familiar with while she slept. But it is not necessary."

"And what if she says no?"

"She won't. As you say, she is in love with you and will do anything you ask."

"I will not threaten her with us breaking up."

"I know that. She will not refuse!"

Jai asked, "What is the second thing we need to discuss?"

"Before we move on, Jai, you didn't answer me. How do you feel about raising a special baby?"

"I know. I have been avoiding thinking about it."

"You must come to an answer because it should be done before you move on to the next assignment."

"That is awfully fast for such a big decision. Is there a reason why?"

"Yes, your next assignment will take you away for quite a while, and we do not know when you will be back."

"What is so important that I might be gone for a long time?"

"You are going to go the jungles of Cambodia to find your military leader. We will give you his approximate location, but since he moves around so quickly and often we cannot pinpoint his exact location."

"Can't Guy or another capable person do it?"

"No, Jai, it must be you!"

"Why?"

"There are many dangers in the Cambodian jungles, some of which only a person with your abilities can escape. Of course you may face none of those. On the other hand, you may face them all. His name is Dorje, and he is just the man you have been asking for."

"If he is so brilliant in battle, why would he join us and follow me?"

"When all is said and done, he, like Amira, will not turn

away from you. He will see a person equal or better than himself with capabilities greater than his. He will honor and respect that, and your credo."

"In just five minutes you have changed my life once again, A Ma."

"Maybe so, but all for the betterment of those who are innocent, and the planet. It is time to face Amira, but before you do know that it is you who will be making love with her, and when you bring her to a state of ecstasy beyond where she has been before, in a state of no consciousness, then you will make the switch. It will only take a few minutes, and she will be back in your arms."

"Really?"

"Yes, he will be brought to the edge of his climax at the moment you withdraw. Please let us not discuss the details of this. It won't make things any easier for either of you."

"What should I tell Amira about the act itself?"

"That is up to you. You know her best, but it must be something that doesn't push her away. You will leave right afterward. Any questions?"

"What if she doesn't conceive?"

"Believe me, child, she will. Start by letting everyone know you will be leaving and gone for a while on a recruiting trip. That you will be going by yourself and will hand out assignments for when you are gone. This will put the two of you in bed with an extra urgency. We too will be ready."

# CHAPTER 44

Jai, still in a mild state of shock, continued mulling over what the A Ma had explained. Pacing around her room, she decided that trying to decipher to see if there use another motive behind this request was useless. She decided to get to work. She called Zelda on her com.

"Zelda, I am told that you and your team have successfully tracked the nuclear material to its final destination. It that correct?

"Yes, Director, it is. I would really like to be a part of the final takedown when it occurs. Is that possible?"

"I'm afraid not. I know you are as capable as any they will send to recover the material, but we cannot under any circumstance expose our organization. You will argue that the chances are slim of that happening, but there is still a chance no matter how slight."

"Yes, Director, in that case we will start our retreat right now. I have relayed everything necessary to Hiroshi, and with your order it will be passed on to the proper people."

"Thank you, Zelda, for another op well done. I will pass

the information on to the president of the United States and ask that he work with the Israelis.

"Hiroshi, please call the senate whip and ask him to pass the information on to the president."

"Yes, Director."

"Where is Amira?"

Hoshi answered, "She has left the compound for a short while and will be back momentarily."

"Understood. Have her join me in my suite when she returns."

Waiting for Amira to return, Jai was in a state of anxiety while trying to gather her thoughts and figure out a way to present this to Amira. *Why would speaking about us having a child seem to be the most difficult thing I have ever done till now? I have no idea her thoughts about having a child, and an alien child at that. And what about me? Am I ready to take on another responsibility? How will a baby affect my willingness to put myself in harm's way? Will Amira, whom I love dearly, decide that approaching her with this new rather strange request be the last straw? After all, just telling her that I was part alien was a big chance in itself. I understand the reasons for having this baby, and I know I brought it about myself by taking Amira to a level beyond what would be considered normal for a female, but how could I not? And if she says no, what do I do? I would have broken her heart, and even if I agreed to walk away from the A Ma, will either of them ever forgive me? There is just no way to know the answers to any of my questions unless I act, and then I will know.*

Jai's com went live and jolted her from her reverie.

"Director, Amira has returned, and she is headed up to your suite."

"Thank you, Hoshi. I will be off com for a while."

"Yes, Director. I will either direct your calls to Denton or I tell them you'll call them back."

Jai heard a knock on her door and said, "Please enter."

"You asked to see me?" Amira said.

"Yes, I did. Come into my arms. I have a deep desire to hold you and feel your body against mine."

Amira, after holding Jai close, leaned back and looked into her eyes. "Jai, why do you look so sad? Is everything all right?"

"Yes, my love, it is. I want so badly to make love with you right now, but I'm afraid that the new level that I may bring you to might be dangerous for your physical or mental well-being."

"I don't care. I just need you to be free to do whatever it is you want to do with me. I love your touch, and your ... well, your everything. I just want to melt inside of you and be a part of you forever."

Jai, taken aback by that statement that gave her the cue she was waiting for, said, "What if we could be as one in another being?"

"What does that mean? I don't understand."

"What if I tell you we can have a baby together?"

"How could that even begin to be possible? Who would carry the baby?"

"You, my love. You."

"But you do not have the male sex organs necessary for me to conceive."

"Remember the other night when I expended my energy to reach deep inside of you?"

"Yes how could I forget? I still feel you there."

"What if I tell you that I can transform my energy into male sex organs with the ability to produce sperm?"

"Seriously? What type of child would we produce?"

"A child who will be far superior to the normal human child. A child who will be able to help humanity progress beyond its miserable state."

"That would be incredible."

Jai, having released Amira from her grip, took her hand and led her to the couch. They both sat down, and Jai continued. "Yes I believe so too. How do you feel about having our baby and then we will raise it together?"

"I must say this is quite a surprise. I am totally confused as to my feelings. Of course I want to have a child with you, but this is so far beyond my understanding that it is blowing my mind."

"It was quite a blow to me also when I found out this is possible, but I know that for so many reasons it is right. I know that we are meant to do this, and I too want so badly to have a baby with you."

"Jai, I love you beyond any words that can express it, but I need a moment to allow it to formulate in my mind. Can you wait for an answer?"

"Yes, of course, but you should know that I will be leaving pretty soon on a mission, and I will not return for quite a while. I really would love for us to try before I go."

"Why? What are you telling me? Is there a chance you won't return?"

"There is always that chance, but I'll only be searching for someone so there should be no danger."

"Who?"

"The person who I hope will lead our military wing. It's a long story as to why he is hiding and you will find out after I'm gone, but for now I would really want us to try and conceive before I leave. I want oh so badly for you to have our child and for me to know that you are pregnant before I leave."

"Okay, my love, let me go to my room and I'll return in a few minutes and I'll be ready for us. Believe me, Jai, I can think of nothing more exciting than us making love and second, me getting pregnant with your baby."

"Our baby."

"Of course, our baby. I'll be right back."

After a long kiss Amira departed and Jai began to think, *I can't believe I told Amira, the woman I love, two very big lies. But honestly I think it saved us a long, drawn-out battle, and the end result would have been the same. Still, now if she ever finds out the truth it might mean the end of us.*

"A Ma, are you here?"

"Yes, my child, we are both here, and he will be ready at the right moment."

"Do you have to be so close? I would rather we be alone until the right time."

"As you wish. The energy created by both of you will attract us at the right moment. It will be done quickly. When you feel my energy touch your forehead, withdraw and lay by her side. Also, you did the right thing in telling her what was to happen. I would have done the same."

"I hope so, for all our sakes."

"Here she comes. Take her beyond where she was last time. It will be easy having been at the level she was before. I love you, my child. I will leave now. She is coming."

"I love you too, A Ma.

"Come in, Amira, and join me in a drink to toast what we are about to create."

"I am really scared, Jai. I just feel that this is such a big decision, and I've had no time to think about it."

"I know, my love, but I truly feel that the journey we are about to undertake is not only right, but something I want badly to share with you."

"I know, I feel the same way. I also know that once the baby is born, I'll forget its alien origins and love it to death."

"Come, my love, take my hand and let us begin by taking the first step."

Their lovemaking started with a wild passion brought on by a hunger from deep within. The hunger for each other seemed unquenchable. They made love as though there was no time or space and no end in sight.

Ninety minutes later, Amira was going crazy with multiple climaxes, one greater than the other. Jai felt she had reached a point of exploding like a supernova. At that very moment, Jai felt A Ma's energy on her forehead. It took her a moment to come back to her senses, and she slid off of Amira and lay by her side. Jai kept her eyes closed tightly, not wanting even a glimpse of Amira with another being. In about one minute, Jai heard Amira moan then scream, and she knew that the male exploded inside Amira. It seemed to last forever until he rolled off and Jai slid back on top of Amira. Amira's hips were naturally pushing upward, trying to hold in every drop of fluid. Jai held her tightly while kissing and licking Amira's face and neck. Tears came to Jai's eyes, and she started to cry. She convulsed with so much passion so that it scared Amira, and she grabbed Jai with a tight hold with her arms and legs. Both women were now crying and speaking of their undying love for each other. Amira finally let go and immediately passed out. Jai just lay there stroking Amira's body and looking at her with love and understanding.

Jai heard the beating of wings and immediately covered Amira with a sheet. The A Ma appeared, smiling. "That was incredible. Jai, you are a great natural lover with abilities you do not yet understand."

"Why is there fluttering? Who is here with us?"

"It is someone your people might call a medical doctor or a shaman."

"Why is he here?"

"She, to see if Amira has already or will conceive. I know from the sounds and body positions that she will without a doubt."

"I sure hope so. I'm not entirely sure I can turn her over to another once again."

The A Ma just smiled and kissed Jai on her head. "We won't need to wait long."

"When will we know if it's a boy or girl?"

"It will be a girl, without question."

"How do you know that?"

"It is the only chromosomes he carries. It must be that way."

"Yes, I understand."

"There. The fluttering has ended, and she is gone.

Congratulations, the two of you will be having a baby girl in nine months."

"Oh, A Ma, I am so happy. We will be the best parents possible."

"I know, my child. Now you have about a week before you must leave. So I will leave you two now to enjoy the coming moments. Do not tell her the sex of the baby. Let her choose when she wants to know."

"Okay, A Ma. I want to thank you for all that you have and continue to do for me."

"It is my distinct pleasure to know and guide one such as you."

Amira, having gone back to her apartment, left Jai with a sense of emptiness at having to leave Amira for what might be a long time.

# CHAPTER 45

Six days had passed since that wondrous night with Amira. Jai thought often about the A Ma, and the nearness of her upcoming quest to find the warrior began to cause her anxiety and sadness. She did not want to leave Amira, but she knew she had to. She shook herself out of her thoughts when her com set alerted her.

"Director, we have conformation that most of the nuclear material has been captured, and the Israelis are on track for the balance."

In the hallway Jai ran into Amira. "Amira, do you want the good news or bad news first?"

"Shit! The bad news."

"I'm leaving later tonight for the Far East, and I won't be back for a while."

"Who is going with you?"

"No one. I'll be on my own."

"Oh Jai, I don't know why you are going and what you will be doing. I am so scared because you are so secretive."

"I know, baby, but it must be this way. It will be over soon and I'll be back."

"You have to promise me."

"I promise."

"Okay, what is the good news?"

"You—I mean we—are pregnant."

"Really? How do you know?"

"I have that ability."

"Oh my god, I am so excited. Please don't go away. Can't we have at least a couple of nights to celebrate?"

"I'm sorry, Amira, but I don't have a choice."

"Damn it, Jai, can I have one thing my way?"

"Yes you may, but not when it comes to the operation of this organization."

"I understand, but how about you get a job that is not so dangerous, like a secretary or something?"

"You are kidding I presume?"

"Of course."

Jai shook her head and laughed over Amira's joke. Soon, however, it was all business as usual. She completed delegating as necessary, and in less than two days she found herself in another world—the jungles of Cambodia near the Thailand border.

A small contingent of seasoned, dedicated soldiers under the leadership of Commander Dorje moved with stealth and resolve through the jungle. They had fought together and won many battles throughout the years, always in the name of freedom for the people. They felt that today would be no different because they had reliable intel on the village and the forces they would encounter.

Having sent a small band ahead to ensure that the invading army had not yet entered the village, Dorje was feeling confident that they would once again defeat a superior force, both in numbers and firepower.

Dorje did not believe in advanced communications because too much could be intercepted, so they waited for his scouts to return. He believed that he would have the time to enter the village, look around, and decide then where his men should take up their positions, and hopefully they wouldn't have to wait too long. These battles, he knew, always resulted in massive bloodshed. Thankfully it was always on the opponent's side.

Upon the return of the scouts, he learned that the opposing force had not arrived and all was quiet. They were able to notify the village people that they were about to enter the village and help repel the invaders; they were welcomed with open arms and swore their allegiance.

One hour later they were on the edge of the village when Dorje told his lieutenants that they should go the heart of the village and work with the elders in setting up the resistance while he went to the highest point in the village to scout the area and decide where the enemy's forces might come from.

Dorje waited and watched as his men walked carefully into the village and on to the town's square. When they were greeted by the town's elders, he turned and headed for the church to climb up the steeple for the best view of the surrounding area.

Jai, having flown into Bangkok, Thailand, the day before, crossed unseen over the border into Cambodia and headed to Lake Tonle Sap, the last place Dorje and his men were known to be. She knew that they wouldn't be there any longer, but she thought she might learn from the people where he was headed.

Two hours after Jai crossed over into Cambodia, Jun Shan, hot on her trail by following a solid tip from his American compadre, also crossed the border. *This time I won't miss. Having her in my sights twice before and not finishing the job has been a great embarrassment and a plight on my reputation. From what I've heard and seen she is close to my ability, but I'll have the advantage of surprise.*

Moving through the jungle Jai was able to use her *lung-gom* ability to cover a lot of ground in a short amount of time. Every time she came to a village she entered as a male native, speaking the local language and inquiring about the mysterious Dorje and his men. At times it was difficult to separate fact from fiction, but no doubt he was a legend in these parts.

After a day of travel, Jai reached a village where Dorje had spent the night. Dorje, having met with the village elders and learning the movements of the government troops and the approximate location of the next village, headed out in that direction. The elders had never heard of the village so they couldn't tell either Jai or even Dorje exactly where to go, just the direction the troops were headed.

Jai, seeking more information from whomever she ran across, learned that she was headed in the right direction and that she wasn't too far behind. She was told to follow the river because that's what the troops were doing.

Jun Shan, picking up the same information from a villager, stole a small boat with an eight-horsepower motor and began down river. It wasn't too long before he saw a figure bounding along the river's edge, achieving great height and distance. *There she is. I'll wait until I have a clear shot and bring her down. This time I won't miss.*

A short distance later, a shot rang out, and Jai felt a bullet nick her thigh as it flew past. Jai headed for the water as fast as she could run. Reaching the shoreline, she submerged her body underwater. Out of air Jai lifted her head and sensed the boat behind her. She ducked under just as another bullet hit the water, grazing her shoulder.

Jai was in only two or three feet of water and felt the mud below her; she crawled and swam when she could, seeking shelter from the sunlight above. The boat neared, searching for her. Jai took a breath and lowered herself to lay on the bottom for as long as she could. She opened her eyes, but everything was a blur. After a few minutes hearing the boat move ahead, she needed to get some air, so she rose to the surface. Her lungs felt like they would burst. The boat had circled back, but she came up at its stern. She took shallow breaths. Looking into the boat, she saw the figure of a man carrying a semiautomatic rifle looking around.

Jai ducked back down and then heard the boat move slowly ahead. She was confused. Who was this person, why was he hunting her, and how did he get to this particular spot in Cambodia? Jai eased herself back under the water and swam to the riverbank. Climbing out, she felt she needed to check her wounds to be sure they were not serious and then dress them up so they wouldn't get infected. She knew that here in the jungle dangerous bacteria ran rampant. Jai luckily had carried a first aid kit in her rucksack, and seeing that both wounds were superficial, she patched them up.

After a couple of minutes of respite she got up, and getting her bearings, she headed down river on a path. Ten feet ahead a spray of bullets hit the dirt behind her. Spinning around she spotted the assassin, who was now on foot and had positioned himself high up on a tree branch. She wondered how he got up there as there were no low branches below.

She was positioned behind a large tree trunk and took stock of what was happening. It happened before—a lifetime ago, in the forests—as then when the fear passed she would plot her actions, her survival. Every moment that passed brought the assassin closer to whatever destruction he was planning. She had to reverse roles. The hunted had to become the hunter. His plans had to be exposed and destroyed before it was too late.

*Move!* shouted Jai to herself as she left the cover of the tree and ran fast along the path, seeking to circle back and get behind the killer.

Circling back, she knew she had to get closer to her assailant in order to block her image from his mind. As she neared him from behind, he suddenly spun around, catching Jai off-guard. As Jun took aim with his rifle, Jai leaped into the air, giving her enough time to block his vison. Now that he was unable to see her, Jai floated down to the ground and began to build her energy while she circled Jun, creating an impenetrable wall encapsulating him.

Jun, frustrated, began firing, but he stood in amazement as the bullets fell harmlessly to the ground. He was defeated and deflated—a feeling he never felt after he had entered the monastery to train.

Jai began questioning Jun but suddenly realized that she was spending too much time away from finding Dorje. Figuring that she would find her prisoner right where he stood after she returned, she turned back to the path and continued down river.

Three hours had passed when she ran into a peasant in an ox-driven cart and learned that the village was just ahead, maybe one kilometer beyond the bend. Jai knew it was time to get off the road and move slowly through the dense forest. She imagined that Dorje and his men would be in the village setting a trap for the government troops. Working her way through the forest brush near the road, she spotted a pin light in the bushes directly across from her. Judging the height and angle of the light, she knew the man was kneeling or sitting. The bushes were very dense where he was and he shouldn't be able to see her, which meant he was not expecting anyone to pass or he was inept.

She went back a few yards to where she couldn't be seen and ran across the road into the underbrush. She tested each step to ensure silence. For a moment, Jai was back in the forests, leading away from the horror that she witnessed at the temple where she studied with her teacher. Forcing herself to clear her mind brought her back to the present, where she was, and what possibly lay ahead. She felt comfortable in this element, a stalker of those that would do harm, destroying innocence and Mother Earth.

Jai took her hunting knife out of its scabbard and lunged through the bushes, hitting the soldier with her knees directly in his chest, knocking him flat. The knife was pressed against his jugular vein.

Speaking in Khmer, the language of Cambodia, the soldier yelled "What do you want? I am nothing but a simple soldier."

Jai said, "Tell me where the rest of the army is or I will skin you alive like I do a deer."

"Okay, okay, but you will be a dead man when they find you. Around the bend eight, maybe twelve kilometers ahead."

"When will this Dorje arrive?"

"We don't know exactly, but we believe it is today. I am one of the men looking for them."

"How many lookouts are there?"

"There are four on the road, and two more in the surrounding hills."

Jai jammed the backside of the hunting knife into the soldier's head, immobilizing him for a good many hours, then moved past him heading for the village.

She worked her way through the underbrush, satisfied with the knowledge that Dorje was still alive.

The next sentry was straight ahead, highlighted by the tail lights of a vehicle that just passed. Jai crawled slowly ahead. Since he was not looking at her, she couldn't force his mind to not to see her, and the brush was too thick to leap high and land on him. Getting close enough, she lunged and slammed into him before he could react. She shoved his head hard into the rocks he was leaning on, knocking him out. She put her arm around his neck in a chokehold and finished the job. He too would be out for a long time.

Moving ahead, Jai snapped a twig and heard movement

from across the road. A beam of light clicked on, looking for where the noise came from. Jai quietly slid away and lay flat behind a long rock about nine inches high. Peering over the rock, she saw the soldier looking around with his pistol drawn. Finally not seeing anything, he gave up and headed back to his post. She thought that since he had his weapon in hand she better just let him go. She couldn't afford a slip of his finger followed by a gunshot.

# CHAPTER 46

After many years of success the man known as Dorje, a name given to him by the people he defended against their communist oppressors, found himself for the first time, trapped. His small army of freedom fighters were all dead.

A trap conceived many months before led him and his men into a blind valley. The villagers they thought they were trying to free from their oppressors were in fact the enemy. When the red army attacked, they were caught in a web of a well-stationed army. They fought bravely, but it was a fruitless attempt. Those few that tried to surrender were shot where they stood with no weapons and their hands raised in the air.

Dorje, the name meaning "one man who was said to be indestructible," was trapped in a cathedral's bell tower half a mile away from the main fighting. He had been scouting the area for defensible positions the battle began, and he was trapped outside the communist main force. Watching his men get slaughtered, Dorje had to make a choice, throw himself into the battle, and sacrifice his life with the others or seek a way to escape.

The fight was over in no time. He watched as the enemy searched the dead soldiers for his body. He would be easy to identify, after they removed the full face mask he wore to hide the disfigurement he had suffered many years ago. He was in a partial state of shock, but when he saw patrols were finally being dispersed to find him, he came to his senses.

Peering out from the rear window, he saw a drainpipe, which led to a freshly trimmed lawn with rows of flowering hedges. He remembered a path that led across the main road through a large stand of trees and into the mountains.

Then Dorje saw a glow from a distant cigarette and realized that they left a contingent of soldiers surrounding the village in case someone was able to break through their lines.

It was growing dark, and he knew that they might have flood lights with sufficient illumination to light the outlying areas.

He had to make his move now if he was to escape.

As he climbed out the window, thinking about which way he would go once he hit the ground, he remembered that the whole town was bordered by a high, heavy-duty rolled barbed wire. They had seen it when they first arrived, and they thought it possibly was to hold in the town's farm animals or to keep out intruders. Now he knew it was so he and his men would not be able escape.

His feet hit the gutter. He inched his way to the drainpipe. Holding on to the gutter, he slipped over the side and straddled the pipe.

He descended by inching his way down. He stopped

when he heard a crash from the room he just left and realized he only had a moment before they looked out the window and saw him dangling there.

The men above smashed the glass window, and without thought Dorje let go and fell to the ground, rolling away from the house. Landing on his left shoulder, he smashed into a rock hard pavement.

With his life in danger, he was impervious to pain. He picked himself up and started to run away from fading light and into the darkness of the trees. The first volley of shots followed crashing into the tree trunks that surrounded him.

Hiding behind a thick trunk, he peered around to see that the shots were coming from the broken window. So far no one on the ground had seen him. He was able to move deeper into the woods.

The shouting started, and the men on the ground were joined by highly trained Rottweilers barking savagely while straining at their leashes. They stood there waiting. Dorje imagined that they were waiting for orders from their commander, who appeared in the doorway of the house Dorje had been in. He ran. The commander ran out screaming orders, but still he was calm and collected. He was gathering his men for the assault on Dorje's position.

Dorje knew the commandant and his men were pigs. The ultimate war machine, killers of all things decent, honoring only their corrupt leaders.

"You are dead, my friend!" yelled the commandant. He opened fire with his AK-47; Dorje threw himself on the ground behind a three-foot-tall root, which created a shield of wood. Bullets were flying over his head and were ricocheting off the surrounding trees.

"Come out, Dorje! Show yourself. It is time for you to die! Show yourself! You're dead!"

Dorje unslung the sniper rifle that was strapped across his body. He laid it across the root and took aim. He made all the adjustments he thought necessary and calmed his nerves like he had done so many times in the past. Took dead aim at the commander's head and fired. In an instant the general's head exploded like a watermelon, and he fell face-first onto the steps.

Dorje heard the yelling of the soldiers spreading the word and realized he had only seconds to get the hell away from his present position. He rose and strapped his rifle across his body and ran with all the speed he could muster deeper into the woods.

He broke out of the trees and was faced with a small out building. He ran to the far end of the building, turned the corner and stopped to catch his breath. It took him a moment to figure out the shortest way to the mountain. The biggest problem was the open field between him and the mountain passes. Then of course there were the rolls of barbed wire to somehow get beyond.

He walked to the other side of the building and spotted a small stand of trees close to the wire. Even though it took him further away from where he needed to go, it might be his only hope of getting across the sharp wire.

He ran from the building, straight across the field. A steady salvo of gunfire started up behind him. It was further away but still close enough to take him down. Zigzagging his way, he reached a small hill and crossed over the top, giving him cover from the bullets that followed.

A bullet just missed his head; it had come from in front of him. He had been seen by a perimeter guard.

He threw himself into the high grass, clawed sideways, and stopped cold. The foot soldier was running toward where he was, and Dorje knew he had to quietly dispose of him.

The moment the soldier stepped past him, Dorje took a single stride and clasped his hands around the man's neck from behind and slit his throat. He took the man's machete and continued on.

Hearing the fierce cry of a Rottweiler coming closer, he knew the animal was near.

Looking toward the howling, he took out the newly acquired bayonet and waited. Suddenly a massive black creature, his eyes red with hatred made sharper by the scent of the wounds emanating from his prey, leaped through the air. Dorje switched the bayonet to his right hand and ran it into the dog's belly. Still the dog was able to tear some flesh from his shoulder. His head was shaking side to side as Dorje, using all his strength, ran the blade higher and tilting it he was able to pierce the creature's heart. The dog howled and died.

Gathering himself, Dorje heard men running toward his position. He knew he had just minutes before they would be on him. He started running toward the isolated stand of trees and possible freedom.

Running blindly, he knew if he didn't gain ground all was lost. He reached the trees and was stumbling over rocks and fallen braches. There was no path, so he had to make one with the machete. His shoulder was throbbing where the dog had bitten into him, taking a small piece of flesh.

He was growing tired—very tired—and losing blood. There was a clearing ahead, and he hoped it was very near the fence.

The moon was now high and shining brightly as Dorje, breaking through the trees, saw the fence and possible escape.

Now he had to find a tree with a limb that would help him cross over the top of the barbed wire.

Sweat was pouring down his face, blurring his vision. He also required a tree he could climb in his weakened state.

The pursuing soldiers were in the trees, now running with their dogs on his scent. He had little time to choose, but he had to find the right tree.

There it was, just twenty feet to his left. A strong, long limb reached across the fence, and there were only two weak limbs below for him to climb up. Not enough!

But Dorje knew this was his only chance. The men and dogs were closing in fast.

He stepped back several steps, setting up a head start, and pushed off with his back leg. Running as fast as he could, he leaped into the air and wrapped his arms around the trunk. Using the sides of his boots and his arms as a hoop, he managed to pull himself up to the first small limb. Stopping for a moment to catch his breath, he focused his eyes on the next limb above and began pulling himself farther up.

Two gunshots were fired, and one of the bullets hit him in his thigh and the other in his shoulder. They found him, and now it was only a matter of time before they would bring him down. His arms and face were scratched raw from the bark, and his strength was almost gone. He wasn't sure he could move even one more step, but he had to try. He couldn't die this way, like a treed animal surrounded by wolves.

Thinking at this point was out of the question. Motion was his only hope. He reached the strong limb that reached out partially over the wire and pulled himself onto it.

His clothes were drenched with blood and sweat, and his eyes were stinging. He took a couple of deep breaths, and when his eyes cleared, he realized he would have to stand up and walk to the end of the limb and leap over the remaining barbed wire.

Not possible! He didn't have the strength or the will.

Panic set in as he heard the remaining soldiers and their dogs closing in.

Only six feet of limb and a broad jump to freedom. How ironic! So many battles, so many dead, so many broken people! Six feet and a broad jump to freedom.

*I was a hero. A god to some. I was a leader, an inspiration.*

*And now I'm a man broken by six feet of limb and a broad jump.*

About to lose consciousness, Dorje heard a voice coming from deep inside his mind. It said over and over again, "Hang on, I'm coming. You will be free."

# CHAPTER 47

Before the action started, Jai decided it might be best to climb the hills about where she could probably see the whole village and possibly the deployment of troops. She scrambled up a hill and out of the forest. Reaching a clearing she used her lung-gom discipline to reach the top of the hill. As she did and began to look around, all hell broke loose in the direction of the village.

She saw Dorje's troops being killed in the center of the town. Surrounded, they had no chance at all. They fought bravely but to no avail.

Jai was depressed and collapsed to the ground, believing that she got there too late and that the man she came to recruit was among the dead. Sitting there she thought about the uselessness of this endeavor. After she assured herself of Dorje's demise, Jai decided she would collect her prisoner and head back home and once again be with Amira and her fellow warriors.

All of a sudden Jai heard a new round of gunfire, loud yelling, and howling dogs. Standing up she saw a man leave the back of the church and run toward the wire, probably trying to escape into the mountains. With a concentrated look at the runner's head, she saw that he was wearing a full face mask like the one described to her about Dorje.

Jai thought she might be too late. Nevertheless, she stood up and headed down the mountain in leaps and bounds. At the base of the mountain she stopped and planned her move. She watched as Dorje leaped onto a tree trunk and started to scramble up in an attempt to get high enough to leap across the wire.

Jai made her move. Gathering all her energy, she leaped to the very top of the tree and started to spin, creating an impenetrable wall of energy. The energy lit up in an array of colors, and she could be seen in the center in her battle outfit of black. The men stopped shooting as they saw their ammo just bouncing off the waves of energy. Jai started to move the wall, creating a roaring sound like a tornado toward the army, and when they realized what was about to happen, they turned and ran as fast as they could.

Dorje in all his pain was able to turn toward the energy wall and stare in amazement. With renewed energy he tried pulling himself to the end of the limb, but he was too weak. He passed out.

Jai returned back to the tree, and realizing the problem, she pushed herself above the limb, and with all her weight she forced herself down, landing on Dorje's back, causing the dead limb to crack and break. Straddling his back, Jai gathered her energy and forced them to flip backward, taking his limp body with her to the ground. Jai, holding him tight to her body, landed on her feet in a crouch, lessening the impact. Thankfully, they landed on the other side of the wire with a clear path to the mountains.

The enemy troops were still in shock, and none made a move to chase them. Jai, using her knowledge of mechanics, lifted and flipped Dorje, carrying him across her shoulders like a sack of potatoes. She began to trot across the open field. She knew that at some point somebody would take charge back in the village and start to pursue.

Entering a mountain path, Jai was thinking, *This is so familiar. I vaguely remember a time when I was carrying a girl on my back moving quickly through the dense forest. It seems to me that life travels in circles. It's just a matter of time before life repeats itself. Then as now I was trying to save a life, maybe two.*

Steadily climbing higher on an old pack animal trail, Jai knew she would have to get off the path and find a place to hide and rest. Unfortunately her backpack with all her food and supplies were on a mountain across the valley. She saw a long flat stretch of meadow to her right and debated whether to take it, but she came to realize that's exactly what any pursuers would think she would do. Checking down the mountain and listening carefully, she saw and heard nothing. She laid Dorje down behind a rock and increasing her previous pace ran across the field, being sure to land heavily with each stride. When she reached the mountain wall, she turned and headed back to Dorje, staying on the loose rocks next to the mountain.

When she reached his position, she decided once again to leave him lying there and climb up to see if she could find an overnight resting place. Using her *lung-gom,* Jai moved up easily down and around the mountain.

On the side of the mountain facing away from the village, Jai spotted a small opening but big enough to crawl into. She walked to it, and getting down on her hands and knees, she crawled in. The hole turned to the left, and then seventy-five feet ahead it opened up to a large cave with shelves of rock seemingly carved out by a fast-moving river. She didn't see any water, but she could hear it running farther back in the cave.

*Perfect, I can leave him here and go get my pack and when he heals a little—if he heals. Then I can either bring help or carry him out. That is if the army doesn't find us first.*

Heading back to Dorje's position, Jai heard the army moving through the meadow. *They have taken the bait,* she thought with a smile. Reaching Dorje she checked and found him still breathing, so she lifted him as before and started on her long, arduous climb up the mountain.

Without the ability to do her *lung-gom,* it took Jai two and a half hours carrying Dorje. The higher she climbed, the further away the sound of the army trying to track them became. Finally reaching the cave, she had to pull Dorje inside by his ankles. Feeling secure, Jai finally had a chance to take a close look at Dorje's wounds. Ripping apart his pant leg, Jai could see and feel that the bullet wasn't too deeply embedded in his thigh. The bullet that went into the shoulder seemed to go out the other side, but the dog bite on the same shoulder was beginning to become infected, and that compounded the problem.

Needing to clean the wounds, Jai looked around to see if there were any materials to start and maintain a fire with but couldn't find anything. Still she felt she needed to cleanse the wounds, so she headed toward the sound of running water deeper inside the cave.

It didn't take long until she found the place where the running water entered into the ground below the surface. Problem was how she would carry it back to him. Not finding an answer, she went back and picked him up then carried him to the water.

Laying him down on the flat rocks alongside the stream, she tore his shirt and pants off and soaked them in the water. Jai washed both wounded areas, hoping that the water was clean. When she finished dressing them with pieces of his and her clothing, she sat back and made a priority outline of the things that needed to be done, starting with the need to camouflage the entrance. Jai went outside to gather the materials while figuring out the rest. Luckily there was some high mountain shallow root vegetation that she could dig or pull out and replant. This satisfactorily done, she again looked for materials for a fire, to no avail.

Jai went back inside to where Dorje lay and heard him moaning. She thought he might be trying to say something, so she reached for his face to take off the mask. As she did so, Dorje grabbed her wrist and while shaking his head no actually managed to scream out the word, "Don't!"

Dorje immediately fell back into a coma, probably from the energy he had expended.

Jai wondered what happened to his face that he didn't want her to see. She figured that sometime soon the mask would have to come off and she would know.

A single day had passed and twilight was upon the mountain, and Jai knew it was time to either cross the meadow or circle the mountains to retrieve her gear. Probably the safest way to avoid the troops was over the tops, but that could take all night and the sky was dark with rain clouds. Her decision made, she headed down the mountain.

Small fire lights lit up the meadow and the far mountain side like blinking stars in the night. Jai made her way alongside the base of the mountain, avoiding any contact. As she approached a large group of soldiers asleep on the open ground, one gave out a small yell as he popped up. He must have been dreaming but his eyes were wide open, and he found himself staring directly into Jai's eyes. Luckily he thought he was still dreaming; he closed his eyes and tried rubbing the sleep out of them. This gave Jai the moment she needed to place in his mind that he could see nothing but darkness, and a glow from the fires. He looked around and laid back down, satisfied that he was just seeing things like shadows and sparkling lights that looked like a pair of eyes.

Jai continued on and started her climb up the mountain side. There she found a sentries post a short way up, which she was able to get around with no problem.

Finding her belongings, she headed back down and across the meadow, avoiding everyone, even the guy who was pissing, along her path back.

In the cave she found Dorje sleeping peacefully, taking in deeper and deeper breaths as the time passed.

Because she was really tired and her energy fairly low, Jai decided to get some rest before she brewed some healing tea for them both. Laying down close to the bend leading to the outside, Jai fell into a deep sleep.

# CHAPTER 48

She was back in the back alleys of the streets in her home city with her brother Peng.

Huddled on the ground Jai was afraid of what her brother would do next. After failing to sell her at the auction or on the streets, she feared the worst. Sitting against a wall, Peng grabbed her and slid her up between his legs. He was talking to himself, questioning what to do with her and what his father would do to him when he got home. Finally coming to a decision, he pushed her away and crawled away. With Peng out of sight, Jai lay there, crying and yelling that she would kill him one day.

Jai jarred awake with the dream fresh on her mind, and shaking her head to clear it she thought, *Brave words for a seven-year-old. I wonder if he is still alive.*

Now awake she went back to where Dorje was lying and saw that his eyes were wide open and he was leaning on the elbow of his good shoulder.

Jai said, "Now that you are on the mend, I will have to leave you for a while. I have a prisoner that I also must attend to. He is an assassin sent to kill me, and I must find out why and who they are. I will be back shortly."

Nearing the site where she left Jun, Jai found that he was gone. Looking around, she saw no signs of him or of his trail. In a slight panic, she decided to return to the cave.

Once back Jai started a fire with the twigs and branches she brought up from the meadow along with her pack. Dorje said, "Who, or should I say what are you?"

"I could ask you the same question," Jai said without looking up from her fire building.

"I am just an ordinary man, as you can plainly see. You, on the other hand, seem to be something different, like a genie or a witch with magical powers."

Jai answered while laughing, "I am no such things, nor do I have magical powers."

"Then what was that I saw back at the village? What you did was not normal."

"Maybe I'm a magician."

The fire Jai was lighting came to life and gave the cave a warm glow. She gathered more fuel before she sat down beside Dorje.

Dorje said, "A magician warrior? I doubt that very much."

"And you, my friend, why do you hide behind that mask?"

"What's behind my mask is too horrible to look at even for me."

"Has it been that way all your life?"

"No, but I'd rather not talk about it. What about you? Were you born with magic in your soul?"

"Maybe, but I too will not speak of it."

"So I'm not to know about the woman who came to my rescue and saved me from what would have been terrible torture?"

"Maybe someday, but for now we should be concentrating on getting you healthy and us out of here alive."

Jai brewed some tea and gave a cup to Dorje.

"What is it?"

"It is a healing and anti-inflammatory brew made from natural herbs and tree bark. It is a very old recipe used for maybe thousands of years and in most cases successfully."

"What about the cases when it didn't work? Did people die?"

"Maybe but not from the brew. It doesn't work if the diagnosis is wrong or if one is trying it as a last effort. Your case is very simple, a dog bite, two bullet wounds, and some scratches. Unless you have some foreign disease, or an unknown malady, you should survive."

"Okay, I'll try it as the doctor ordered. Tell me, what you are doing in these mountains? Such a strange place for a beautiful woman to be, especially alone."

"I came to find you."

"What? Why?"

"Simply put I represent a militant group of highly trained people with the latest in all weaponry and technology, who are fighting for causes important to the health and welfare of this planet and its people."

"What is the name of the group?"

"What does it matter? It's what we fight for that matters. Anyway, you have never heard of us."

"What exactly are these causes you speak of?"

Knowing the causes close to Dorje's heart, Jai answered, "We fight to save the planet from those who will destroy its water, land, and air and oppress its people. Our past and present world leaders have failed in one way or another to act with the rapidity or on the large scale needed to protect citizens from potential catastrophe."

Jai continued, "The executive director of the *Bulletin of the Atomic Scientists*, in a news release said. 'The failure of our leaders to act and that failure of leadership endangers every person on Earth.' Need I say more?"

"Yes much more, but so far you make a good case. One I have been fighting for most of my adult life"

"And successfully I might add."

Dorje suddenly slumped over.

"Are you okay?"

After a bit he replied, "No, not really. I am thinking about the men I lost and how it was my arrogance that led them to their deaths."

Jai said nothing. She knew instinctively that she could say nothing at the moment to relieve his mental pain.

After feeding him more tea and looking to the redressing of his wounds, Jai said, "I quote, 'Action is the true sedative for pain and time heals it to a large degree."

"Maybe, but those people fought alongside me for years. We were more than brothers in arms; we were brothers."

After a bit Dorje asked, "What brought you to the point of becoming a militant leader? I am guessing that you are a leader of men."

"That is a very long and painful tale—one I may tell you if and when you agree to join us in our fight. For now it is almost daybreak and I can hear a lot of movement in the meadow. I had better go outside and check around. We need to know that they are heading off in the opposite direction from our position."

For three days the hills were quiet, giving Dorje's wounds time to heal. He slept most of the time while Jai tended the fire, kept watch, and took care of his dressings. They chatted about many things, including the state of affairs of the world, but not once did either bring up their pasts.

Then on the morning of the fifth day, Jai said, "It is time to leave this place. You are well enough to travel, and I must get back to my life."

"And what life is that? I still don't know a thing about you."

"As I said before, if and when you agree to join us I will tell you, not before. So have you given it any thought?"

"Yes, that's all I have been thinking about. That and my wife and child."

"So you are married. Where do they live?"

"In a small village in Nepal."

"That's a long way away from here. When do you see them?"

"Very seldom, and that is a problem for me. My ideology and need to fight the oppressors of these lands have kept us apart. It would not be safe for them to be with me."

"That is sad. But I want you to know that if you join us, they can safely live within five kilometers or so of our headquarters."

"That will make it a lot easier coming to a decision. Where would that be?"

"All in good time, my friend."

"Would I be working with you?"

"Yes, and for me. I am the sole director of the organization. I want you to be the overall commander of our military arm."

"How many people are we speaking of?"

"We keep our teams small. When we need more people on an op, we join two or more teams. When I get back I'm hoping that we have four or five teams, including a new team of women. This team will be specialists in certain fields. All have already proven themselves in battle under stressful circumstances. I have great people working together, but we are missing a man like you, and possibly one other important person. You would report directly to me."

"Can I see the operation and speak to the people before I commit?"

"No, I'm sorry, but that is not possible. All of us, including me, committed because of our belief in the causes. You should not be swayed by our technology, weaponry, or people. This has to be a personal decision based on commitment to the causes we fight for."

"There is one piece missing before I decide. I know you said more than once you will not talk about who or what you are, but I must have these answers so I know, at least somewhat, what I am getting into. I also would need to know if you are capable of that type of leadership."

Jai thought for a moment and said, "I will tell you some things about me, but you will only know what I am capable of when you hear of our successes, and if you see me in action."

"Now tell me about your journey to becoming a famous military general."

"It is a simple story. Many years ago deep in the Tibetan Himalayan mountains I was residing and training in a temple that housed fighting monks. One day we were overrun by a company of Chinese Communists."

Jai listened carefully, holding her breath, hoping beyond hope to hear what she had hoped to hear, for many years.

"There was an explosion from a canon that tore apart the building I was inside with two other monks. A flaming beam fell on us and landed on my left side, including my face. I was on the bottom, knocked out, and the beam kept on smoldering. It probably saved my life because when the soldiers came and looked at three of us, they saw that the top two were dead and didn't want to move the beam and see about me.

"Three days later a group of monks from another temple came to investigate and luckily found me alive, if just barely. They tended to me for days, and when I was in some condition to travel they took me across the border to a Nepalese hospital, where they were able to heal everything except where the log lay. It was there that I met and married my wife, who was my primary doctor.

"After a while stories started to filter out of the mountains about a young girl who single-handedly slaughtered the company of invading soldiers. The tales were being spread by one of the soldiers who escaped. Of course many of us thought this to be a ridiculous exaggeration, but there was the fact that almost the whole company of men were found dead just a few miles from the temple. As time went by the tales grew grander, and the girl became a folk hero, almost a god to be worshipped.

"A couple of years after the mass murder of my friends and thinking about that girl, I just couldn't stand around doing nothing anymore, so I went back into the mountains and started a crusade against the red Chinese wherever I found them. Soon I was joined by more and more men, and we fought battles wherever they needed to be fought. That is until a few days ago when we were trapped by my arrogance and stupidity. That's it."

Jai, again finding herself hoping, asked, "Were you just a simple monk, or the abbot?"

"Just a simple monk."

"Did you have a protégé at the temple that you personally were training?"

"Yes, but she was probably murdered with the rest of them."

Jai, with a lump in her throat and feeling sixteen again, said, "Watch carefully!"

With that Jai leapt into the air and landed on a small platform at the roof of the cave. She called out, "Teacher how did I do?"

Dorje looked in amazement at the feat he just saw, but still he didn't recognize his old student. Jai landed back next to him, saying, "Jinhai, look closely at my face. Do you not remember me?"

Dorje couldn't believe what he was hearing. He shook his head and said, "It cannot be. What is your name?"

"Jai, Teacher, Jai, your student from the temple."

"Oh my god, it can't be. How did you escape?"

"I wasn't there. Remember, I was at my meditation retreat. When I returned, I looked all over for you. I only felt a very weak essence of your energy, but it seemed to be fading fast. I went back to the cave, hoping that you were there looking for me. Back at the temple I searched again, but I couldn't find you or even any physical evidence that you were among the dead. I thought I would or even should die, but I came to my senses and chose to live and find my way out."

"You called me Jinhai, my real name. I haven't been called that for years. Tell me, where did you learn to do some of the things I saw you do?"

"That I will tell you when I know you'll join us in our fight, but only then."

"One other thing. Jai, was it you that fought and defeated the Chinese company?"

"Yes is was, but I am no god or hero. It was blind hatred that drove me and a lot of luck that I succeeded."

"Did you use some of this magic back then?"

"There was none, and there is no magic now."

"Then let me hold you against my body once more and I will give you your answer."

Jai immediately thought of Amira and the baby, also Makeen and his love for her, and debated what to do. Deciding she said, "Yes, that is right, but you should know that I am in a committed relationship and it can go no further than that."

"I too am in a committed relationship, and I will never break my vows. I just need to feel the energy we had once before once again. I lived with the thought of you for so many years. I must now feel it for one last time."

Their first moves toward each other were awkward. They pressed into each other, ending the years of hurt and pain. Thousands of moments of longing were washed away with the tears that they both shed. Their bodies pressed harder against each other, their lips came together, and their tongues parted their lips, searching for the final release of all their anguish.

They pushed back a little and lay side by side, their breaths heavy with the promise of things that should naturally happen. Fighting against every instinct, they released each other, knowing that the time had passed for them.

The time had come for his decision, and Jai just looked into his eyes and didn't say a word. Dorje finally said, "You were the love of my life then, and you will always remain so. But circumstances have forced us apart for too long. Had we met again two or three years ago, I would have said no, because I wouldn't be able to be so close to you every day and not want you in my bed, in my life as my woman. Now that we are back together again, I do not want us to be separated again. I of course will join your organization in whatever capacity you see fit for me."

Jai stood up with joy on her face and in her heart said, "I am so happy and relieved. I too wouldn't want to lose you again. We will make an awesome team, and I can't wait to meet the lucky woman who snagged the best man on Earth."

"And I hesitantly want to meet your man."

"Woman."

"What do you mean woman?"

"The person I am in love with is a woman. Her name is Amira, and she is carrying our child."

"How is that possible?"

"That is a big part of all I have to tell you. We will start from the beginning, and as we head down the mountain and across the world to your new home you will learn it all."

"Okay, but first I must go to Nepal and get my wife and child, and our things."

"Of course, you won't need much except the things that you all are emotionally attached to. Everything else you all need can be bought were we are going or on the way. There is one caveat. She must never know who you work for, what you do, and where you work out of. This is for her and the child's protection. Okay?"

"Yes, of course. That is no problem. She lives with that premise now."

"I have a small thing I have to take care of in Macao, and then we will head to Nepal on one of the organization's private jets. How does that sound?"

"Wonderful! I feel like I'm being unnecessarily seduced."

# CHAPTER 49

The travel between Cambodia and Thailand was full of danger in the depths of the thick jungle. But Jai and Dorje were able to make it out of the mountains to Bangkok.

Finally aboard the company airliner, Jai retrieved her communication devices and called headquarters.

Hoshi answered, "Director. Oh, thank goodness. We have been so worried about you. It's been over a month since we heard from you. Is everything all right? How are you? Are you hurt? Wait one moment; I have to notify Amira."

Hoshi came back on, and Jai said, "Yes I am really fine, and everything is great. We have our new military commander. His name is Dorje, and so it was worth the trip."

"Jai, Jai?"

"Yes, Amira, it is me. I love you."

"I'm going to kill you as soon as you get home. Oh, and I love you more."

"How are you feeling? Is everything okay with the pregnancy?"

"All is well. I got a call from your A Ma, and she has a special doctor she wants me to see. I must tell you it scared me."

"She is the last person on this planet you should be scared of."

"When will you be home?"

"We need to stop in Macao, and then we will be heading to Kathmandu to pick up Dorje's wife and child. After that I'll be heading back to you. Now let me speak to Hiroshi."

"Hurry home! Bye."

"This is a beautiful plane. Are all your planes like this?" asked Dorje.

"No, we have fighter jets, transporters, helicopters, and one other like this. All of them equipped with the latest of everything and more, much more."

"Okay, this is going to be a different kind of war than I'm used to fighting. Are you sure you have the right person to lead when he knows nothing of this kind of equipment and arms?"

"Anyone can learn to use this stuff. It is the natural instincts, the leadership ability, the willingness to die for a cause, and of course a friend in a high position that counts."

"Right. And is there someone in your organization that is promoting me?" Dorje said, laughing.

"Actually I had no idea who you were when I came for you. It was your reputation that did it."

"We are about to land in Macao, China. We'll check into the Mandarin Oriental. First, I will give you some money. I want you to buy some great outfits."

"What is going on? What are we doing here?"

"I will explain it all to you once we are checked in. We have a two-bedroom suite reserved in the name of Doctor and Mrs. Denton. Here is your passport. The photo is blurred, but since your face is mostly covered due to a recent accident, that should explain everything."

On com Jai asked, "Hiroshi, did you find whom I asked you to?"

"It wasn't easy, but yes I found him, and his home and business addresses. He is the leader of a major gang, with a reputation of a sadistic killer. Everybody is afraid of him, and the other gangs leave him alone. Do you want them now?"

"No, send me an e-mail. I'll get it after I'm settled in."

After Dorje left to do some shopping, Jai opened her e-mail and took down the addresses. She located them on Google maps and left the hotel in a rental car.

She drove out to an exclusive area in the outskirts just outside of Macao and found the house she was looking for. Making three or four passes outside the acreage, she was able to spot just what she suspected: a heavily guarded property both electronically, and with human guards and dogs. She couldn't see the house, but she guessed it was magnificent.

To get a better look, she figured she would need to *lung gom* her way inside, landing in a tree high above the ground. Driving once more around the property, she found what appeared to be a good landing spot possibly thirty feet inside the high wall and away from the entrance guards.

Jai parked the rental car in an unobtrusive place, changed into her battle outfit, and jogged back about half a mile to pick up enough speed to make the leap. She started to run when she heard a car approaching from the main street and headed to the gate. She stopped and waited, hoping to get a glimpse of the people inside the car, to no avail as the stretch limo's windows were darkened. She started her run once again and timed the leap perfectly, landing silently high above the ground in position to see the main house, and the limo pulling into the front drive.

A young girl got out, and the limo headed to the rear of the house to park. There were two guards at the gate and two guards at the front door. When the door opened to allow the girl to enter, Jai saw another guard. The door closed.

Jai counted at least six guards, including the driver. There was no one on the roofs of the two residences, Jai guessed that was the second house was where the guards slept, and possibly the servants. The other thing she was not sure of was there just one shift or more?

Jai figured that questioning one, maybe two of the guards was the only way of getting the answers. She decided to wait and see if any of them would leave the grounds. Capturing them outside the gate was the best way.

Ninety minutes or so later, a small sedan pulled up to the gate, and it was opened. The car drove directly behind the servants' quarters, and two men got out and entered the main house. Shortly after two others came out and headed for their cars. Jai figured their shift was over, so with one long leap she jumped outward and glided down to the ground outside the wall.

Luckily both men left the compound together, and Jai figured this was her chance. She waited to see which way they turned after leaving the gate, and they happened to turn directly toward her. Jai thought, *Well, Dorje, too bad you are not here to witness a little magic, as you call it.* When the car was one hundred feet from where she stood, Jai leapt to about ten feet and held that position. With one hand on her hip and the other stretched out, palm facing outward, Jai raised her energy and lit up the area around her.

"What the fuck is that?" one of the guards said.

"I don't know, but don't stop."

Jai saw the car speed up and knew she had failed to stop it peacefully. Quickly building her energy, Jai shot two laser like bolts from her fingers at the front of the car and melted the grill and the engine. The guards sat there stunned, and Jai said, "Come out of the car quietly, lay your weapons on the ground, and kick them to me. If you don't do as I say, I will melt you down to a puddle of hot fat. Now move."

The men did exactly as Jai said. She floated to the ground and told the men to go to the rental truck and sit in the front seat. She picked up their revolvers and emptied the clips and then threw them over the wall.

Jai slid into the backseat and said, "Now I want answers to my questions without hesitation. You'll speak when spoken to. You in the driver's seat, how many guards are inside the house, and how many outside?"

Jai quickly got the information she needed and the men's agreement to join Jai in whatever she was planning. "When does he leave again?"

"Tomorrow."

"Now the two of you just sit quietly. There are some things I need to take care of."

On her com, she said, "Dorje?"

"Yes, Director. By the way this, com system is really great."

"My time table has been pushed up. I need you to be at my location at seven thirty tonight. Hiroshi, give Dorje directions."

"Who is the girl that arrived earlier?"

The driver side said, "The boss's mistress. She is really pretty."

Jai explained what her plan was and their parts in it. They both agreed with enthusiasm. The three of them left the area and drove to a sleazy part of town, where Jai, once again looking like a man, went into a few shops and bought a few things she thought may come in handy. They went back to the house and waited until the time was right.

The clock approached seven thirty, and it was time to move. The driver of the rented truck pulled up to the gate, and acting pissed off, they explained they had been called in early to help move some big items going into town the next morning. Jai, using her mental abilities, made sure they gate guards could not see her. About halfway to the house Jai left the car and using the tree line trotted to the side of the house and waited.

The two men parked directly in front, and when they started up the stairs to the front door, the house guards stepped forward to question what was going on.

"We were called in to help pack and get ready to move some heavy cabinets to town."

At the same time they pulled their weapons and told the guards to put their hands on their heads or they would blow them away. Jai slipped in behind them, and with a hand on each neck, she pressed the right arteries and they passed out.

"Okay, they will be out for quite a while, but we will tie them tight with the wire I bought. Gag them and then drag them into the trees."

Back on the porch Jai tried the door handle, and the door opened. The three slid inside, and the men led Jai to where they believed everyone was.

Reaching a corner, Jai peeked around and saw the final guard outside the master bedroom door. She motioned to the two men behind her to take care of the problem. Luckily it went down easily and quietly.

Jai said, "Be prepared for any other people in the room. One sweep right, one left, and I'll cover the middle."

They nodded in understanding, and Jai opened the door.

Next to a bed where his mistress was lying down masturbating, the boss was on a love seat in just his underpants playing with himself.

Jai called out, "Hold it, both of you. Don't make a move or we'll shoot both. Of course we will not kill you just yet. There are things that need doing first."

At that very moment Jai heard Dorje in her ear. "Director, I am outside."

"Come on in, and wait a moment. You'll be escorted to my location."

"What is your name?" Jai asked the girl.

"Lian."

Facing the love seat, Jai said, "As for you, Mr. Boss Man, if I see you even flinch I will place a bullet in your groin, and you'll have nothing to play with ever again. Understand?"

"Yes, ma'am."

"What is your name?"

"Niu, ma'am"

The door opened, and Dorje walked in.

"Do you know who I am, lady?" asked Niu.

"Oh yes, I certainly do. You are a scumbag and pimp, with a penchant for torture, killing, and selling drugs. And you just love to watch your mistress take apart young women's lives with her sadistic sexual behavior. How am I doing so far?"

Niu said nothing.

"You two gentleman, grab that piece of shit and tie him to the back of that straight chair over there."

Jai walked over to the bed, pushed Lian down, and kneed her legs. She took out her gun and put it up against the girl's mouth and said, "Open up and strip off your clothes."

Jai turned to Niu and asked, "Well, big shot, how do you like watching your lover as you did so many other young girls?"

"I'll kill you, you whoring bitch."

"Oh I doubt that."

Jai faced Dorje, who was in a state of revolted anger, and said, "Now, my dear friend, you will learn why we are doing this, and you will have some of the answers you have asked me for many years.

"You two guys bring the girlfriend here and kneel her in-between scumbag's legs."

Jai walked over and said to Niu, "Now grab her head and make her suck you off."

"I won't do it," he said.

"What's the matter, big boy, you forgot how?"

"What the fuck are you talking about?"

Jai reached back and slapped his face before she said, "What is your name?"

"You know my name."

Jai slapped him again, and with her thumb she put pressure on his left eye and said, "What is your real name? Say it or I'll poke your eye out."

He took in a deep breath and said, "Peng."

"Now, Peng, take your girlfriend's head and make her suck you dry like you wanted me to do when I was seven years old."

"Jai? Is that you?"

"Yes, you piece of shit. It is me, the sister that you tried to sell into slavery and then forced me to commit sexual acts with you. Me, the seven-year-old that you left in the filthy back alleys to fend for herself with no money or clothes. Yes it is I who will now take apart the empire you built on the backs of young girls and boys that you sold into slavery working for the auction house you tried to sell me at. I know you eventually killed the owner and took over the business and from there managed to win the favor of the imperial boss and move rapidly up the chain until you finally killed him also and became the head honcho.

"Dorje, please bring me my laptop from my bag."

"Peng, I'll show you a summary of your accounts around the world. Let's see your password—which stupidly enough is the same in all your accounts—is Chinese emperor. Here we go, look at all your balances and read them out loud."

"This cannot be. It says I have one dollar in each account. Impossible."

"Oh it's not only possible, it is correct. I left you a dollar in each to show you that I am much more generous toward you than you were to me. Now finish the job I told you to do. And you, Lian, you better not spill a drop."

Jai turned to Dorje and asked, "Any questions or comments?"

"Nope, I'm satisfied."

"Okay, then please leave us alone."

After they all left the bedroom, Jai walked over to her brother and said, "It took a long time, Peng, but justice is almost done."

Jai took out a big syringe filled with heroin. "Don't worry, Peng, I'll only give you enough to get you well hooked like you do the kids on the street. Then I will leave you in a filthy alley like you did me. Oh and one other thing." Jai raised her energy and pointed her finger at Peng's groin. Then she let out a burst of laser-like vibrations that caused his penis and scrotum to shrivel to a handful of dead meat. Peng, already high on dope, gave out a weak yell and passed out.

"Okay, everybody, put Peng and Lian in the trunk, and drop them in a back alley off the main street of downtown. Then we'll drive the women home."

Dorje asked, "What about the two guards who helped us?"

"Just leave them. They too will not remember. Now let's get going. It's been a long day, and one that has finally set me free from my past, but to tell the truth I feel no satisfaction with my revenge."

Jai thought to herself, *Now I know what the A Ma was referring to; my lower human nature was in control of my actions today. Guess in some ways I'm no better than them.*

# CHAPTER 50

After landing in Kathmandu, Nepal, Jai checked into the Yak and Yeti hotel. She knew there were places she wanted to visit in the three districts that made up Kathmandu. She was especially interested in the Buddhist community and its temples. Their devotion to the idea of compassion and peace intrigued her. Based on what she knew of the world's people and their hatred of one another, mostly grounded in religion and prejudice, she was anxious to know if the Buddha's true teachings had lasted throughout the centuries. Sometime ago she had discussed this very topic with A Ma, who had mentioned Nepal among a few other Buddhist communities, and that it would benefit Jai to see and speak to some of the Buddhist leaders about the Buddha's words on compassion.

Dorje didn't waste any time in the capital city. He stocked up for his fifty-five-mile mountainous trek to Hetauda, the village where his wife and child lived. He told Jai that they would return by vehicle as soon as he could pack up their belongings and buy a car, or if not possible then buy some mules with the money Jai gave him.

That night after dinner, Jai suddenly realized she was exhausted and her energy was very low, probably dangerously so. She contacted Hiroshi and had him make arrangements for Makeen to fly to Nepal ASAP. She gave it a priority label.

Jai was notified by the front desk that Makeen would be landing in Kathmandu later that afternoon, so she decided to spend the day in Old Thamel shopping in the little hippie-type boutiques. She walked around, trying to avoid being run down by one of the many cows roaming freely in the streets. The old city, a tangle of narrow alleys and temples immediately north and south of the central Durbar Square, was full of life, where tall family dwellings blocked out the sun, open shops crowded the streets, and vegetable sellers clogged the intersections. Everywhere she turned there was a stupa with people making donations and offering a prayer.

Time flew by, and Jai was headed back to the hotel in anticipation of meeting Makeen when she felt a surge of familiar energy. She knew immediately who it was because she had faced this man in the jungles of Cambodia. She sensed that he was close and coming closer. She needed to put some distance between the two of them so she could plan her strategy.

Jai turned quickly, making her way through the crowds toward the Ring Road, apologizing whenever she made contact with someone. Another lesson learned, one she should not have had to learn. Keep on alert whenever and wherever you are. Stop your mental babbling. *Okay, this is not a jungle where individuals could face off without innocents being harmed or killed.* Jai feeling she couldn't do her *lung gom* and bring awed attention to her movements so she began to run toward the "monkey temple."

Jai slowed down; something was not right. A woman was standing in front of a food stall talking to the vendor. Jai thought she had seen her likeness before, but she didn't know where; then suddenly she turned and faced Jai and Jai began to remember—a blurred vision, and then it began to clear. Being so out of context it took her awhile to understand.

Jai involuntarily gasped, and the girl looked up, recognition of being caught in her eyes. She turned away her hand slowly moved toward her pocket. Jai was stunned. Was she actually reaching for a gun? It all appeared insane. Jai considered turning and racing back in the direction she came from, but she knew it was pointless; the assassin was closing from that direction. Jai made a decision and began walking directly towards the girl.

"There you are. I've been looking for you," Jai yelled.

The girl stood still in shock, unable to speak. Finally she blurted out, "Jun? He told you I was here?"

"Yes, he did."

Jai was close enough now; she made a quick run at her and tackled her to the ground. "What the hell is going on?" Jai yelled, making her words heard above the traffic. "You look like someone from my past. Who are you?"

"My name is Mai Shan. I am the daughter of the general you killed in the forests of the Himalayas. I have sworn an oath to kill the legend you became at the expense of my father at whatever cost. Soon you will be dead at the hand of my brother, Jun."

Jai felt this Jun person closing in from behind. Knowing she couldn't just let Mai go, she zapped her with a large bolt of energy, and it took her life.

Needing to put some space between them in order to figure out what to do, Jai raced out into traffic in an attempt to cross the road. Halfway across with a car bearing down on her she leapt in the air and with an additional bound made it to the other side and kept on running.

Apparently safely away, Jai sat down on a grass knoll and thought, *This is no good. It has to stop. I have to end it here and now, but I need to find a way to do it without anyone else getting hurt.* Jai formulated a plan she thought might work. Looking directly across the Ring Road, she spotted Jun approaching Mai. She stood up in hopes of him seeing where she was, and just before he reached her, he saw Jai.

Jai watched as he zigzagged across the road; she lay down on the grass and calmed herself. Almost upon her, Jun pulled out his dagger, and when he reached her she remained still. Feeling rather cocky he straddled her, and as he did so she slid between his legs, coming up facing his backside. She zapped him with a burst of energy, and he flew off the knoll and crashed into a tree, dropping the dagger. Seeing the dagger leave Jun's hand, Jai rushed forward, but Jun, groggy yet aware, pulled out a semiautomatic pistol from his jacket and took aim. Jai reacted instantly and was able to put up a wall of energy just in time to deflect the bullet that was headed for her head.

Jun was stunned for a moment as he watched his bullet fall harmlessly to the grass. He froze as his prey began to spin, creating an energy wall all around her. He finally guessed what she might be attempting and again raised his pistol, put it on automatic, and began firing. When the clip was out, he immediately shoved another into place and continued firing. He was in a daze as he watched his bullets fall to the ground.

Jai kept on spinning, building her energy higher and higher, causing the wall to get taller and wider. Jun emptied his second clip in a frenzy and without thought of danger rushed Jai, intending to do hand-to-hand combat, where he believed he was superior. He ran headfirst into the wall of highly charged energy. Jai watched as Jun's body melted into a puddle of liquid fat, bathing her with a stench she wouldn't soon forget.

Jai allowed her energy to drop to a normal level, looked down at Jun, and thought, *No one will be able to identify him.* Two police were approaching from behind, and when they got closer, she blocked her image from their minds and walked away.

Jai, in a semi state of shock, was shuddering as she headed back to the hotel to wait for Makeen.

After a quick reciprocal greeting, one of respect, Jai told him the whole story of Jun and Mai. Jai finished the tale with tears in her eyes, and after she calmed down, they had high energy–producing sex, leaving Jai renewed and Makeen exhausted.

Makeen, after resting a while, said, "Jai, this may not be the right time because of all you've been through, but I want and need you to know something important."

"I hope whatever it is it will not affect what is necessary for me to remain who I am."

"I don't think so, but also I hope not.

"To say this simply, I am very fond of a woman, and I believe I will fall in love with her. I know this could make things very complicated for us, but I'm hoping that won't be the case."

"Does she know about us?"

"No, and I never would tell her."

"Do I know her?"

"Know her? No, I don't think so, but you may have seen her."

"Who is she?"

"She is one of the new Black Ops soldiers who joined us. I have been training her. The harder I push her, the harder she pushes back."

"When did you know that you were falling for her?"

"One morning while training she pinned me, and we found ourselves looking deeply into each other's eyes. I had this feeling come over me, and I believe she felt it too."

"How far has it gone?"

"That's it. I purposely have not scheduled her for training with me. And I have avoided any place I might run into her. What do you think?"

"I see a lot of good coming from this, but I must know that if you take the relationship to a sexual level it will not affect the energy you give me."

"Will my energy be tainted by hers?"

"I don't know. I will have to speak to the A Ma. She will decide. Truthfully I hope she will say it's okay. I know how you feel about me and I also know that you will never lose that, but I want you to have a full life, and it can't be with me."

The following day Jai visited the Boudhanath Stupa, the

holiest Tibetan stupa outside of Tibet. It has a sixteen-sided wall with frescoes in the niches and prayer wheels around the base along with the 108 forms of the Bodhisattva Avelokiteshvara. The mantra of Om Mani Padme Hum is carved on the prayer wheels. By constantly intoning the mantra, you can attain an indivisible union of practice and wisdom. When you reach a certain level, you can transform your impure body, speech, and mind into a pure body and mind likened to a Buddha.

It was at this stupa that Jai had the pleasure of speaking with a number of high-ranking monks, discussing the variations of the Buddha's teaching and the religion as it is practiced during this era. She found the same problem existed in Buddhism as in Christianity and Islam. The prophet's words were seriously bastardized by the minds of the church leaders seeking their own agendas.

That night Jai felt as though a great boulder had been lifted off her head. She thought about her dreams and nightmares and realized that she had been watching a movie of her life. Now having settled all past scores, she knew she was ready for her future with Amira, their new baby, and her position as director of a truly worthwhile cause. She smiled when she thought of the incredible people she would be working with and for.

Dorje and his family arrived the following day. Jai noticed right away how pretty his wife and child were. The five of them spent the balance of the day in Kathmandu's Dubar Square (a place of castles) walking around and buying a few mementoes. Their final stop was the Kumari Chowk Palace, home to the living goddess, a virgin girl chosen at an early age. Though it was a great honor to be chosen, when the year was out, she inevitably had a difficult time finding a man. After all, who would marry a goddess?

A quiet dinner at a great Indian restaurant topped off the day. By ten o'clock the following morning they were in the air headed home.

# CHAPTER 51

Twenty minutes after checking Dorje's family into a hotel eight kilometers from the entrance to headquarters, Jai and Dorje walked through the security chambers into the lobby.

Without hesitation Amira ran into Jai's arms with tears rolling down her cheeks and held her tighter than she ever held her before.

"I love you," she whispered in her ear, "but next time you disappear where nobody knows where you are and without a com device, I will kill you."

Jai pushed her back, looked into her eyes, smiled, and said, "Okay, but you better have someone like me to take care of you and our baby."

Dorje, a little uncomfortable, cleared his throat. Jai said, "Sorry, Dorje, I'd like you to meet my housekeeper, Amira. Amira, this is Dorje, the reason I've been gone so long."

Amira playfully punched Jai in the arm, and looking into Dorje's eyes, she said, "Nice to meet you, but I'm her woman and the mother of our baby, and more, so much more."

"Okay, playtime is over. Hoshi, ask the department heads plus you and your brother to meet me in the conference room at four."

"Yes, Director."

Turning to Amira, Jai said, "You should be there also. In the meantime I'll show Dorje the facilities."

After the tour was over, Jai asked, "So what do you think of our operation?"

"I can't believe what you people have here. You say the world hasn't seen a lot of this equipment and armament?"

"That is correct. A lot of it was designed and manufactured right here."

"I'll tell you my problem. I wouldn't know how to best utilize all this. Again I think you might have the wrong person to lead your military."

"Utilization of the armaments can be learned in a few months, but what you bring is so much more in terms of leadership and instinct in and out of the field. Plus you are a proven winner, a man who can win against great odds. No, my friend, you are perfect for this position."

Jai went up to her apartment to think things out and rest when she heard, "Welcome back, my child. It is good to see you."

"You too, A Ma. Tell me, did you know what Dorje was to me before you sent me out?"

"Yes, child, of course we did. It is one of the reasons we took so long deciding whether to send you to him, but we figured that in the long run it was the right thing."

"Why, did you think it might not be?"

"Because there is a lot of negativity surrounding that part of your life and also the love you had for your teacher. You have moved on to a better, more productive life, and have a new and powerful love. We weren't sure how you would react to bringing everything full circle."

"After Macao I feel a great weight has been lifted off my shoulders. Plus knowing that my former teacher, who saved me from a miserable existence, is alive, healthy, and has a great family—I can't tell you how happy that makes me."

"I believe you, Jai. Now there is something you want to talk about."

"Yes, it's the matter of Makeen and his possible relationship. If it turns sexual, which he and I both think is very possible, how will it affect the energy I need from him?"

"It is true his energy will be somewhat tainted, but as the relationship continues, he will purify hers to the point where it won't affect him or you in a negative way."

"So then he should pursue his feelings as I did mine?"

"Yes."

"That's great. I'll tell him ASAP."

"Well, my dear, you have accomplished a lot and know you have a full and great team, and I'm confident that you will accomplish a great deal more. There is so much that needs to be done. I'll be on my way and let you get started."

"Thank you, A Ma, for everything you have given me. I hope we can live up to your and our people's expectations and needs."

"You will, my child. You will."

The A Ma faded away, and Jai called Hiroshi, "Have Makeen and his friend meet me in my suite now. He knows who I'm speaking of."

Makeen and Heather appeared at Jai's door, and both looked extremely anxious. Jai pressed the button unlatching the door, and when they entered, Jai asked them to be seated on her couch. Makeen introduced the woman, and Heather said, "I am so happy to finally meet you, Director. I have heard so many wondrous things about you and your abilities."

"I am sure that most are exaggerated," Jai responded. "Did Makeen explain you why you are here?"

"No, he hasn't."

"Well, simply put, Makeen tells me that the two of you would like to start a relationship that goes beyond trainer and student. Is that correct?"

"I'm not aware of any such thing," Heather said, looking a little shocked.

Makeen jumped in. "All I said was that I felt a definite connection between the two of us at our last training session and told the director that I would like to pursue it. Was I wrong?"

"No, I guess that's true, but we never said a word about it. As a matter of fact, I haven't seen you at all since then."

Jai said, "Before we go any further, I had better ask if that is something you would like to pursue with Makeen."

"Yes it is, now that we are allowed to speak of it. I've wanted that since the day I met him."

Jai smiled and said, "Would you be willing to take me on in the ring, and if you win one out of three matches, I'll give you my blessing?"

Heather answered with a frown. "From what I have heard, I couldn't begin to compete with you; nobody can.

But if that's what it takes for him and me to get together, I will certainly give it my all."

"Your willingness to fight me for your man is all I needed. The two of you have my blessing with one caveat: the two of you cannot go into the field together. We cannot have emotions play in any decision that needs to be made. Understood?"

Both said yes, and Jai said, "Okay, I have to go to a meeting. Good luck to both of you."

In the arena area, Jai introduced Dorje to the assembled company as the new military commander of the entire outfit, saying, "For those of you who have not heard of him, let me just say there is no better military leader in the field. Now sitting next to me is Guy from the Alpha Black Ops team. He will head up military strategy. Any questions?

"No? Then I want you to realize how proud I am of all of you that have been working so hard to improve yourselves both physically and mentally for the upcoming conflicts. I believe we have put together the best fighting force on the planet, and that includes the support teams, design and manufacturing geniuses, and medical staff. It has taken time and some weeding out, but the results will prove the process. We are a conglomerate with a definite purpose, one that bears up against any scrutiny in relation to the salvation of this planet and its people."

From the crowd came the hum of *amen*, followed by a single male voice, who whispered, "And women."

# EPILOGUE

Jai, finally alone and lying on her bed napping, heard the A Ma whisper, "Wake up, my child."

"Yes, A Ma, is there a problem?"

"No, Jai. I and my people have come to a decision that you should, once again, visit our home, but only for a short while."

"Oh my, I have been thinking about that for a long time now. When can we go?"

"Immediately!"

"Do I have to pack?"

The A Ma laughed and said, "No, just lay back and close your eyes. I will do the rest."

Jai did as she was told, and the A Ma put her hand on Jai's head, and in a moment's time Jai and the A Ma were walking the path that led to the gateway. The A Ma said, "All your animal and alien friends are waiting for your return visit."

Jai asked, "Will Amira and the baby be allowed to enter here someday?"

"It is too early to say, my dear. We will see. We must allow events to unfold."

Crossing the threshold, Jai heard fluttering wings and

saw her friends the deer and unicorn, among many others she fondly remembered, standing before her. She bowed her head as tears streamed down her face. *It is so good to be home.*

# ABOUT THE AUTHOR

S. A. Stitz was born and raised amid the steel and concrete of New York City. His craving to travel drew him to explore the idea of creating an adventure travel company. While exploring parts of countries seldom visited by tourists Stan met and talked with chieftains, ascetics, and shamans as he sought to gain knowledge about the legends, myths, and folklore of their regions. Stan's awareness of mystical events and lore from vastly different countries brought clarity to the notion that there is a great deal that today's societies are not privy to. Stan's first attempt at a novel was inspired by much of the folklore he collected and firsthand spiritual experiences he was fortunate to be a part of. Combining that with what he learned while visiting martial arts training and meditation centers, the idea of Jai came into being. Stan presently resides on a beautiful rain forest island in the Caribbean.

CPSIA information can be obtained
at www.ICGtesting.com
Printed in the USA
LVOW08s1506190417
531396LV00002B/264/P